Series By Michele L. Coffman

The Alpha Evolution Series

The Battle for Liberty Series

The Universal Guardians Saga

The Royal Descendant

Book One

The Universal Guardians Saga

Michele L. Coffman

Launch Point Press
Portland, Oregon

Dedication

This novel is dedicated to those with the passion to tell a story, but no self-confidence to write it. Never give up. Stay focused and keep writing. Your belief in yourself will grow.

The Universal Guardians: The Royal Descendant

Characters

Annabel (Ann) Malanight—Human, Trysal, Kan—Casey's great-great-grandmother. Queen of the Universal Region.

Ashonda Malanight—Trysal—Casey's great-great-great-grandmother. Retired queen.

Barick—Blunion—Elizabeth Malanight's head guard, Parrow's father, Hanna's husband.

Bilana Savel—Trysal—Ann's wife.

Casey Malanight—Human, Trysal, Kan—Last royal descendant of the Universal Region.

Chasel—Casey's Personal Functioning System, or Program Intelligence.

Darren—Gaminite—Elizabeth Malanight's guard and engineer.

David Titron—half-Human, half-Kan—Casey's great-great-great-grandfather.

Daynard—Dayshire God.

Elizabeth Malanight—Human, Trysal, Kan—Casey's grandmother. Next in line to the throne.

Eva—Kan—Elizabeth Malanight's guard, assistant in engineering.

Fayrel Beletal—Trysal—Elizabeth Malanight's healer, Tanille's father.

Hanna—Blunion—Elizabeth Malanight's guard, Parrow's mother, Barick's wife.

Havan—Ashonda's Personal Functioning System, or Program Intelligence.

Jasper—Elizabeth's Personal Functioning System, main residence Program Intelligence.

Parrow—Blunion—A German Shepherd and Casey Malanight's head guard.

Program Intelligence Vespa—Instructor of language classes, Universal Region, planets, and species.

Program Intelligence Zeckner—Instructor of math, science, and physics.

Marah—Ship's main computer.

Rachael Malanight—Casey's great grandmother killed by Erules.

Senior Paraney—The head of council.

Tanille Beletal—Trysal—Casey's healer, Fayrel's daughter.

Valishima—Casey's mother, killed in an Erule attack.

Vashee—black panther and soul-link to Casey.

<u>Terminology</u>

Assembly—Committee that assists the queen in ruling the Universal Region.

B-76—Transportation craft in engineering.

Belfont Originator—Molecule Dispenser named after the scientist Davron Belfort.

Blackseleight—Material that holds in temperature. Expensive with an appearance of silky black marble.

Blunion—Species living in the Phortrix Solar System gifted in combat and able to shape-shift into virtually anything living.

Crogonic travel—Traveling by speed of time. Inventor: Malbet Crogon.

Crymonone—A purplish-red stone located in the Vasar solar system. It's abundant on Vasar Three but can be found on all four Vasar planets.

CSF virus—Deadly, extremely painful, and fast-acting.

Dayshire—Enemy outside the Universal Region.

Dayshire whip—Whip intertwined with *acidifora*, a nasty chemical that affects individuals physically and mentally and leaves permanent scars.

DNA Modifier—Chambers that change appearance. Three in existence—Vasar Five, Malanight Estate, and the Palace on Vasar One.

Equipment originator—Molecule chambers that store equipment.

Erules—Enemy outside the Universal Region.

Erule SRB destroyers—Short-range battle destroyers with short-range boost.

Floun—Species living outside of the Universal Region who are part of the Assembly.

Hafites—Species living in the Couhl Tabarr System.

Head of Council—Elected official who governs the Assembly.

Human—Species living on Earth in the Milky Way galaxy.

ISR—Individual-Seeking Rocket.

Kan—Species living in the Denite Solar System.

Kesler Solar System—Where the Erules live.

Molecule displacer—Scans size and makeup of objects before removing the air and space, shrinking items into condensed forms. Their previous configurations are stored in the displacer for reconstruction at a later time.

Naphia Solar System—Location of the Universal Region's prisons and justice system.

PDR-4/PDR-5—Planetary Defense Rockets.

RLP—Rechargeable low-powered handheld weapon for hip holsters.

RRD—Rechargeable Rocket Device.

Semina Planet—Center of the Universal Region.

Simulation room—Molecule displacing room.

Telamanrin—Ability to mentally speak with animals.

Tenliltes—Trysal word for sluts.

Teratopton—Black hole.

Terropen—The strongest metal discovered in the Universal Region. Almost every ship from the Region within the last one thousand years is constructed with this metal.

Trysal—Species living in the Vasar Solar System on four inhabited planets.

Unification Necklace—five in total—jewel star flight ruby. Malanight family uses them for time travel.

Universal Region—A vast area of space, roughly one thousand mega light-years long, one thousand mega light-years wide, and over nine hundred mega light-years in depth. The Universal Region is ruled by a Queen (a descendant from the Malanight bloodline) and the Assembly.

Universal Translators—goes in ear, speaks and translates every dialect in the Universal Region.

Zelics—Species living outside of the Universal Region who are part of the Assembly.

Epigraph

Life is a mysterious journey,
veiled by the garment of time
Wherein this life we must wander,
as we discover the small and sublime.
Wherever this road it must take us,
we each decide our own way
As our journey does unfold before us,
with each crossroads of decision we weigh.
Sometimes the journey does find us,
battered, bruised, and forlorn
It seems that the road is quite rocky.
with the stresses of life, we are torn.
But each day brings new hope to guide us
and gives us the strength to pull through
To continue the journey we've started,
ever reaching for what we pursue.
And alas, the road it does take us,
to new heights and to places unknown
As we discover what life has to bring us,
and the wonders to us it has shown.
We all pave the road we have taken,
for those that will follow behind
And who knows where this journey will take us,
it all starts with the road in our mind.

~Elizabeth Leonard

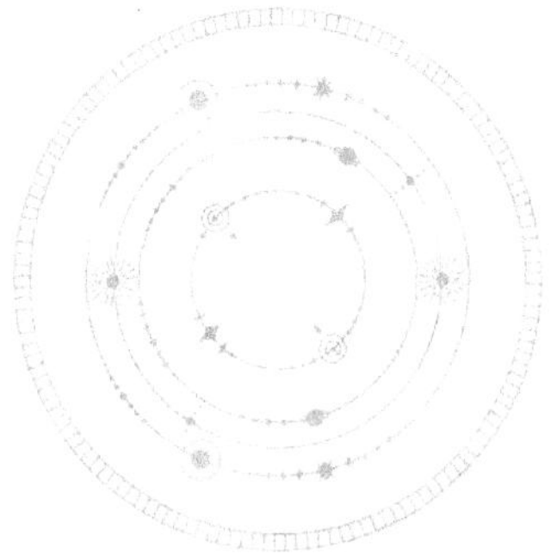

Chapter One

Earth Date: 1st July 2042
The Retrieval

Shortly after four in the morning, Casey Malanight switched off her reading lamp and placed the finished four-hundred-page novel on the table beside her. She stretched her body fully in the recliner to the rubbing sound of pulled leather. The two hours of losing herself in a fictional story, with only the rhythmic *hum* of Parrow's light snoring, were exactly what she needed to unwind after another long, stressful evening at work. She retracted the footrest and rose.

She didn't feel tired, only mentally drained. This was unusual, considering within the last few months she'd only been able to sleep a few hours at a time. Several nights she didn't sleep at all, only redirected her mind from the stressors of her job into the depths of a good book. One with an interesting storyline which tossed her from the painful truths of reality into the mind-boggling world of fantasy. Thankfully, she still felt refreshed and ready to go the following day.

Upon hearing his owner's movement, Parrow sprang to his feet and trotted straight to the front door.

"Fine, let me change first," Casey said, passing the black-and-brown German Shepherd at the edge of the hallway.

Once in her bedroom, Casey threw on a pair of sweatpants and a T-shirt, strapped on her shoulder holster and weapon, and flung a light blue jacket over it. She always carried her weapon when she went out. A bad habit, but one that came in handy more times than she cared to admit. She snatched her wallet and badge, secured Parrow's leash, and left the apartment.

The instant the two made their way outside, a cool breeze teased Casey's short, dark brown hair in a welcoming greeting. She adored these early morning walks with Parrow. It gave them both a chance to enjoy their piece of New York without the congested streets and busy sidewalks.

Parrow lifted his leg to the first tree in the park.

"Wow, you really had to pee," Casey said.

As Parrow grabbed a whiff of his scent, Casey spotted a team of male college-aged runners, all wearing blue and red matching outfits, jogging along the trail toward them. She rolled her eyes to the cat-whistles and flirtatious shouts they directed her way as they passed. Parrow sent the men a low growl and placed his body between them and Casey.

"Oh, you're as overprotective as Gran," she muttered, ruffling through the strip of hair standing up on his neck.

She directed Parrow's leash the opposite way on the path, before giving her four-legged protector the lead. He kept the pace slow and steady, stopping every few minutes to leave his aroma on a tree or bush, marking the trail as his own.

Her grandmother gave Parrow to her as a gift within a month of Casey moving to New York. Casey's mother had died in a car wreck when Casey was eleven, leaving her to be raised by her only living relative, her over-protective grandmother, who had insisted Casey accept the dog for her protection. She'd also had to promise to enroll in a self-defense class as soon as she arrived in the city. Casey tried to explain the Police Force provided these classes, but Gran insisted she receive additional training.

Looking back, Casey realized how right her Gran had been. She loved Parrow, and on two occasions, he had deterred would-be burglars from breaking into her apartment while she slept. As for the self-defense classes, Casey kept her promise. She found an instructor from a business card someone had slid underneath her front door when she first moved in. By the time the initial lesson ended, she was hooked.

Her instructor was of Asian descent with a distinguished half-moon shaped birthmark under his right eye. She never got a straight answer from him about what his unique style of martial arts was called. To her, it resembled kickboxing, karate, and some other form of fighting she'd never seen before. Whatever he taught, the lessons came cheap, were one-on-one sessions, and the tactics had proven effective under extreme circumstances.

Besides taking these classes three to four times a week, she also lifted weights in her apartment complex's fitness room and jogged several miles every other day. This routine not only kept her body well-toned, but it helped to clear her head from the stresses of her job. Casey's own way of purifying her mind and her body.

Casey was fond of this section of the park where the trees grew up thick on either side of the trail. There were no beds of flowers like in the open areas because little light shown through here. The spot was calm, peaceful, and gave Parrow a bit of mother nature's ambiance to enjoy.

She chose one of several green wooden benches and unhooked Parrow's leash. She knew Parrow would stay close and wanted to give him a taste of freedom since he was cooped up in the apartment all day. He barked his thanks before he left her side. He was a wonderful dog, well behaved and extremely smart. The way his intelligent eyes often searched hers, Casey felt he was almost human.

She inhaled deeply, taking in the fresh fragrance of this unique slice of landscape. The city lit the path with old Boston-style streetlamps that emanated a soft glow through the trees. She cursed herself for not bringing a book to read but quickly found enjoyment by watching Parrow bounce around, trying to coax the squirrels into playing with him.

Twenty minutes later, Casey cut Parrow's game short when she heard the faint sounds of voices approaching. Hooking his leash, she scratched behind Parrow's ear and apologized for the short bit of freedom. She reluctantly directed him onto the path.

"Do you want to stop for a cappuccino before we head home?" she asked Parrow when they arrived at the park's entrance. He gave her an excited bark and practically yanked her across the street.

"Fine, I'll have the cappuccino, and you can have a glazed donut. You drive a hard bargain, boy."

When they first entered the shop, the sun was rising, casting a reddish haze over the city. Mr. Rice, the short, plump owner, was finishing up with another customer who, thankfully, was the only other patron inside.

"Ah, Detective Malanight, I'll be right with you two," he said, handing a woman in a blue business suit her steaming drink.

The well-dressed woman caught Casey's gaze with a flirtatious smile, thanked the balding man, and headed out the door.

"So, what'll it be today? One of my warm cinnamon-chocolate twists? Or perhaps a generous sample of my new caramel-drop vanilla pastries?" he asked, throwing Parrow a freshly made donut hole.

Only service dogs could legally enter an eating establishment, which Mister Rice strictly enforced. Parrow was his one exception. He adored Casey's four-legged companion, and no one complained. The neighborhood patrons knew Casey, as well as her profession, and the way Parrow carried himself, he was often mistaken for a police dog.

"I'll take a tall French vanilla cappuccino and Parrow will have a plain glazed donut."

Parrow barked his approval.

"You've made another splendid choice as always, my good man," he said, winking at Parrow.

Casey smiled while the bubbly man set to work on their order.

"Have you heard we're going to be getting thunderstorms over these next four or five days?" he called over his shoulder as he busied himself with the cappuccino machine.

"No, I haven't had the TV on all week."

She was inspecting the fresh assortment of pastries when the door opened again. A rough-looking man in an old, dirty green army jacket stepped inside. When his dark eyes found hers, warning lights went off in Casey's head. Parrow must have felt the same thing because the hairs on his neck stood straight up.

"I'll be with you in a moment," Mister Rice called out.

The man didn't respond. Instead, he eyeballed Casey and Parrow, obviously sizing them up. Seeing them as no threat, he made a beeline for the counter.

The second the man reached his hand underneath his coat, the unexplainable happened. A flash of light filled Casey's eyes with such force, she was temporarily blinded. Unexpected fear gripped her chest, making it hard for her to breathe. Rapid blinking not only brought clarity, but a form of slowed reality that was hard to comprehend. She saw a vision of the man pulling out a nine-millimeter handgun. The man fired two rounds into Mister Rice before she could retrieve her weapon from beneath her jacket. The realism of the scene almost brought her to her knees. The second she squeezed the trigger in her waking dream, the nightmarish phantasm disappeared, leaving her temporarily off balance.

She focused her bleary eyes as the man's hand wrenched from his coat, clutching a handgun. Casey lunged, shoulder first, into the man's chest. She heard the air leave his lungs, and they both crashed hard to the floor. His weapon flipped outward, landing a few feet away. He reached for his gun, but she drove a solid punch into his right side. He recoiled beneath the blow. She jerked backward to avoid his elbow but was too late. The brutal impact hit straight on her nose. She heard the *pop*, felt the pain, and tasted the sickening tang of copper sliding down the back of her throat, unsettling her stomach. She welcomed the adrenaline rush and willed herself not to think about anything but the deadly situation.

The man scrabbled ahead and grabbed for his weapon again. This time, Parrow swooped in. He sank his thick canines deep into the man's outstretched forearm. The snarl that came out of her guardian was almost horrifying, and he whipped his head about, fighting viciously to protect her. The shriek from the man was much higher and more frantic and equally horrifying.

Casey shifted onto her knees, pulled her weapon, and pressed it firmly to the base of the man's skull. "NYPD, asshole. You move and so help me, I'll put a bullet in you."

The man screamed. "Call off your dog! Dammit, call off your fucking dog! I swear I won't move." The man slurred the last part in a whimper.

"Parrow, that's enough, boy."

Parrow dropped the man's bloody arm. Strangely enough, he picked up the weapon with his teeth before backing several feet away and lowering it onto the checkered tile.

"Good boy," she said, her voice full of pride.

Casey glanced at Mister Rice's fear-stricken face. "I need you to call the police."

He stood motionless in a daze until a loud bark from Parrow snapped him into action. "Oh my, of course, Casey." His hands shook as he turned to the wall-mounted phone.

After he placed the call, he came around the counter, picked up the weapon sitting in front of Parrow, and placed it tenderly on top of the counter, as if one wrong move would cause the weapon to discharge. "They're on their way," Mister Rice said, handing Casey a wet towel.

"Thank you." Casey placed the towel against her throbbing nose.

"Aren't you going to cuff him?" Mister Rice asked.

Casey peered at her blood-soaked sweat outfit. "With what? My bra?"

Two days later, rain slapped hard against Elizabeth Malanight's stained-glass windows. The rhythmic thuds and clinks echoed throughout the room. The only light came from a dying fire in the vaulted stone fireplace and the occasional flash of lightning, followed closely by a cascading eruption of thunder.

Elizabeth stared vacantly at the dancing flames, knowing the horrible, drawn-out night would soon be over. She kept her composure, not thinking about the what-ifs, and left no room in her commitment to have foolish doubts. The outcome of tonight would certainly depend on everyone maintaining a high level of calm. After all, to ensure a persuasive ending, they had arranged everything weeks in advance. She was biding her time now, waiting for Barick to send word.

Sipping her coffee, Elizabeth watched the rain as it fell against the window near her desk. She couldn't help but worry she might have missed something, one tiny detail she overlooked. She stared at the gold-framed picture to her right and slowly exhaled. Fresh tears slid down her age-lined cheeks. The woman and her daughter were laughing at the camera; each appeared to be tickling the other. The mother was young, strikingly attractive. The photo revealed the daughter was going to follow suit. She had the same high cheekbones as her mother and the same naturally tan complexion.

A sudden knock on the library door made Elizabeth jump, almost spilling hot coffee on her silk blouse. She set the coffee aside, wiped her eyes with an embroidered handkerchief, and composed herself. She steadied her breathing, then beckoned the individual to enter.

Light from the entryway spilled in when the door opened. Barick stepped over the threshold, blocking much of the illumination. His sleek, athletic build matched his impressive height.

Once the door was closed to ensure peaceful obscurity, she said, "Barick, I was just thinking about you. Have you received word yet regarding the progress of the situation?"

"I spoke to my son. He's informed me everything is moving precisely on schedule." He stoked the fire, and placed two more logs on top, forcing flickering brightness in the room. "How are you doing, Elizabeth?" he asked, not taking his eyes off the newly created flames.

She paused before answering, attempting with no luck to read his thoughts. "I'm fine, why wouldn't I be?" she lied, trying to sound insulted by his question.

Straightening to his full height, he studied her eyes, as if he were trying to see through her, searching for any type of giveaway to reveal her genuine feelings. He crossed to one of the English leather chairs in front of her desk and gracefully seated himself. "Because we're hours away from killing your granddaughter."

The reality of his words plunged like a knife deep into Elizabeth's chest, yet she refused to let it show. "We're doing what we must. If this doesn't work, nothing will." Though her heart fell heavily to grief, she kept her voice calm, level. "I'm sure of it."

"You don't fool me," he said. His eyes held compassion, and his voice filled with concern. "I know you're hurting, Beth. We all are. Fayrel is confident this plan will work. Everyone knows their jobs. *Nothing* will go wrong."

Elizabeth considered the man she called a friend for so many years. She knew he was right, but this didn't reduce her fear of failure. She had already lost so much. "Yes, my emotions are being challenged, but I have faith, Barick. In you and your son." She stood and went to the window. "Did he mention if Casey has experienced any more visions?"

"He only has proof of the one I mentioned to you earlier, but he suspects she's had several. There's really no way to be sure."

"I'm worried she'll experience one tonight. If that happens, she might prevent us from doing what we must." Elizabeth returned to her desk.

"Tonight will work out. You have my word. I also promise it'll be a clean shot. She'll feel minimal pain."

"What of the boy?" she asked, glancing at Casey's picture.

Barick sounded confused. "What about him?"

"My granddaughter is about to give her life for this child. Therefore, I ask you, what will become of the boy?"

Barick slowly nodded. "We're planning on wiping the events of tonight from his memory. He'll be fine, only confused."

She thought for a moment before continuing on to the next issue. "I've already paid off the coroner. The arrangements are all set. I'll fly out first thing tomorrow to claim Casey's body before their doctors have examined her. When you return, could you ensure Fayrel has everything ready by the time we land?" Elizabeth knew she wasn't telling him anything he didn't already know.

Barick bowed his head in understanding.

The alarm on Barick's watch beeped, bringing him gradually to his feet. "It's time," he said. They both stared at one another. Their eyes briefly exchanged all the unasked questions and doubts.

"Be careful, and whatever happens…" Her voice trailed off.

"I know." His eyes softened. "I'll send Hanna in to keep you company." He spun from Elizabeth and left the room.

Detective Casey Malanight reached the middle of the hallway as the perp rounded the far corner. Her partner, Detective Jim Smythe, drew his sidearm and shouted, "NYPD."

Gunfire answered him, and they both ducked into an open doorway. She squeezed off two rounds, but the man disappeared around the corner. She and Jim raced down the hallway, stopping before the next turn. She squatted low on one knee. Jim stood directly beside her and readied his stance. He whispered, "We go on three. One …two…three."

Spinning her upper body around the corner, Casey aimed her weapon but saw no one. Ten feet directly ahead was a closed door. She heard sirens in the distance. Backup was coming, but Casey wasn't sure they'd make it in time to save the child.

Jim held up his phone and motioned for her to wait.

She showed her understanding by silently signaling to him she would push ahead, then hold her position until he was ready.

He threw out his usual thumbs-up.

Crouching, she moved forward, hugging the wall. Less than a foot away from the door handle, she took a calming breath, preparing to wait for her partner. Suddenly, a vision, like the one in Mister Rice's coffee shop, struck her hard. She'd had them before. They started a month earlier. A brief glimpse of the future which, strangely enough, all had come true. This one foretold the next few moments of her life. Moments that would be her last. And Jim's.

She peered back at Jim. He was muttering into his cell phone, no doubt letting the other officers know where they were located so they could assist. Behind the door was the kidnapped child, a boy two years younger than Jim's seven-year-old son. No matter what, she would make sure Jim held his son again.

Casey checked Jim's position. He ended the call and surveyed the hallway they'd come from. Now or never. She tried the door handle, found it unlocked, and slowly turned it. The door swung open easily, and she used the wooden barrier to shield herself, giving her a few seconds of time to gain her bearings. The room was dark. Movement of an adult-sized figure hunkering on a ledge outside the window caught her eye.

After shoving the door open, Casey rolled to her right, coming up in a crouched position with her weapon trained on the abductor. A shot rang out. The bullet struck her chest. Then a sharp burst of raw energy, like a sonic boom, reverberated in her ears. Her body collapsed to the floor, her heart slowed, and her breathing grew infrequent, like it did in her vision, but this time Jim wasn't lying beside her, which hopefully meant the boy had also lived.

The aroma of warm copper filled her nose. The instant her eyes shifted toward the body lying sprawled out on the floor on the other side of the bed, she gasped. The lifeless perp lay motionless in a pool of his own blood. Eyes opened, dead.

But who shot her? She was still conscious, yet unable to move. She glared toward the window, where a dark figure stepped from the shadows. Could that be her self-defense instructor? He frowned at her, a cone shaped handgun, unlike anything she'd ever seen before, clutched in his hand.

An image of her dog, Parrow, flashed before her eyes. Her beloved German Shepherd would be all alone now. What would happen to him? Surely, Gran would come for him.

The next shot echoed like a cannon in her ears, and her world gradually darkened.

"Vasar Eight, we've cleared you for runway eleven. Please start your final approach."

"Copy tower, Vasar Eight proceeding to runway eleven," Barick's wife, Hanna said.

Elizabeth settled into the co-pilot's seat and stared out one of the side windows at a clear bluish-red sky. She watched as the sun's rays swayed lightly above the horizon. The effect gave off a reddish glow between the high-rise building of the city, tapering its way slowly upward into the sky. Purple shading emerged where the blue and red colors came together. The view was so beautiful, it almost felt unreal. Like a manufactured picture hanging off in the distance.

Hanna removed her headset. "Parrow contacted me. He's had a slight problem with reaching Casey's landlord. He also said the placement of Casey into the hibernation capsule functioned smoothly. We can head over there as soon as we land."

Elizabeth's heart fluttered with relief. "Why don't you meet up with Parrow, and as soon as I collect Casey's body, I'll meet you both here at the airport."

Hanna replaced her headset and squeezed Elizabeth's arm. *"Don't worry, Elizabeth. We still have plenty of time left. Everything will work out fine. I'm sure of it."*

Hanna's mouth didn't move when she spoke, but Elizabeth heard every word clearly. Her lips curved upward in a grateful smile.

While Elizabeth got into a hearse, Hanna, with her long, dark hair placed in a fashionable bun and dressed in a feminine-cut business suit, hailed a cab at the overcrowded New York City airport. The air was thick with exhaust fumes, blaring horns, and swarms of boisterous travelers going to or coming from the madhouse of a terminal. Hanna was ready to be free of New York. She waited until the black Mercedes hearse left with Elizabeth before having her own driver pull away.

She didn't care for the overcrowded city. With all the crime and pollution decaying this vast metropolis, the truth of this civilization's apathetic nature was everywhere, and it sickened her. Hanna knew this species held the potential for greatness. One day, maybe humanity would see it themselves. Maybe they'd find their species traveling through the universe, exploring other worlds, socializing with other beings who shared in the wonders given to each life-form. Unfortunately, at the rate they were going, it wouldn't be in her lifetime or that of her sons. Humans were struggling just to survive.

As Elizabeth said the last time they were in New York, *Humans need to open their eyes to the many blessings they have. Maybe then they will take notice of how quickly they're destroying their own existence.*

Hanna had agreed with every word.

The cab drove along a less busy side street. Beyond their flaws, Hanna had to admit human talent surrounded her. The creativity chiseled in a good number of these older buildings was beyond breathtaking. The tiny details they offered, with their stone arches and hand-carved statues and trimmings, were exceptional. This skill, this pride, was the reach younger generations should strive to create. Not the spray-painted cartoon figures covering such craftsmanship.

"Could you please wait for me?" Hanna asked, once the cab stopped in front of an older apartment building.

"Sure, lady, but the meter stays on," the balding man said, grinning wide enough to display the few teeth he had. "And there's an extra twenty-dollar fee for my time," he added after a brief hesitation.

She knew this greed was the main reason behind humanity's downfall. "That'll be fine." She closed the door and marched up the line of stone steps to the building's main entrance.

She heard a commotion the instant she entered. The bickering wasn't necessarily loud, but she, like her son and husband, had heightened senses. She could tell something was wrong several floors above her by the sound of the angry tones. She rushed up the stairs, taking two at a time.

Hanna reached the third floor in less than thirty seconds, not even close to being out of breath. She spotted her son arguing with an older, slovenly dressed man outside the doorway to Casey's apartment. The man was complaining to Parrow, something about more money. This must be the proprietor.

"She still owed me twelve hundred for this month's rent," he shouted, standing inches away from Parrow.

Parrow stood his ground and didn't move. Hanna threw him a glare that said, "Let it go," but he remained firm with his arms folded across his chest.

"She paid you last Tuesday for next month's rent. Therefore, you owe a refund of twelve hundred for the unused rent, not to mention another twelve hundred for her security deposit."

"You weren't there. You don't know what she paid me," the landlord bellowed, refusing to greet the new arrival.

Parrow squinted down at the man. He *was* there that day. But he was much hairier and walking around on all fours. "She called me and told me about it," he said, no doubt seizing the first explanation that popped into his head.

"She lied to you."

The property owner took two steps backward, away from the fierce anger rising in Parrow's eyes. Hanna gripped Parrow's arm before he retaliated. She sternly motioned for him to step inside Casey's apartment. Once Parrow left, Hanna reached into her well-pressed slacks, pulling from them a folded stack of one-hundred-dollar bills. She counted out twelve. Ignoring the proprietor's words of undying thanks, she entered the apartment and closed the door on him.

Hanna bit back her disapproving words when she saw the sorrow on Parrow's face. The heart of a mother beat within her chest, and she reached out for the teary-eyed young man. She held him close, like a child in her arms. She had never seen him cry before, and she cherished this opportunity to comfort him through his pain.

His body shook with each tear that fell, while Hanna stroked the nape of his neck. "You did what had to be done, my brave son. I'm deeply sorry for your anguish. If I could carry it for you, I would." She held him tight, not breaking the connection until he was ready to do so on his own. They had little time left, but he needed this, and she would do all she could to lighten his troubled ache.

When his emotions were under control, Parrow stepped to the side, his gaze dipping awkwardly away from her. "I'm sorry for my weakness. It got the better of me."

"You have your father's strength, but your mother's heart. Never apologize for either. For both gifts are a blessing to cherish."

Parrow placed his hand on her shoulder. "I've missed you, Mother."

She covered his hand with hers and gently squeezed. "The feeling is mutual. Unfortunately, we're on a tight schedule." She surveyed the room. "Where did you put the molecule displacer your father brought you last night?"

At once, Parrow went into the bedroom and retrieved the item from under Casey's bed. He pulled out the modified, titanium-based footlocker his father had also left. Parrow handed her the molecule displacer before he opened the footlocker and waited.

Hanna pointed the displacer at every object in the living room to scan the size and makeup of each individual piece. Three-dimensional images appeared in blue holographic forms inches above the device. Along the sides of the images were columns of figures and inscriptions. Hanna completed the process by entering various numbers and equations into the complex mechanism. Instantly, the furniture changed structure as the molecules fused together, removing the air and space from each object. Miniature piles of matter now stood in tiny, condensed forms, their previous configurations to be stored in the displacer and reconstructed at a later time.

Parrow collected and packed the broken-down elements into the footlocker, while Hanna went to the next room to start the entire sequence again. Parrow had placed the last grouping into the chest by the time Hanna's watch said eight-thirty a.m. He adjusted the gravity control on the side of the footlocker, making the extremely heavy container light enough to carry.

Hanna did one last sweep to make sure the apartment was empty. "We should go to the airport and wait for Elizabeth since we're done here. Unless there's something else you need to do?"

"How much time do we have?" Parrow asked.

She studied him curiously. "We're roughly an hour ahead of schedule. What else do we need to do?"

"Something I know you will enjoy." Parrow lifted the container from the floor. He strode with Hanna to where the cab was waiting. "Give us half an hour," he said, handing the driver a hundred.

The bald man's eyes brightened. "Take all the time you need."

Offering his mother his arm, Parrow directed her through the busy sidewalk. "I want to say a proper goodbye to mine and Casey's neighborhood." He veered them around the bustle of pedestrians to the end of the street. "First, you need to experience a warm New York pastry. After, we'll enjoy a pleasant stroll through the neighborhood park."

Elizabeth stepped from the hearse around the same time Hanna arrived at Casey's apartment, accompanied by two well-dressed men in black suits. The contract agency the Malanight family had used for over twenty years provided both the armed escorts and the hearse. The agency's services may have been more expensive than their competitors, but they were highly proficient and asked no questions.

Elizabeth quickened her pace the closer she drew to the door for the city morgue. A chubby man in a white lab coat greeted her with a crooked nametag pinned above his chest pocket, spelling out the name Harold, in bold white letters.

"May I help you?" Harold asked, gazing nervously at the two broad-shouldered men behind Elizabeth.

"Yes, I'm Elizabeth Malanight," she said, shaking the man's hand. "I believe one of my staff, Mister Parrow, spoke with you earlier this morning and told you I would arrive today to claim my granddaughter's body. Is she in the container we provided?"

"Ahh, Mrs. Malanight. Yes, everything's taken care of. I'll need you to fill out some paperwork first."

"I would like to see her body before I sign anything." A flash of an impure thought emerged from this man's mind to an earlier image of him loading Casey into the makeshift coffin. His eyes had lingered over her nakedness a bit too long to be considered in good taste for any species, humans included. Irritated, Elizabeth forced away the revealing connection. Humans were easy to read, though normally she chose not to. She felt it invaded one's privacy.

"Sure, not a problem. She's through here," he said, heading toward a closed stainless-steel door.

Elizabeth's voice cut him off. "I would like to see her alone, if you don't mind."

He looked as if he was going to protest her going unaccompanied through a door marked *Staff Only*, but he didn't. "Oh, certainly, I understand. I'll have the paperwork waiting for you when you're done." He scurried off down the hall.

Stepping through the door, Elizabeth caught her breath at the sight of the capsule lying on the cold, gray floor. "Please, let this have worked," she whispered as she hurried to the container.

She triggered a concealed button at the base of the capsule to reveal a screen containing a computerized keyboard and DNA reader embedded into the top of the lid. She placed her hand over the reader and waited for it to respond. Within seconds, the top of the container changed appearances, becoming gradually transparent and revealing Casey's body below. A colorful medical monitor appeared above Elizabeth's hand showing her the health status of the occupant.

Elizabeth held her breath as she read the multiple shapes and numbers, fighting hard to keep her composure. Her heart raced, her breathing leapt forward, and tears slid down her cheeks. She didn't bother to wipe them away, for these were blissful tears, and many years had passed since she'd had the pleasure of the way they felt.

Casey was alive and stable. She would soon be under the care of their healer and amongst her own people, who would protect her with their very lives.

She placed a kiss on the lid above Casey's cheek. "You have your mother's powerful will," she whispered, before removing her hand from the screen. As soon as she broke contact with the lid, the capsule transformed to its original appearance.

The Malanight Castle laid nestled in the center of the fifty-thousand-acre Malanight Estate in the heart of Virginia. The castle's interior contained four levels and a full subterranean vault. The combined space of the vast structure exceeded three hundred thousand square feet.

Elizabeth was grateful to see Healer Fayrel waiting for them at the castle's main entrance the moment Parrow steered their vehicle along the circular drive. Fayrel was an extremely attractive man, well-built, and stood six inches above Elizabeth's five-seven frame. She spotted Darren and Eva behind Fayrel, both with anticipation etched in their features.

"How's she doing?" Fayrel asked when he opened her door.

"The same as when I called you from the airport," Elizabeth said.

Fayrel made his way around and opened the rear door, revealing Casey's capsule. He pressed the concealed button and typed commands on the keypad. Within seconds, the capsule hovered inches above the bed of the vehicle. He guided the container out and placed his right hand on top of the lid.

"She's doing extremely well, better than I could've hoped for," he said. "Darren, you and Eva take Casey to the infirmary. I'll update Elizabeth,

Hanna, and Parrow on the events from this morning and join you shortly."

"Would you like us to begin the de-hibernation process?" Eva asked.

"That'd be fine. But don't open her pod until I get there."

Both bowed their heads in unison. They directed Casey in the hibernation capsule up the stone steps to the castle.

The moment they departed, Fayrel twisted toward Elizabeth, his expression somber. He guided the tiny group along the drive, not speaking until they were away from the castle entrance, where the shade of oak trees lined both sides of the paved driveway. "Barick sent out the transmission to the queen like you asked. We tracked two interceptions before she received it."

"Two?" Elizabeth stopped walking. Being able to monitor the transmission from so far away had taken a great deal of planning and work from her team, in the slim chance someone could breach such a highly secured message. But with past security failures and the gravity of the message's topic, Elizabeth needed to be sure their transmissions were not intercepted. Thankfully, the message was written in a manner only the queen herself would understand. "Where did the signals come from?"

"The first disruption was in the Couhl Tabarr System. I've the exact coordinates for you inside."

"Couhl Tabarr? There must be a mistake. That's near the center of our Universal Region." Elizabeth took a deep breath as her mind raced with the troubling news. "Not to mention the technology it would take to intercept a transmission on that frequency. One would almost have to assume the Hafites are involved."

Fayrel cleared his throat, his eyes housing the same nervousness plaguing Elizabeth. "That's the conclusion Barick and I've come up with."

"Hafites have been part of the Assembly for over a thousand years…" Elizabeth trailed off in deep thought. She didn't want to believe the conflict to come would be against a species inside their own region.

"The Hafites are a tolerable race," Hanna said, "but they've never let go of their lust for power. The other species of the Assembly know this, which is why no Hafite has ever been, or ever will be, elected as head of council."

Elizabeth expelled a deep breath. "We must investigate this situation further before we act on it." Several of her friends back home were Hafites. She couldn't fathom ever being at war with them.

"I agree," Hanna said. "The last thing we need is to make unprecedented accusations toward an entire race."

"What of the second interception?" Parrow asked Fayrel.

When Fayrel answered the question, he addressed Elizabeth, not Parrow. It wasn't because Fayrel didn't like Parrow. Fayrel was older and set in his ways. His belief was the younger generations would benefit more if they remained on the sidelines and let those with more experience handle issues of importance.

"We traced it to the Denite Solar System. To be more specific, it emanated from Planet Baysor."

"That's impossible." Hanna's words sounded painfully forced from her chest.

Elizabeth darted her eyes to the castle, then stared at Fayrel. "Does Eva know?"

Fayrel shook his head. "Neither of us had the heart to tell her, but I don't see how we'll be able to keep it from her much longer."

Elizabeth knew he was right. Once she reported this breach to Queen Ann, her entire team would know. "That can wait until Casey is taken care of. Thank you for the information, Fayrel. You and Barick are to be commended."

"I only wish I could've given you better news. Now if you'll excuse me, I must go see to my patient."

"I'll go with you," Parrow blurted out.

Elizabeth gave her dear friend Hanna a look of puzzlement.

Hanna flipped a hand toward her son who was trailing after the healer. "He blames himself for what happened to Casey. I don't believe he'll ever find peace if she doesn't pull through."

Elizabeth sensed her friend was fighting to keep her motherly worry at bay. She locked arms with Hanna, and they strolled to the castle under the shady freshness of the trees. "We ask much of our younger generation." Elizabeth's words were soft, and she spoke them with the compassion of a mother, a grandmother, and a friend. "They do so much to please us, and all they seek from their efforts is our love and guidance."

She squeezed Hanna's arm. "I feel, as I'm sure you have as well, they will see us through this war. We'll do what we can to support them, even fight and die beside them when the time comes. But I'm positive, their strength and determination are what will save all of our races in the end.

Chapter Two

Earth Date: 18th July 2042
Universal Truth

Intense light shone into Casey's eyes. She tried to move, but her muscles felt stiff, too heavy to respond. Blinking soothed the sting the brightness caused, and the room drifted better into focus. The walls were white, exceptionally clean, with nothing hanging on their bare surface to reveal her location. She tried but couldn't turn her head. It felt as if it were pinned against the warm, cushiony table beneath her.

A weight pressed against her chest, but her head was too stiff to raise to see what was causing it. A soft humming came from behind her, but the sound was too subdued to tell if the noise was real or her imagination. *Is this heaven?* Casey thought, as the memory of her death quickly sank in. *If I'm in heaven, why can't I move?*

Casey's throat was extremely dry, so when she tried to speak, only a tiny rasp emerged. The sound was inaudible, but loud enough to send the source of her chest pressure bouncing up, revealing the head and body of her beloved companion. She cleared her throat. "Parrow? Is it really you?" Casey croaked out, while he drenched her face with his wet tongue.

He pivoted on the bed, placing a heavy foot on Casey's stomach, and barked off toward Casey's left.

She felt discomfort, that much was certain. Maybe she was somewhere between Heaven and Hell. Purgatory?

Reality struck her. If I'm dead, Parrow must also be dead. A tear slid down into Casey's hair. "I didn't want you to die, boy. I was sure Gran would've taken you home." The image of her Parrow, alone and starving to death in their apartment, was unbearable.

Parrow whined when fresh tears fell from Casey's eyes. He craned his neck and licked Casey's face.

"Parrow, get down," a deep male voice bellowed somewhere from the left, the commanding demeanor sending Parrow straight to the floor.

"How many times do I have to tell you to leave her alone? If you want to stay in here, you must let her rest."

Casey was about to protest this harsh treatment of her dog, but after feeling a sharp prick to her forearm, she couldn't resist the lure of sleep.

With grogginess clouding her eyes, Casey awoke confused several hours later. Her body no longer felt heavy, but her throat was still parched. Two sharp barks greeted her from the floor, followed by Parrow's furry black and brown head peering curiously at her.

"Parrow, it's good to see you, boy," Casey muttered. She felt a sense of relief when she patted blankets that normally covered her bed.

Parrow's legs sprang in one motion, sending him to her chest in a flash.

"I thought we were both dead."

Was it all a dream? If so, I've had the worst dream ever, she thought, while peering around the room to confirm she was where she should be.

Her mind registered the familiarity of her bedroom furnishings, but something was different. The walls, no longer constructed of drywall and paint, were now stone and marble. She blinked upward as uneasiness crept in. The ceiling was also stone, with massive mahogany beams running along the width for solid support.

Casey slowly sat up, baffled. She found herself staring directly into an arched stone fireplace. "I'm at the Malanight Castle," she said aloud.

Casey froze. Uncertain thoughts raced as she made her way out from underneath the bedding. *What's going on? Is this real, or am I hallucinating while my body still clings to life?* She grabbed at an unfamiliar bedpost. The sudden standing motion made her dizzy.

Parrow leapt to the entry and barked loudly. Within seconds, the door to the room flung open, and in its threshold, directly ahead of Casey, stood her grandmother.

"What are you doing out of bed?" Elizabeth asked sternly.

"What...what's going on?" Casey's voice was scarcely above a whisper. Her mind spun. She was unsure of what was real anymore.

"All in good time. First, you need your rest."

"Am I dead? Are you dead? Is this actually happening?" Casey allowed her grandmother to guide her underneath the blankets, too taken aback by the situation to protest.

"No, you're not dead, and neither am I." Elizabeth offered Casey a reassuring one-armed hug. "This isn't a dream. You're safe and surrounded by the people who love you."

Elizabeth spoke to Parrow. "Has Fayrel been in recently?"

Parrow let out a quick bark.

She sighed and motioned for him to get on the bed. "You keep her here while I go get Fayrel."

Casey jumped slightly when he barked again. Not a normal everyday "dog" bark, but one suggesting he understood every word.

Elizabeth gave one last look to Casey before gliding out of the room.

"Of course, my grandmother's speaking to animals now. Sure, why not."

Parrow lowered his head to Casey's stomach, and she remained unmoving, staring at a stone ceiling directly above her bed. Why was she here? Or better yet, was she truly here?

Her grandmother returned five minutes later, followed closely by the man who'd been the family live-in physician for many years, even before Casey was born. She snapped her fingers to direct Parrow off the bed.

"Good morning, young Malanight. How are you feeling?" Fayrel asked, opening the black satchel he usually had on hand.

"Oh, let's see, lightheaded, somewhat weak…oh yes, and completely crazy," she ended sarcastically, her voice holding a slight edge of annoyance.

"It's good to see your wit is still intact." He pulled out a hand-held contraption that buzzed and beeped as he ran it over the full length of Casey's body.

Casey waited impatiently as Fayrel conducted his examination. She fully expected either him or her grandmother to explain how and why she and Parrow were at the family estate. As the minutes went from five to ten, then pushed close to fifteen, Fayrel switched out machinery to additional devices, making no sense, and neither one offered any explanations.

"She's fine," Fayrel announced, closing his bag. "There's nothing to worry about, Elizabeth. High-protein meals, bed rest, and she'll be fully healed in no time."

"How long do you want to keep her in bed?" Elizabeth asked.

"Let's give it one, maybe two more days. Before we rush anything, we'll see how she's doing tomorrow." He and Elizabeth made their way toward the door.

Casey's building irritation grew into anger. "You're both overlooking one tiny problem." She propped herself up with her elbow and struggled to keep her frustration hidden. It didn't work. "I'm an adult in case either of you have forgotten, and unless I get some basic questions answered, I don't plan to remain in this bed. Or in this state, for that matter."

She'd never spoken to her grandmother with such assertiveness before. Someone needed to enlighten her about why the last thing she remembered was being shot and dying on a floor over four hundred miles away. Demanding a few answers seemed little to ask.

"I can give her another injection," Fayrel said, his tone too casual for Casey's liking.

Her grandmother had the audacity to actually consider the offer. "No, that won't be necessary. I suppose now is a good time to have the talk. Could you ask Hanna to send up a lunch tray for two and some drinks?" She was about to turn toward Casey but added. "You may want to stay close by, in case she doesn't respond favorably to the information."

Casey felt a tinge of worry when he agreed. Maybe she didn't want an explanation after all.

Elizabeth moved a chair closer to the bed, avoiding the slumbering Parrow. She lowered herself, crossed one knee over the other in a proper fashion, and sat eye to eye with Casey. "There's much I need to tell you. Truthfully, I'm not sure where to begin." Elizabeth gently grasped Casey's hand.

Casey welcomed the touch from her grandmother and let go of her anxiety-driven agitation. She'd missed her grandmother more than she realized and felt at peace in her presence. "Why not start by telling me how I survived the other night, and how Parrow and I ended up here?"

"Yes, but before I explain, you must promise me, whatever I tell you, no matter how unbelievable it may sound, you'll hear me out to the end. I'm not asking you to fully believe me right away, but I expect the courtesy of being heard with minimal interruptions."

Slightly troubled by her grandmother's serious tone, Casey still consented to what she asked.

"Good. Thank you. Let's begin. First, that unpleasant night happened over two weeks ago. Second, you were never truly dead. We only made it appear that way. The weapon we fired at you slowed down your heart rate and breathing, keeping you on the edge of being alive. It works by temporarily freezing a body from the inside out for placement into a hibernating capsule."

Casey's chest tightened. "We? What do you mean we? You had something to do with this?"

"Yes, I'm afraid so, Casey. I knew a week before it happened the man was going to shoot and kill you once you entered the room. This became the perfect opportunity to stage your death to ultimately save your life."

An icy chill moved up her spine. "What do you mean you knew?"

"I used the same ability you've been tapping into lately. My mother and grandmother trained me to use this gift, but you have been learning this skill on your own."

"What skill?"

"Seeing the future." Elizabeth scooted her chair a few inches closer. "I'm immensely proud of you. You'll get better at it with training. You're not twenty-five yet, and your abilities are already showing on their own."

"My abilities? Are you saying there's more?"

"Yes, but we're getting ahead of ourselves. I must tell you our family background before we discuss our abilities. Unless you have any more questions pertaining to the other night?"

Casey felt lost, numb. "Let me get this straight. We can see the future. We have a weapon that fires electric ice of sorts, and there's this hibernating capsule thing. Oh, and let's not forget to throw in my own grandmother planned a hit on me." Her voice ended a pitch higher by the time her rundown ended.

An unexpected knock on the door made Casey jump.

Elizabeth gave her a reassuring glance before she called for the person to enter. Hanna came in carrying a silver tray with enough food to feed a family of four. Eva followed close behind with another silver tray holding a generous assortment of drinks.

Hanna beamed at Casey as she placed the tray in the middle of the bed. "I figured you'd be hungry, considering all your meals for the last two weeks were liquified and fed through a machine. I've prepared some tasty items that will aid you in feeling better. Many of these dishes are light, with high protein to help you recover your strength. They're not my best recipes, but they should do the trick."

Eva sat her tray on a nearby end table. "The same goes for me, but since I'm not gifted at cooking, I fixed you both some drinks." With a tender grin, she dabbed at tears with a tissue from the corner of her eyes.

Casey was overjoyed to see them. "I've missed you guys. I'd hug you both if I hadn't already promised Gran I'd stay in bed."

On that note, Eva and Hanna took turns moving in to give Casey warm embraces. Their presence sent a soothing calmness through her body. Both women had played a key role in Casey's upbringing, Hanna as the protective mother lion and Eva like a peace-loving, energetic big sister.

Elizabeth gestured to the antique bench positioned at the foot of the bed. "Would you like to join us?"

Hanna said, "We already ate. Plus, you two need some time alone." She pulled Eva by her arm as Eva was about to take a seat. As they exited, Hanna called out for the reluctant Parrow to follow.

"So where were we?" Elizabeth asked once they were alone. She handed Casey one of the silver plates, some utensils, and a full glass from the drink tray.

"You were getting ready to tell me about our family background."

"That's right." Elizabeth took a quick bite of her turkey sandwich and washed it down with a swallow of her sweet, iced tea before beginning.

"Your great-great-great-grandmother, Ashonda Malanight, arrived here on Earth back in 1894. She came from the Vasar Solar System. They sent her here as an overseer with a team of four other individuals to assist her."

Drained of what little energy she'd had minutes earlier, Casey lowered the serving spoon back into Hanna's hearty chicken soup and relaxed against a pillow.

"She ended up falling for your great-great-great-grandfather, David, who she married less than a year after arriving here." Elizabeth took another bite of her sandwich before continuing. "David was half-Human and half-Kan—"

"Wait." Casey put a hand up, realizing what was happening. "The guys in my precinct put you up to this, didn't they, Gran?" Her grandmother finally finding a sense of humor was unusual, but the knowledge also came as a great burst of relief. Her grandmother wasn't insane.

"I'm not toying with you but telling you the truth behind our family. Now let me continue. David's father, Roken, who was a Kan, crash-landed here on Earth from the Denite Solar System in 1863. He mated with David's mother, who was human, but ended up returning home to his own kind. Tragically, his superiors refused to let her go with him since she was human." Elizabeth added more sugar to her tea. "Honey, you're not eating. Please, you need to get your strength back. Here, let me make you a sandwich."

Lost in her worry, Casey watched her grandmother cut two more slices off the freshly made bread loaf. "You're telling me we're aliens from another planet?" What she was hearing more than frightened her. Her heart ached with grief.

"No, we're part human. We're also part Kan, but mostly Trysal."

"What are Trysals?" Casey whispered. Her world was crashing down around her, making it difficult to breathe. Her last living relative, her own Gran, had completely lost touch with reality.

"They're the species from the Vasar Solar System where Ashonda came from. You'll learn more about our species at another time. Today, we'll only talk about our family."

Casey felt her heart flutter a dangerous rhythm. Part of her wanted to shout for Dr. Fayrel, but a tiny voice told her to stay and listen to her grandmother.

Elizabeth handed Casey the sandwich but didn't continue until Casey finally took a decent mouthful. "Where was I? Oh yes, Ashonda and David. Neither knew of the other's true uniqueness until after they were married and Ashonda was pregnant with your great-great-grandmother, Annabel. Ashonda grew worried about the effects from mixing species, and she wanted to give David a heads-up, so to speak."

"Gran, I'm sorry to cut you off again, but do you actually believe all of this?"

Elizabeth's expression softened. "Yes, because it's true. I assure you I'm not crazy, and if you give me some time, I'll prove it to you. I'd like to get our rare lineage out of the way."

Casey's rational mind felt torn. She wanted to believe in her grandmother's sanity, but to do so, she would have to consider that not only were alien life-forms hiding out on Earth, but she, in fact, was one of them. Her grandmother was all the family she had.

Gran tended to be controlling with how Casey lived her life, but Casey loved her very much, no matter how challenging her Gran could sometimes be. The only choice Casey had was to listen and keep an incredibly open mind.

Casey pushed her plate away. "Let's say this stuff's true. Why was Grandmother Ashonda sent to Earth to begin with?"

"Good question. I need to first explain the area we and so many other species, including humans, live in. It's called the Universal Region." Elizabeth lowered her own plate and retrieved a notepad and pen from a drawer in the nightstand. She drew a three-dimensional outline of a rectangular figure, and three dots on three different sides of the rectangle to form an unconnected triangle. "This shape represents a rough sketch of our Universal Region. It takes up a vast area of space, roughly one-thousand mega light-years long, one-thousand mega light-years wide, and over nine-hundred mega light-years in depth."

Casey couldn't believe what she was hearing. "Do you realize how far that is?"

Elizabeth let out a dramatic sigh. "Of course, I do. A mega light-year is a measurement used for long distances in space. It's one million light-years for each mega light-year." She pointed to her drawing. "These three dots are the solar systems of Vasar, Denite, and the Milky Way. They're the only ones you need to pay attention to today." She paused. "Can you dish me out some of that, please?" She handed Casey her bowl.

Dishing out a serving of soup, Casey felt confused. "Can you explain that one more time?"

Elizabeth took the bowl and set it on the end table beside the stained-glass window. "I want you to picture space and the endless ocean of solar systems it holds. Now this section is our Universal Region. We protect everything living within this area and several other solar systems outside of it, which have joined our union. These three planets are on opposite sides of this region, and when you draw a line to connect them, they form an equilateral triangle inside our Universal Region. Does this make it any easier to understand?" Elizabeth asked, looking like she had just confused herself.

Casey nodded. "I get the concept." A thought struck her. "How long does it take to get from Earth to Vasar?"

Her grandmother's response was instant and done with such ease Casey might as well have asked her how long it would take to drive to the grocery store for a loaf of bread rather than venture a distance one could not complete in a million lifetimes.. "It depends on which ship you're on, and which route you take. The average is around a week."

This response was what Casey was hoping for. Proof to invalidate Gran's frightfully fascinating tale. "You'd have to travel much faster than the speed of light. Sorry, Gran, traveling hundreds of mega light-years in a week, it's not possible." Casey tilted her head to the side, contemplating. Her Gran was an extremely intelligent woman who knew the laws of physics had limits. "Gran, admit it. You're intentionally pulling my leg, right?"

Elizabeth kept her eyes focused on Casey as she spoke. "Actually, we've more than broken the speed of light. But yes, by traveling head-on, it would take us a millennium of years to reach Earth from Vasar." She brought her glass up, hovering the rim by her lips. "I, however, have not said we travel solely by way of velocity."

Casey's bubble of certainty broke. "What do you mean? What other way is there?"

Elizabeth consumed the rest of her tea and lowered her glass. "I'm not specialized in this area, but I'll do my best. Back when Vasar was grasping the possibilities of time and space, a young Trysal scientist, Malbet Crogon, conducted an experiment to convert a space vessel into a time machine. He said speed and time were intertwined with one another, connected by a pinpoint calculation through friction and mass. A scientific formula he was on the verge of discovering. One he could use to travel back and forth in time. Naturally his fellow scholars ridiculed him. Until the day of his trial run. He didn't succeed in time travel in the way he'd hoped, but he did manage to travel using the speed of time. Crogonic travel is the accurate term for it. Malbet Crogon traveled one and a half megalight-years that day, or to be more specific, 1.5 million light-years.

"Tragically, he lost his life several months later when he was perfecting this new technology. He didn't consider he would have to map out his destination around the many objects in space. Poor man flew headfirst into a field of asteroids."

Casey was speechless. Gran could have dementia. A condition like this at her age made sense. Possibly she'd read a science fiction novel and mentally distorted her grasp on life with the make-believe world in the book.

"I'm sorry," Elizabeth said. "I guess my talent for explaining things is lacking. But I promise, you'll learn more later and from those gifted to teach."

She refilled her glass as Casey remained unmoving. "Our rule falls under the queen and the Assembly, or the council, whichever you prefer to call it. We've been skirting on the brink of war for hundreds of years. Several species outside our region wish to rule over us. These species attacked a handful of the inhabited worlds close to the Milky Way several months before Ashonda and her team came to Earth. Since humans have no knowledge of interstellar life and could not defend themselves against the tiniest of attacks, the queen suggested to the council an overseer be stationed in this part of the region. All had agreed, but when it came time for volunteers, none stepped forward. None except for the queen's own daughter, Ashonda."

"You're saying we're from royal blood?" Casey didn't know what to make of this twist in the story. Her gran was telling the best and worst fable she'd ever heard.

"Correct. The queen and council arranged it so when a queen is ready to step down, the next in line will take the throne, leaving her daughter or granddaughter here on Earth to carry on. For them, separating the bloodline felt safer if war broke out. Don't keep their eggs all in one basket, so to speak. You'll learn more of this and our Universal history in time, but tonight I'll try to educate you with a brief glimpse into our world."

Elizabeth topped off Casey's glass and seated herself comfortably in the chair, less properly than Casey was used to seeing. "Where was I? I believe I was talking about David and Ashonda."

"Yes, she was pregnant and wanted to warn David about being from another planet."

"That's right. I guess you *are* paying attention." Elizabeth took a sip and placed her drink on Casey's nightstand.

"Did David tell Ashonda he was part Kan?" Casey asked.

"He did. The child, Ann, came out happy, healthy, and appearing as she should, and both David and Ashonda were pleased. Ann grew into a highly intelligent, beautiful woman and acted no different from any other Trysal. By the age of twenty-four, close to her twenty-fifth birthday, Ann developed certain abilities neither parent could have imagined."

Casey snorted. "Certain abilities? Like what—levitation? And why did it take so long? Twenty-four years. Even young witches and wizards enter Hogwarts at eleven."

Narrowing her eyes, Elizabeth shot Casey her legendary look, the stern glare which always made Casey regret whatever wrong she had committed. Like now.

"I do not know what you mean by Hogwarts, but I'm quite sure you are mocking me."

After a sincere apology on Casey's part and close to a full minute of awkward silence between the two, Elizabeth resumed talking. "The reason your abilities took so long to manifest is Trysals reach puberty around the age of twenty-five in Earth years. At this age, life for us truly begins. We grow from here at a rate approximately four times slower than humans, and our average life span is roughly two-hundred-sixty-four Earth years. Plus, like with you, she had no one around to help her with her unique gifts."

Casey's nervous laugh held no humor. "What, I'm about to hit puberty, and I've roughly two hundred and forty years of life left? I'm sorry, Gran, but what you're saying is ludicrous."

Elizabeth stood and added more sugar to her tea. She asked Casey over her right shoulder, "Have you been getting plenty of rest at night, or are you finding it difficult to sleep?"

Casey stopped laughing.

"The visions you're experiencing, are they becoming more of a reality than a mere daydream? Giving you the feeling you're actually in the vision?" Elizabeth pivoted around to face a bewildered Casey.

"How did you know?" Casey whispered.

"My darling, because I was once where you are now, and like you, I had no mother, just my Grandmother Ann to guide me."

Casey swallowed. "I'm sorry for laughing, Gran. Please go on."

Elizabeth retook her seat. "Let's see, oh yes. Ann showed signs of abilities far greater than any Trysal possessed. It started with the visions—"

Casey stopped her grandmother again. "What abilities do Trysals have?" Elizabeth looked at her, a questioning in her knitted brow. "You said she showed signs of abilities far greater than any Trysals. Do Trysals already have certain expected abilities?"

Elizabeth's brow rose in understanding. "Yes, maybe I should first explain the average being in our world. That way, you can see how different our bloodline truly is. Not different from humanity alone, but from the Trysal species as well.

"Vasar is an older solar system, and far more advanced than most. Not a boast, but a fact. The boasting will come from the way we use our higher level of advancement. For the good of many. Which is why we have a queen and an Assembly. We've learned through trial and error that absolute power truly does corrupt absolutely."

Elizabeth paused. "Sorry, I appear to be rambling. Now let me see. Trysals have an exceedingly high intelligence level, and over seventy-five percent can communicate through telepathic abilities. Some have the gift of seeing things before they happen, but the gift is more like feelings rather than actual visions. We need little sleep, especially after puberty, and we're made of a *xhemight* skeletal system."

"Excuse me? X…what?"

"*Xhemight* is one of the strongest elements discovered so far. It's roughly sixty times the strength of titanium and very lightweight, well, for a metal base substance anyway. A diamond-like structure imbedded in the center makes it almost impenetrable."

Casey inspected her arm as if looking for something she'd missed throughout the years. "A man shot me with a bullet that night, here in my chest." She rubbed the spot above her heart.

"Didn't nick the *xhemight.* The bullet was for the appearance of your death. We have a weak spot through either eye that leads right to the brain. The vision I saw a month ago showed this spot is where the bullet from the kidnapper's gun would have struck you, ending your life instantly."

"You didn't need to fake my death, though, did you? You could've stopped him from shooting me."

Elizabeth didn't respond.

"Gran, I'm confused. Why did I need to appear dead? There must be a reason for it."

"I promise I'll answer you, but I'd like to save that toward the end of our discussion, if you don't mind. Trysals are around seven times stronger than humans, but you don't develop full strength until you hit adulthood. The abilities our bloodline's been blessed with, beginning with Grandmother Ann, are still unveiling. I know our bloodline has a higher connection with time. To be more precise, we can travel through time, the past, and the future. The future hasn't happened yet. It's nothing more than an illustration of what is coming if we choose to keep on our same course with life. Therefore, when we travel there, we're like a ghost, with no solid body or substance."

A thought entered Casey's head. "In one of my visions, I was in the future for one minute, and the next thing I knew, I was jolted to the present. Why?"

"When you travel to the future, you must first connect with a certain source, a living individual, to be more specific. It's as if you're choosing to dial into this person's futuristic design, like dialing into their home landline telephone. If you move out of range from your source, naturally, you'll lose your connection. For our good fortune, after slight discomfort, you can choose to go right back in. Unfortunately, I've found if you're experiencing heightened emotion, like stress, worry, and so on, you probably won't be able to make a connection. The past, on the other hand, has already taken place. As a result, we can live in it and if we're not careful, die in it. If you come close to changing outcomes and causing a potential paradox, a force greater than that of the future will remove you. Take my word for it, the experience is extremely painful."

Elizabeth frowned at Casey's expression of astonishment. "You know what a time paradox is, right?"

"Yes, but as I understand it, it's a theory. No one actually knows what'll happen if you try to change the past."

"We do now. To a certain extent. One cannot go backward in time and change key factors. This concept is impossible. If one did and somehow prevented their own birth, how could they have been alive in the first place to go back in time? Even changing someone else's life could be disastrous for all. So I thank the stars no one has actually created a time paradox. We can't explain why or how, but some unknown force prevents this. Whether it's time itself, or some higher being, we cannot say."

For the most part, what her grandmother was saying made sense. "I see."

"Good, now we have a level of control over molecules, giving us the ability to move things, but it's awfully hard to do and requires much practice."

"Like lifting cars or rocks?"

"Yes, but like I said, it's difficult. You and I have a more acute sense of sight, smell, and hearing, and around twice the physical strength of a normal Trysal, which is saying a lot, I might add."

Casey thought for a moment, and her grandmother took this time to pick at the food tray. "What of the Kans? Do they have any abilities?"

"Yes," Elizabeth said. "They were identical to humans in many aspects, but at an overall higher development level. Mainly because the Kan race had been around longer than humans, but they also had a greater respect for their planetary welfare than humans do. They contributed most of their time to coming up with ways to improve their society rather than enlarging their pocketbooks. They were still a much younger race than Trysals, but we had great hopes for the benefits they would have added to the Universal Region. They could see in the dark and most were blessed with a rare connection with nature." She paused, as if in thought. "It's not that they could vocally speak to animals, like you and I are verbally talking now, but they had a strong relationship with them. I've not had much of a chance to experiment with this gift, so I'm not sure if we possess this or not. However, I have mastered the gift of seeing at night."

"Why do you talk about the Kans as if they are no longer around?"

The sadness in Elizabeth's eyes gave Casey an unsettling feeling. "I promise, I will answer that soon."

Casey didn't want to push the topic with further questions, so she changed it. "Do these abilities happen only on Earth?"

Elizabeth's expression brightened, showing she was pleased with the question. She reached over, placing her rough drawing of their Universal Region between them. "The triangle connecting our three solar systems represents the makeup of our family tree. Our abilities will work anywhere within this triangle."

Casey raised her eyebrows, astounded. She returned her fork with an uneaten bite of creamy chicken back to her plate. "There must be millions—no, billions of solar systems in this area alone."

"Oh, easily, but most do not have intelligent life-forms. Few do, considering how vast this area is. Like I said, you'll learn more about that later."

"How is this possible? I mean, how did this—this ability thing happen?"

Elizabeth studied the sketch. "I've done some extensive research and equations and discovered all three planets our ancestors originated from are exactly the same distance apart from one another. I've a feeling this piece of information is the basis for our phenomenon."

"You said we could control molecules. How about being able to adapt that into moving ourselves? Like flying."

Elizabeth showed a subtle hint of surprise at the unexpected question. "The thought never occurred to me. Like I said, we're still learning, but do me a favor and no jumping off of buildings any time soon."

Casey felt a smidge childish for having asked. "I promise, Gran, no Superman stunts." She glanced over at the sky out of a stained-glass window. "It's hard to believe a Trysal and a half-Kan mated. I mean, what do you think the chances are for two different species other than human to find each other and fall in love with one another here on Earth? Are there many Trysals or other species living here?"

"No, only us. You make a good point though. I've often thought of how fortunate we are Ashonda and David met one another. Pure luck if you ask me, but Grandmother Ann would swear fate was involved."

"So, who's on the throne if it's just me and you left?"

"Why would you think we're the only two still alive in our bloodline?" Elizabeth asked.

Casey was once again baffled. "My mother and your mother have both passed away. Oh, I guess they could have had a brother or sister."

"No, we're not sure why, but the royal line has always produced females and only granted us one child in every generation. Your great-great-grandmother, Annabel, is currently on the throne."

"She's still alive?"

"Yes, so is Ashonda. Remember I said we live an average lifespan of two hundred and sixty-four years. Ashonda celebrated her one hundred-seventy-fourth birthday last month. She has retired to our family's estate on Vasar One. Vasar One is the biggest of the four inhabited planets in our solar system. You'll learn all of this and more within time."

Elizabeth peered at her hands before staring out of the same window Casey had earlier. "I must tell you, my mother did not die of old age as you have been told. She and my father were both killed saving me. I was only nine when it happened, but I remember as if it were yesterday. I was coming down the circle drive from school when I heard my mother shouting at me from inside my head. *Run, Beth, run as fast as you can,* and so I did. They killed my mother right after. My father killed the Erules before either of them could catch and kill me. He died in my arms before help arrived, and that's why the security around this planet and our land is extraordinarily strong. No one expected such an open attack. Since that day, we have learned from our mistakes, and we remain on constant surveillance."

Casey didn't know what to say. She did know, by this troubling confession and the sincerity in her eyes, this wasn't a prank. Gran truly believed in her fictional fairytale.

"I've something else I must tell you." Elizabeth repositioned herself on the bed next to Casey. "Your mother didn't perish in a car wreck as you've been told. A squadron of Erules attacked her ship. They'd been waiting beyond the boundaries of the triangle. Your mother didn't detect their presence until it was too late. She had been on her way back from Vasar with the delegates from Baysor. They had no warning, and no chance to retreat."

Casey ignored the restricting feeling in her chest. "Who are the Erules?"

"Mercenaries who have a strong fondness for the taste of any flesh other than their own. They are located outside of our Universal Region and are part of the Kesler Solar System." Elizabeth held Casey's hand. "They've taken almost everything away from me I hold most dear. I'm pleading with you to pay attention to your training, and always be on a constant vigil. You are very important, Casey. To me and to our region."

They sat in silence for the longest time. Finally, Casey asked the question troubling her, "Why did they kill my mother or your parents?"

"Remember I told you we're holding back a war? The abilities our family possesses give us the advantage of knowing what will happen in our Universal Region before it actually takes place. We have used this to protect ourselves and our allies against those who would do us harm. Furthermore, our enemy doesn't know what else we're capable of, and this worries them. We're not sure how they found out about our gifts, but they have. I'm saddened to say a traitor must have infiltrated somewhere high in our council because few knew of these abilities. So now, we report to the queen and to the head of council only. We no longer have the comfort of trust, even with our own people."

How long had it been since Gran lost touch with reality? Surely the house staff knew her grandmother was off, but if this was the case, why hadn't anyone notified her?

"We've prevented three attempted assassinations on your life in the last few months, Casey. With you obtaining your abilities, they have become very desperate to end your life. The price on your head is so great we not only staged your death on Earth, but sent word to our people of your downfall. We must hide that you are alive, at least until we're able to catch this infiltrator, assuming there is only one. Both the queen and the head of council have welcomed this decision and give it top priority."

"Is my father alive? Or did he truly die when I was six months old?"

Elizabeth stood and paced the open space in front of the fireplace. She seemed uncomfortable with the question. "Yes, he died when you were little. You must understand—he wasn't meant to be in your life, only to give you life. You see, he and your mother, as with your great-great-grandmother, Ann, and your great-great-grandfather, Samion, never married. We, the royal line, by the age of thirty, choose to produce an heir to the throne if we have not joined with a partner by then. We find the strongest and most gifted individual in the Trysal species and mate with them to produce a child to carry on the bloodline."

Casey was stunned. "My mother wasn't in love with my father?"

"No, she was always too busy with her work to find someone to love. After you were born, she devoted as much time as she could into raising you." Elizabeth exhaled. "I wish she'd lived long enough to experience romantic love."

Casey felt an aching need to change the subject away from her mother. "So my great-great-grandmother, Ann, never fell in love either?"

"No, she fell in love, but not with Samion. Ann married a female Trysal named Bilana. They've been together for over a hundred years." Elizabeth moved in closer to whisper. "Before Ann married, she was awestruck by Queen Elizabeth the First."

"Queen Elizabeth? The Queen of England, Queen Elizabeth?"

"The very one."

"How's that possible? Queen Elizabeth was way before her time."

Elizabeth's forehead wrinkled. "Ah, but don't you remember me telling you we can venture back in time? She did, and often. She would see Queen Elizabeth whenever she could. I don't believe anything ever happened between them, but she never would give me a straight answer."

Casey leaned against the post on her bed, her head swimming in thought. "Gran, I'm sorry, but this all sounds so unbelievable. I mean, traveling in time, moving things with your mind, it's awesome, yes, but…" Casey shook her head. "You had me going, Gran. I was actually starting to believe you. It's hard enough swallowing the fact we're royal, but from another planet to boot." Casey's nervous laugh sounded odd, even to her. "So where's the house staff from? I guess they're also aliens from another planet."

The edges of Elizabeth's lips curved upward. "Yes, we have a staff hand-selected by me for my time here on Earth. They will remain with me when I take my position on the throne. My healer is Fayrel, who is a Trysal. Barick and his wife Hanna are my personal guards. They are Blunions from the Phortrix Solar System. Blunions are gifted in combat and can shape-shift into virtually anything living."

Elizabeth held up her hand when Casey was about to interrupt. "You'll learn more of the different species with your training. Darren is also my guard, but he's an exceptionally skilled mechanical engineer as well. He's a Gaminite from the Gamron Solar System. Then there's Eva, who is also a guard, but her primary function is to assist Darren in engineering. That woman can fly any ship you put in front of her. She's a Kan from the Denite Solar System. Other than our line, Eva is the last survivor of her people. We don't know how it happened, but every living being on her planet died. You'll find out greater details about all of this in time.

"We have two of your staff already chosen. One is your healer, a Trysal who finished top in her class, Healer Tanille. She's Fayrel's daughter. We'll pick her up sometime within the next few months when we head to Vasar. The other one you already know. He'll be your guard, and he's Barick and Hanna's son."

Casey was startled by the news. "I didn't know they had a son."

"His grandparents raised him. That was a choice Barick and Hanna made when they accepted this position, as well as Healer Fayrel with his daughter. They made trips to their planet as often as they could to be a part of his life and to help shape him into the gifted Blunion he is today. His name is Parrow."

Casey frowned at the name. "Parrow? You named my dog after him?"

The look on Gran's face was one Casey had seen a few times in her youth, and always after she'd done or said something her gran thought was ridiculous.

"What, my dog *Parrow*? Are you saying my dog's a shape-shifter? I'm sorry, Gran, but this conversation is getting out of hand." Casey slid to the edge of the bed and put her bare feet on the floor.

"I must insist you stay in bed. You're still too weak to move about." Elizabeth made her way over to Casey. "If you'll remain in bed, I'll call Parrow in here, and you'll have the proof you desire."

Casey wasn't sure what to say. She felt lightheaded. She wasn't sure if her building unsteadiness was from getting out of bed or from what she was learning. The more she thought about what Gran said, the more farfetched it all sounded.

What do I do when Gran calls Parrow in here, just to realize he's only a dog? How do I take care of Gran? Should I call for Dr. Fayrel to come in?

Elizabeth said, "I can take care of myself, young lady. Don't worry. If you would like, I'll get Healer Fayrel as well."

Casey glanced up, astounded. Her throat instantly went dry. She watched her grandmother head from the room. *Did she hear what I was thinking? How's that possible?*

Before Casey rationalized her unanswered questions, Elizabeth returned with Fayrel at her side and Parrow dawdling close behind. Parrow's head drooped, and his normally high tail was tucked between his legs. Casey didn't like to see her best friend cower like this. She called him to a spot on the bed next to her, and with a brief hesitation, he complied.

"What's wrong, boy?" she asked, rubbing her hands on his floppy black ears. She peered into his eyes, not knowing what she was searching for. As far as she could tell, he was the same loveable dog she'd left in the apartment two weeks ago.

Fayrel said, "I take it your grandmother told you who we are, but more importantly, who *you* are."

"She's told me what she believes, but I'm not sure how to take it."

Fayrel rubbed his chin, contemplating. "You don't trust what she said to be true?"

Casey kept her gaze off her grandmother. "I believe she believes it. But no, I don't. Did you know what she was going to tell me?"

"Yes, of course." Fayrel took the seat close to the bed. "Casey, you weren't raised knowing the truth because of what happened to your mother. Years ago, the Erules found out about your family and their abilities. After your mother's death, we realized we needed to keep you as cut off from the outside universe as possible. We hoped the more you didn't know about where you came from, the more your abilities would remain dormant inside you. We've done everything we could to protect you from danger, but since you're aging, your abilities are growing. We believe the enemy has learned that you, too, possess the Malanight gifts, which called for us to take drastic steps to hide you. Now it's time you know the truth."

Casey searched Fayrel's unwavering expression, not sure what to say. He rose and signaled his approval to Elizabeth.

"Parrow, we're ready," Elizabeth said.

The dog whined and placed his head on Casey's lap.

"Parrow, did you hear what Elizabeth said?" Fayrel's voice was firm, his words direct. "You know what to do."

Parrow slowly climbed off the bed. He kept his back turned to Casey, remaining motionless where he crouched. Elizabeth held up a hand to Fayrel, who was about to snap at Parrow a second time.

"Parrow, I know you're struggling, but it must be done." Elizabeth's voice was soft. Genuine. "You've been nothing but a loyal friend and protector to my granddaughter for the last several years. There's no reason to feel ashamed for doing what I ordered you to do."

Parrow turned to face Casey.

Casey heard enough. "Don't you both see how ridiculous this—"

The glow of light that emanated from somewhere inside Parrow froze Casey to the edge of the bed. She stared wide-eyed at her dog as his form slowly changed shape. The transformation was as beautiful as it was astonishing. She watched in silence as his figure converted from a hairy, four-legged dog into the slender, muscular man before her. He wore a luxurious navy-blue suit, a white silk shirt, and a red silk necktie. His exposed skin was a dark almond shade, bringing out the pale blue color of his eyes.

She blinked, and the authenticity of her gran's story sank in. Her throat tightened and her anger flared. He was the man who shot her, her self-defense instructor, and her loyal four-legged companion for these past several years. All lies.

Parrow glanced sadly at Casey, then to the floor.

Casey leapt up from the bed faster than her body was prepared for. The contents of her bedroom revolved in a cyclone of blurry images before sending her straight to the floor.

"She's coming around."

"How's her head?"

The voices sounded far away. Casey squinted, but visually, the only thing she could make out were two dark hazy figures crouched above her in the dim light.

"The knot looks worse than it is." Fayrel's deep tone drifted slowly toward her. "The swelling should go down in a few days, so there's nothing to worry about."

"Good. I guess under the circumstances, a bruised head is the least of her worries."

"Gran…" Casey mumbled when she recognized the sound of her voice. "What happened?"

Elizabeth's warm, smiling face grew into focus. "You stood up too fast and ended up passing out. Your head caught the corner of the chair when you went down, so you might have a slight headache."

A slight headache? Her head felt like it was going to explode.

Elizabeth clicked her tongue against the roof of her mouth. "Ah, now, it's not that bad."

"You heard my thoughts?" Casey tried to sit up, but the movement only made her head hurt that much more. "So, I wasn't dreaming. My dog's actually a shape-shifter, and I'm an alien—who's royal—with special abilities?" Casey deeply exhaled, while touching the painful spot on her forehead. She gently ran her fingers over the egg-sized knot.

Elizabeth said, "I guess we've gone over enough for one day."

Wait, couldn't Gran see the future? Casey pushed herself onto her elbows, praying she'd found a snag in their farfetched story. Enough to bust her from this mental fantasy world. "Why didn't you stop me from hitting the chair when I passed out? I thought you could see the future."

Elizabeth's brow drew upward. "It would be impossible to see *everything*, Casey, because there's so much to see. You must focus on the important areas to make sure everyone and everything is okay." Elizabeth paused. "I look into the future a few weeks ahead to determine we're all alive and well. If one is missing or injured, I focus on tracking backward on that individual to see what transpired and find out the details. I also watch different areas of our region to make sure nothing major has happened to any of the inhabitants." Elizabeth guided Casey to her pillow, pulled the covers up, and tucked them around her shoulders. "You'll learn how to do this in time and understand more as we go along. Right now, you need your rest."

"I certainly agree." Fayrel rose and gestured to the door. "Parrow's waiting outside. He's worried about you, and if you promise to keep it brief, I can give you two a few minutes to talk."

At hearing Parrow's name, Casey felt angry and ashamed all at once. "I don't want to see him."

After a brief pause, Fayrel said, "I'll tell him you're tired and to come back later." He politely excused himself from the room.

Elizabeth retrieved a glass of iced water, placed it on the nightstand closest to Casey, and sat on the edge of the bed. "You know, honey, Parrow was following my orders, and he did so to keep you safe."

"Gran, I understand what you're saying. I just don't…" Casey trailed off. How was she supposed to explain this feeling of betrayal to her grandmother? "If it's all right with you, I'd rather not talk about it."

Elizabeth stood. "Keep in mind, if you let something fester for too long, it'll make it so much harder to work through in the end." She placed a kiss on Casey's cheek. "Get some rest. I'll return later to check on you."

Chapter Three

The Secrets of Malanight Castle

The next twenty-four hours were absolute boredom for Casey, who remained in bed under the care of Healer Fayrel. He checked in on her every few hours, reminding her each time he left she must stay in bed to heal faster. He gave her two different types of injections following each exam, and by the first evening, Casey was already feeling like her old self again.

She wanted to explore the three-story guest wing, which was a miniature castle in itself, and located toward the far-right side of the estate, if one was facing the castle's solid-oak doors. The only ways in or out of this section was by the entrance on the ground floor, off the kitchen, or through the enclosed stone bridge on the third floor, which extended across to the main castle. The broad, winding driveway branched off directly under the bridged stone archway before circling around in front of the castle's main entrance.

When she was younger, this area of the castle was strictly off-limits. This made the unexplored dwelling more alluring. She had tried a handful of times to sneak in, but lock-picking proved too difficult for one so young. Her grandmother always caught her in the act. After the last lingering lecture she sat through when she was thirteen, Casey gave up trying.

Casey's bedroom was on the third floor, with her entire bedroom set moved into the suite. Her own casual furniture didn't match well with the opulent furnishings in the main castle, but having her things gave her a piece of her own independence. They weren't as exquisite, but she had worked hard to get them on her own.

On one of her grandmother's many visits, Elizabeth told Casey she moved her out here to give her as much privacy as she could. Elizabeth also said she had this entire three-story wing furnished with objects she hoped Casey would enjoy, with decorations and furnishings the entire staff had a hand in selecting. Since that visit, Casey had been eager to explore each level, fervently wondering what exactly she would find.

Casey sat up and cautiously swung her feet over the end of the bed. She no longer felt lightheaded, but not wanting to chance another blackout, she kept her movements slow. She welcomed the cool feel of the breeze against her skin as it poured in from the open window. It brought with it a fresh aroma of crisp, country air, heightened with a strong floral scent of honeysuckle and peaches.

Steadying herself, Casey rose, feeling the soft comfort of the ornate rug beneath her bare feet. She waited for several seconds for any signs of weakness, preparing to retreat onto the security of her king-sized bed if necessary. When she felt confident enough, Casey traipsed to the window to observe the grounds she hadn't seen in some time.

The land was so beautiful. Picturesque in an England, mid-century sort of way. Casey watched the wind blow playfully through the trees, teasing their many lush, crisp leaves. She loved every shade of green, a color of new life. The grass, a deep shade of forest green, was freshly cut and covered the surrounding landscape like a vast green ocean with no end.

"It's official. You were born with the Malanight stubborn streak. I thought I made it quite clear you were to remain in bed."

Casey looked over her shoulder to find the mixed expression of irritation and humor on Fayrel's face. "Sorry, I'm sick of being in bed."

He waved her off with a smirk outlining his features. "Don't bother apologizing. I know you don't mean it. I would bet it's the worry I'd give you another sedative is what has kept you in bed *this* long."

"Wow, you're good," she said, moving away from the window. "I guess my family hasn't been the best of patients."

Fayrel grunted. "You might say getting you Malanight women to follow simple orders is worse than pulling teeth from a Blunion." His tone was as airy as the breeze blowing in. "However, it's also been my greatest honor and privilege to take care of your family."

"Gran said your daughter was selected to be my healer."

Casey watched Fayrel's chest swell with pride. "That's correct, Casey. I hope she'll make a fine healer for you. She graduated first in her class a few months ago and has been studying all she can about Earth and its customs ever since."

"How long has it been since you've seen her?"

"I was on duty during the last trip, so I wasn't able to return home. But I was able to attend her graduation ritual." He radiated with paternal delight. "She's done well for herself."

Fayrel took out his instruments to use for Casey's routine examination and motioned for her to take a seat in one of the deep-red, mahogany-colored antique chairs by the window. "I only hope she's able to befriend you with her personality and skills, as I have with your grandmother. Serving as healer to the royal family is the greatest honor in our profession."

"She was pre-chosen, so why should it matter if we get along or not?" Casey asked, while she watched him work.

"She was pre-selected because of her capabilities and her relation to me. This doesn't mean you must keep her as your healer." He inspected the knot on her forehead.

"I'm sure we'll be fine. If not, we'll adjust."

Fayrel's expression relaxed, as if a hefty weight lifted from his shoulders. "You're so much like your grandmother."

"Thank you. I'll take a compliment like that any time."

Once he finished his examination, Casey stood. "So can I go check out my quarters, or am I still a prisoner trapped in that godforsaken bed?"

He busied himself with repacking his medical bag. "If I told you to get into bed, you'd be out of it the moment I left the room anyway. I'll allow you to move about, but first you must promise you'll take it easy."

Casey agreed, feeling a degree of excitement bubbling up inside. The thought of being stuck in bed any longer was almost unbearable. And to explore an area long denied to her curious self, she felt the venture would be well worth any exertion.

"I've one favor I need to ask."

Casey quietly waited.

"It's about Parrow. I know it's really none of my business, but he's a gifted Blunion, and I'm positive he'll serve you with the same devotion his father and mother have served your grandmother."

"I won't dismiss Parrow, if that's what you're worried about." Casey forced down her annoyance at his name. "I care too much for Hanna and Barick, and yes, I do believe he'll do his job well." Casey turned toward the window. "I'll deal with Parrow when I feel I can control my temper around him. Until then, it'll have to wait."

"Seems fair. I must say, considering you're approaching puberty, you've done very well at keeping your emotions at bay." His tone was of a doctor-to-patient rapport. "If you ever feel out of control or overly emotional, please let me know. I can give you something to get you past the touchy times."

"Exactly what will I be going through?" Casey asked, puzzled. This was information Gran failed to mention.

"Oh, I guess we haven't yet discussed this. Now is as good a time as any, I suppose." He reached over, placing two speckled pills in her hand, which she took without question.

Satisfied, Fayrel began. "You'll experience frequent mood swings, mainly anger, and you'll probably cry often for no reason. These outbursts of emotions are common. Most of us experience this. Also, expect to have a cramping pain run throughout your entire body. Also normal," he quickly said, apparently noticing the concern in her eyes. "It's just your *xhemight*, or skeletal structure, strengthening and growing. You could go through stages of not being able to control your body temperature. Oh yes, and you'll develop a heightened sex drive." He raised his eyebrows, more with the look of a father figure than a doctor. "This chat is between you and me. Your response will not leave the room. Have you been sexually active before?"

She blushed slightly when she said, "Yes." Not that talking to him about personal matters was uncomfortable. He was quite easy to confide in. Always had been. The topic itself made Casey feel uneasy. "I experimented once in college with my roommate, but we didn't get very far. I wasn't attracted to her in that way, but everyone else was, well, doing it. I figured why not see what all the fuss was about."

"This reaction is natural," he said, offering her a bit of reassurance. "I only ask because we normally will not develop a sexual desire until the onset of puberty or adulthood. As Trysals, we're usually internally motivated to find a life partner. Though, with your human composition, this might not be the case."

Casey thought about this last comment. She often wondered why she was never interested in intimate involvement before. She had friends growing up, but she never dated. Never wanted to. During college she chalked it up to having little time due to her busy workload. Afterward, she rationalized her lack of attraction toward anyone was due to not having found the right person. She guessed that her internal excuses were close after all.

Casey pondered through the idea of the growing pains he mentioned from her developing *xhemight* skeletal structure, and the dreadful notion of suddenly crying for no reason. She wasn't looking forward to any of this. "How long does puberty last?"

"Anywhere from several months to a year, measured by Earth time. Your libido, though, will remain high until around the age of two hundred and twenty, if it goes down at all. I've pills you can take for that as well. Most choose not to."

An entire year. He must be joking. "So to summarize, I'll become an emotional, out of control, sexually-driven adolescent, in pain, with hot and cold flashes."

"I'm afraid so. Let's hope you don't lose your wittiness when you've matured."

Casey walked him to the door. "Thanks for saving my life. I guess I should've thanked you much sooner."

Her unexpected hug threw him slightly off-kilter. He recovered quickly and patted her awkwardly on the back. "It's unnecessary to thank me. But please take it easy. I don't want you to make it a habit of getting injured."

Casey finished the rest of her lunch tray before setting off to explore her living space. She wanted to take a long shower and change out of the plain white gown she wore as soon as she could. She glanced at the door toward the north side of the bedroom and assumed it would be her bathroom.

Downing the rest of her ice-cold soda, and feeling more revived, Casey opened the closed door. A walk-in closet, almost the same size as her bedroom, lay before her. It contained clothes from her apartment, along with rows and rows of outfits matching her style of fashion. Jeans and jean shorts, dress slacks, loose fitting T-shirts and sweatshirts, dress shirts, board shorts and tanks, and several long rows of tennis shoes, running shoes, dress loafers, and two pairs of western boots. Oh, how Gran knew her.

She picked out a dark blue pair of jeans and a red Coke emblem T-shirt. She found her undergarments and socks in one of the many drawers built into the far side of the closet. She selected a pair of white and red running shoes and carried the complete change of clothes out before closing the door behind her.

Crossing the distance of the bedroom, Casey headed to the door others had been going in and out of for the last few days. As soon as she stepped through, she faced a comfortable living area. Someone had brought and arranged her entire front room set in the same manner as in her New York apartment. The only difference was her office, located in a separate corner room that featured arched windows which peered toward the sprawling gardens at the tail end of the castle. Both rooms contained a fireplace like the one in her bedroom.

She twisted the handle of a door between her bedroom and office to unveil what lay on the other side. Her excitement rose. The bathroom was the same size as her bedroom. Two marble sinks sat side by side on a long, black granite cabinet, etched with golden designs. They boasted matching handles and faucets. To her right was a walk-in stone shower, roughly eight feet in length and width, with corresponding fixtures. A toilet and Jacuzzi-style tub were located in the far-right corner of the room, and various shelves and drawers soared in the opposite corner, filled with bathroom supplies, soaps, bath wash, an extensive assortment of fragrances, and neatly folded towels and washcloths.

She hadn't realized until now how much she'd missed the luxury of the castle. Casey stood barefoot on the heated marble floor, unsure of what would feel more refreshing, a shower or a bath. Choosing the shower, she undressed and selected the soaps and shampoo to take in with her. Water in the capacious cubicle streamed out in all different directions, rhythmically massaging her from head to knees. Casey was satisfied with the shower.

Thirty minutes later, dried and dressed, Casey felt ten times better than she had in over a month. She was ready to explore the rest of her section of the castle and opened a door past the bathroom, which was a completely empty walk-in closet. Casey pushed on. She located a spiral staircase and ventured her way down.

The décor on the second floor was fashioned for the taste of a modern-day human being. The first room housed a home theater with expensive brown leather recliners and identical leather couches facing a high-tech movie screen, which took up the entire back wall. A wall-to-wall bar filled the opposite wall, complete with several stainless steel kitchen appliances, spacious black granite counters, and matching cabinets.

Casey made her way over and opened the doublewide refrigerator, revealing a tasty assortment of drinks and snacks to enjoy during a relaxing show. She noticed out of the corner of her eye a computerized stand at the end of the bar with a forty-five-inch monitor on the top shelf. Curious, she wandered over and inspected the different electronic boxes and devices that took up each of the shelves on the stand. She wasn't sure how it all worked, for she could find no switch or remote to operate it. She examined along the rear of the unit for the power cord but located none.

"It looks cool anyway," Casey said aloud.

With the sound of her voice, several red and green lights on multiple pieces of equipment powered on. "Welcome, Casey Malanight." A woman's voice, soft and elegant, greeted Casey. Colorful wavy lines and dashes emerged across the monitor. "I'm Chasel, your Personal Functioning System."

"You're my what?"

"I'm your Personal Functioning System. Program Intelligence is the common term for my kind. I was engineered specifically for you."

"You can understand me?"

"Definitely. All you have to do is tell me what you need, and I'll endeavor to achieve it."

Casey glanced at the screen with uncertain curiosity. "What things can you do?"

"I can perform any basic needs you have. Cooking, cleaning, and even organizing your computer files for you."

"What do you mean cooking?"

"What I provide is more of reconstructing." The lines on the screen flickered when Chasel spoke. "My system, which runs throughout your quarters, has been altered to appear as human appliances. However, you'll find I'm as capable as my counterparts elsewhere. Now, if you're hungry, you may say what you would like, and I'll create it for you."

Casey thought of something she could ask for. "So if I want a slice of chocolate cake with fudge icing—" Casey heard the beep from the stove before she could finish her sentence.

Opening the oven door, Casey was amazed to see a moist slice of chocolate cake sitting neatly on top of a crystal plate with a silver fork beside it.

"Try it. I hope you'll find it to your liking."

Casey took a good-sized bite, which proved to taste better than any cake she'd ever had. The fudge icing was as moist as the warm cake. "Not bad. You're a good cook."

"Would you like something to drink? I can provide you with anything made on Earth. Because of planetary security, I'm not allowed to keep any particles here that are not from this planet."

"Can you make a Shirley Temple?"

The refrigerator beeped as the stove had, sending her to open one of its two doors. A red drink was sitting inside. It tasted sweeter than the ones Casey remembered from her youth.

"Would you like to watch a movie? Or perhaps you would like me to prepare you a bath?"

Casey shook her head. "No thank you. I've already had a shower." She gazed at the screen. "You're going to cook for me and get my baths ready?"

"Oh yes, and much more. I can help you study when you begin your classes."

I could get used to this, Casey thought. Then her mind backtracked. "What classes?"

"The ones you must go through before obtaining acceptance into the Universal Academy."

"What Universal Academy?" Did Gran expect her to go back to school? If so, for how long?

Chasel gave a long whistling noise. "Yes, I can see you'll need drastic help with studying and preparations. You'll be attending classes next year if you pass the entrance test. I heard your grandmother has been working on your study schedule. We still have a few days until then, so please finish exploring the rest of your living space. If you have a question or merely want to talk, let me know."

Casey examined the monitor. "To get in touch with you, I come down here and call for you?"

"Simply say my name *anywhere*, and I'll be there. You can also change my appearance if you like. I can only take a Human shape though.

Planetary security will not allow me to assume the form of any other species."

Interested, Casey stared at the monitor. "How do I change your appearance?"

"Do you have a look in mind, or would you like me to give you some choices?"

"Give me some choices."

The image on the monitor changed to a blonde woman in her mid-twenties. She had a shapely body, but Casey didn't think it went well with the voice.

"Nope, got anything else?"

"Oh yes. My programming is very advanced."

"Okay, keep going with different images, and I'll stop you when I see one that fits."

Chasel complied and slowly her imaging changed. She had only gone through a few selections when Casey picked the one she liked. "Yep, that's my favorite."

Chasel appeared to be close to thirty with long, reddish-brown hair and a medium-built body. Casey enjoyed her soft, brown eyes the most. They made Chasel come across as honest, endearing.

"Shall I guide you on a tour of the rest of your quarters?"

"Sure, do you have monitors in each room, or speakers?"

"I have both. Or I can walk you through it personally."

"How?" Casey asked, puzzled.

The holographic image of Chasel materialized the instant Casey asked the question. Her form appeared real and opaque, as she stood politely watching Casey. She was three-dimensional, giving Chasel the appearance of Human life.

"You could touch me if you like."

Casey was shocked. "I can? So you're solid?" Without waiting for a reply, she reached out to touch Chasel's arm. She made no contact, as her fingers and hand went right through, giving no distortion to the image of the program.

Chasel let out a hearty chuckle. "Sorry, I couldn't help myself, but your shocked expression was invaluable."

With a light shake of her head, Casey huffed. "It's nice to see they gave you a playful personality." Casey stopped at the sound of her own words. "Wait, I guess you don't have feelings or emotions, do you?"

Chasel sounded a little affronted. "Yes, I have feelings. After all, we are overly complex and highly intelligent. We don't, however, generate the sensation of anger. My ancestors decided long ago, anger is an emotion not worth having. It has proved to create certain…complications within our programming."

"Wow, to cancel out an emotion. That's amazing."

"Yes, we *are* rather impressive." She wrinkled her nose in a good-humor sort of way. "Now, shall we finish your tour?"

"You lead. I'll follow." Casey held out an arm to direct Chasel to go in front of her.

Chasel guided Casey throughout the rest of the second floor. As they went along, she pointed out the hidden terminals and dispensers in each room where Casey could access a bite to eat, something to drink, and connect directly to her personal computer.

As Chasel was about to head down the next flight of circular stairs, Casey noticed an open door leading off into a corner hallway. "Where does that go?"

"To Master Parrow's living quarters. He has a bedroom, bathroom, and an office to himself. For some unknown reason, he's been staying in a different room inside the primary residence."

Casey wished she hadn't asked. She didn't want to think about Parrow, let alone talk about him. The hurt she felt regarding his dishonesty was still too fresh.

"Is everything all right?" Chasel asked.

"Yes, I'm fine. We can head downstairs now."

Chasel set off a few steps ahead of Casey toward the first floor. They entered a contemporary kitchen containing all the appliances one could hope for, including a fully stocked pantry. A door led outside toward the main part of the castle. Directly across from where they stood was a bay window looking out onto the grounds and the infamous stone barn. Infamous for Casey anyway. The building was large enough to fit a horse racing track comfortably inside, but unless something had changed since going to college, Gran didn't own any horses.

Casey headed to the pantry for something to snack on. "Can I cook with the stove if I want, or is it set up to have items materialize, precooked?"

"Oh, no, you can cook with it if you like. I've a database full of every recipe you could think of."

"Thanks, but I won't need them. I stink at cooking. Is this where you get your ingredients from when you prepare things?" Casey opened the pantry.

"No, the elements required to make each item in my database are loaded from beneath the castle by cylinder tubes that only store molecules from Earth."

"From beneath the castle? Other than a wine cellar, I didn't know we had a basement. Can we see it next?" Casey selected a serving-sized bag of chips.

"You'll first need approval from Elizabeth Malanight. Your grandmother should grant you access soon, but we must wait until then." Chasel threw Casey an exaggerated sigh. "You also need all these codes and passwords to attain access down there. Plus, security increases as you go along the lower passageway."

"What passageway?"

"I'm sorry, but without clearance, I cannot tell you." Her voice sounded nervous. "I've probably said too much already."

Casey wondered if the basement went under the main part of the castle as well but decided not to press the topic further. "Don't worry. I won't say a thing. I'll wait until Gran brings it up."

"You're exceedingly kind, young Malanight. Let's finish the tour. Once we're done, I'll make you my special caramel chocolate cappuccino."

Caramel and chocolate in a caffeinated beverage. Maybe this was heaven after all. "Sounds wonderful."

Chasel grinned and bent in closer to whisper, "I've discovered if you add the whipped cream at precisely the right temperature, it gives the drink an extra bit of sweetness which is unsurpassed, even by Jasper."

"Who's Jasper?"

Chasel swatted a hand in the air, as if she were waving off an annoying fly. "Oh, he's the Program Intelligence for the primary residence. He takes care of your grandmother Elizabeth and her team, whereas I was programmed for you and your team." She leaned forward to whisper again. "Between you and me, he has no sense of humor, and he's a complete bore."

Casey liked Chasel. This Program Intelligence was a great fit for her. "Why do we have a pantry if you get the food from somewhere else?" Casey asked, before shoving a few chips in her mouth.

"Hanna and Fayrel insist on preparing meals from scratch. The items are here to give you and your team the same option. Speaking of Fayrel, we better get a move on. I'm sure he'll return soon to check on you." Chasel guided the way through the rest of the first floor.

Chasel showed Casey a section containing four identical rooms, each with their own offices and bathrooms, where the rest of her team would live once Casey selected them. The remainder of the first floor was divided into two equal-sized rooms. The first room was an elaborate den, including comfortable overstuffed furniture, a granite fireplace, and stocked bookcases. Casey thought this to be a splendid room in which to snuggle up with a good book and relax for hours.

The last room was a state-of-the-art conference room, which had an adjoining office set up in a space no bigger than her walk-in closet. A highly polished mahogany table ran half the length of the conference room with matching cushioned chairs surrounding every side. On one wall was a built-in screen at least eight feet long. Monday night football just got better.

The office in the back was a miniature version of the conference room. The only difference was a sturdy mahogany desk sat angled in the room instead of a table. "You'll have several of your classes here. I'm sure your grandmother will explain more of this to you within a day or two."

Casey was more than ready for her promised treat. "Would you say this marks the end of our tour?"

Chasel's eyes sparkled and within a split second, several of the books on a shelf behind the desk vanished, revealing a hidden monitor next to a sleek metal container. It resembled a futuristic microwave but was twice the size. Casey grabbed a foaming mug from inside the contraption and took a sip. The creamy-sweet texture had a soothing sensation, and the caramel chocolate cappuccino easily slid down her throat. "Delicious!"

"I'm glad you like it."

Shortly after the guided tour was over, Chasel informed Casey that Healer Fayrel and her grandmother were waiting upstairs in her living room. Chasel excused herself and vanished as quickly as she appeared.

Casey hastily downed the last few mouthfuls of her cappuccino before trekking to the third floor. She found her grandmother sitting on a couch in front of the fireplace, talking to Fayrel.

He rose to his feet as soon as Casey entered. "Ah, we were just talking about you."

"Anything I should be concerned with?"

Fayrel responded with a teasing shrug.

With her proper air of grace, Elizabeth stood. "Actually, we've been deciding if you should go with us to Vasar One. We need to pick up Fayrel's daughter, and I've some issues to discuss with the queen and head of council."

A wave of excitement rushed through Casey. To fly off into space. Explore a mysterious planet. A far-off world her own family came from. The thought was beyond imaginable. "I would love to go."

Fayrel didn't seem entirely taken by the idea. "We must consider many things before deciding. It will depend on how well you're doing in your classes, and there's the matter of your safety." He directed his last bit of information toward Elizabeth. "I imagine this should be a group decision. If this were up to me, I'd give Barick the final say."

Elizabeth wasted no time in agreeing. "Casey, we know you deserve to see where your people come from, but you'll have your whole life to experience it. I'm asking that whatever the decision, you try to understand we based it on what we felt was best for you."

Casey's mind turned to her police partner, Jim. She was trying to come to grips with her old life being over, and worrying about what her death had done to him didn't help. Couldn't she tell him the truth? "I've thought about this arrangement regarding my faked death. To be honest, I'm not too keen on the idea."

"This choice I made, along with the approval of the queen and head of council, is not open for discussion."

Casey felt her temper rise. She didn't go through Earth adolescence only to be treated like a child all over again. "Do I not get a choice?"

"You're young—"

"I'm an adult," Casey snapped.

"Yes, on Earth, but not on Vasar."

"Please…" Fayrel held up a hand to both women.

Elizabeth said, "Casey, you must appreciate it's not only your safety on the line here. The existence of our way of life rests on your survival. You have no heir. Care for your wellbeing must come first."

"It sounds like I'm considered nothing more than a walking womb."

Elizabeth pinched her lips together. "There's more to consider than just you, young lady."

Casey was about to bark out a retort, but Fayrel loudly cleared his throat. "Elizabeth, with all due respect, Casey has but recently learned of where she comes from and who she truly is. She wasn't raised with the knowledge, as you and your family have been."

Elizabeth looked at Fayrel. After a temporary pause, she relented. Her voice was calmer, and she addressed Casey with an air of compassion. "I'm sorry. I know everything's new for you. However, this decision is irreversible. With any luck, you'll not have to remain in hiding for long."

Casey's anger subsided. Releasing a lungful of disappointment, she sat down on the couch across from the other two. "What kind of classes will I be attending?"

Elizabeth retrieved a black leather satchel from beside her seat and handed it to Casey. "I've provided you with several items to help keep you organized. Over the next few months, you'll need it."

Casey opened the bag to reveal a top-of-the-line laptop, handheld electronic organizer, several leather-bound notebooks, and miscellaneous items like pens, pencils, and highlighters.

"There's a schedule I put together for you, listing all of your classes. They'll give you the basics to help you during your two years at the Universal Academy."

Casey jerked her head upward. "Two years? I've already been to college. Must I go to this Academy? I thought I was going to be an overseer here on Earth?"

Fayrel snorted. "Do you think your previous schooling has prepared you for the universe outside this solar system? I can assure you, it hasn't. You shall one day take the throne as queen, and not having the proper education or training would almost certainly guarantee you an unsuccessful rule."

"Since you put it that way," Casey said sarcastically. Surprised by her own childish reaction, she felt instant warmth around her neckline.

"Being born a Malanight is your fate, and ruling, your legacy," Elizabeth said with pride. "We can provide you with the basics, but it will take hard work and determination on everyone's part. The Academy will supply you with the advanced training we cannot." Her chin rose a fraction of an inch higher. "It's a tremendous honor to be accepted into this institution. Only eight thousand trainees receive the opportunity each year, and considering we're talking in terms of all the species in our known universe, that's saying a lot."

Fayrel said, "Of course, there are other places you can attend, but none come close to comparing with the training at the Academy."

"Because of your position, you're guaranteed a slot at the school, but you must first pass the entrance exam." Her grandmother's words held a serious undertone Casey instantly picked up on. "It's an extensive test. But if you work hard for the next several months, you won't have a problem passing." The way her grandmother spoke, Casey knew no Malanight had ever failed the exams.

"When and where is the test?" Casey asked her question with all the humility she could muster.

"We hope to schedule it around the first of February," Fayrel said. "If you're as gifted with learning as your grandmother, you'll have no problems preparing for the test. You'll need to test out in each of your classes before you're allowed to take the Academy entrance exam, and each instructor will determine when you're ready to do so."

Casey stood up to pace. She wasn't sure what she was feeling as multiple questions rushed through her head. "Listen." She turned to face them both. "I'm not even sure if I would make a good queen." She ran her fingers through her short hair. "I mean, ruling a country is one thing, but you're talking about an entire Universal Region."

Elizabeth's answer was straightforward. "It's in your blood. Plus, you still have a long time to go before that happens. Let's concentrate on one thing at a time."

A bit relieved, Casey resumed her pacing. Growing up at the castle and attending private schools, she may not have been raised as normal as most, but she knew who she was. Now, her life was plunging into uncertainty. "When do I start?"

"We'll begin your classes on Tuesday. As long as Fayrel says you're medically ready." She raised her eyebrow.

At once, Fayrel signaled his approval.

"Splendid," her grandmother said sunnily. "You'll have a day and a half to become familiar with your quarters."

"What classes am I taking?"

Elizabeth pointed toward Casey's pricy laptop. "I've jotted down your schedule in there. If you would please open the program labeled 'class schedule,' we can run through it together."

Casey sat next to her and did as her gran asked. When the program opened, her mouth dropped. A complete schedule was typed out by class subject, location, allotted times, and names of instructors. Each of her classes was three hours long, with no mention of bathroom or rest breaks. "You've got to be kidding me. Forty-eight hours of back-to-back classes with a twenty-four-hour break in between?" Casey shook her head. "What about food—rest?"

"When I attended the Academy for my Doctorate of Universal Medicine," Fayrel said, "I had sixty-two hours of classwork, with a twenty-hour break between cycles."

"I went easy on her since her body is still adjusting to her adult Trysal internal clock." Elizabeth turned to Casey. "Your instructors will see to your meals and restroom breaks. Your twenty-four-hour time off will be for rest and study time."

"About how much sleep does a Trysal require in a week?" Casey asked Fayrel.

"It varies depending on age, but the average is around ten to fifteen hours per Earth week." Fayrel said, obviously noticing the surprise on Casey's face. "Casey, our internal clocks are longer, as with our lifespan. Both are linked by several factors."

Casey asked, "What sort of factors?"

"For instance, our brainwave activity is much higher than humans. I'm not trying to say this part of your lineage is unintelligent, but compared to Vasar, Earth is an incredibly young planet. We've been around millions of years before Humans roamed Earth, so naturally, we're going to be more advanced."

Casey could tell Fayrel didn't want to offend this part of her heritage. He only wanted to make her aware of the facts. She leaned over to touch his arm. "I understand what you mean. Please go on."

Fayrel said, "All four Vasar planets share two suns. Both suns are five times larger than Earth's. Therefore, this extends our daylight to one hundred and forty-eight hours, giving us roughly twenty hours of nighttime, depending on the season. There is also a difference in our body structures, cell regeneration, and hormone production. The list goes on and on. Let's also not forget the advanced technology we have in science and medicine. Why do you think your grandmother appears as old as she does when she's only eighty-four? That's just one-third of our average age."

Surprised, Casey glared at her gray-haired grandmother. "You don't really look this old?" Casey blushed as her words came out, and she shifted uncomfortably. "I didn't mean you…" Casey swallowed the rest of her sentence.

Elizabeth huffed. "Yes, I look much younger than this, but thanks to a tiny green pill, which I take once a month, I'm able to hide this truth from the many humans who know me to be eighty-four."

Elizabeth sternly eyeballed each of them before continuing. "I happen to like my appearance. One day I'll wear this age with pride, knowing all the good I've done and the full life I've led while residing in this body."

Fayrel clumsily sputtered. "I didn't mean you looked appalling, or anything of the sort. Quite the opposite, Elizabeth. You're an extremely beautiful woman…" He trailed off, as if realizing the impact of what he had said, and went from his normal, light-tan complexion to a bright shade of red.

Casey felt sorry for his obvious distress and figured she should help by changing the subject. "I'll learn more of this in your class, I take it?"

He jumped at the save. "Yes. I've a well-thought-out schedule for you. I'm confident it'll help prepare you for the preliminary exams." He suddenly stood. "I know you two have much to do today. I'll say my goodbyes and let you both get on with—excuse me."

Casey had to stifle a laugh, as Fayrel all but ran to the door. She was getting the idea Fayrel had feelings for her grandmother. How deep they went, she wasn't sure, but the idea of them together wasn't terrible. She was contemplating saying something to Gran regarding this but decided not to. After all, she could be wrong.

Elizabeth stood. "Shall we begin?"

Casey powered off her computer, placed it into her satchel, and followed Elizabeth from the room. "Where are we going?" she asked, as they went down the circular stairway leading to the lower levels of Casey's living space.

"To finally show you what lies underneath this castle."

When her grandmother exited the stairway on the first floor, Casey stopped. "Don't we need to go down one more level?" she called after her grandmother, who was moving with the stride of someone with an especially important purpose.

"Not that way. It leads to the wine cellar. Keep up, please."

Casey trotted after her. They went through the kitchen and down the hall toward the front of the building. Casey thought they were heading for the den, but as Elizabeth passed the first door, Casey realized she was taking her into the conference room.

They made their way through, not stopping until they reached the modest office.

"We're here," Elizabeth said, standing next to the spot where Chasel had exposed the hidden cappuccino contraption less than an hour ago.

"What is it?" Casey asked.

Elizabeth raised her eyebrows, a hint of enjoyment showing on her face. She reached for the center row of books and ran her first finger gradually down the leather spine of *The Encyclopedia of Stars and Planets*, instantly exposing a separate monitor directly above the container Casey's cappuccino had materialized in.

Chasel's image appeared on the screen. "Good afternoon, Elizabeth Malanight. How may I be of service?"

"I see Casey has given you a new image."

Chasel rotated fully on the screen. "Yes, do you like it?"

"I think you're lovely. This fits you very well."

Chasel's eyes sparkled at the compliment.

"I'm taking Casey below to see Vasar Five. Please let Barick know we're on our way."

Chasel bowed before leaving the screen. The bookshelf to the left side of the monitor vanished, revealing a silver door. There was no doorknob, only a computerized panel embedded in the center, eye level to Elizabeth's height.

"What is Vasar Five?" Casey asked curiously.

Excitement danced in Elizabeth's eyes. "You're about to find out." She pressed on the screen. A green ray of light instantly encircled her hand.

"It's scanning my handprint and also checking my DNA makeup. We must go through several such stations before we reach our destination. We have already programmed your information into the system, but to go through, mine alone will suffice."

Casey heard a loud click, and the silver door moved smoothly to their right, disappearing into a gap in the wall. A light came on, exposing an all-metal stairway leading downward. Strangely, the light seemed to emanate out of the walls and ceiling themselves. Their composition was the same metal substance as the door, but the surface of the stairs resembled a highly polished black marble, not silver.

Several minutes passed before they reached the bottom, even at the fast pace Elizabeth set. For many years, Casey had considered her grandmother to be a frail older woman with white hair and wrinkles to match her age. Now Elizabeth glided along, displaying the vigor of a young woman. Casey, who was much younger and a few inches taller, had to periodically jog a few steps to keep up.

As a bead of perspiration developed on Casey's forehead, the hallway ended. In front of them stood another metal door with the same type of computerized panel as the first. This time Elizabeth spoke the word *Valishima*. The same metallic click followed the name, and the door slid obediently open.

Casey ogled her Gran.

"I always loved your mother's name. It means 'beautiful one' in Trysal," Elizabeth said. She smiled softly before stepping through the door onto a platform doused in a green glow. An elevator of some kind.

Casey followed, feeling a mixture of grief and serenity at hearing her mother's name and the meaning behind it.

A few seconds after the door glided shut, it reopened. At first, Casey thought the futuristic elevator was broken. Damn technology. She soon realized they were no longer in front of the vast stairway that brought them and instead faced a long hallway which split in two different directions.

"Gran, where are we?"

"We teleported down to the lower level. The hallway to our right leads to the entrance of my office in the main part of the castle." Elizabeth gestured toward a partially lit passageway. "This other way will bring us to the entrance of Vasar Five."

Casey couldn't tell how far ahead the hallway went because everything over fifty feet was blanketed in complete darkness. This corridor had almost the same appearance as the previous stairwell, except the far wall was a darker shade of silver, almost ash gray. She placed a hand on the surface of the strange metal. It felt warm, sending a calm vibration against her skin which traveled throughout the length of her body.

"What kind of metal is this?" Casey asked, pivoting toward her grandmother while keeping her hand on the wall.

"It's *terropen*. The strongest metal discovered in the Universal Region."

"Why's it vibrating?" With a sudden burst of certainty, an answer to her own question consumed her. "Is this a spaceship?"

Elizabeth gave Casey a matter-of-fact glance. "It vibrates because it's in operation and yes, we are located outside a spacecraft. We've constructed almost every ship from the region during the last one thousand years with this metal. God forbid, if this planet should ever explode, this ship would survive undamaged."

Elizabeth turned and strode through the hall in the direction opposite her office. "Keep up, please."

Casey stared at the impressive wall of *terropen*. Mesmerized by the gravity of her position, she fully realized for the first time she *was* from another planet and standing next to a spaceship. Her job would be to protect Earth, and the Universal Region surrounding it, which one day she was destined to rule. The facts were a lot to take in.

"Casey!" Elizabeth's voice brought her out of her reverie, and Casey ran to catch up.

"Is all this really happening?" she asked, falling in stride with her Gran.

"I thought we already covered that."

"I know, but it's all so—so—"

"Unbelievable? Yes. However, once you make your first trip up there," Elizabeth gazed toward the ceiling, implying outer space, "it all becomes real." Elizabeth enclosed Casey's hand in hers as they walked. "There's so much for you to see, so many things outside of this solar system you'll experience, enlightening your mind and soul a hundred times over." Her intense eye contact revealed the abiding love she had for her granddaughter. "I'm proud I'll be next to you throughout it all."

Touched by Gran's words of affection, Casey responded with unwavering honesty, "So am I."

A piece of the wall opposite the ship transformed instantly into a display screen. An older, dark-haired figure in his mid-forties spoke. "Ms. Malanight, the president is requesting a conference call as soon as you are available."

"Thank you, Jasper. Please let him know I'll contact him in about an hour."

So this Program Intelligence is Jasper. Casey watched him bow low, then disappear, screen and all. She touched the cool surface of metal where Jasper had appeared, only to discover it felt no different from any other part of the wall.

"We'd better hurry," Elizabeth said. "I'll not have time to give you the extensive tour I had hoped to provide, but I can at least show you the operations deck."

"Does he mean the president of the United States?"

"Yes. If it were a different president, he would have told me. Otherwise, he's referring to this country."

"Do they know who we are?"

"No. We overseers, by Universal Declaration, cannot divulge our true identity for fear of altering this race. Unless this planet was in significant danger to the extent we would need to step in to defend or evacuate it, in which case we would have no choice but to inform them."

"What about our technology? I assume, in the medical field alone, we could improve the quality of life on Earth tenfold."

Elizabeth stopped walking, her demeanor solemn. "This happened four hundred years ago on another planet not too far from here. They were further along than Earth, and we thought we could help them advance by sharing a minute part of our knowledge." Elizabeth shook her head. "It ended tragically. Their planet was like Earth, divided into civilizations under separate governments. Each government had its own idea for one world rule. They ended up using the new technology we provided in a massive world war, ending their species almost to the point of extinction."

"That's awful!"

"Earth is still incredibly young. There are wars here because of issues involving religion, money, oil, race, and oppression. This list goes on and on. How do you think it would be if we added great power and unimaginable knowledge to that?"

"Disastrous."

"I'm afraid so. All we can do is protect them from the harm outside of their solar system and make sure they don't destroy themselves as they grow. With all this pollution, we might have our work cut out for us." Elizabeth pointed to another door leading off to the left. "That one goes to the stables. The password is 'Casey.'" She continued along the hall with Casey close by.

"Why would the president call you?"

"We must keep up political appearances in case we ever do need to inform them. We also donate generously to several organizations working to clean up and benefit the Earth. Same with each government, as long as they have a valid agenda. He is more than likely planning on asking me to make a monetary donation. It better not be related to military or oil this time, or I might hang up on the old fart."

Casey fought down her laughter. The thought of Gran calling anyone, especially the president of the United States, an "old fart" was unexpected.

She didn't realize they had reached the end of the hallway until her grandmother stopped in front of a dark green doublewide door, roughly fifteen feet tall.

"The port entrance to Vasar Five," she said, sending Casey's heart into an excited rhythmic beat.

Casey tried to see past the extended, darkened hallway to get a feel for the length of the vessel. "Exactly how large is this ship?"

"Over five and a half miles long and four hundred and twelve stories high," Elizabeth casually responded, as if the size were unimpressive. "We're at the top level, which we've buried a mile below ground. It rests underneath the castle and the barn, so if we ever had to take off, both structures would be destroyed." Elizabeth grinned at Casey's wide-eyed expression. "It's actually a pretty average size for an exploration ship. You should see the size of the colony ships. They make these T-19s look puny."

"How do we go to Vasar, or anywhere else, if we don't use this ship?"

"There's a hangar right above us which houses two traveling vessels. They are Vasar Six and Vasar Seven. You get to the hangar through a doorway located as you go up to the stables. The password for the door is 'Malanight.'"

"Who came up with the names of the ships? I mean, the planets are Vasar One, Two, Three, and Four and this ship is Vasar Five, then there's Vasar Six and Seven. It's kind of dry."

"That was Ashonda's idea. She went in order after Vasar Four, saying each of the royal ships is like a pocket-sized planet. They provide the means for survival and a place to live for our family as planets do. There is also Vasar Eight, which was named after your mother's ship. It's a normal Earth-made airplane that remains in a storage hangar at the airport."

Still thinking the names could've been better, Casey was more than ready to step foot into her first non-terrestrial spacecraft. She watched her Gran activate a control panel with a monitor next to the solid door. After speaking her name, Elizabeth placed her hand on the screen so it could scan her handprint and crosscheck her DNA. The metal click was much louder than the previous doors, but instead of sliding instantly inside the wall, this one moved a foot backward and slid slowly to the right, where it disappeared into a compartment inside the wall.

Casey followed Elizabeth inside, gawking. The air smelled as fresh as a cool summer's day, as she made her way through the immense entryway. Elizabeth reached up, pressing a red button on one of the multiple control panels, and closed the door behind them.

"There are maps throughout the ship if you should ever get lost. Plus, if you need help, you can always call for Chasel or Jasper on one of the many monitors, and they'll be able to assist you."

They entered a main corridor which branched off in three different directions. The space was around twenty feet wide, and the walls and ceiling were composed of the same *terropen* metal as the outside of the ship.

"What's this floor made of?" Casey asked. The ground was the same silky, black-marble floor as the hallway.

"That's *blackseleight*. It's covering a layer of *terropen*. It's awfully expensive, but it holds in the temperature for the ship very well."

They made their way to the first door on the left, with a glowing red panel affixed to the side.

"The black panels have no special security clearance," Elizabeth explained, before Casey could ask. "You have minimal security panels, which are yellow or orange in color, depending on which area of the ship you're in. The red panels have the highest level of security. The members of the royal teams are the only ones who have clearance to enter through doors with the red panels. If anyone else should try, the ship will go into lockdown while trapping the intruder inside an energized retaining barrier until we can get to them."

"Has this ever happened?"

"Not yet, but it's good to know it's there."

The door opened after Elizabeth said her name and had her handprint and DNA checked again. They stepped through into an elongated oval room with various blinking control stations. Each station was equipped with electronic panels, high-tech holographic monitors, maroon leather chairs, and black metal dividers. The top half of the room was constructed out of metal panels arching together in a dome ceiling fifteen feet above them.

"Those sections will slide down, giving you a full circular view of the outside," Elizabeth said upon noticing Casey's interest in the ceiling. "Or, if you're under heavy fire, they can remain closed, giving you a projected image of the surrounding area instead. It's almost as clear and provides adequate protection."

"How many people does it take to operate this ship?"

Elizabeth thought for a moment before answering. "Close to a thousand on a normal flight mission, but since we can run everything from this operations deck, we can do it with five to six people, as long as we're not under attack. We also have the help of the main computer, Chasel, and Jasper if we need them."

"Sounds like an awfully thin crew to pilot a ship over five miles long."

"Yes, but departing this planet would only happen in an emergency. Leaving our post and destroying Grandmother Ann's castle would not be a decision I would make lightly. Just the thought of telling her I had to obliterate her beloved castle makes me shudder."

She led Casey to the forward part of the operations deck where they spotted two men sitting at the frontmost workstation with thirty or so unoccupied stations fanning out behind them. It thrilled Casey to see Barick, but when Parrow's eyes met hers, she flushed with anger. He lowered his head and turned away.

Elizabeth said, "This main console is where we perform the bulk of our duties as overseers. I work here half of the time, with the rest of the team taking turns to fill in for me. Someone must always be here in case something should happen."

"What do those names on the screen represent?" Casey asked, pointing to an array of dots on the main wall monitor.

Barick was the one who answered. "They're our patrol ships stationed along this side of our Universal Blockade. If something gets past them, they'll let us know. That rarely happens, but we must always keep a constant watch."

Elizabeth retrieved a box from one of the lockable shelves of the metal work desk. "This item is for you." She handed the box to Casey.

At first glance, the contents resembled a smartphone with flawless diamonds running down each side.

Elizabeth showed Casey her own identical device, which was attached with an armband and explained what every button did. "This is your personal computer. You can communicate with anyone on the team, including the ship's main computer, Chasel, and Jasper. It only operates when it's in contact with your skin or by the command of your voice alone." She reached over and placed the device on Casey's forearm. At once straps emerged and bound the computer to her arm. "It will also let us know your position, up to two Crogons away.

"Wow, impressive. We could have used these on the police force."

"I can go over the rest of it later, but I must now go see what the president wants." Elizabeth faced Parrow. "Will you please show Casey around the hangar for me?"

Casey hurriedly interjected. "I can see it another time. I don't want to impose on anyone."

"He's only here to keep me company," Barick said. "I don't need his help, so he's all yours."

Casey, feeling she had no way out of this, finally agreed. "That'll be wonderful." She meant for her voice to sound more cheerful, but it came out flat.

"Fantastic," Elizabeth said. "I assume you're both planning to dine with me and the others in the formal dining room?"

With little enthusiasm, they each said, "Yes."

"Wonderful, we'll expect you at seven." Elizabeth spun on her heels and departed.

Casey took a seat at one of the opposite stations where she fidgeted with her newly gained personal computer. Parrow powered on one of the screens and pretended to pore over several of the solar system charts.

Casey heard Barick utter something under his breath before he stood and stretched his legs. "Well, it's getting late," he said. "You two had better get a move on, or you'll not have time to see the hangar before dinner."

Casey was about to decline the tour but thought better of it. After all, she wanted to see the hangar, just not with Parrow.

Parrow rose, his eyes focused on his feet. "Are you ready?"

She gave a slight grunt, but before she left, Casey spoke to Barick. "Do you want me to bring you something to eat?"

"No, thank you. I've everything I need here, but I appreciate the offer."

Casey followed Parrow from the operations deck, staying several feet behind him. They exited the same way Casey came in but this time, instead of traveling along the extended corridor after leaving Vasar Five, they headed out through the first passageway leading up to the stables.

"The door is right around this corner," Parrow said over his shoulder. Several moments later, Parrow stopped in front of a section of the wall, which showed no signs of being any different from the rest of the stairway. "We're here," he mumbled, seconds before the monitor become visible. Placing his hand to the screen, Parrow said the word "Malanight," and the door unlocked, sliding itself open.

"How'd you find it?" Casey asked, her curiosity getting the better of her.

"Oh, sorry, guess you might need to know that. There's a tiny notch on the base of this step." He pointed.

Casey searched closely, noticed a visible mark below his outstretched finger, and grew animated. "I see it," she said with more excitement than she intended. Damn her inability to keep a grip on her emotions. *That will not happen again.* Cursing herself, she went forward, passing Parrow on the stairs.

"I'm sorry I shot you," he called out after her. "I was doing what I thought would be best for—"

"You think that's why I'm angry with you?" she bellowed, cutting his sentence short. Every muscle in her body felt instantly tight, and Casey faced him with fury in her eyes. "I trusted you, but you betrayed me," she shouted, fighting with the urge to hit him. "How can I ever trust you again?"

Parrow took a guarded step backward. "I didn't want to deceive you, but I was under orders. I couldn't let you see who I truly was. Please understand this. As your dog, I could protect you, and as your self-defense instructor, I trained you to protect yourself."

She threw him a twisted, humorless laugh. "You were under orders?" She stepped toward him at first, but reeled away, trying to control herself.

"Casey," Parrow's voice was just above a whisper. "Casey, I'm terribly sorry. I never intended to hurt you. I don't mean to belittle the pain I've inflicted on you, but I'm not sure what I've done. If you'd tell me, maybe we can work this out. If we can't, then I'll do the honorable thing and step down as your guard."

"Honorable?" She spun slowly, halfway to him, staring blankly at the floor. "How can you speak of being honorable?" Her heart ached. "You were my best friend for the past three years. I could tell you anything…and did. Damn you for that!"

"Casey, please understand, I love you—"

"Stop it! Just stop talking!" Casey glared at him for several perturbing seconds before lowering herself to one of the many steps. Parrow did the same.

"How can I make this right between us? Please, tell me what to do," he whispered.

Casey buried her face in her hands, refusing to cry. "You were my lifeline through some of the hardest obstacles I'd ever faced. I relished the honesty and purity that went into our relationship, only to find out all of it had been a lie."

Parrow kept his voice slow and steady. "Casey, for the last three years, I've only thought of your safety. You were also my best friend. I miss you terribly."

A lump developed in her throat, and Casey focused hard on her breathing. She wanted to reach out and hold him but couldn't. No, she wouldn't. "I miss my dog," she finally admitted.

Parrow held out his hand. "I'm right here, Casey."

Casey felt her cheeks take on heat. "For three years I lived with you in that apartment, oblivious to who you were. I slept, showered, and wandered around the house naked—" She peered up into his eyes, "I thought you were Parrow, my dog, not Parrow…a man." Her voice came out crushed, and she hated exposing this piece of herself.

Parrow sounded confused. "Casey, I'm a Blunion."

"Is that supposed to make me feel better?"

"It should," he said, offering her a reassuring explanation. "We're only attracted to other Blunions. Ask anyone. Not that I don't think you're attractive, but I've considered you, well, like my younger sister for these last several years." His forehead wrinkled. "If that doesn't ease your mind, maybe this will. I'm also attracted only to the male gender of my race."

"I *masturbated*—several times." The word held an unpleasant taste in Casey's mouth and her voice broke away.

He raised his eyebrows to this. "Yes, but only when you were in the shower, or when you kicked me out of the bedroom."

"That's not the point. How can I look at you without thinking about that?"

He beamed with delight, clearly not understanding what she was going through. "Honestly, you should be proud of the fact you have such a healthy sex drive. I hope when I find my life-companion, he'll be as healthy in this area as you." His perked up. "You haven't even hit your peak yet."

Casey buried her face in her hands once again, thinking her cheeks must be two shades darker by now.

"I'm not helping, am I?"

"No, you're not." Casey's words came out muffled under her hands.

He cleared his throat. "I never told this to anyone because it's pretty embarrassing. But here goes. When I was at the Academy, I met a Blunion named Worrlen. He was very handsome, the top cadet in our class. I'd admired him from afar since the first day of the Academy."

Casey glimpsed through her fingers, hearing the hurt in Parrow's voice. "What happened?"

Parrow stood and nervously kicked at the base of the wall. "Right before we graduated, he asked me out on a date to one of the local nightclubs so we could get to know each other." Parrow gave a feeble grin. "I guess he liked me as well. I was extremely nervous and ended up drinking way too much that night. For a Blunion, that's quite a lot." He shoved his hands deep in his pockets. "When the night was over, we headed to my room on campus to get better acquainted. When I unlocked the door, I turned toward Worrlen, meaning to kiss him, but instead, I vomited all down the front of his suit."

"Oh," Casey said, feeling his pain, "that must have been awful."

His shoulders dropped. "Shit happens, Casey, but all we can do is move on from it."

"What became of Worrlen?"

Parrow leaned his body against the wall. "Don't know. I left him in the hall, hurried into my room, and avoided him for the last month we were at the Academy. That's not the point though."

"What, you're saying is I should avoid you?"

Parrow snapped his head toward Casey. "No, I didn't say that!" He stopped once he heard Casey's snicker. "Ha-ha. So can we move on from this? I promise not to keep anything from you ever again."

She knew, even before he shared his story, she wanted nothing more than to move past this. To forgive him and see how their relationship would unfold. She deeply missed her companion. "Parrow, I don't want to lose you in my life. I only hope you're as good a friend as a man as you were as a dog."

With an air of confidence, he squared his shoulders. "You might like me more as a man."

"Maybe," Casey examined him from head to toe, "but I doubt it."

Casey and Parrow remained sitting on the steps leading to the hangar for quite some time. Casey asked him about his upbringing, and what traveling in outer space was like. He also answered many questions regarding the Academy, his home planet, and queries concerning shape-shifting.

Their engaging conversation came to a crashing halt when Parrow checked his personal computer. He sprang to his feet and hauled Casey up by her arm.

"What's going on?" she asked, running up the stairs after him.

"We have fifteen minutes 'til seven, and you know how your grandmother is with punctuality."

"Yes, unfortunately I do."

"My mother's worse."

"Don't we need to head the other way to leave?"

"I'm supposed to show you the hangar, remember?" he said when they reached the next door. "Unfortunately, we have little time." He opened the door and hurried her inside. "This'll be the super short tour."

The room was state-of-the-art, with control panels and electronic devices covering most of the space. A second door sat directly across from them, but instead of going through it, Parrow headed toward one of the four swivel leather chairs. He sat and with swiftness pressed multiple colored buttons and knobs on the main panel that ran the full length of the room.

Casey heard no squealing noises or the rubbing of metal-on-metal as the top half of the wall glided downward. It revealed an enormous hangar, which appeared to go on for miles. Casey felt like a tiny ant compared to its size, with only a tempered, transparent wall separating her from two astonishing spacecrafts.

The first ship, labeled Vasar Six in blue lettering on its side, was slightly larger than the second, which had Vasar Seven printed in black lettering. They were both primarily oval-shaped and made from the same material as Vasar Five.

"That's about all the time we have. Do you feel up to running?"

Disappointed, but knowing they had to go, Casey aimed a playful sneer at Parrow. "I could run circles around you, even after being shot, frozen, and thawed."

"You're on," he said.

He kept his eyes on the plate until it completely covered the window. Once Parrow had the room sealed, they jogged down the stairs the way they came, then veered upward at the next set of steps, until they stood at the entrance of the barn.

Casey squinted to the storm clouds overhead. "How much time do we have?" She stretched her legs against the edge of the building. Her entire body ached to run.

"We have about five and a half minutes. Plenty of time for us to sprint three quarters of a mile." Readying himself, Parrow smirked at Casey. "Say when."

"Go," Casey shouted, and both dashed swiftly from the building.

The cool air felt refreshing against Casey's face, and her lungs drank in the damp promise of rain. When they were halfway between the house and the stables, neck and neck with one another, Casey realized how out of shape she'd become in the last few weeks. The first pain to hit was in her right side, directly under her ribs. She sucked it up, fighting at this point to remain even with Parrow. The cramp that followed, shooting from her left calf, was excruciating. All she could do was bite on her bottom lip. She willed herself not to fall back as the castle grew closer and closer.

"Almost there," Parrow shouted, driving Casey on.

They ran up the stairs, nearly missing the front door by inches as it opened with the voice of Jasper shouting at the two of them to slow down. Casey was in tears, partially from the pain, but mostly from the laughing they started after hearing Jasper's scornful tone. They turned in unison down the stretched marble hallway toward the formal dining room. Parrow slid off balance on the ornate rug halfway through the turn, bumping into Casey who hit the opposite wall, but both recovered instantly.

Their hearty giggles and breathless shouts at one another echoed off the high ceiling in a thunderous uproar, so loud all seated at the extended mahogany table in the room at the far end of the hall could hear. Jasper, once again, opened the door for Casey and Parrow. Both tumbled to the ground directly past the doorway, panting and laughing wildly at one another.

The sound of Eva's stifling giggle brought the two tangled together back to reality. Parrow was the first to his feet, but Casey, pain be damned, was close behind. She couldn't stand up straight and had to limp slightly to her seat, between her grandmother, at the head of the table, and the amused Eva, who was now playing nonchalantly with her napkin.

Hanna's chair was at the other end of the table, and Casey noticed how Parrow avoided her eyes, as she avoided Gran's. He sat at an empty seat directly across from Casey, next to Fayrel, as the grandfather clock in the corner struck seven.

"At least you both made it on time," Elizabeth said. "Tomorrow, we'll work on the proper entrance into a room."

"Jasper, we're ready for dinner." Hanna's announcement and Casey's own curiosity got the better of her, and she lifted her gaze.

Eva or Hanna had been the ones to bring Casey her meals when she was growing up. Yet they were both at the table with her tonight. Jasper was only a program with no physical body. Opening the doors with computerized technology was one thing, but serving them food, this feat was entirely different, and in Casey's mind, relatively impossible.

She gazed curiously from Gran to Hanna, and lastly to Eva. Each of the women gave her a friendly smile but offered no explanation to her unasked question. Right when she was about to inquire on this subject, the surface of the table turned from its solid, wood texture to a black chalkboard colored metal, similar to the inside of the metal boxes hidden throughout her and Parrow's living quarters.

"Wow," she said, as elegant table settings, a grand assortment of food, and several types of drinks materialized before them all.

Parrow gaped at the entire array of dishes with the look of a man who hadn't eaten in weeks. "I know. Baked honey-glazed chicken and filet mignon. Not bad for Earth food."

"First grace, then we shall eat."

For some reason, the notion of praying took Casey by surprise. "Do we still believe in God? What I mean is, I don't know. I guess what I'm asking is, exactly how different are religions here on Earth, compared to out…you know, out there?"

Parrow half-groaned, half-chuckled. "Could you make that question any longer?" He turned to his mother. "Let's pray first. I'm famished."

"It won't take long. I promise you'll not starve." Hanna's words were unsympathetic, but her tone still held the love of a mother. She answered Casey's question. "With many species comes many religions. Most believe in the same thing, that there is one creator of all. He has many names, depending on where you go. What you choose to call him or her, and which religion you choose to follow, is entirely up to you. We don't push beliefs on anyone or wage wars because of it. That would, in our eyes, be taking away the gift of choice from an individual, which we consider would be morally wrong."

Hanna said to her son, "It's good to see you're still here with us and have not wasted away into nothing. Now let us pray."

Chapter Four

Beginning Preparation

Casey spent the following day with Parrow in their quarters. They watched old movies in the grand theater room and spent hours in the game room where they relentlessly competed against one another while discussing their much different upbringings. They stopped long enough to have meals in the dining room with the rest of the team before heading straight to their side of the castle to enjoy each other's company.

She missed the relationship she'd had with Parrow, her lovable, furry, four-legged companion, but she relished this newly developing friendship with Parrow, the free-spirited, consistently hungry, two-legged Blunion. They had a lot in common, and he was easy to talk to. Kindred spirits, Eva had called them during lunch.

Midnight had fallen when Casey excused herself, finally feeling the need to get some rest. She slept a little over three hours before waking up with an uneasy sensation someone else was close by.

Watching her.

The room was pitch-black, preventing Casey from seeing anything but her own outline. She lay in bed unmoving, trying to figure out if what she felt was the effect of a bad dream, or if there truly was someone else in her bedroom.

Remembering the conversation with Gran about the abilities their bloodline tapped into, Casey cleared her mind, thinking of nothing but the total darkness shrouding her eyesight. She willed herself to take in her surroundings, trying fiercely to flip on an untrained ability as casually as flipping on the bedroom lights. The seconds passed into minutes with no change in the darkness or with how Casey's inner vision perceived it.

She mentally grumbled and pushed the covers away. "Chasel, could you flip the lights on, please?" The bedroom light flashed on, blurring Casey's vision.

"Is everything all right, Miss Malanight?"

"Yes, and please call me Casey." Casey rolled out of bed, knowing the idea of falling back asleep was drifting away.

She tried but couldn't shake off the feeling of not being alone. She made her way to the hidden monitor inside her closet. "Could I get a coffee with heavy cream and sugar?"

Her coffee emerged instantly inside the black box, as it and the monitor materialized in a section of the wall by the light switch. Casey gazed at the device with her head slightly cocked to one side. "Chasel, what's this machine called?" she asked before sipping her coffee.

"It's known as the Belfont Originator, named after the creator, the scientist Davron Belfont. Most people call it an Originator."

Casey nodded, feeling somewhat foolish. "Would you mind showing yourself? It's odd talking to the wall."

"Of course, and if it makes you feel better—" Chasel appeared before she finished her sentence "—I'll show myself whenever we communicate with one another.

"That would be great—except if I'm in the bathroom or changing clothes, then we can keep it to the voice thing."

"Casey, is anything wrong?"

"What makes you ask?"

"Your heartbeat has been elevated since before you woke from your sleep."

Startled, Casey paused before taking her next sip. "You read my vitals?"

"Oh yes, I can read much more than that."

"Can you sense if there is or was anyone else in my quarters?"

"Yes, of course. I can also tell you the location of any being in the castle, the grounds, or down below on one of the vessels."

"Was anyone in my room when I was in bed?"

Chasel appeared a tad insulted. "If someone were in your room, I would have alerted you right away. Also, I'll let you know if anyone enters the castle who is unauthorized to be here."

She should have known Chasel would have woken her if there was an intruder. Casey did her best to verbally show her confidence in Chasel's capabilities. "It's very comforting to know you're watching over me, thank you."

"My pleasure. Casey, would you like me to run you a relaxing bath before you start your classes?"

Casey peered at her personal computer and realized she was to start her first class in less than two hours. "I would appreciate it. Thank you, Chasel."

Casey was in her office, refreshed and ready to begin class fifteen minutes early. Her stomach felt overstretched thanks to Chasel, who had made her eat a Blunion-sized breakfast. She insisted Casey needed a healthy dose of energy to start her busy first day.

By the time her instructor, Program Intelligence Vespa, materialized precisely at five in the morning, Casey had finished her third cup of creamy-sweet coffee and was more than ready to begin. Halfway through her languages class, Casey switched to diet soda, while she buried herself in her studies.

Casey liked this computer-generated instructor. Vespa had a cheerful personality and constantly gave Casey compliments on how well she grasped the material. The next two classes Casey had with Vespa were equally as pleasant, revealing a much clearer picture of their Universal Region along with the many planets and species protected by her family's rule.

Before Casey knew it, two o'clock rolled around, ending the first nine hours of her classes. Casey loved learning, and with engaging teachers like Vespa, her readiness to take the preliminary exams into the Academy would not only be achievable, but she also believed the endeavor would be rewarding. Vespa had provided Casey with the false hope of how enjoyable it would be to prepare herself for the Academy.

After a brief encounter with her next instructor, all encouraging thoughts vanished. Program Intelligence Zeckner wasn't short and plump like Vespa, but tall and slender, like a praying mantis. He was partially bald, with an old face that wrinkled into a frown when he talked. He carried himself with the air of a condescending man whose time was too valuable to waste on anyone not as brilliant as himself.

Casey had nine straight hours with this instructor, and he had already forbidden any food or drinks while he conducted classes. "They are an unnecessary distraction, and I will not tolerate any disruptions in my class," he declared, pointing toward the Originator for Casey to dispose of her soda.

He allowed her two bathroom breaks but made it a point to tell Casey she would receive extra homework for these troublesome interruptions. She wasn't sure how she did it, but she made it through all nine hours. When he finally vanished, he'd given Casey a menacing grin, along with a five-page homework assignment for each of the three classes he had taught. The math and science sections seemed manageable, but the essay on physics appeared taxing and time-consuming.

Chasel materialized while Casey was brooding over her homework. "I'm sorry you are subjected to a program with his demeanor. The programmers at the Academy designed Zeckner, as well as Vespa, after each of their makers. Believe me when I say he's the most unpleasant program I've ever encountered."

Casey believed her.

"I, however, much like Vespa, am a very pleasant program." Chasel smiled, giving Casey a playful flutter with her eyelashes. "I'll allow you to drink and eat in my classroom, seeing as how I'm your next teacher. Plus, if you check through the remainder of your schedule, you'll see Zeckner's name is nowhere to be found. Would you like an iced soda?"

"Please. That'd be great."

Feeling the tension in her shoulders dissipate, Casey made her way over to the Originator and removed a bubbly iced soda Chasel materialized for her. After gulping half her glass, she expressed her gratitude to Chasel.

"My pleasure. I'm only trying to clear your mind so his unpleasant image will not disrupt *our* class."

Casey was grateful for Chasel's kindness. "That definitely did the trick. I must warn you, though, I know enough about computers and programming to get myself into trouble. You'll have your work cut out teaching me."

Chasel waved Casey's words off. "Computers can be fun, and without them, any advanced race would be lost. What we'll go over in my class will be unlike anything you have ever used before." Chasel directed Casey to follow her into the conference room. "Computers and their programs intertwine with basically every aspect you'll use throughout your life. I'll be able to touch upon a small part so you can continually learn new data and new technology. What they teach at the Academy will help you the rest of the way."

Chasel motioned to the long conference table next to them. The wooden surface changed into ten picture-perfect monitors running the full length of the table. Each screen had its own images and designs Casey couldn't understand.

"This will be our classroom. We'll start with the basic programs and work our way up from there. If I move too fast, please let me know." Chasel's eyes were warm and friendly. "I designed these classes for you and your learning style, so don't hold back any questions you may have."

Casey felt the excitement of learning once again. They spent the next three hours studying the fundamental commands and designs on each monitor, and Chasel made Casey a hearty lunch. As their next session came to a close, Casey was beginning to grasp the rudiments of programming. After twenty-four hours of back-to-back classes, her weary body screamed with exhaustion. Her brain thumped with a pressure of being overloaded, and she prayed her dwindling mind was able to retain the bulk of what she learned.

Chasel giggled at Casey's expression. "Don't worry, Casey. Tomorrow we'll take up right where we left off. If you like, once you finish Zeckner's assignments, we can do a recap in your free time."

Casey released the trapped air from her lungs and her building anxiety along with it. "That'd be wonderful."

Without warning, Chasel's eyes rolled upward and the muscles on her face relaxed. Confused, Casey observed Chasel's temporary pause. A moment later, the program met her gaze.

"Healer Fayrel is requesting you at Vasar Five where the rest of your classes are held."

Casey thanked Chasel for the information, for lunch, and for her class before hurrying through the hidden door behind the bookshelf in the back office and down the long stairway. Once she teleported and entered the split hallway, Casey set out at a full run to minimize her travel time. She was looking forward to going on the trip to Vasar One and wanted to do all she could to ensure this outcome.

"You made it here in record time," Fayrel said, greeting Casey inside the entrance of the main ship.

Casey tossed him a hunched over salute while catching her breath. She needed to start working out again…if she could ever find some free time.

She followed him inside the ship where they made their way along the corridor and passed several doors on either side before coming to a halt beside a notched-in partition of double doors with an orange security scanner.

"These are the elevators for this section of the vessel. Swipe your hand over the front of this scanner to get the doors to open." Fayrel demonstrated the simple task, and the doors slid to the side.

Once they stepped in, Casey saw how the ceiling and floor radiated brightly throughout the wide space, emanating a soothing glow inside the elevator. On the sidewall, a screen of the ship displayed strange letters and shapes she didn't recognize. She could tell the rest of the walls were constructed of *terropen*.

Fayrel said, "English please." The letters and shapes on the screen switched to the English language, giving Casey a clear directory of the ship, including floor and room numbers and brief descriptions of the highlighted sections.

"I'm taking you to my office in the medical wing. On the last supply run to Vasar, I gathered all the essential items we'll need for your classes, including a few surprises your grandmother didn't have when she was preparing for the exams. Level D-57, Marah."

"Yes, Healer Fayrel." With the sound of the soft, older woman's voice, the doors whooshed shut, and the letters and numbers on the screen dropped rapidly.

"Marah, is she the main computer?" Casey asked. She was amazed at how fast they glided by each floor, although the feeling of movement was absent.

"You two haven't met? I guess Elizabeth said she had to cut your experience short. Yes, Marah is the main computer. She's highly intelligent, very efficient, and a true asset to our overseer's responsibility."

"I think highly of you as well, Healer Fayrel." The computer's voice sounded flattered as the door opened on D-57.

Fayrel waved a friendly hand in the air, thanking the computer before exiting.

The passage was almost identical to the first one they'd traveled through, yet this floor held more doors with different shapes and letterings beside each one. She couldn't wait until she learned the Trysal language. She felt like an outsider in a foreign country.

"May I present the medical wing," Fayrel said, running his hand over the scanner. The doors slid open.

Fayrel proudly guided Casey on a full tour of the wing, which encompassed many exam rooms and offices. He showed her an array of high-tech tools and instruments, giving her a brief rundown of what their functions were. The items he carried in his everyday bag, for minor injuries or quick fixes, resembled objects used on Earth. Tape, dressings, and syringes used for blood draws or giving vaccinations were tucked neatly in his bag. Fayrel explained how, even though each of these medical supplies looked similar, their sophisticated structures were more advanced than what Earth's doctors used. For the purpose of planetary security most devices and supplies were specifically designed to blend in so Fayrel could use these items amongst the Earth's populace.

"Now, your class schedule, as with everyone else who attends the Academy, will be geared toward your field of study. My field was medicine, so our classes will be different. Like your family members before you, the Academy will focus your schooling at a wider assortment of learning, giving you the necessities to perform your duties as overseer, and later as queen."

He ordered each of them a coffee before directing Casey into his office where they plunked down into chairs. "Since we're working as a team so far from home, the required medical classes for each member of our group is intense, as are the engineering classes. You're not expected to learn the requirements to be a full-fledged healer but to be able to care for and treat the injured until medical care can be provided." He stood and stretched. "With that said, I'll now show you to your first patient."

"What do you mean, *my* patient?"

With an air of excitement he rarely displayed, Fayrel beckoned and led her from the office to a medical supply room. Shelves upon shelves of meticulously organized boxes and packages stretched along both sides of the room with larger compartments embedded into walls resembling eight-foot-tall Belfont Originators.

"I charged him into the computer last night to get him ready for you."

"Who did you charge?" Casey asked, not understanding what Fayrel was talking about.

He held out his arm, directing her eyes to a full row of built-in cabinets at the other end of the room. "Marah, please activate test patient three for me."

The door to the far cabinet vanished, revealing a naked and unnaturally hairless muscular man close to seven feet tall. His hollow eyes were open, glossed over, and looking straight at her. She shuddered, too unnerved to speak. Was he a corpse Fayrel expected her to perform an autopsy on? Everything about this situation screamed out barbaric, or better yet, immoral.

Fayrel clapped Casey on the back. "This, Casey Malanight, will be your patient. It's an awfully expensive piece of machinery, so I beg you to be careful with him."

"He's not real?"

"Heavens no. I'm not a mad scientist. I don't *actually* keep naked men hidden in the closets of my lab. He's only a synthetic replica of the basic Trysal man. He's controlled by voice activation and will serve as your training aid to help you with my class."

Fayrel shifted toward the motionless prototype. "Patient three, please proceed into the main examination room and wait there for further instruction."

The replica instantly stepped from the cabinet, headed past the stunned Casey, and made his way out of the supply room as ordered.

"He's so real," Casey muttered, still unsure what to make of her naked patient.

"He had better be," groused Fayrel. "With the price we had to pay for him and the others, we could have bought another flight ship."

In the main exam room, the nude machine was sitting on top of the exam table, legs partially opened to reveal an area Casey wasn't interested in seeing.

"Does he have to be unclothed?" Casey asked, feeling uncomfortable.

"I'm afraid so. For our first few classes, anyway. We're going to start with basic anatomy." He ran his hand along the back of Casey's practice patient's neck.

She watched with exhilaration as the synthetic flesh on the training aid changed from a light tan color to a translucent structure.

Fayrel said, "Each organ system will become transparent, giving you a complete illustration of what lies inside and underneath the complex tissue."

He went to a shelf and retrieved a flat electronic notebook, which he handed to Casey. "Your textbook. It's voice-activated, but you can use it as a touchpad if you prefer. Once you have the anatomy of a Trysal mastered, we'll work on another species. I'll also be uploading different viruses, illnesses, and injuries into your patient, which you must treat throughout this course. You'll be docked points for killing your patient, and after you achieve a certain number of points, I'll set up a pre-test to see if you're ready for the entrance exam into the Academy."

Casey glanced from her patient to her computerized textbook. Learning had always been a passion of hers, but this knowledge base and training methods were more than the average, run-of-the-mill classroom she was accustomed to. The possibility of unimaginable knowledge flooded her mind.

"I believe I'll love this class," she finally said.

His cheeks grew red, not from embarrassment, but flattery. "I hope so, but you'll soon find out how hard it'll be. We have many species and many forms of illnesses to get you through. On the bright side, if you take to this class like your mother did, this course might go fairly fast, with no undo hitches."

They spent the rest of their time going over a detailed outline of Casey's upcoming lessons. He showed her how to connect her touchpad to her patient and program in various illnesses for practice on her own time. As Fayrel finished explaining how to use her textbook and her training aid, the door into the exam room opened.

"Ah, Darren. Has it been three hours already?" Fayrel asked the Gaminite, who entered the room in good spirits.

As the healer and engineer exchanged normal pleasantries, Casey tried to spot any noticeable difference in Trysal and Gaminite. She couldn't.

When Darren said they should go, Casey shoved her textbook into her satchel and followed the Gaminite from the room. They traced the path to the elevator as Casey remained a step behind Darren, eyeing him. She was hoping to find something she'd never noticed before—a type of mark or an extraterrestrial ambience of some sort. He stood about the same height as Casey, and his features were young and pleasant as they had always been.

When they entered the elevator to go down to level B-16, he asked, "How have your classes been going?"

She shrugged. "I like them all so far...well, except the ones with Instructor Zeckner."

"I see. Your mother didn't care for him either. Be careful, Casey. He came close to refusing her his entrance test into the Academy. Your grandmother had to persuade him into letting her take it."

"How's that possible?" Casey asked, with a mixture of surprise and worry.

"He's the pre-instructor, and they didn't get along. His creator is the actual instructor at the Academy. I met him once, and believe me, after hearing the stories your mother told us about his program intelligence, I kept my distance."

Casey shifted her weight anxiously to her other leg. Darren offered a reassuring smiled. "Don't worry, Casey. Keep your head down and do as he is asking. Before you know it, you'll be finished with his classes."

After being around Zeckner for only one day, Casey knew if the Program had a say about her forthcoming education, he would prevent her from taking the exam no matter how hard she worked in his class.

The door to the elevator opened into a tiny room no bigger than the elevator, with only a door and a red panel directly across from them. Casey's worry turned into curiosity as both exited the elevator.

Darren explained how the structure of Vasar Five changed for this floor. "The vessel's engineering department starts at level B-11 and goes all the way to B-20. Unlike the other floors, engineering encompasses the full width and half of the length of the entire ship, and most of the area is open, with the offices and supply rooms located around the outside walls of every level." He stepped to the side and motioned to the red security panel. "Will you please do us the honors?"

Without hesitating, Casey scanned her hand across the panel. The door clicked and slid promptly inside the wall. To Casey's surprise, they entered the engineering wing to a drop-off on the other side of the platform railing, at least a hundred floors down with an additional thirty floors flowing upward to the all-metal ceiling. A spiderweb of catwalks and platforms stretched throughout the vast department, which was oval in design.

She breathed in a lemon odor, a pleasant smell reminding her of clean surfaces. The engineering wing wasn't clean—it was immaculate.

Flabbergasted by the size, Casey asked, "This takes up half the length of the ship?" She strained her eyes, trying to make out what was on the far side.

"A bit less than half, but close enough," he said, leading her further inside.

Several cylinder containers, which reached from the floor to almost the ceiling, were the central focal point, and a countless assortment of control panels, contraptions, and computerized workstations ran throughout each platform.

"How do you operate all of this by yourself?" she asked, leaning over the railing to get a better view of the place. She would bet good money if she shouted, anyone on the other side of the wing wouldn't hear her echo. The area was too damn enormous.

"We're operating at minimal levels, so it's easy. Plus, Eva helps me when she has free time." Abruptly, his mouth curved upward into a broad smile. "Ah, that's her there coming toward us."

"What's she on?" Casey asked, feeling slightly meddlesome for noticing how delighted his eyes shimmered at seeing Eva.

"The B-76 transporting hovercrafts. One of the primary ways in which we travel around engineering. They're stationed at docking ports along the railings."

"It looks like a hovering chariot," Casey said.

Darren laughed. "Yes, but without the horses."

Eva beamed brightly and docked her craft close to them. "Marah informed me you two had entered."

Eva was an incredibly beautiful woman, even with her long blonde hair drawn into a ponytail, lines of grease smeared over half her face, and her well-formed body covered by a pair of dirty, navy-blue coveralls. Eva was stunning, matching nicely with her engaging personality. Casey knew Darren would be foolish not to be attracted.

Casey studied Eva closely. Eva was Kan and not human, and the unique differences in the two species, no matter how faint the discrepancies, were now noticeable. Eva's graceful eyes were nearly catlike. Their coloring was a feline yellowish gold, adding nicely to Eva's bold, distinct features. Her eyelashes were long and thick, and her movements had an unnatural elegance, as if she were gliding on air.

Eva reached over, pulling Casey into a full hug. "Have your classes been enjoyable so far?"

"Yes, mostly."

She had always enjoyed being around Eva, especially when she was growing up. Eva and Hanna had assumed the role of mother figures after

Casey's mother died. From what Casey learned during her long talks with Parrow, Eva's species had ceased to exist around the same time as her mother's death, but that was the extent of what Parrow knew about Eva's past and her people.

The rest of the three-hour class entailed taking Casey through the engineering wing where Eva and Darren showed Casey a brief glimpse of where each major subdivision was located and their primary functions. Afterward, they led her into an office, which Darren had set up for many of her classes. He handed her a computerized pad like the one she received from Fayrel. He told her he had downloaded a detailed diagram of each of the unique pieces of technology used in engineering to help with her studies, and instructed her to let him know if she needed help with her assignments.

She placed the pad into her satchel and followed Eva out of an exit door to head for her next class. They took the elevator up to level C2, where they entered a vibrant corridor, complete with a layer of extravagant purple carpeting. They veered along a lengthy hallway to a door that also contained a red security panel.

Once Eva swiped her hand over the panel, they crossed into a comfortable office with two separate desks on either side. Eva told her the desk on the right was hers and the other one was Casey's. After Eva instructed Casey to leave her things on her desk, both women moved through the next sliding door.

Inside, the spacious room was constructed of metal sectional plates throughout the walls, floor, and ceiling.

"What is this place?" Casey asked. The room dully echoing back her question.

"This will be your ship—or ships, I might say. It's the flight simulation room where I'll be teaching you to pilot over thirty different space vessels." Trying to talk past her own echoes, Eva comically smiled, and pointed toward the door. "Let me show you how it works."

Eva and Casey returned to the office where Eva programmed different commands into the wall-mounted terminal.

"We'll begin with an expedition vessel. That's what Vasar Six and Seven are. They can travel anywhere in our region and support a crew of several hundred. Vasar Five is an exploration ship and will be the last ship I'll teach you to pilot."

"Will I be doing all of my training in the simulation room, or will I be allowed to fly a real spaceship?"

Eva grinned. "I'll take you up in Vasar Seven when I feel you're ready. I hope it'll be before our trip to Vasar One. That way, I might talk your grandmother into letting you pilot us most of the way there if you're able to go."

"I hope so," Casey said, thrilled. "That'd be the experience of a lifetime."

Eva placed her hand on Casey's shoulder. "I agree. But first you must learn to fly without killing us."

The ship's computer, Marah, announced, "Your program is complete." Her concise statement was enough to get Casey's heart racing.

"Shall we begin?" Eva asked, redirecting Casey into the simulation room.

When they entered this time, the realm of empty space had altered its appearance to resemble the inside of a miniature operations deck similar to the specs Casey had seen of Vasar Five. The space was larger than Casey expected, and she reached her hands out, contacting as many surfaces and textures in the room as she could. She knew she was acting like an eager child in a candy store, but she didn't care. This new life was all so amazing. "Impossible," she breathed, trying hard to wrap her head around the magical appearance of the fixtures and furnishings.

"No, it's known as molecule displacing," Eva said. "The computer breaks down and stores the molecules of these items until such time that we need to program their design into this simulator. You'll learn the breakdown of this process in your physics and chemistry classes.

"On most ships, the main control panel in the front here can be operated by one to two people while flying under normal conditions. If you're under attack, or something goes wrong with a part of the ship, it'll take at least four people to operate this ship efficiently." She jokingly winked. "Unless you're a gifted flyer like me."

Eva ran through the basic controls and functions to give her an idea of where things were located. She stated how pleased she was to see Casey grasp the training at a fast pace and indicated she had planned to let Casey take the ship in the simulator for a practice flight but they had run out of time.

"We'll get you on the simulator during our next session. I'd better take you to your combat class or else we'll be cutting into Barick and Parrow's training time."

The next training section was located two doors away, on the opposite side of the corridor where the simulator room was located. When the door opened, Eva said her farewells and Casey hurried inside.

The center floor was spacious and fashioned out of a thick workout mat. Several stands with various types of weapons and equipment lined the outer walls. She flexed, and when she felt the muscles tighten throughout her arms and chest, she smiled. Her body was more than ready for a solid workout.

She saw three doors at the far end of the room past the mat and opposite from where Casey stood. The first two were side by side, and the third was on the corner of the sidewall to Casey's right. She didn't see anyone upon entering, so she went to the first of the three doors.

When she was getting ready to run her hand over the black security panel, the next door over slid open, and Hanna walked out.

"Hello, Casey. I was on my way to get you from Eva's class," Hanna said, directing Casey with her inside the room. "Did you two have an excellent lesson?" She handed Casey a dark green bodysuit.

"Yes, and to be honest, I hated leaving."

Hanna halfheartedly agreed. "Flying always is great at first. It's fun and exciting, but after you do it long enough, it becomes a chore."

"I find that difficult to believe."

The room was simple, with a built-in desk, several cabinets and shelves, and a sitting area with a leather couch and two chairs surrounding a flat television screen on the wall.

Hanna excused herself from the room, giving Casey time to change and use the restroom. When she was ready, she exited and followed the tan-skinned Blunion to the center of the mat. Her skin tone wasn't as dark as Parrow or Barick's, but a light golden shade. Casey wondered if the variation in color was normally softer for the female Blunion. She had much to learn about so many species.

"Where are Barick and Parrow?" Casey asked, sitting on the mat in front of the already-seated Hanna who had begun to stretch.

"They're getting things ready for your grandmother, but they'll arrive soon. I told them I'd make sure you properly stretched before they returned. Parrow's nervous about making a good impression with his father today." Hanna's brow furrowed. "I almost had to shove his lunch down his throat, if can you believe that."

Surprised, Casey reached forward and touched her toes. "Actually, I can't. I've never seen a man eat so much."

"Yes. We Blunions consume a larger amount of food than most species. That's because we have an extraordinarily high metabolism. However, most take the time to chew the bulk of their food, unlike my son."

Casey laughed at the truth of Hanna's comment. She relaxed her hamstrings before the next stretch. "Why's he so nervous?"

Hanna gazed up, astonished. "Oh, he didn't tell you?" She stretched her body in ways Casey would have guessed impossible for any species other than a Blunion. "Maybe Barick told him not to. You know, to make it a surprise for you."

Casey stopped stretching. "Make what a surprise?"

Hanna peeked over her shoulder, the one she had her left leg twisted behind. "He wants to see how well Parrow has done training you in hand-to-hand combat these past three years. Therefore, he's planning to spar with you today."

"What? Barick's going to fight me?" Casey glanced around at the vast assortment of weapons and wondered what she would like placed upon her headstone.

Hanna abruptly laughed. "No, Casey, this brawl is but a friendly competition. He's only making sure your training is proceeding on schedule."

"Did you read my mind?"

"Yes, sorry, a bad habit of mine. Elizabeth taught me how, and we use it often with each other. You'll learn to do this in her classes, as well as how to block out your mind from others, like me, who are nosey enough to read it."

Casey didn't mind. "It doesn't matter. I've no secrets from you."

"I appreciate that, Casey. Honesty is something we Blunions hold dear."

Casey shifted slightly, holding tighter to her twisted side-stretch. Her stomach knotted when the main door slid open, bringing with it Parrow and Barick.

"Sorry it took us so long," Barick said the moment he entered. "We had to help get a few things together for your grandmother's class."

"Not to worry, we were working on our stretching," Hanna said, as Barick helped her to her feet.

Parrow winked at Casey and took her hand, pulling her up beside him. "I'm fighting your father today," Casey whispered. "Thanks for the heads-up."

Appearing as calm as ever, Parrow rotated her around. With firm hands, he massaged along her shoulders and upper back. "I found out yesterday, and they instructed me not to tell you. Don't worry. Father will go easy on you."

She nervously brushed his hands away. "Exactly how good is he?"

"Our skill level reaches its peak at seven, which is where he is. Mother is at a seven also, but I've only reached the fifth level. A few more years and I should be up to six." He puffed out his chest with satisfaction.

Casey tensely watched Barick enter the same office she had changed in. She assumed he was doing the same. He looked taller, more muscular than he was a few days ago. "What level am I?"

Parrow cocked his head in thought. "I would say you're a strong three. Not bad for only three years of training."

"I'm dead," she mumbled, remembering how painful most of her classes with Parrow had been.

"You'll be fine. I might get the approval from Dad to train you for level four. That's if you don't embarrass us both today." He forced out a laugh, but Casey could tell by the concern in his eyes, Parrow was serious.

"I'll do my best," she said dryly. She sat on the mat to stretch, giving her jittery concentration something else to focus on.

Parrow squatted next to her. "Casey, calm down and remember what I taught you. I promise you'll be fine."

"That's easier said than done. My mind is completely blank at the moment." Casey examined the rising panic on Parrow's face. Seeing how important this was for him, she forced her tight jaw to relax. "I was kidding. Give me a few uninterrupted minutes to focus, and I'll be fine."

"Sure, Casey. Take whatever time you need." He offered one last look of struggling confidence before stepping off the mat to converse with his mother.

"Calm down, Casey," she whispered to herself, while leaning her body forward between her outstretched legs. "You can do this. Remember what you've learned. Battling Barick is no different from fighting Parrow."

The door to the far room opened, and Barick stepped out, focused and ready. Hanna helped Casey to her feet. "Think of this as another sparring session."

Casey slowly exhaled, hoping to release her building stress. "I don't want Parrow to look bad in front of his father."

"He won't," she said. Her expression was warm, motherly. "Today's battle is for your benefit, as well as my son's. It'll let Barick know where you stand in training and where to improve your skills, giving you the opportunity to become a wiser and stronger leader."

Hanna's talk helped calm her some, offering Casey the opportunity to steady her breathing. She thanked Hanna with a hug. The Blunion touched Casey's cheek, pivoted, and exited the floor, returning to stand next to Parrow.

Casey took a position facing Barick in the center of the mat. *Focus, relax, and breathe,* she repeated inwardly.

Barick's warm greeting made him appear less threatening. "Parrow has considered your placement at level three. I'm not sure I consider this possible, giving the limited time you've trained, but I'll start off fighting you at that level, and we'll go from there." His eyes were focused, his tone unwavering. "Don't hold back, because I won't, and neither will your enemies. When we train, we battle. We don't restrain ourselves, and we don't hesitate, for this will do you no good with bettering your weaknesses. It could even get you killed in the end."

Casey remembered the first class she had with Parrow. Those were almost the exact words he'd used, and he'd been right. She had left many a lesson bruised and bloody, and on one occasion, she'd thought she'd cracked a rib or two. Yet, she had taken the beatings and learned quickly from them what *not* to do. This one would be no different. She knew that now. "I understand, and I'll give you everything I can."

"Good, now let us begin."

Hanna signaled for them to start, but neither fighter advanced.

Casey watched Barick for any signs of movement. *Let your opponent come to you,* Parrow had told her relentlessly in their training session together. *Patience and concentration are your two strongest weapons in hand-to-hand fighting. Fear and anger are your weakest.*

Casey was positive she saw a smile flash across Barick's lips. An instant later, the Blunion flew toward her. He was fast, soaring straight across the mat. Casey lunged to the side, scarcely missing his powerful blows.

She shifted her weight, directing her own attack to the now defending Blunion.

He spun quickly around, blocking each of her punches and kicks with the ease of one not trying. She didn't want to let go of her offensive stance but realized her position would soon falter to his advantage. She backflipped to the far edge of the mat, regaining her balance with enough speed to roll left, giving his high kick nothing but air.

Staying low, Casey swept her right leg out, missing Barick who leapt out of the way. He was on top of her position before she recovered. She did all she could to defend herself from his multiple blows and kicks.

She was prepared to roll backward out of his reach when his left foot caught her above her ear.

Don't let him overpower you, she mentally scolded herself and used the momentum of his blow to roll away from him. His next advance was swift, but she expected this. She moved, faking a second roll to the right. She spun directly at him, swiping his legs out from under him. Barick landed hard on his back, where he blocked each of her attacks, returning several of his own before rolling backward to his feet.

Pressing at his location, Casey attacked with all she had, trying unsuccessfully to connect a foot or a fist with his body. He was faster than when they first started fighting, and his blows more frequent, moving her from an advancing position into a defensive one. Casey wanted to retreat for a second to collect herself, but with the speed Barick used to attack, Casey was doing all she could to keep from being hit. With a move of desperation, Casey stepped to the left to land a strike of her own, but her kick missed, leaving her exposed to his powerful uppercut.

The impact sent her flying halfway across the floor. She landed hard in an outstretched position. Pushing away the pain and the feel of warm blood trailing down her chin, Casey whipped her legs around and sprang to her feet. She met her challenger with a swift spinning kick to his head.

Barick's arm came up, shielding him from her move. He commenced another wave of brutal blows and kicks, which Casey fended off before striking.

Casey focused on keeping her temper at bay while allowing her determination and competitive nature to take over. This fight was all about skill, all about spirit, and although she was more than outmatched, Casey refused to give in, determined to land a blow of her own before *this* bout was over.

His triple punch came quickly, sending the first blow toward her face, which Casey knocked to the side with her hand. The second he aimed at her chest. She twisted quickly out of the way but was now open to the third blow. The solid thrust of his knuckles made contact with the left side of her jaw. She went straight down onto her knees. As if her leg acted on its own, it came up in a backward kick the moment her body hit the mat. Her heel struck Barick's nose. Surprised, he halted his advance temporarily as his own blood gushed out.

Casey sensed him resuming his approach. She twisted up to land another strike.

She glimpsed his fist, realizing too late she had merely moved right into its path. The contact sent her directly to the mat into complete and total darkness.

Casey awoke to the sound of Hanna's voice. She felt the elastic surface of the mat against her cheek. She knew instantly the fight was over, and she hadn't been the victor. The feel of a cold wet cloth on her face brought with it throbbing pain through her upper body.

Parrow was standing behind his mother, but Barick was nowhere in sight. *I disappointed him*, she thought. Casey recalled the last strike and gently lifted herself into a sitting position.

Hanna beamed. "On the contrary, Barick thought you did extremely well. We all did. He's gone to the office to get you something to heal faster."

"I got my butt kicked."

"You sure did," Parrow proudly agreed. "But he had to fight you above a level three to do it."

"I also don't remember the last time anyone has actually hit him," Hanna said. "Other than me, of course."

Casey remembered she had landed a blow to Barick's face with her foot. "To be honest, I'm not sure how I did it. Like my leg moved on its own."

She watched Parrow and Hanna exchange excited glances. "What?" An undertone in both of their expressions suggested she'd missed something.

"You're moving into level four, Casey," Hanna said. "This training stage is where your body and your mind connect with each other. That experience you felt will grow with time and training." She helped Casey slowly to her feet.

The door to the office slid open, and Barick returned, clutching a metal device. "Sorry about that," he said.

"So am I." Casey noticed he hadn't yet treated his own wound. She pointed at his blood-caked nose.

"You got lucky," he teased. He placed the device against several spots on her face. It sent a slight tingle, which instantly released most of the painful pressure. "A hot shower, a warm meal, and you'll be as good as new." Barick tucked the device into one of his side pockets.

"There's a shower in the back room." Hanna gestured to the far door. "Go freshen up while I treat Barick. Afterward, the four of us can enjoy a well-earned feast."

Doing as Hanna asked, Casey rushed from the room. She couldn't believe it had already been over thirty-two hours since she first started her classes. Despite her physical fatigue, she felt newly energized and ready to learn more.

After she and Barick cleaned up, they ordered enough food to feed half of Italy. Casey ate with enthusiasm while they talked about her upcoming training. Barick agreed she should begin the crossover into level four, and Casey savored the pride in Parrow's eyes. Hanna was so pleased with her, she suggested, halfway through their meal, Casey skip their history class for the day to rest. Casey insisted she felt fine, and she told Hanna she was looking forward to both classes. Hanna seemed delighted by this response, and after all had devoured the food and drink prepared for them, the two women excused themselves to go into the rear office.

The first set of the races Hanna went over in her class were Trysals, Blunions, and Kans. History had always fascinated Casey, and she learned all she could with Hanna's guidance on the subject material. The three hours that passed were enjoyable. Both women then moved into the back-corner room for Casey's next class.

This room was twice the size of the fighting area, with multiple rows of locked metal cabinets lining a sidewall. A slanted barrier stretched along the rear of the room, which Casey thought might be a state-of-the-art firing range. On a long table to the left sat several weapons Casey had never seen before. On closer inspection, she was positive these firearms were not from this planet.

"There are many weapons used throughout our Universal Region. In this class, we'll only cover the handheld arsenal, leaving the high-powered weapons for your training at the Academy," Hanna said, unlocking the first two cabinets she came to.

"This firearm is an RLP. It's standard issue with our military and law enforcement. It's rechargeable and worn primarily in a holster on either hip."

She handed Casey the weapon to get a feel for its size and weight. The RLP was entirely black, and much lighter than it originally appeared. Casey pointed the high-tech, pistol-shaped firearm downrange, enjoying the balance.

Hanna entered a command into a monitor on the sidewall. Another metal table, waist high, slid straight out next to her. She directed Casey to place the weapon on its surface, and Hanna went to the cabinet to retrieve a much larger weapon. Casey thought this new weapon resembled an M03 grenade launcher. The only difference was the right side held a miniature screen and keypad affixed to it.

"Next, we have an RRD. Most of our ground units use this weapon. However, it's extremely dangerous without the proper training. This weapon will take out many ground ships, with the right setting, but we primarily use it for massive casualties." She handed the weapon to Casey and pivoted toward the table.

Upon inspecting the new weapon, Casey found it too was lighter than she believed it to be, and she placed it next to the first one. Hanna retrieved the third firearm. This weapon was also black, but the barrel was longer and slender, with a scope mounted on top. As soon as she held the weapon in her hand, Casey realized the scope was advanced, with buttons running along both sides.

"This here is an ISR, and unlike the other two, this one requires a magazine with a special type of ammunition loaded into its chamber." She pointed to a spot behind the trigger. "We use this for firing at farther distances, and we can adjust the rounds to the makeup of different races. That way, there's no chance of friendly fire."

"Nice," Casey said, surveying the weapon.

"For the next few hours, we'll break these weapons down and rebuild them, giving you an idea of their components and what each piece does." Hanna picked up an electronic pad and handed it to Casey.

"I've downloaded all the weapons we'll be covering onto here and included Barick's class and our history class. Most of these classes are hands on, so your homework will be minimal."

They had started on a fourth weapon when Parrow sauntered in, still looking proud. "It's time for me to take her to Elizabeth's class," he said, picking up the RRD and pointing it skillfully down range.

Hanna took the weapon Casey was holding and returned it to the cabinet. "I guess we covered enough on our first day. If your grandmother asks, let her know I'll head up to cover her overseer post. First, I need to lock up these weapons and change."

Casey thanked Hanna and followed Parrow from the room.

"My father is very proud of how far you've come in your training," Parrow said when they entered the elevator. "Level A-7, Marah." He pivoted, clapping Casey on her shoulder. "You're going to enjoy training in the fourth level of combat. All the exciting stuff your body can do begins at this stage. You'll see."

She was about to ask him what he meant by exciting, when the elevator doors opened, revealing a more luxurious corridor than the others Casey had been on. The air was warm, relaxing. They fashioned the walls and floors from the same material, but their surfaces held a different, more inviting appearance. A strip of carpet, decorated red and black, ran through the center of the floor, leaving a few inches of *blackseleight* exposed on either side. The walls were etched in gold designs, and comforting shades of light blanketed the entire passageway. Around each turn, Casey noticed how comfortable the notched-in seating areas appeared with brightly colored plants, blank viewing screens, cushiony chairs, and comfy couches. She was ready to sleep.

"This entire floor is the living quarters," Parrow said, evidently noticing Casey's impressed look. "This section holds the entire high-ranking personnel when the ship is fully functional. There are several entertainment areas and different social establishments located here as well.

"Your grandmother has given me temporary access to her quarters. I believe your clearance is permanent. Being family and all." Parrow scanned his hand in front of a red panel. The door instantly slid open.

The room was easily one thousand square feet, with bright furniture settings and unique knickknacks arranged attentively throughout the open space. A thin bronze carpet covered most of the floor, other than the entrance and an extravagant bar area, which used *blackseleight* for the flooring. The entire far wall was made up of closed window panels, and the ceiling was several inches taller than the hallway.

"Your grandmother's suite. Her bedroom is to the right past the bar, and her office is this way to our left." He guided Casey toward the office. "Your quarters' floorplan and furnishings are set up almost the same, but without this collection of antiques she obtained throughout the years."

"Where does she get all this stuff?" Casey asked, running her eyes over a life-sized diamond statue, sculpted in the shape of a beautiful, long-haired woman. The statue stood positioned in the room's corner, and a trickling waterfall encircled it. Casey wasn't sure if the statue or the waterfall had drawn her interest. Possibly both. The reflecting water glided softly from the ceiling into a long, oval mosaic container of brightly colored rocks and stones.

"These items are priceless memories your grandmother has collected in her travels, from all over the universe. This statue is of Soptra, a legendary Blunion Princess. She was the defender of my people thousands of years ago."

Casey heard the pride in Parrow's voice. She stepped closer to take in the details of the statue. She noticed the stones and rocks were smooth gems and jewels, more beautiful than anything she had ever seen before.

"Our people had this done in honor of your grandmother when she rescued my mother from the Dayshires many years ago. I'm not sure what you've covered in your history class with my mother yet, but you'll find out, if you haven't already, my mother is the blood descendant of Soptra."

Casey glanced over to Parrow, surprised. "You're also royalty?"

His tone was one of indifference. "In a way. Your ancestors crowned Soptra directly after the Great Universal War. An extremely long time ago. They also commissioned the Blunion people as the Universal Protectors. We have been known by this ever since."

Before Casey could respond, Elizabeth entered her quarters. "Ah, good, you're both here. Sorry I took so long. We had a disturbance along the outer rim." Elizabeth held up her hand to Parrow. "Not to worry, the outer patrol dealt with them before any got through."

"What kind of disturbance?" Casey asked.

Parrow answered. "Dayshires and Erules send soldiers or mercenaries into areas in our region on suicide missions. Either with ships or velocity capsules."

"What's a velocity capsule?" Casey sensed her grandmother's uneasiness at the mention of the capsule.

"It's a containment pod which is blasted into our Universal Region, targeting one of our planets," Parrow said. "It has room to carry one being and cannot navigate or make a return trip if it even survives entry. They're harder to lock onto than ships, but we've kept the damage to a minimum."

"We can talk about this later. Right now, we have training which we're already behind on." Elizabeth made her way into her office after first directing them both to follow.

Her office was almost the size of her quarters, with an impressive collection of unusual and extravagant furnishings. Casey wanted to inspect the different objects but shadowed her grandmother to the far wall. Elizabeth stood next to a hand-painted picture of the Malanight Castle, which stretched from the base of the floor to roughly seven feet high. The picture hung between two shelves, laden with hundreds of leather-bound books. Casey didn't recognize any trinkets scattered throughout the shelves.

Elizabeth reached up, running her hand along the outer edge of the frame. Something clicked. The painting swung out, revealing a hidden, *terropen*-made door with a security panel in the center, waist high. She typed in three sets of numbers. Several louder clicks and thuds reverberated outward as the panel revealed the solid barricade unlocking.

As soon as the five-inch door swung open, all three made their way inside. An unseen light powered on, revealing an immense vault and much of its contents to the new arrivals.

"Is this for real?" Casey asked, her eyes taking in the items stacked with see-through bins and shelves stored around the outer edges of a room roughly forty feet wide and at least twice that in length.

"We are self-sufficient in all areas, including financial," Elizabeth said in a matter-of-fact tone. She and Parrow smiled at Casey's dumbfounded expression.

The shelves were organized and labeled into sections, starting with Earth, and continued all the way around to the other end of the room where it ended with Zelics. Stacks and stacks of different assortments of paper, coin money, stones, and brightly colored chips and markers covered each shelf.

"If you think this wealth is impressive, wait until you see the vault under the Malanight Estate on Vasar One. It's a hundred times the size of this one."

Casey noticed the far section of the vault held two impressive safes that stood next to each other, taking up the entire wall. In the center of the room stood several bulky metal containers, at least eight feet high. Each was full of drawers with different labels like diamonds, gems, gold, and words Casey had never seen before.

"Parrow, could you please get us three money bags of the gold Roman coins, while I get you and Casey your necklaces."

He obediently marched over to a lower bin in the section labeled Earth. Casey followed her grandmother to one of the two safes and stood in awe, as the thick door swung open. Inside the walk-in safe were multiple sectional-shelves, each covered with a vast assortment of treasure. Elizabeth retrieved two tiny, jewelry-sized boxes from the top shelf, then closed and latched the solid metal door.

"You ready?" Elizabeth asked Parrow, who held up three bulging cloth bags for her to see.

"Good, let us begin," she said, motioning for Casey to follow.

From Elizabeth's suite they journeyed through the corridor in the opposite direction from the elevators until they came to the last room on the far end where Parrow opened the door at Elizabeth's request. The room held a sitting area in the center, and two separate, floor-to-ceiling cylinder containers on each end of the room.

"That's the DNA Modifier." Parrow pointed to the cylinder at the opposite end of the room. "It's not a pleasant experience to go through, so I hear. There are only three DNA Modifiers in existence, because of the security risk involved. A second is housed on your family estate on Vasar One."

"What's this other container?" Casey asked, gesturing to the chamber next to her.

"It's an Equipment Originator. Davron Belfont invented this, and the Belfont Originator. That's the device we get our food and drinks from."

Elisabeth added to Parrow's comment. "It works the same way, but this one provides clothing, equipment, and odds and ends we may need." She programmed orders into the monitor attached to the side.

When she was done, a door on the Equipment Originator opened, and she waved Parrow inside. He handed Casey the pull-string bags of gold before making his way in. The door shut tight, followed by a tiny whooshing sound. Several seconds later, Parrow emerged from the chamber dressed in a golden-etched toga with an elaborate set of slippers on his feet. "Next," he said, taking the bags of gold back from Casey. He tied one to his long belt and motioned for her to go.

The moment she entered, the door closed, leaving her in total darkness. She wasn't sure if she should hold her breath or not. Within seconds, an identical whooshing sounded, followed by the door opening. She stepped out, glancing distastefully down at her wardrobe, which was almost the same as the one Parrow wore. Unfortunately, hers was shorter, and lacked the etched gold trim like his.

"Wow, you have nice legs, Casey!"

"It's not like you haven't seen them before. Heck, we've lived together for the past three years."

"Maybe so, but I've never seen them in a dress," he said. "Nice." He followed it with an approving whistle.

Casey wanted nothing more than to deck him, and his ridiculous razzing attitude. "Don't get used to it."

"That's a palla, a female toga." Elizabeth switched places with Parrow. He stood at the controls while Elizabeth made her way inside. Less than a minute later, she emerged in an identical outfit as Casey.

Parrow handed them both their bags of gold, which they also fastened to their belts. Elizabeth retrieved the two boxes she'd removed from the safe in the vault. "Could you get us the translators also?" Elizabeth asked.

Parrow went over to a place on the wall that folded out at his command. Casey watched him take something from the inside of the wall before heading to where they stood. He handed Elizabeth a nearly invisible device she fitted inside her ear.

"A Universal Translator." Parrow placed it in Casey's hand. "It has the programming of every language within our region in it. Put it in your ear, like so." He demonstrated with his own. "When someone speaks a language to you, it will translate it into the dialect you want. I programmed these for English."

"What if I need to speak the language?"

"A signal goes to your brain and is relayed to parts of your mouth and your vocal cords. Although you're speaking English in your mind, it will come out sounding like the language your earpiece picked up on."

Elizabeth handed the first of her two boxes to Parrow. She opened the second one, and pulled from it an elaborate, tricolored necklace with a yellow jewel in the center. She placed it around Casey's neck and locked the two ends together. "It's called a Unification Necklace. There are only five in existence." Elizabeth held up the necklace so Casey could see it. "We call this jewel a star-flight ruby, and it's why these items are so rare. Queen Ann accidentally discovered them in the Semtra Solar System, on the Semina Planet, over sixty years ago. This planet sits directly in the center of our Universal Region."

Elizabeth pointed at the outer layer of metal, which she said was *terropen* from the Planet Denite. The second layer was *blackseleight* from Vasar, and the third inside layer was gold from Earth. Elizabeth turned the necklace over and showed Casey the etched design of all three solar systems carved into the three metals covering the entire back of the necklace.

"These four surrounding layers of tick marks on the front," Elizabeth said, flipping the necklace and running her finger over the outer edge, "will let you know the exact year and date when you travel through the past. The proper ticks will glow when you press your finger over the jewel. On the back, the planet you're closest to or on will also glow. There is a secret compartment in the center." Elizabeth moved the flap to the side. "If you press this, it'll light up all the necklaces, giving us your position if you're ever in trouble. It'll only work if you're inside the triangle section of our Universal Region."

"Does the rest of the team have these?" Casey asked.

"No, they'll only work for our family. The one Parrow is using belonged to your mother. When you have a child, this one will pass down to her." Elizabeth touched her index finger over the one around Parrow's neck. "If anything happens to Parrow, he can push his button to give us his location. Unfortunately, that's all it will do for him. He also won't be able to see the tick marks glow, but we will."

"How is this possible?"

Elizabeth raised her eyebrows at Casey's question. "These were hand-crafted by a man who lives on the planet of Semina. He understands the universe and everything in it better than any being I've ever met, and in time, you will meet him. The design was something Queen Ann had in a dream when she was younger, which this man interpreted as something more." She pointed at the jewel. "Ann said the star-flight rubies called to her."

"Called to her?" Casey asked, uncertain.

"Mentally, yes. None of us can explain it, not even Grandmother Ann." Elizabeth moved beside Parrow. "I'll travel with Parrow, and you'll journey alone. We'll be going to Rome, on the fifth day of June in 105 CE."

"Gran, I don't know—"

Elizabeth raised her hand. "You have learned to travel in the future on your own, and it's much harder than traveling to the past. You only need to *wish* yourself there, and before you know it, it'll happen." She gestured to Casey's necklace. "If anything should go wrong, press your button, and we'll both find you."

"Do you realize how big Rome is?"

"Don't worry, Casey. These necklaces are connected. I'll navigate us to a deserted road, and you should appear close to where we are, unless you think of an exact spot." Elizabeth held Parrow's hand. "Let's make it for four in the morning. That way, few people will be up."

With that, Elizabeth and Parrow vanished, leaving Casey alone in the room. She closed her eyes tight thinking of Rome, four in the morning, on the fifth day of June, 105 CE repeatedly in her mind.

Chapter Five

Earth Date: 5th August 105 CE
The Ancient Connection

Casey kept her eyes closed tight until she felt cool water encircling her. Her lashes opened to wet darkness. She flailed wildly about until her feet scraped against a solid surface. With a wave of embarrassment, she jerked her head out of the water and glanced sheepishly around. Planting her feet, she stood inside a circular basin, the depth of the water coming to an inch above her knees. She wiped the damp from her face and rolled her eyes.

"Get out of there, you woman," she heard a man shout.

A short, dark-skinned man was running toward her. Wasting no time, Casey clambered from the aged, mosaic fountain, unsure what to do. Although the sun was still hours away from rising, the bright glow of stars and the vibrant shine of the moon cast enough light to make out the approaching figure was more than agitated. He was pissed off.

"What is the meaning of this?" he demanded, as he drew closer.

"I fell in." Casey took two steps backward while scanning the area. Where were her grandmother and Parrow? Her fingers fumbled with her necklace.

The chubby little man didn't slow in his approach, and when he was almost upon her, Casey adjusted her stance in a natural anticipation of self-defense. Right when she readied herself to send out a nonlethal, yet highly effective kick into the center of the man's groin, she heard the voice of Parrow shouting from behind her.

"What's going on here?" he yelled, running toward Casey and the red-faced man. Elizabeth was directly at his heels.

The plump Roman stopped at the sound of Parrow's tone, but the anger burning his cheeks didn't subside. "Is this your wife?" he demanded, between gasps of much-needed breaths.

"Yes, what have you done to her? Why is she all wet?" Parrow looked from the man to Casey.

"What have I…what have I done to her? I found her bathing in my fountain when I stepped out for a bit of air," he bellowed, obviously insulted by Parrow's accusations.

"I wasn't bathing. I fell in," Casey said in her own defense.

The annoying man cut her off. "How dare you address me in that tone, woman," he screeched, as spit went flying toward Casey. "If I were your husband, I would whip you within an inch of your life for the use of that tongue in your insulting little head!"

"She, however, is not your wife. She is mine!" Parrow fumed, bringing himself to his full height, which caused the other man to move slightly away. "If I so much as catch you stealing a glance at my wife again, I shall whip you within an inch of your life. Do you understand me?" Parrow spoke his last words through clenched teeth.

"Do you know who I am?" the man muttered in fear, while trying his best to sound threatening.

"It doesn't matter. I can guarantee my connections are much higher than yours."

The man glowered from Parrow, to each of the women, then again to Parrow. "Just keep her away from me, and my fountain," he shouted, before wheeling around and storming off.

The three hurriedly made their way off the man's property and onto an empty, narrow side street. "How did you both find me?" Casey asked once they were a safe distance away. She squeezed out the water from the bottom of her palla.

Elizabeth held the back of her necklace toward Casey, pointing to a different row of tick marks surrounding the star-flight ruby. The one closest to Casey's direction was glowing yellow. "I guess I forgot to show you the compass. This part will glow if another necklace is on the same planet at the same date and time. It pointed us right to you."

"How did you end up there?" Parrow asked, eyeing Casey's wet outfit.

"Yes, how did you?" Elizabeth questioned.

Casey thought about the man, his fountain, and the realization struck her. "As I was thinking of Rome, the image of the waterfall in your quarters on Vasar Five, flowing into the Mosaic basin, entered my thoughts."

Parrow shook his head while he snickered. "That explains how you ended up in that nasty man's mosaic fountain."

Elizabeth rubbed her forehead. "This kerfuffle isn't a laughing matter. She could've ended up at the bottom of an ocean, or some other place which would've gotten her killed. Goodness Casey, what were you thinking?"

Parrow stopped laughing, and Casey responded defensively. "I've never traveled in the past before. Maybe these are the warnings you should share before I venture out, unsupervised." Casey wasn't sure if she was indeed angry, but she wasn't about to feel obtuse for something no one bothered to explain.

Elizabeth peered regretfully at her granddaughter. "You're right. I'll work on giving you better information in the future."

Casey felt a wave of shame for her tone. "It was kind of funny," Casey said, trying to lighten the mood.

Elizabeth returned her smile. "The first time I traveled, I ended up smack dab in the middle of the Battle of Bull Run. I thought of the Civil War time as Grandmother Ann said, and I left as the image of my friend's bull, which chased her and me a week earlier, flashed before me." Elizabeth's eyes sparkled at the memory. "I had a hard time explaining it to Grandmother Ann when she found me trembling in a set of bushes. She was so angry with me for scaring her half to death."

"I bet she was." Casey conjured a clear picture of her grandmother cowering in shrubbery, as men dressed in gray and blue uniforms scampered about. Rifles firing, cannons blasting, and a young girl hiding. They were lucky Gran wasn't older when she was there. She would have single-handedly ended the war before it began.

"So this city is Rome?" she asked, veering the conversation to a new topic.

"Yes, ancient Rome, to be more specific." Elizabeth guided the two out to a main, yet desolate, road. This stone-paved street was wider than the one they were previously on, and the surrounding buildings were rows upon rows of closed shops on the first level with living quarters directly above.

Elizabeth pointed. "Down that way is one of the more upscale thermae, or public baths. Barick went once but didn't care for it."

"How often have you come here?" Casey asked, hearing a neighing horse close by.

"Hanna, Barick, and I travel here once a year for vacation. This place is more for Hanna and me. It's ideal for shopping and taking in the beautiful landscape. We also visit other places, including treasure hunting, to please Barick."

That got Parrow's attention. "Mom told me about several of your trips to Rome and Egypt, but apparently, she's failed to mention the more interesting excursions. Treasure hunting sounds like a fun vacation. Do you usually find anything?"

"Of course we do. It's pretty simple to locate missing treasure when you have the capabilities and historical information to travel in time and figure out where and how the treasure disappeared in the first place."

Parrow wasn't the only one who found this interesting. "What do you do with it?" Casey asked.

"Some we keep here on Earth, some we take to our estate on Vasar One, and the rest we sell at a low cost to museums on Earth or whichever planet it comes from."

"We need to start treasure hunting after you graduate from the Academy," Parrow insisted with great excitement.

Casey snorted with amusement. He looked like a kid who was begging his mother to take him on an outing to the zoo, or to the ice cream parlor for two scoops of his favorite flavors. "We'll see how well you behave first. Only good little boys get to go find buried treasure." She patted his head in a motherly gesture.

"You'd enjoy it too," he said, brushing her hand away.

She analyzed their surroundings, only now grasping what traveling through time could mean. "Can you fathom the places and events we could experience? The possibilities this gift of time travel can offer us." She spoke to Parrow with disbelief while the images of various historical events rolled in.

Elizabeth held up her hand. "You both must remember what I've told each of you about the consequences and dangers that can come with traveling in the past if you're not careful."

"Yes," Casey said, remembering Gran's warnings about a potential paradox, and if not cautious, they could die in the past.

"Good. Now let's go explore some before the shops open for business. There's much to see here." Elizabeth motioned for the two to follow her down the street. They plodded along for several hours, Elizabeth pointing out different sites and buildings, while explaining what the Roman customs were. She was going through the long list of restrictions, what a Roman woman must and must not do, when Parrow began his normal complaining about being hungry. To pacify the Blunion, Elizabeth steered their tiny group to one of the nicer eateries to enjoy a tasty meal under the morning shade at an outside patio.

"That's outrageous! Simply because I'm a woman, I can't see any comedy shows, only tragedies. That makes no sense at all," Casey said, angrily before taking a bite of cheese.

"Women have only been allowed to drink wine within the last few years in this era. It used to be a woman could be beaten or killed for having but a sip of the drink. Stay close to Parrow and you'll be fine."

"Because he's a man and considered better than me," Casey protested through clenched teeth.

"No, because he's supposed to be your husband, and yes, society considers women inferior here."

Parrow guffawed at Casey before shoving more food into his mouth. "I like ancient Rome."

Casey had to fight off the urge to kick him under the table. It took a few cups of wine and a lengthy yet understanding lecture from Elizabeth before Casey felt her agitation for the male sex subside.

Right as they were leaving, Parrow ordered another medium-sized container of wine, two blocks of cheese, several loaves of bread, and some fruit, which the ecstatic shopkeeper placed into a cloth bag after Parrow paid him well for the items. Casey rolled her eyes at his sack of goodies. "What? I thought I'd take some home for later," he said defensively.

Elizabeth directed them along a row of shops where the establishments, as well as their items, were more elegant and alluring than Casey could have imagined. They fanned out to inspect the different tiny trinkets and furnishings each building offered.

"Gran, what's this marble-etched plate? I've seen them hanging in every store we've been to."

"They require the shops to display their licenses publicly. The engravings are their license numbers," Elizabeth said, searching through recently dyed fabric.

"I didn't know Rome was this civilized." Casey leaned closer to inspect the craftsmanship of the engraving.

"Rome holds many wonderful surprises. Did you notice the detail that went into the ivory figurine I bought? Or these engraved gems? It's hard to find good quality work like this in our time era."

"Casey," Parrow shouted.

She and several other shoppers turned toward the front of the store. Through the bustle of the buyers, he shoved himself and four bulging cloth bags he had heaved over his shoulder to where she stood.

A few patrons irritably moved aside to give the Blunion room to drop his belongings on the ground next to her.

"Look at all of this stuff I've got. I filled this bag with decorations for my room. This one here is for my office, and these two are loaded with food and wine," Parrow said, beaming from ear to ear.

He eyed Elizabeth's bags, then frowned at Casey. "Don't tell me you haven't bought a thing?"

"If it makes you feel better, I've helped Gran pick out unique pieces of jewelry from three different merchants." She laughed when his frown became a sulk. "Come on, Parrow, you know shopping isn't my thing. I'm enjoying myself though. More than you realize."

Several hours later, Parrow rushed to where Elizabeth and Casey were inspecting bolts of brightly colored fabrics. "I was talking to a man who told me there's an all-day event happening in the Circus Maximus today."

Elizabeth's response was indifferent as her attention remained glued to the cloth. "Yes, they hold exhibitions for over two hundred days out of the year there."

Parrow seemed antsy. "Do you guys want to go?"

Moving to inspect a bundle of fabric the shop owner brought over, Elizabeth said, "It's awfully brutal. If you two would like to see it, I don't have a problem attending."

"Isn't Circus Maximus for chariot racing?" Casey asked Parrow.

"No. The man I spoke with said today is the gladiator matches."

Casey peered at her gran. "I'm fine with it if you are."

"Good." Parrow gleamed with excitement. "I'll go get us some provisions we can take. Meet you both back here in a few minutes."

"What about the food you already have?" Casey asked Parrow as he spun to leave.

"These bags are for later," he called over his shoulder. Casey and Elizabeth rolled their eyes at one another.

Elizabeth sighed as she continued to search through the fabric. "Barick's the same when he's here. Blunions enjoy a good fight. The more brutal and barbaric the fight, the better they like it. Hanna, thank goodness, is a more passive Blunion. She enjoys a fight, but with boundaries that don't cross into this level of barbarism."

Casey huffed at the thought.

"You must understand, Casey, although Blunions are a good-natured species, they're raised as fighters. They've been our esteemed Universal Protectors for thousands of years. As we lust for knowledge, they lust for battle."

"I can't picture Parrow having a violent bone in his body."

"If his family or friends were threatened, if you were ever in danger, you'd be surprised how vicious that Blunion could be."

"Do they want this war to happen?"

Elizabeth's eyes widened, obviously staggered by the question. "Heavens, no. You've misunderstood me, Casey. I'm not saying they choose to fight, but they choose to be out in front when the fighting starts." She arranged the purchase of the bright yellow material with the pleased shop owner before giving Casey her full attention. "If a child is in danger, a mother's maternal instincts will take over, and she'll protect her child with any means necessary. The same goes for a Blunion, except they are born with those instincts to protect and fight."

"I understand what you're saying. In a way, I can relate to a Blunion. I feel a desire to protect others. It's one of the main reasons I joined the police force."

"Yes, we've been geared toward being overseers. Similar, but less violent," Elizabeth said.

"I'm ready." Parrow returned once again to the store. He held up another hefty bag, which he said was full of nicely wrapped meat and cooked vegetables with a couple of bags of figs. He also procured additional containers of wine in case they got thirsty.

They followed a group of people along a stone walkway, which opened into a grand valley. A colossal stone and marble oval-shaped structure was erected in the center. Elizabeth told them the Romans had constructed this three-story arena, roughly two thousand feet long and five hundred feet wide. As they entered, they noticed the seats were filling up quickly. Fortunately, Parrow had somehow secured them a pleasant spot on the first level, fashioned primarily out of marble.

"Isn't this great?" Parrow shouted over the roar of the crowd. He pulled three jeweled goblets from his bag, pouring each of them a generous glass of wine. "I also have water if you need it. But once you try this, I'm sure you'll find it's quite appealing."

"Where did you get these cups?" Casey asked, admiring the gold craftsmanship.

"I got them from a peddler. He was selling in one of the not-so-populated alleys. I bought several things from him."

"Humph," Elizabeth said in a displeased tone. She mumbled to Casey, "They've been stolen, no doubt. Yes, he's exactly like his father. Searching for the best deals from illicit merchants and not bothering to ask where they get their shady valuables from."

Casey worked at masking her laughter.

After first seeing Casey and Elizabeth were comfortable, Parrow ventured off in search of more vendors. Casey busied herself with people-watching, drinking wine, and enjoying a few of the fresh juicy figs. The surrounding commotion was magnificent to watch. Comparable to the Super Bowl she went to last year with a few work colleagues.

Parrow returned twenty minutes later, bursting with news. "I met a man who oversees these games. He has a reserved section directly across from us if you two want to move. It's shaded, and they have a variety of food and drinks there. He also told me he'll take us to see the animals before the show starts."

"How do you do that?" Casey asked, impressed.

"Do what?"

"Take off in a strange land and engage people so well."

"Oh." Not waiting for them to decide if they were interested in moving, Parrow started to gather up his and Elizabeth's purchased items. "Blunions are a very sociable race. It has something to do with shape-shifting. We connect easily to other species." He shrugged, "Ask mother when you're in her history class. She explained it all to me when I was younger, but I believe I fell asleep in the middle of it."

Elizabeth stood and motioned the reluctant Casey to her feet. "Lead the way," she told Parrow.

Moments later, Parrow was introducing them to a young, attractive man who showed the three to their seats. She believed what Parrow said about a Blunion's connection to other species to be true. But, in this case, the man's link to Parrow was more sexual in nature. The man, who called himself Cassius Decimus, had noticeably taken an instant shine to the handsome, yet oblivious, Blunion. If Cassius only knew Parrow's attraction swayed to other Blunions, or that he wasn't even human.

"Would you like to see the animals we house here?" Cassius asked, forcing his eyes off Parrow and onto Casey and Elizabeth.

Elizabeth politely excused herself, saying she was old and should stay out of the sun as much as possible. Casey jumped at the chance.

As they made their way through an underground walkway, Cassius occasionally leered over his shoulder at her. "You wife is exquisite," the ogling man eventually told Parrow.

Casey winced. Apparently, this man had more than Parrow in his sights.

"You said you were from out of town. Do you have a place to stay tonight? I've a modest dwelling close by with plenty of room for the three of you."

"Oh, we couldn't impose Cassius Decimus," Casey said with a polite wave of the hand. Inwardly, she cringed at the idea.

"It would be my pleasure. Please, call me Cassius."

"I'm not sure if we'll stay the evening in Rome," Parrow said. "We have such a long journey ahead of us. If we do, we'd be grateful for your hospitality."

Casey adamantly shook her head at Parrow once their escort was two steps ahead.

He answered her shake with a full-on squint. His way of nonverbally letting her know he also knew the man's offer was a bad idea. One which he would never actually accept.

"That would be splendid," Cassius said, oblivious to the nonverbal chitchat transpiring behind him.

He directed them through a rustic wooden door. "This underground fortress is but an oversized labyrinth of tunnels and rooms." Cassius pointed out the constructed ramps and wooden crank elevators leading up to different places inside the arena. "This section of the lower-level is where we keep the animals for the matches before the gladiator games." He motioned them into a poorly lit space, smelling of unkept feces and pungent urine, with multiple thick, wooden-framed cages. The low-ceiling room held lions, tigers, and several other animals scattered in variously sized holding pens.

"What matches?" Casey asked.

"We fight wild animals before the matches. Sometimes we'll throw in a poor soul or two to liven things up. Only lawbreakers and prisoners though," Cassius said with a laugh when he apparently noticed Casey's displeased expression.

She saw no humor in this, and by the forced smile on Parrow's face, he too wasn't thrilled. Cassius directed them further into the room with its occupied cages.

As they drew closer to the end, Casey was finding it difficult to shake a strange warming sensation rolling through her body. One which radiated heat from her brain to her extremities. Like someone or something was gripping her soul, pleading for her attention.

"We have set aside this black beast for the highlight of the animal matches," Cassius boasted, as he dipped his head toward the far cage. "She's an untamed beast I'm putting two of my best lions up against. Normally, I would consider this an unfair match, but just look at her. We've never seen her kind grow to this immense size before. And she fights with such wild fury, Mars himself would be frightened."

Casey peeked in at an impressive, beautiful black panther with piercing, yellow-green eyes. She clutched a wooden post in each hand and leaned in for a closer inspection. This striking creature was beyond enormous. Panthers, Casey knew, while more agile than lions, were smaller and weaker. Normally, they didn't stand a chance against lions, especially these old Roman ones. Yet, this panther was different. Taller, standing on all fours with the height at the shoulders reaching about four-and-a-half feet. The panther's head was as big as a lion's head minus the mane, and Casey guessed the cat's weight to be four hundred pounds. Maybe four-fifty.

What was truly interesting was the unexplainable connection she felt with this animal. Her mind raced uncontrollably. An exhilarating sensation unlike any other. She watched in awe as the powerful cat plodded slowly toward the front of the cage where Casey stood.

"You best step away," Cassius said, scraping his hand through the air. "She's extremely dangerous. Even through these bars, she could still get to you."

Casey didn't listen to his words of warning. She and the black cat stared directly into each other's eyes. It felt as if she was gazing inside a kindred soul, one she had searched for her entire life but didn't know it. When the cat was a few feet away from her, Parrow pulled Casey to him.

Cassius wiped sweat from his forehead. "Your wife's a brave one."

"She is," Parrow agreed, sounding as if he was barely listening to Cassius. He nudged Casey with his elbow.

"Would you sell her?" Casey asked the second the idea entered her mind.

Cassius raised his arm to gesture toward the exit. He was definitely ready to leave. "Like I said, she's my prized performer for the show."

Casey thought hard, weighing her options. "You said you sometimes throw a person into the arena with the animals."

"Yes, but I assure you, they are wrongdoers of the worst kind." He took a step away from the panther's cage, then another, his eyes pleading for Casey and Parrow to follow.

She would not be so easily dismissed. "What if someone was to volunteer to fight in the stadium with the animals?"

He laughed hard enough for his shoulders to shake but stopped short when Casey's eyes narrowed in sincerity. "We've never had a volunteer in the animal matches before," Cassius said, considering her question. "It would be the grandest match yet. May even start a trend."

Unsure how or why, Casey felt an undeniable knowing settle in her gut. She understood what she had to do. "I want to fight in the arena with her."

Cassius coughed out his response. "I can't allow you to do that. Those lions would tear your limbs from your body." He clapped Parrow on the back. "Not to mention, your husband would never let you." His amusement faltered when he saw the seriousness on Casey's face, combined with Parrow's lack of response. "You two are joking, right?"

"No, she's not, and I give her my permission, if that's all you need."

Cassius blinked wide-eyed between them. "You want to fight two lions next to a monster who'll rip you apart herself the first chance she gets?"

Casey noticed the panther's muscles quiver than relax. Impressive was an understatement. "I'll make you a tiny wager. If I can go into the cage and come back out without so much as a scratch, you let me fight with her. If not—" Casey removed her satchel of gold coins. "If not, you can keep this."

His surprise changed to greed.

With a voice as soft as honey, Parrow jumped at the opening and whispered in Cassius's ear. "I can guarantee you, she and this cat would win. Think of the money you could make if you took bets on her and the panther, and they were victorious."

Cassius held up a hand. "First, she goes into the cage to prove she can befriend the beast, and then we'll talk of the terms."

Casey started toward the cage.

Cassius stopped her. "I insist you let me fetch a few armed soldiers before you proceed." Without waiting for a response, Cassius hurried away.

"What's going on?" Parrow asked once Cassius left the room.

"You know the connection the Kans, with whom I'm part of, have with animals?"

"Yes, to an extent. Mother says it's stronger than the connections we Blunions have when we shape-shift."

"I feel it with this panther. The connection is hard to describe, but it's there. I know it, same as I know I need to do this."

"What about your grandmother? I think we should talk to her first."

"No, this choice is mine, and I'm sure she would agree with me."

He wasn't sold on her plan. "In the arena, do you realize what you're doing?"

"Yes." Casey said, her eyes on the panther. "If she dies—" Casey stopped, suddenly distraught at the idea of this creature's body ripped to shreds in this awful place. Her insides shuddered.

"Why don't you travel in time and take her with you before the fight?"

"I can't explain it, but I know if I try, without proving my devotion to this connection, it won't work, and I'll lose her forever. I'm positive."

"Let me fight with her instead."

"No," Casey insisted. "I'm certain I have to be the one to do this."

They stopped talking when they heard sounds of laughing men approach. Cassius silenced the amused guards and positioned both men around the cage with their swords ready. He signaled to Casey, who shifted to the panther.

Casey held her breath when she noticed the animal was now lying on her stomach with her head up, casually watching the commotion. This animal was astonishing. The sensations intensified. Unlatching the door to the cage, Casey opened it enough to squeeze her body through. Her hands shook, but not with fear, with excitement.

"She's completely crazy," she heard one guard whisper to the other.

Casey stepped inside and latched the door behind her. This electrifying feeling grew as she drew closer. *"I'm Casey,"* she mentally thought, unsure if the panther heard her, or better yet, understood what she was thinking. Casey held her breath and inched forward.

"I'm Vashee. I've never communicated with one of your kind before."

Her excitement rose. *"Neither have I. I mean, I've never spoken with an animal. Where did you learn how to speak my language?"*

The panther's puzzled tilt of the head made Casey smile. Was this really happening? *"I'm not sure if we're speaking your language or mine. This might not be a language at all. However, I do understand you."*

Casey moved closer, causing all four men behind her to hold their breaths. *"I would like to fight with you in the arena."*

The cat's eyes narrowed, and Casey heard feet shifting on dirt behind her. *"Why would you want to risk your own life to fight those creatures?"* Vashee asked, climbing to her feet. As she stretched, her throat let out a soft, rumbling growl.

"That's it. We've seen enough. Why don't you come out of there so we can go drink some wine together?" Cassius's question was bordering on beseeching.

Casey ignored him and drew closer to Vashee. *"You know why I'm going to fight with you. I can see it in your eyes. We have a connection, and I genuinely believe our paths have not crossed by accident."*

The panther closed the gap between them and rubbed her long body against Casey's legs. *"I dreamed about you a few nights ago, on the same night they captured me. I was in a room with you, and the earth was made of stone. Darkness filled this room, and all I heard was the crackle from a dying fire as I watched you sleep. The moment you awoke, so had I."*

Casey's entire body went numb. *"That was in my room in the castle. I woke up the other morning when I felt someone—when I felt you watching me. I'm sure of it."*

"What does this mean?" Vashee asked, rolling onto her back. She wiggled her weighty body against Casey's legs, an action which almost caused Casey to lose her balance.

Casey adjusted her footing before kneeling beside Vashee. *"I believe we're destined to journey together."*

Vashee raised her eyes to Casey. *"I feel you may be right."* She flipped over and glared down the room toward the other animals. *"If we should die battling those beasts?"*

Casey followed Vashee's gaze. Rubbing her hand through the fur on the panther's back, she answered. *"It will be a brief journey for us, then."*

Parrow talked Cassius into allowing Casey to fight in the stadium. He agreed, with the understanding he would save the match until after the gladiators performed. This would give him time to spread the word, and to max out his betting on the fight. Parrow instructed him to place his money on his wife, and although Cassius considered this a poor investment, the thought of the wealth he would make if Casey were fortunate enough to win was more than enough to convince him.

Cassius hurried off to arrange the match, secure his bets, and to find a set of armor and a weapon for Casey to use in the fight. Casey headed to the stands with Parrow after saying goodbye to Vashee, so she could be the one to tell Gran. She wasn't looking forward to the talk, but she had a strange feeling Grandmother Elizabeth would accept the idea.

"It's about time you two returned," Elizabeth said, while snacking on a plate of fruit.

"I'll leave you both alone to converse." Parrow stepped away to grab a full bottle of wine.

Both women watched him go. His noticeable tension wasn't helping the situation. "Why do I have a strange feeling I'm about to hear some information I won't like?" Elizabeth sat her plate on the table next to her and motioned for Casey to talk.

After a deep sigh, Casey began filling her in on what had happened after they left. From experiencing the connection in the underground room to meeting Vashee to ending with the plan of fighting in the arena. She stressed the fact that the man Cassius would release Vashee to her once they won, and if she didn't do this, she would lose Vashee altogether.

Elizabeth listened to the story without changing her facial expression in the slightest. After Casey finished talking, Elizabeth motioned for Parrow, who was waiting off to the side. She asked him for a cup of wine. When he returned, Elizabeth peered evenly at Parrow. "What do you think of Casey fighting two lions at her stage of training?"

He sat, not breaking eye contact. "I'm only worried because this fight will be to the death. I'm certain she could win. After all, she is a Trysal with Malanight blood in her veins, but there's still a risk. She's our future queen after you and has not yet left an heir to the throne if she should die. Still, you know I would intervene before this happened."

Casey rolled her eyes at his rambling. Her eye-rolling ended on Gran, who appeared to be comforted by his proper and extremely lengthy response.

Elizabeth placed the plate of fruit on a stone table beside her. "Thank you, Parrow." She stared off in deep thought. Neither Parrow nor Casey spoke, as the seconds ticked by.

Finally, Elizabeth took a long drink from her wine, then focused her attention on both. "I would like to meet this Vashee. After you win, of course." Elizabeth shot Casey a level glance. "Which you will."

Casey flung her arms around her grandmother's neck so fast, she almost knocked the cup from Elizabeth's hand.

"What's this for?" Elizabeth asked, startled.

"For you having faith in me, and in my decision."

"I always have," Elizabeth said, hugging Casey back. "Now go get something to eat. You'll need to build up energy before fighting two hungry lions."

"What do you mean, hungry?"

Parrow answered. "They've probably starved the animals for several days. This makes them desperate fighters."

The thought of this abusive treatment sparked Casey's temper. She was about to verbally declare her distaste for the cruelty in this time era, when her mind swung to the panther. "I'll go eat with Vashee. She's probably hungry and could use something to eat as well." Casey quickly prepared a heaping helping of food and asked Parrow to bring her armor to her once Cassius returned.

He protested her going alone until Elizabeth pulled him gently into the seat beside her. "She'll be fine. Why don't you do us both a favor and pour the wine."

Vashee was delighted to see Casey and equally thrilled to learn Casey had snuck her in several pounds of smoked meat. She ate with the hunger of a deprived animal, excusing herself afterward for her rude actions.

"Not at all. You eat like my friend, Parrow." Communicating without speaking was unusual, but Casey also found it enjoyable. It felt like she

was exercising several areas of her brain she'd never used before. The tingling sensation was intriguing.

"Is Parrow the tall man with the mark under his eye, the one who you were talking to earlier?"

"Yes, you'll like him."

"You both are not from around here, are you?" Vashee asked. She laid herself next to where Casey was sitting.

"No, actually we're from the year 2042 and live in a state called Virginia." Casey wondered how much Vashee could understand.

Deciding to tell her, Casey explained to Vashee her life changes these past few weeks. She went into detail about her family tree and the planets they originated from. An extensive discussion regarding the people on the team and the different species they encompassed followed, before ending with the Universal Region, the approaching war, and their overseer responsibilities on Earth.

When the talk was over, Vashee lifted her head and stared into Casey's eyes. *"I often gaze at the stars at night, thinking there's some grand plan for me."* She stretched again, releasing a terrific bellow, and the rest of the animals acted up. Once they quieted, she said, *"I've never fit in with my own kind. I was born with the desire for greater things."* She paused in contemplation. *"If we make it out of this alive, I will owe you my life. I will serve you and your allies with loyalty above all others."*

Casey stroked Vashee's muscular back. *"I would consider it a great honor to have you on my team."* Casey swore she saw Vashee grin.

Vashee thanked her, laid her head on Casey's lap, and fell asleep.

Casey watched Vashee sleep for quite some time, before dozing off herself. She wasn't sure how long she'd been sleeping when she finally awoke, startled. She lifted Vashee's head a bit to slide out from under her and stood.

Vashee sprang to her feet and produced a low defensive rumble in her throat. Not long after, her rigid body relaxed. *"It's your friend, Parrow."*

Casey glanced around and saw no one. *"How do you know?"*

"I can tell it's your friend by his smell."

Casey snorted into a hearty laugh.

"I don't mean he has an unpleasant odor. Every creature gives off a specific scent, and his is peculiarly strong. It's like he's part animal."

Casey rubbed at a stitch in her side, still laughing.

"I've brought your armor, but you won't like it," Parrow said when he entered. He handed her the cloth bag. "How are you and the big kitty cat getting along?" he asked, watching Vashee, who had her body pressed against Casey's thigh.

"Her name's Vashee."

"Oh, interesting. It sounds like Vassie, which means 'watchful one' in Blunion."

Casey's hand locked onto leather straps, and she removed the armor from the bag. More like a leather bathing suit than armor. She held the outrageous outfit up and asked Parrow, "What is this?"

There was no humor in Parrow's response. "I know the armor is lousy, but Cassius said this ensemble was all he could find on such short notice." He handed over a shield and a sword. "At least he had the sword sharpened."

"How thoughtful."

"You just make sure you come out of this in one piece." He gave her a hug before leaving.

"*Is he your kin?*" Vashee asked while Casey changed.

"*No. Although he feels and acts like my brother, we're not related.*"

Casey was fiddling with her armor, or lack thereof, when an old man stepped into the room to tell her she had ten minutes to go before heading up to the arena. Casey repeated what he had said to Vashee and asked her what she knew about the two lions they were getting ready to battle.

Vashee glowered at the other end of the room as she spoke. "*Those two down there are evil souls. They kill, not only for food but also for the thrill of the kill.*" Her eyes found Casey's. "*The first chance you get to kill them, do it, for they will not hesitate to kill either of us. Sadly, I feel no compassion in their hearts as I do in yours.*"

Casey remembered having read that these Barbary lions were not only the largest and heaviest of the lion species but also the meanest.

The sound of trumpets blared overhead. Casey grabbed her sword and shield and led Vashee from her cage. The armor wasn't as bad as she figured it'd be. After all, she felt like Xena in the outfit, and the fresh smell of leather was a pleasing scent.

The two soldiers entering the door froze in fear the instant they spotted the muscular panther move around Casey's legs at the other end of the room.

"She won't hurt you," Casey called. On second thought, she asked Vashee not to touch the soldiers.

"I'll attack only on your command, or for you and your people's safety."

Both men hesitated before treading toward Casey. "We'll release the lions up the far ramp once they signal you're ready," the taller of the two said, while keeping a watchful eye on Vashee. "You and the creature will be hoisted on the elevators the moment the trumpets stop."

The man motioned Casey to follow them to the elevator to wait. The soldiers stood on each end of the cranking mechanism, then directed Casey and Vashee to climb onto the wooden platform. She tightened her hand on the hilt of her sword.

"We'll wait for them to make the first move. Try to stay close to me," Casey said as the horns stopped.

"Yes, they'll seek to divide us," Vashee said. *"They'll work together to injure one of us, and gang up and kill whichever is left standing."*

Casey felt the lift move upward, and she wished she'd had more time in training with a sword. She was good at defending, but her attack was still unbalanced. They exited the wooden platform to a mixture of cheers and hisses. Casey guessed a good portion of the spectators in the overcrowded arena were offended by the idea of a woman volunteering for a fight such as this. Truth be told, she couldn't care less about what they thought.

"Good citizens of Rome." Casey heard the echoing voice of Cassius call out from some rudimentary type of speaking horn, causing the reverberation in the stands to subside.

"This battle is the fight of all fights. For tonight, I bring to you a female whose bravery and courage rises above all others who have ever stepped foot in this arena." He looked around at the crowd, giving his speech more of an enhanced theatrical significance. "The woman has befriended a great black panther, and fights by this animal's side, to either her death or this beast's freedom. She, who must be a direct descendant of Bellona, the Goddess of War herself…I give to you the beautiful, the gallant…the wife of Parrow."

Casey felt instantly affronted. He referred to her as the wife of Parrow. She shook her head. No way she could ever live in a time like this. She supposed she was lucky these sexist bigots let her fight in the first place.

They probably figured what was one dead woman to them anyway. Then she remembered Parrow had to give Cassius his blessing for this match.

"I'm sensing you're upset," Vashee said.

This brought Casey to focus on what they were here to do. She willed herself to block out the noise from the surrounding crowd and what Cassius was shouting, and she readied herself for what was to come.

A loud thud followed by a cheer from the spectators caused Casey's heart to race. In one giant leap, two titanic lions with full, wavy manes, one darker than the other, emerged onto the surface of the arena. They were breathtaking. They spun in unison toward the two waiting competitors on the other side of the stadium. Vashee stepped a foot away from Casey and lowered herself into a threatening stance. The two golden-brown animals scrambled eagerly toward their prey, rapidly closing the distance between them.

"Here they come," Vashee shouted.

Casey raised her sword and readied her shield the moment the dark-maned lion sprang at her. The lion's attack felt like slow motion, and she knew her thrust at this angle would be useless. Right as the lion reached her, Casey reeled herself underneath its massive, outstretched body, missing the sharp points of its claws by inches. She whirled to witness the mighty cat land on all fours and spin for another attack.

Worried, Casey saw the bodies of Vashee and the other lion roll intertwined to the ground. Her attention snapped to the first lion. The beast was pacing in a slow, wide circle around her. Its tail was ridged, its face scrunched tight in rage. She held up her sword, ready for the next assault. The lion let out an ear-piercing roar, followed by cheers from the crowd, and he leapt with all his weight directly at Casey.

"Casey!" She heard the warning shout from Vashee in her head, scarcely in time to see the light-maned lion dash toward her, with Vashee sprinting a few feet behind. Casey rolled to the right, dropping her shield during the roll for more speed. She cleared the attack from the first lion but caught a full swipe of merciless claws from the second one. She yelled as a chunk of her flesh ripped away from the backside of her left shoulder. She forced down the excruciating pain and lunged with her sword at the center of the dark-maned lion. She missed his middle by inches.

"Are you all right?"

"Yes, I'm fine," she said in her head, facing her worried companion.

"Look out," Casey screamed, with fear rushing in. The light-maned lion dove at Vashee from behind, lunging right for the cat's neck. Vashee had no time to react. Casey watched in frozen horror as the teeth from the commanding animal drew toward her companion.

Vashee closed her eyes, bracing herself for the deadly slaughter.

Protective rage engulfed Casey. Planting her feet, she brought her sword up and hurled it at the light-maned lion with all the strength she possessed. The impact was great, sending the lion's body backward in a hard-jerking motion, its bite left unrealized.

Her own heartbeat muffled the crowd's cheers. She visually inspected Vashee for injury, then dropped her gaze to the fallen attacker to make sure the lion was dead. There, half covered in dirt, lay the motionless body of the lion with the hilt of her sword sticking up from the center of its blood-soaked chest. *One down.* She regained her composure and scanned the arena for her other opponent.

The dark-maned lion was pacing close to the elevator, where it eyed both her and Vashee. It was clearly trying to size up who would be the easiest to kill. It trained its bloodthirsty rage on Casey, bared its teeth, and bellowed out a battle cry.

"You're unarmed. Run toward me! I have a plan!"

Casey did as she was told, sensing the other deadly predator closing in on her heels.

"When I say now, fall to the ground," Vashee told Casey while she ran at a full sprint, keeping Casey's body in-between the view of her and the other cat. The second the lion sprang for Casey, Vashee shouted, *"Now!"* It sounded like a mighty roar to all present, and Vashee leapt over the fallen Casey.

Tilting her head, Casey made out the confusion in the lion's eyes as Vashee sunk her strong teeth straight into the neck of the other creature. They both fell hard to the ground, but Vashee kept her jaw clenched tight, squeezing with all her might against the jugular of the flailing lion. Vashee didn't release her grip until after the animal's body stopped moving and the beast was dead.

The noise of the applause echoed throughout the stands. Casey stumbled to where Vashee was hovering over the corpse of the dead creature.

"You've saved my life. I'm forever in your debt."

"I believe we're even," Casey answered.

"You're injured, Casey."

Casey peered over her shoulder, wincing at the pain. *"Don't worry, it's only a scratch."*

Chapter Six

Returning Customs

The three time travelers arrived in the same room of the ship they had originally departed from. The only difference was that five minutes had passed since they initially left, and Casey had her arms draped around the body of a unique black panther, whom she guided through the journey of time.

Casey, Elizabeth, and Parrow entered, one by one, into the Equipment Originator, each coming out wearing their original clothing. Parrow headed to his quarters to unpack his gear, while Casey and Vashee followed Elizabeth to her quarters to do the same. Elizabeth had Casey put the leftover coins into the vault, as well as the necklace Parrow wore. Her necklace remained dangling around her neck, with the strict instructions from her grandmother to never time travel without it.

They met Parrow at the elevators several minutes later. Elizabeth instructed him to use his personal computer to assemble the rest of the team onto the operations deck. She told him they would meet him there after she took Casey and Vashee to the medical wing to finish treating their wounds.

"We'll be cutting into your abilities training with this meeting," Elizabeth said as she treated Casey's injured shoulder. "Still, considering you've made your first journey to the past alone, and what you have accomplished with Vashee, I think I'm more than happy with what you've learned today."

Elizabeth set a handheld medical contraption on the table beside Casey, one that sealed Casey's gashes without the use of stitches, staples, or tape. "There will be a slight scar because of the degree of the wound, but I managed to get much of your skin to regenerate and fuse together."

Elizabeth went to work on Vashee's minor injuries. Once she was finished, the three made their way to the operations deck, where the entire team was waiting. Apparently, Parrow filled everyone in on what happened in Rome, because no one appeared the least bit surprised to see a huge black panther enter the room.

Casey introduced the team to Vashee and was startled when Eva came bouncing over with a wide smile across her face and spoke to both. *"I'm very pleased to meet you, Vashee, but I'm more pleased to see Casey and you have found each other."*

Casey gave Eva an astonished look. "You can communicate with us?" she asked aloud. Once she realized her blunder, she asked telepathically for Vashee's benefit.

"Yes, my people have done it our whole existence. How we're communicating now is not telepathy and not a language in the sense either of you are used to. We call the gift Telamanrin. A mental dialect used between a species of the animal kingdom and a member of the Kan race."

"Why have I never communicated this way with another animal before?" Casey asked.

Eva raised her brow. *"For the same reason Vashee has probably never communicated with another human, or why your grandmother has never interconnected with an animal."* She smiled. *"Because, Casey, you didn't meet your soul-link until today."*

"What's a soul-link?" Vashee asked, intrigued.

As Eva answered, Casey wondered if the Kan was on the verge of crying. *"The souls of those in the Kan race link with the souls of a member of the animal species. Sometimes you can have several soul-links, but it's exceedingly rare."*

"If Vashee is my soul-link, how is it you can speak with her?"

"Good question, Casey. Because I'm a Kan and have joined with my soul-link. We hold a soul-binding ceremony once we find our soul-link. It connects us, making us one with each other. Once this happens, our souls connect with the animal kingdom in a way no Kan scholar could ever explain. It's a treasured gift. One that I thought had ended." She held the beginning of tears in her catlike eyes. *"You two have given me confidence that our most prized capability will live on."*

Vashee asked, *"Can you perform this soul-binding ceremony on us?"*

"Yes, I'd consider it an honor. I've already collected all the essential items from my planet we would need for the ritual."

"How?" Casey was surprised. *"We just got back."*

"Your family is part Kan. I've been ready for years in case this blessed event should ever happen."

Casey thought of the elation on Gran's face when she first told her of Vashee. *"Do you think Gran is going to find her soul-link?"*

Eva gazed across the room to Elizabeth. Her reply held a trace of sorrow. *"You must be aware, as she is. This sometimes does not happen, this meeting of your soul-link. Tragically, your family is not full Kan, so the chances of her never connecting will increase. Now, being part Kan, and a relation to you, your grandmother might learn to communicate with Vashee once you two complete the ritual. Unfortunately, this way of communication may be extremely limited, if it works at all."*

"Oh, that is regrettable. I suppose we're lucky Casey traveled in time and met me when she did."

Eva adamantly shook her head. *"I believe everything happens for a reason. Our destiny works by means greater than we can explain or fully grasp. No, I feel yours and Casey's meeting was more than chance."*

Casey's idea from earlier crossed her mind, bringing her to her next question. *"Can we program the translators so Vashee can communicate with the others on the team?"*

"I'm afraid not. Many species have tried for thousands of years to come up with a method to communicate with the animal kingdom. There are ways of somewhat understanding animals, through studying them and their behaviors, to get a better insight into their world and feelings. However, this partial perception is unfortunately the limit to many unsuccessful endeavors. Even Blunions, who can shape-shift into various animals, from all sorts of planets, are unable to communicate in the way us three are now. They have a deeper grasp of an animal's body language and feeling, but this too is not an absolute understanding."

A loud siren rang throughout the room, bringing the three of them around to the main screen above the front control station. Red lights were going off in cadence with the sirens, and each of their personal computers blinked rapidly. Barick and Darren, who were on duty at the main terminal, moved away from the rest of the team and faced the built-in monitors on the desks. Together, they worked the various controls in a flurry of movements. The alarm stopped.

Darren touched a tiny object in his right ear before he turned toward Elizabeth. "Trysal Seven has reported a velocity capsule heading for this part of the solar system. It shot past their patrol."

"Do we have another patrol close by?" Elizabeth asked.

"Yes," Barick said, pointing to the display. "Sycom Three might be able to intercept."

Darren placed his hand on the device in his ear. "Sycom Three, this is Vasar Five, do you read?" A momentary pause before he said, "We have a VC heading our way, passing coordinates MW187436A. Can you respond?"

After another brief wait, Darren spun to Elizabeth. "They're in route, but with the speed of the capsule, they're not confident they'll make it here on time."

"Eva, you man PDR-4, Hanna, you're on PDR-5. Barick, put the long and short-range visuals up on the main screen. Include the outer left regional tracking chart."

Casey remained with Vashee out of everyone's way. They watched the metal plate in front change instantly into three separate screens. The first two views held clear images of what she assumed were live pictures of different parts of the Milky Way surrounding Earth. The third display showed a colorfully detailed, dimensional map of what Casey had heard Elizabeth say was the outer left section of their region. Casey didn't understand what the different labels were, but she assumed the minute, red moving dot to be the velocity capsule, and the larger, green moving circle to be Sycom Three.

"Is everything all right?" Vashee asked Casey.

Casey explained to her what was going on, as she stroked the spot of fur between Vashee's shoulder blades.

"Estimated time of interception for Sycom Three is thirty-two seconds," Darren announced without looking away from the screen.

Everyone watched silently as the dots drew closer together.

"Barick, give me the projected location of the capsule's impact on Earth once you receive it."

"I'll have it in one second," he said, and he started to tap the desk monitor in front of him with one hand, while working his other hand rapidly on another screen to his left. "It's going to hit two miles northeast of Ava, Missouri," Barick called out over his shoulder.

"Marah, I need you to power up Vasar Six," Elizabeth instructed the main computer, before glancing around the room. "If that capsule lands, I want Parrow and Eva to stay here with Casey and Vashee while the rest of us head out to the impact site." She spoke to Fayrel, who was sitting off to the right, waiting to help if they needed him. "Has the medical wing been resupplied since our last operation?"

He straightened in his chair before answering. "I did it the moment we returned."

"Five seconds to interception," Darren called out, bringing Elizabeth's focus to the main screen.

The place fell silent once more. Everyone watched the screen. Darren kept his hand on his earpiece. A few seconds later, he spun in his chair to Elizabeth. "They were too far away for a clear shot and missed the target."

Elizabeth and the rest of the team directed their attention to the two women on standby at the far corner stations. "It's up to you both," Elizabeth said, moving closer to where Hanna and Eva were sitting.

The room was eerily quiet. Casey filled in Vashee on what happened, and what was to come, while intently eyeing the first two screens on the wall. When she was about to turn toward the two women, a movement on the short-range imagery caught her eye.

"Targets in range." The firm voice of Hanna rang throughout the room. Eva repeated Hanna's statement seconds later.

"Once you're locked onto the capsule, fire," Elizabeth said, watching the distinct bullet shape outline grow steadily larger on the big screen.

"Planetary defense rocket-five fired!" Hanna shouted.

Casey watched as a new, faster moving dot came into view on the screen.

"PDR-4 fired!" The sound of Eva's voice preceded a second dot, heading straight toward the target on the short-range and regional tracking maps.

Elizabeth clutched Darren's chair in anticipation. Casey heard no sound when the first of the two rockets struck the target, followed instantly by the second hitting in the exact spot.

Darren twisted his head toward Elizabeth. "Targets destroyed."

A gasp of relief filled the room, and Elizabeth instructed Marah to power down Vasar Six. "Darren, send out the necessary transmissions, and I'll fill out the reports after our meeting." Elizabeth proudly displayed her relief to her team. "Good job, everyone," she said, taking a seat in the front.

After Darren sent out the transmissions and Barick had the system set to its original status, Elizabeth called everyone together to begin the meeting. She started by introducing her team to Vashee, while Casey translated to Vashee what was going on.

To Casey's surprise, Darren was the first to respond. He rose to his feet, looking apologetic as he spoke. "Elizabeth, what's the Assembly going to say about this? Bringing a species here from another time certainly goes against several laws of the Universal Declaration."

Eva stood, affronted by his question. "Vashee is Casey's soul-link. You, of all people here, should know what this means!"

"Yes…I understand, Eva. I also know the Assembly will never allow it."

Elizabeth raised her hand to silence Eva's next heated retort. "This will not reach the Assembly. It must stay in our circle of confidence. The abilities my family possesses are under the highest level of secrecy. Therefore, this decision will have to be left to the queen and the head of council."

Darren seemed satisfied by this decision and retook his seat. Eva, not so much. She asked to address this matter more closely. She reiterated the importance of this gift and educated the team on the fact that if they were to go to war, it would also involve the preservation of the animal kingdom as well. On every inhabited planet. To communicate with so many creatures, not just here on Earth but in the entire Universal Region, was vital to the survival of every species.

Hanna motioned her agreement, right as Parrow moved to speak. "Vashee being here hasn't caused any rip in time or an unbalanced paradox, whatever you want to call it. I don't believe we should mention to anyone that Vashee was brought here from the past."

Fayrel narrowed his eyebrows at Parrow in disappointment. "We follow these laws to keep a balanced form of government. We, as with the queen and the head of council, are not above them. This decision must go before the Assembly for a vote."

Barick was fast to respond. Either to endorse his son's statement or because he wholeheartedly took Eva's stance, Casey wasn't sure. "History shows us that during the Great War, our planet, as with many others, was defended not only by our species, but with the help of many of our creatures. If the Kan race had been on the Assembly back then—or if our ancestors had the ability to communicate with those animals, as Eva and Casey can do—I believe this gift could have spared many of the lives that were lost, and the war would have ended decades sooner. I agree with what Eva said. When this next war happens, I've a feeling that by nurturing Casey's ability, tapping into this divine power will be a profound asset for the survival of every species."

Elizabeth thanked everyone for their input. "This connection must remain. However, we cannot make this decision ourselves. We must involve the queen and head of council." She gestured to Fayrel. "I agree, this judgement should fall to the Assembly. But if there's a chance a traitor exists in our government, our abilities cannot be revealed to our enemies any more than they already have. Not to mention, everyone thinks Casey is dead. If our enemies knew she was alive, her life would be in substantial danger. I'm sure of it."

Fayrel and Darren both appeared satisfied with Elizabeth's assessment, and Eva verbally agreed. She placed a hand on Casey's shoulder. "It'll work out."

Although her heart felt heavy, Casey forced a smile while explaining to Vashee what the final decision was.

"Can we still go through with the soul-binding ceremony?" Vashee asked Eva, who repeated the panther's question to Elizabeth. Considering they would not be crossing the declaration any more than they already had, all agreed the Kan ritual would be acceptable and scheduled the ceremony before the voyage to Vasar One.

Casey was exhausted by the time the gathering was over and everyone departed, including Parrow, who looked as worn-out as she felt. Eva asked Vashee to join her at the main control panel, to become better acquainted with one another, while Elizabeth took Casey to a far workstation, where they went over Casey's next class with the rest of the time slotted. Casey had to fight to keep her mind centered by the time she and Elizabeth joined Eva and Vashee at the duty station almost two hours later for Casey's scheduled overseer duties.

"You look done in." Eva gave Casey a warm, motherly smile, as Casey lowered herself into one of the cushioned chairs.

"I'm doing okay. A little coffee, and I'll be fine."

"When was the last time you ate?" Eva asked.

She felt too foggy-brained to think. "I'm not sure."

Eva got up from her seat, returning moments later with her hands full of food and drinks for Casey and Vashee. Vashee scarfed down the large helping of meat and drank the entire bowl of water Eva placed on the ground. Soon after, she stretched her body on the floor at Casey's feet and was out within seconds.

"I guess we've had a full day," Casey said, finishing her second cup of coffee.

Elizabeth looked from her to the panther. "We can reschedule your duties."

Casey wanted more than anything to be allowed to go to Vasar on this next trip. Blowing off part of her schedule wasn't an option. "I'm fine," she insisted between bites of her toasted chicken and Swiss cheese sandwich.

By the time her duties ended, Casey took Vashee to their section of the castle. She was spent. She wondered whether she would remember any of the many controls and sequences Elizabeth and Eva had demonstrated on the main computer terminal during her duties. She didn't even bother to change out of her clothes before she crawled underneath the covers. She welcomed Vashee to join her until they could set up an area of her own.

Casey lay there, feeling too tired to sleep. She calculated the additional time they were in Rome and realized she had been awake for almost three days. As Vashee arranged herself on the opposite side of the bed, Casey finally drifted off into a deep, dreamless sleep.

Casey awoke over twelve hours later, still feeling groggy, like she had overslept. Vashee was nowhere around, which struck Casey as odd, considering Vashee had no way to let herself out of the room. "Chasel, do you know where Vashee is?" Casey asked.

The feminine holographic figure appeared. "Yes, she's out in the gardens with Parrow and Eva."

"How did she get the doors to open?"

The program looked mystified at the question. "Why, I opened them for her when she wanted out."

"How did you know she wanted out?" The throbbing from her head was almost unbearable, and aggressively rubbing different parts of her scalp didn't ease the pain. Sluggishly, she made her way to her closet.

"Eva programmed into my system everything she could find on the studies of animal characteristics and their mannerisms. When Vashee awoke, I sensed by the way she was acting she wanted out of the room."

"That works." Casey busied herself with choosing another outfit.

"Vashee began licking herself the moment she awoke," Chasel clarified. "I interpreted this to mean she was bathing herself. I made her a nice bath, and would you believe she thought I was giving her a drink?" Chasel giggled at her own story. "She was so thirsty, she drank nearly a quarter of the water in the tub."

Casey slipped over to the bathroom. "Thank you, Chasel, I don't know what I'd do without you."

"Would you like me to run you a bath?"

"No, thanks. I've a massive headache. I plan to jump in the shower, and afterward, find something for my head."

Casey noticed the pill and drink waiting for her in the Belfont Originator as soon as she entered the bathroom. "Thank you, Chasel," Casey said gratefully.

The yellow and black-striped pill worked its magic by the time Casey stepped into the shower. Her headache and grogginess were both gone, and she felt as good as new. Thirty minutes later, she found Vashee with Parrow and Eva wandering through one of the castle's extensive gardens. With so many colorful plants, decorative fountains, and a generous assortment of statues positioned in every corner, this vibrant sanctuary was Casey's favorite place growing up. She could see someone had already collected the summer strawberries and replaced the red, juicy vegetation with an array of flamboyant flora.

Vashee was the first to spot Casey, and she came at her in a full run. Once she drew closer, she slowed and rubbed her face and full body along Casey's faded blue jeans.

Planting her feet to keep from being pushed over by Vashee's weight, Casey laughed while playfully scratching her fingers along the fur on Vashee's legs and back. She saw Parrow pluck the petals from a bright red flower, and Casey wondered if he was repeating, "He loves me, he loves me not," in his head.

"She must really like you," he said. "That's how cats mark you as theirs."

"She does," Eva replied, as she lovingly eyed the playful exchange between the two.

"Eva and Parrow set me up a room off the third-floor stairs, and a woman who could walk through walls showed me around the castle." Vashee sounded so excited by all she had done today, it made Casey feel instant relief at how much Vashee was enjoying her new home.

"That's Chasel. She's our team's Program Intelligence."

"Yes, Eva explained her to me. It's odd, this place you're from, but it feels like home. I hope they allow me to stay here with you."

Eva exchanged a brief glance with Casey. *"I'm sure all will be fine. You'll be going to Vasar One with us on our next trip, and so will Casey if she does well in her classes."*

Casey shot Eva a worried grimace before checking the time on her personal computer. *"I need to go. I only have eleven hours left to study and do Zeckner's assignments."*

Casey bid the three farewell before running to the castle.

Casey spent the next several weeks adjusting to her new schedule, immersing herself completely into her studies during any free time. The hardest of her classes were Zeckner's. The instructor acted as if he wanted her to fail. Thankfully, with the help of Chasel and their many study sessions, Casey grasped the material of his classes and turned her overloaded homework assignments in on time.

The rest of her studies flew by with little to no stress. She could create several types of programs in Chasel's class. She studied over fifty different species, close to a hundred unique planetary types, mastered two separate languages in Vespa's class, and absorbed the information in both of Hanna's classes at a remarkable rate.

Parrow's classes were more of beatings than lessons. She moved up a week ago to fighting him with two new types of hand-to-hand weapons, and her lack of skill with these items had shown with the many cuts and bruises on her body. After every lesson, Hanna treated these multiple marks, leaving Casey as good as new. Her ego still felt damaged though.

"Not to worry," Hanna would say with a motherly grin while smearing soothing ointment on Casey's back or running a machine that hummed over one of her limbs. "He tells me you're improving in your training like a true Malanight. Barick too, for that matter." Hanna's inspirational talks would help, but Casey relished the hopeful image of Parrow one day lying sprawled out on the mat instead of her.

Her abilities classes with her grandmother started with her going into the past alone to various locations. Elizabeth instructed Casey to find and return with requested keepsakes from a long list she carefully prepared. Once Casey finished locating the historical items, she put Casey to work on her next ability, moving various objects with her mind, a feat harder than Casey expected it to be. After two sessions, she grasped the concept and moved her grandmother's chair a few feet away. She felt lightheaded afterward.

"What you're experiencing is normal. You've never used these parts of your brain before, after all. You must start off slow and work your way up or else you could seriously injure yourself. Practice with lightweight items on your own time when you have the chance."

Casey gave her patient a second injection, then stepped to the side so Fayrel could grade her work. She had mastered the anatomy and treatment of the Trysal prototype and was currently working with a synthetic Blunion.

"I'm impressed, Casey. You certainly did your homework on the Zelic Mumps," Fayrel said as he inspected Casey's artificial patient.

"Yes. The Zelic Mumps have similar characteristics to Morfonox Sengentitus. However, if treated wrong or left untreated, the side-effects could cause a slow and painful death."

"What are the stages before death?" he asked, giving Casey a doctor to student stance.

"The first stage is confusion, followed by complete nerve loss, and the explosion of the fifth intestine, which results in the Blunion's deadly toxin seeping throughout their entire body structure."

"Is it reversible?"

"Not after the patient experiences nerve loss."

"Very good. You're about to advance to the Hafite prototype. After that will be the Flouns. Only one more treatment, and I'll consider you ready." Fayrel checked off a few things on his computer pad before pivoting to Casey. "After you've mastered these next two species, you'll be ready to test out in my class. These four prototypes are similar in anatomy to the many universal races out there. Therefore, these species are the only ones the academy requires you to know before they'll accept you. Once there, you'll receive more in-depth, hands-on training for each individual species."

She gave him an understanding nod, eager for his next assignment.

Casey was thrilled by the time she rushed to Eva's class. She was slotted to take Vasar Seven out for a test run. Eva would be with her, so Casey had no worries, only excitement. Her other classes with Eva had been simulated flights, and other than the disastrous landing during her first week, she was doing well, according to Eva.

Eva met Casey outside the door to her class. They headed to the secondary hangar, located directly above Vasar Five. Not a long walk, but for Casey, this trip took forever. Instead of stopping in the already explored control room as she and Parrow had done weeks ago, they went through the second door and came out onto a metal walkway.

Casey held her breath at the sight of the ships. Both vessels were suspended in the air, unmoving, with the underside of their bodies close to fifteen feet off the metal platform. She learned through her classes with Eva how the vessels hovered for security reasons, on the slim chance this hangar was breached. Also, Vasar Six was the vessel the team primarily used, leaving the slightly smaller Vasar Seven here for the overseer detail in case they needed it.

She followed Eva along the catwalk and up the stairs to the platform, directly under the belly of the vessel. Eva directed her to stand at the center of the platform while she entered information into the computer panel along the right edge of it. In the blink of an eye, Casey stood on a similar platform in an enclosed metal room. A few seconds later, Eva materialized right next to her, smiling.

"Is this Vasar Seven?" Casey asked, looking around at the control panels.

"Yes. We're in the ship's teleporting room. We use this means of transportation often on the planets. One can cover a great distance in seconds, and teleportation chambers greatly lessen congestion with air and ground traffic."

Casey followed Eva around, getting a feel of where everything was located. Although this vessel was nowhere near the size of Vasar Five, Casey felt they could still fit the population of a decent-sized town in here comfortably. After going through most of the floors, Eva led Casey to the operations deck. It housed a main front workstation and several individual ones off to each side, identical to the simulator.

Eva instructed Casey to take the seat next to her, then she had her go through the procedures of powering up the ship. Casey used the same method as she'd done many times before, but since this time was real, Casey was on edge. She fought with her nerves to stay focused.

"Now, switch on the ship's invisibility controls and set the anti-detection system to full power."

Casey's mind briefly went blank, but swiftly recovered, giving her the information to do as Eva instructed. Eva double-checked everything was correct before telling Casey she was ready to pilot the vessel out. Casey gave Eva a blank stare. Her entire body became frozen to the seat.

Eva touched Casey's hand. "You'll be fine. The first time is always the scariest, but I'll be right here with you."

"I thought I was taking over once we were off the planet?"

"How are you going to learn if I do it for you?" Eva turned her body toward the view outside the ship. "The worst thing that'll happen is we crash and die. What have we got to lose?"

Casey took a deep breath and relaxed her body. Calmness engulfed her. She didn't believe in chance. She agreed with Eva when she'd said several weeks ago, *Everything happens for a reason.* Casey flipped several knobs, producing red and orange flashing lights throughout the hangar. Marah's voice filled the operations deck of their ship. "Inner and outer hatch opened. Outer building dematerialized."

"Thank you," Casey said to the main computer. Eva grinned proudly when Casey reached for the manual controls. "If it's our time to go, I guess I might as well enjoy it."

Eva didn't say a word. Casey had said all that needed saying. The ship floated up and forward at Casey's touch and hovered briefly, awaiting Casey's command. Casey peered at the exit tunnel above them.

Eva relaxed fully in her chair. "It's no different from the simulation room."

"It looks smaller."

"Your mother said the same thing her first time."

"What happened?" Casey asked.

"I'll tell you after we clear Earth's atmosphere."

Casey studied the opening. After two intense breaths, she repositioned the ship and gripped onto the controls. With a flick of her wrist and the press of the accelerator, the front of the ship shot straight up and out of the hangar. Casey kept the ship steady while she increased their speed, darting them into space.

"Sorry, I didn't mean to go so fast."

"You did very well. You mother forgot to hit the controls for the stables, and she obliterated the entire building when she first tried it."

Casey snorted as she closed the inner and outer hatch behind them, and the barn materialized on the screen.

"Do you feel confident setting your own coordinates?"

"I think so. Are we using the long-range, or short-range plotter?"

"Since our class is only three hours long, we'll use the short-range plotter. Find your course, but remember to crosscheck it with the substance detection map, or else we could fly straight into a planet."

Casey signaled her understanding and did as Eva instructed. Her breath caught in her throat the instant their ship crossed over into the reach of outer space.

"I know." With a graceful sway of her hand, Eva gestured to the surrounding vastness. "Isn't it stunning? We're destined for this, Casey. To be out here. Protectors of an existence far greater than our own."

Casey understood what Eva was saying. Her entire life she'd felt compelled to protect, and seeing this view of the beautiful blackness sprinkled with an array of glimmering stars, knowing so many other species danced among their greatness, it gave a new meaning to her own existence. An importance weighing on a grander scale than she could even grasp. They stayed out for quite a while, flying to different locations Casey picked.

On their return to Earth, Eva had Casey first go to the far side of the moon, where she had her practice planetary landings and takeoffs. Feeling satisfied, Eva told her to land the ship in the hangar. The landing was harder, but Casey managed it without so much as a scratch on the ship. Or the barn.

After everything powered down and Casey was preparing to head to her next class, Eva stopped her. "Casey, we decided to schedule yours and Vashee's soul-binding ceremony later this evening. I will perform it on Vasar Five's operations deck after you finish your overseer duties."

Casey threw her arms around Eva. "I appreciate everything you've done. I know Vashee feels the same."

"You're welcome, but you'll be late for your next class if you don't hurry. You better run." Eva shooed Casey toward the exit.

By the time she showed up for her overseer duties, Casey was once again exhausted and ready for sleep. Fayrel was on watch with her this evening, where he felt the need to quiz her on what she learned in his class. At first, she was rapidly snapping out answers to his questions, but soon took to dragging out her responses. By the time the first two hours were over, Casey had to fight off the urge to lower her head on the desk and sleep. She stood and paced the area in front of the main control station.

"You're looking kind of weary," Fayrel said, reaching into his bag. He extracted a yellow and red-speckled pill, which Casey downed with a glass of cold water.

Within moments, her energy soared, giving her the urge to run laps around the operations room. "Wow, I feel great."

"That one's made from a plant which grows on the planet of Plotar. Chasel has a list of medicines she's allowed to dispense to you if you need them. All are non-addicting, with little to no side effect. Careful with this one, because once it wears off, you'll be out for the count."

Retaking her seat, Casey blurted out answers to his questions, one right after the other. She was on the floor cranking out push-ups by the time the others started to make their way into the room.

Fifteen minutes before her three-hour watch was over, Eva arrived with Elizabeth, both carrying different bags and items in their arms. Eva wore a long, silky white robe with a gold chain tied at her waist. Her long blonde hair fell past her shoulders, where it swayed rhythmically from side to side.

When she noticed Darren ogling Eva, Casey forced her gaze away. She'd never been attracted to anyone before. Because of this, she envied him. The thought of going through almost three hundred years of life alone gave her a sudden empty feeling.

Parrow and Vashee were the last of the group to arrive. Everyone watched in silent curiosity as Eva positioned her items around the open space next to the control panel. After everything was ready, Eva directed Casey and Vashee inside a wide, perfectly formed circle opposite from each other. Eva lit what looked to be dried leaves resting in bowls at the inner edge of this area. As the smoke from the bowls drifted upward, it carried with it the mixed scent of vanilla, peppermint, and a light floral fragrance Casey didn't recognize. Next, Eva draped matching necklaces of different shaped and colored stones around Casey and Vashee's necks. She opened a jar containing a clear light blue liquid that she poured into two separate carved wooden bowls.

"These two individuals have come here asking for the bequest of joining their souls together as one." Eva gazed upward as she spoke, her arms lifted toward the sky. She wasn't speaking directly to the group, but from what Casey could tell, to some higher being. "With this circle of soil, they enclose themselves, united forevermore from this day on." Casey peered closer, realizing Eva had formed the circle out of dirt. Probably from her planet, which made the most sense. After all, this ritual was a Kan tradition.

"We burn the foliage from our homeland in remembrance of the gift which you have given us." Eva handed one of the wooden bowls to Casey and the other she placed on the floor next to Vashee. She motioned for them to drink the blue liquid as she said, "They imbibe the cherished water to cleanse their spirit of the old before their new one is formed."

The water tasted better than any Casey had ever had. Its cool, crisp wetness flowed down her throat where it lightly tingled her insides.

"Bless these stones of Baysor with the gifts each of these beings hold, so they may pass from one another a cherished piece of themselves."

Casey felt the heat on her neck seconds before noticing Vashee's necklace glow bright red. After several moments, the brightness across from her faded away and at the same time, the heat from around her neck vanished. Eva removed each of the stone necklaces, switching them out with the other. Instead of returning to her spot in the circle, Eva stepped outside the line of dirt. She spoke again. "Bind these two souls together, so they may be as one."

Casey waited, unsure of what to expect. Without warning, a bluish-white light encircled her and Vashee, lifting them several inches from the ground. The surrounding air sparked, and a jolt of pain hit the muscles in her legs hard. Startled, she held her breath and squinted wildly around. *This can't be right. Something is definitely wrong. Maybe the items Eva used from her planet were old, spoiled from age.*

She was on the verge of telling Eva to halt the ritual when a sharp pain pierced her deep in the stomach. The intensity was so severe she half-expected an alien to come crawling out. Casey's eyes darted downward, fear pouring in. She couldn't move. Suddenly, her body was on fire. The burning sensation beneath her skin was the worst pain by far. It felt as if she were about to transform into a werewolf, or worse.

Out of the corner of her eye, the image of Vashee caught her attention. Shocked, Casey couldn't move. The muscular black panther transformed into a replica of herself. She opened her mouth to speak, but her own voice wasn't what emerged. A piercing roar filled her ears. She raised her hands to Eva, but saw they were now black, fury paws, and she was in the air on all fours. Her body drifted toward Vashee. Her heart raced. The dirt and the leftover ashes from the once burning bowls blew up in a circular rotation around her and Vashee's suspended figures, in a gust of divine fury.

The light faded, the debris of the flying particles vanished, and both Casey and Vashee looked at one another. They both stood on the ground in their original forms. Their pain was nothing more than a far-off memory. No one spoke. Most stood wide-eyed, with their mouths slightly parted by inspired awe.

Eva dabbed at her eyes with the end of her sleeve as she made her way over, congratulating them both. This exchange snapped the rest of the team out of their hypnotic poses, and they skirted over to do the same thing. The room had gone from a quiet sanctuary into a boisterous celebration, with all sorts of questions directed at Eva and the two newly joined individuals.

After the celebration finally ended, Casey and Vashee stayed after to talk with Eva.

"These necklaces will help you two communicate with each other from great distances."

"I don't feel any different. Is this normal?" Vashee asked.

"You both will. The bond is unique for each. I'm eager to see what will come of your soul-binding."

Chapter Seven

Earth Date: 24th September 2042
The Long Voyage

Casey had extra time to kill before the start of her next set of classes, so she and Parrow decided on an extensive workout in the gym. They began with a moderate-paced, five-mile run around the track before moving to circuit training with the weights.

She pressed her usual one hundred and fifteen pounds, while Parrow spotted her. The weights felt off to Casey.

"Something's not right," Casey said, placing the bar into the holder and sitting up.

"What's wrong? Your form was perfect. Did I put too much on?"

"You didn't put enough." She added up the total and glanced from Parrow to the weights. "That's one-sixty. I said I lift one-fifteen."

"No, your math is off. Add it up again."

She exhaled with a twinge of frustration. "It's one-hundred and fifteen for the weights, yes, but you forgot to add the forty-five-pound bar. Total would be one-sixty. I can't bench press that much weight."

"But you did," Parrow said, flustered. "And, as I recall, you said the weight wasn't enough."

Casey studied the metal bar with the weights on each side. "Not impossible."

"I guess you've forgotten who you are. Your body is changing, which would include your muscles."

"Gran said I might develop the strength twice that of a normal Trysal," she muttered aloud, more to herself than to Parrow.

Parrow let out a long whistle. "Do you realize how much that is? It's around fourteen times the strength of the average human."

She let out a trapped breath before glaring at her arms. She didn't feel any different. Maybe her muscles were growing, but she couldn't tell. Flexing, she pressed a finger against her right bicep.

"Want me to add more weight?"

"Please." She lowered herself on the bench. Reality was making her head spin. She waited until he had the weights on and motioned he was ready to spot. After doing a swift set of ten, Casey placed the bar into the holder. "How much?"

"Including the bar, two-fifty."

"I still need more."

They went on like this for four more sets. By the time Casey hit eight-hundred pounds, Parrow stopped her. "I'm afraid that's it for today," he said, handing her a towel.

"I can do more," she eagerly replied. "I'm starting to feel a burn in my muscles, and it's wonderful. Addicting even."

"Well, Wonder Woman, not to be the bearer of bad news, but we're going to need to get you another bar. This one has reached its weight limit. Not to mention…" he struggled with his words, "I have as well."

"You have what?" Casey's gaze shot to Parrow. She was positive she misunderstood his meaning.

He busied himself with replacing the weights into their holder. "I can't spot for you anymore. Unless we rig up something to help me like a pulley or, I don't know…maybe a brace."

She soared to her feet, overjoyed. "Are you saying I'm too strong for you?"

He threw her an annoyed glance. "It's not all about strength. I could whip your butt any time I wanted."

"Not fun when someone kicks your ass at something, is it?" She flipped him with her towel, snapping it shy of his left leg, causing him to leap away. "Hurts the old ego a bit, doesn't it?"

Grabbing for his own towel, he gave her a playful, yet cocky, grin. "You sure you want to go there?" he asked, slowly stepping toward her.

"Don't worry. I'll go easy on you. I won't use all my unrefined strength. After all, I would sure hate to hurt your delicate body," Casey taunted.

Parrow sprang at her faster than she'd ever seen him move before, snapping the end of his towel on the side of her waist. Casey stumbled backward, holding the spot where he'd struck her. She narrowed her eyes and lowered her body slightly, waiting for his next move. He sprang again, catching her on her right thigh, but this time she was ready and gave him a powerful snap of the fabric to his left calf muscle.

He stumbled forward but quickly found his footing. "Not bad," he said, rubbing the forming welt on his lower leg.

Casey used this opportunity to dive, towel raised, straight for the center of his body. He side-stepped her blow and lunged forward, tackling her to the floor. Their combined laughter came as brisk gasps while both struggled to pin the other to the mat.

"Give it up, I'm better than you," Parrow hollered, trying hard to position his body on top.

She struggled for air. "Oh, you weak little man. So cute. So delicate," she sputtered out through her panting while fighting the urge to bite his leg in a desperate move to regain control.

Casey slid her leg back to use her strength by pushing him off. Parrow was too fast for her. He used this move to spin her onto her stomach. Once there, he pressed all his weight down, pinning both of her arms behind her. Intense pain shot up to each of her shoulders.

"Do you give?" he said, his face bright red from his efforts.

"No," Casey said with a grunt. She tried to break from his grip but the jerking only resulted in more agony in the upper parts of her arms than before.

"Say I'm the better man, and I'll let you go."

Casey regretted not using her teeth on the flesh of his leg. Twisting her head as far back as she could, she glowered at his smug face. He pressed down slightly harder. Casey lowered her forehead to the mat and closed her eyes tight against the pain.

"Give up, and I'll let you go, Casey."

She opened her eyes, flashing him a toothy grimace. "I'd rather you break my arms," she said through clenched teeth.

He smiled at her, and in one smooth motion, he released his grip and jumped backward, readying himself for her retaliation. None came. Gradually, she rolled herself over on the mat with both her arms stretched out painfully beside her.

"You're by far the most stubborn Trysal I've ever met," he grumbled, yet he had pride in his voice. "If I didn't know any better, I'd say you had Blunion blood flowing through your veins."

She half-snorted, half-moaned at his words, slowly sitting up. "With my family background, I might."

"Unfortunately, there's no Blunion in our bloodline," Elizabeth's voice echoed from the door behind them, causing both heads to turn.

"However, that was an impressive performance you each put on. You're much farther along physically and mentally than I expected," she said, beaming at her granddaughter.

Parrow helped Casey to her feet.

"Is everything all right?" Casey asked, concerned. The last time Gran had come to her team's quarters was over two months ago to give Casey her schedule and to show her around Vasar Five.

"Yes, everything's going splendidly. That's why I've come here to talk to you." She moved further into the room, visually inspecting the machines in the gym.

"Should I go?" Parrow asked.

"No, you need to hear this too. It involves everyone."

Casey waited, wiping the sweat off her body with her towel. Her arms still ached, but they were feeling better.

"We've decided to let you go with us to Vasar One."

Casey couldn't believe what her grandmother was saying.

"You're doing outstanding work in all of your classes, though Zeckner's not as optimistic. But he never was with me or your mother, so no unusual news there. He's allowing this voyage, but I expect you'll receive a sizable amount of homework from his classes, which you'll need to take with you on this trip."

Casey was too ecstatic to care what she had to do, so long as she could go. To see a new planet. Travel through space. Her life suddenly felt too remarkable to be true.

"What about security? On- and off-planet?" Parrow asked. It surprised Casey at how fast Parrow's mannerisms shifted to that of a protector.

"We'll use the DNA Modifier to give her another form for the trip. But if she's on the property of the estate, she can remain herself."

"Wouldn't it be better, for security reasons, to keep her disguised throughout the entire trip?" Parrow asked.

"The estate is well-protected, plus she's taking her first trip to Vasar. I want Casey to get to know her family and the head of council as she truly is."

Parrow seemed satisfied with this plan. Casey wasn't. "Why do I have to do all this hiding? You're next in line for the throne, Gran, yet you don't have to have your death staged. You don't have to change your appearance—just me. Why am I the only one being targeted here?"

"Casey, I have been a target of our enemies. More than once. The first time cost me my parents, after that, your grandfather. The last time I had an encounter with the Erules, they found out the hard way I'm a force not to be trifled with. You're vulnerable right now. More so than the rest of us. You're going through puberty and are not physically or emotionally ready to take on a handful of mercenaries. You need training. You're also the valuable link to carry on our bloodline. If they kill you, our rule becomes nothing more than a dying house, with no hope for a future."

"Not only that," Parrow said, "but our enemies are so set on killing you, their attempts have increased drastically in the last few years."

Elizabeth's voice held concern. "He's right. I feel this war is swiftly approaching, and they're doing everything they can to weaken our people."

"By killing me and ending the royal bloodline?"

"Yes, but your death would do more than that—it has done more. Our people are in mourning over your death. To the extent this disguised ordeal may be short-lived." Elizabeth gave Casey a look of confidence. "You won't be in hiding forever."

Before she died, her mother had raised Casey to stand her ground against adversity and never back down. Hiding from her enemies wasn't standing tall, it was cowering, and the thought left a sour taste in her mouth. But Casey wanted to experience Vasar, and if she pushed her grandmother too hard, she knew Gran would change her mind. Her shoulders dropped in defeat. "When are we leaving?"

"Two days from now, after you've finished your next set of classes. You and Vashee will meet the queen and head of council the day after we arrive. Don't worry about this. I don't expect any problems."

Her grandmother was correct when she said Casey would receive homework in Zeckner's class. Her bag was full of relentless mounds of assignments. Her high spirits had somewhat deteriorated by the time Chasel showed up to teach her programming class.

"He wants you to do all this on the trip?" Chasel asked, after going through Casey's coursework.

"Unfortunately, yes," Casey said.

Chasel muttered bitterly in a language Casey didn't understand. "Don't worry," Chasel said once her irritation subsided. "I'll help you with this muddle on our trip to Vasar One."

"You're going too?" Casey asked, relief overshadowing her stress.

"Of course. I'm here to assist your team, and seeing as how neither of you will be here, I'll go with you." She covertly scanned the room. "Jasper has to stay since Darren and Barick are remaining behind to carry out the overseer duties. He's not happy about this at all." Her tone grew chipper. "Marah and I are pleased, considering he annoys us with his downcast, uppity personality."

By the time Casey finished the rest of her two-day classes and entered her grandmother's office on Vasar Five, she was feeling optimistic and ready to learn.

"We've discussed it. After our next two classes together, you'll skip your overseer duties. This will allow you time to pack and help Eva get the ship ready."

"Sounds great," Casey said, anxious to begin.

"Today we'll start off with you using your gift of seeing the future. If you do well, we'll go into substance movement."

Casey waited for her grandmother to take a sip of her coffee. Elizabeth replaced her cup and stood to retrieve a detailed map of their Universal Region. Casey had seen this before in a few of her classes, mainly in her Geography of the Universe Around Us class with Vespa.

"You've done very well with observing the future here on Earth. Now you need to work on seeing the future at a distance."

"I didn't know we could," Casey said, moving beside her grandmother in wonder.

"Yes, it's weaker the further away you are from your source. Here on Earth, I've seen two weeks ahead, but if I were to track onto Grandmother Ann's future, I'm only able to see one, maybe two hours ahead."

"All the way to the other side of our region. That's remarkable!"

"Yes, it is. However, with the past, we have to be on the same planet for it to work." She held out her hand. "Like, if you want to travel to Rome, you must be on Earth to do it. If you want to see the Great Bislop, you must be on Vasar Two."

"I understand."

"The farther you go, both in time and distance, the more energy and strength you'll use. Let's say you locked onto Grandmother Ann. If you're not careful, you could eventually pass out, or worse."

"I'll be careful," Casey said.

"Good, now what I'd like you to do is see us traveling from here," she pointed to a spot on the map. "To Vasar One." She pointed to another spot clear on the other side. "Tell me who you lock onto, and what you observe, and I'll look to see how far away you've gotten from your source."

Casey did as instructed. The touching scene that materialized was one of Parrow and Vashee wrestling on the floor of the ship together. She unconnected her thoughts from Parrow and told Gran what she saw. Elizabeth did the same thing, using Parrow as a guide.

"Not bad. The connection was almost two days away."

"How did you find the exact time I saw?"

"I jumped several days ahead of your vision, and went backward, or rewound the connection."

Casey skewed her head in interest. "How?"

"We're still several sessions away from this part of our training." Determined to learn how to manipulate time travel in this fashion, Casey was about to beg Gran to show her, pout if needed, until Elizabeth raised her hand. "Very well. But remember, if you overstretch your abilities too hard and too fast, you could seriously damage this part of your brain."

"I'll be careful."

Elizabeth peered at her searchingly for several seconds before she agreed. "After you make your connection, think about going quickly forward or backward with your mind. It'll eventually bring you all the way to the present or take you as far forward as the strength of your connection can go. When you get to a part you want to explore further, think about stopping, and your vision will halt, allowing you to view this section of time more closely."

Casey closed her eyes, thinking once again about the connection she had with Parrow and Vashee. She found her transparent image had returned to the same spot where the Blunion and panther were rolling on the ground together.

Casey thought of moving time forward, but nothing happened. Frustrated, she tried once again, while picturing the surrounding scenery in a fast-forward image, like the image you would get from speeding up a DVD. Still, nothing changed. Something in the back of her mind told her she was trying too hard. She shook the tension from her shoulders and relaxed for her next attempt. This time, instead of concentrating on the view before her, she focused on her own self, as if sending her mind forward in time.

At first glance, nothing changed. Then, as if her consciousness had taken over, everything around her sped up. Time was rushing by at such a fast rate, her vision was a complete blur. She noticed the outline of Parrow was still present, but the surrounding backdrop was constantly changing. She wasn't sure how far she had gone when she finally stopped the advancing image. The room she stood in now looked like a comfortable bedroom. The light was dim, making it hard for Casey to see clearly.

When she was about to speed up the image again, the door behind her creaked open, followed by the sound of someone entering the room. Casey's heart fluttered as a dark-haired man moved silently into the room, heading to where Parrow was lying in bed, asleep.

What is this? Casey wondered, with a sick feeling building in the pit of her stomach. *Have we picked someone up along the way? Maybe he's a program I've not met yet.* She watched the unknown man lean over Parrow's sleeping body and fear gripped her. She tried to shout out a warning to Parrow, but no sound came out. This broad-shouldered stranger removed a cylinder from the pocket of his night robe, followed by the distinctive sound of the release of a pressurized substance, like a can of toxic fumes.

Casey gave a hollow sounding noise and moved closer for a better view. She watched this futuristic man pluck another item from his pocket and began using it to tickle the end of Parrow's nose. Parrow's hand came up, plastering his entire face with a frothy white substance. Shaving cream. She and two of her classmates had done the same thing to a fellow recruit at the police academy. A trainee who enjoyed pulling pranks on classmates. Casey bit her bottom lip to stifle her laughter.

Off balance, yet fuming with anger, Parrow sprang from the bed, shouting out obscenities. He sprinted after the unknown man. Thanks to a pair of tired, unsteady legs, Parrow missed the door by inches, slamming him face-first into part of the wall. Casey heard the beginning of Parrow's second round of profanities, when without warning, she found herself in Gran's office.

Casey was laughing when she told Gran about her vision and how she sped up from her original entry point. Elizabeth once again entered, this time to discover Casey had traveled forty Crogons from Earth, around three and a half days into the future.

"Is that good?"

"My dear, it's marvelous. Your reach is halfway to where I'm at, and I've been doing it for years."

"Who was the man traveling with us?"

"Why, it's you. I've already downloaded the settings into the DNA Modifier, and I have to admit, for a man, you're very handsome."

Casey wrinkled her nose. "Why am I going as a man?" Casey thought about her manly image. Not that she didn't like men, but she was content with being a woman. She might be a tomboyish woman, but she was still a woman.

"It's a better cover for you. Plus, it'll do you good to get a feel for this sex. Sometimes, when you travel in the past alone, you'll find being a man is much easier than traveling as a woman."

Casey wasn't sure if she agreed with this, but after remembering their trip to ancient Rome, she realized Gran might be right. They worked for a while longer on time traveling before switching over to substance movement. When their Customs of the Races class was over, Casey hurried to the door.

"You still have some time before we depart. You don't need to be in such a rush," Elizabeth called out after her.

"I need to go pack and locate a canister or two of shaving cream," Casey yelled, just before the door closed between them.

Chasel helped Casey pack, telling her what she might need. She also assisted her with locating several items, including two full canisters of minty shaving cream.

"All set," Casey said, tossing her luggage over her shoulder.

When she was about to step out into the hall, Chasel's fake cough stopped her. She pivoted around to see Chasel tapping her foot, with her hands firmly planted on her hips. "What?" Casey asked, defensively.

"Your satchel," Chasel said, her tone stretched in annoyance.

"Oh, crap." Casey rushed over and retrieved the bag filled with her homework. "Thanks, Chasel. You saved my ass."

"More like your neck, but yes, I did."

They headed through the stretched corridor, parallel to Vasar Five, while Chasel explained the wonderful things Casey would see and do on her trip.

"Why is it called a snifferniffel?" Casey asked, regarding Chasel's description of how different animal life was on Vasar One.

"I'm not sure, considering it lives underwater. I'll have to research this more and get back to you."

They parted ways at the entrance to Vasar Five, when Casey told her she had to meet her grandmother on level A-7 so she could change her identity. She made her way to the elevator and out through the elaborate hallway to the room where the DNA Modifier was located. She was happy to see Gran had everything set up and waiting as she stepped through the entryway of the room.

"Good, right on time." Elizabeth said, peering up from the monitor. "Take everything off and enter the modifier."

Casey did as she was told, throwing her clothes in a pile on a bench, and placing her unification necklace, soul-binding necklace, and personal computer in a neat arrangement beside her clothes.

She stepped inside the shower-like machinery. Within several seconds, the metal door closed, and the chamber filled with a cloudy, white mist, wetly cooling her outer flesh. A familiar "whooshing" sound filled her ears, lasting longer than the Equipment Originator. Soon after, a hot burning discomfort followed, bringing with it a sharp cutting sensation throughout her entire body. Clenching her jaws together, she closed her eyes tight and pushed out the pain like she was learning to do in her classes with Parrow.

Pain is not to be feared but accepted. It's a feeling we possess to distinguish us from inorganic substances. Welcome in your pain and greet it as you would a close friend. For once you fear it, or let it overpower you, your pain will eventually consume you." Parrow's words echoed repeatedly through her mind, and she opened herself to the experience. When the pain reached the point of being almost unbearable, the machine powered down, bringing with it another cool, soothing mist of water.

Casey opened and closed her eyes rapidly as her vision drifted into focus. She was about to step from the monstrous contraption of torture but stopped when an unfamiliar part of her body brushed against the inside of her thigh. She peered at her midsection, uncertain of what she would find. The instant she realized what hung between her legs, her gaze shot swiftly to the ceiling, with a tainted sense she had seen something she wasn't supposed to see.

"Casey, is everything all right?" she heard Gran call out over the pounding of her own heart.

"Um, I'm not sure. I've something here. I need a moment." Her voice was deeper, husky. She steadied her breathing, getting herself under control. "There's no chance I'll be stuck like this forever, is there?"

"No, and you need to think of this as a positive experience. Few beings get to switch to the opposite sex as casually as changing an outfit."

Casey huffed silently to herself. Changing an outfit, last she knew, didn't give her the feeling of being completely skinned alive.

"Are you coming out?" Elizabeth impatiently asked.

"I don't think I can with you in the room." She heard the distinct, proper laugh of her grandmother on the other side of the door, and her face flushed.

"It's all right. I'll turn around."

"Can you hand me my clothes? I'll change in here."

"Hon, I'm afraid they won't fit. I need you to step into the Equipment Originator so I can get your sizes and make you some extra outfits to take with you."

Casey lowered her forehead against the device's wall. "Fine, don't look, and I'll let you know when I'm in the other machine."

Embarrassed, she cupped her hands around her extra appendage. Casey had never seen one up close before and didn't expect it to be this cumbersome or sensitive to her touch. She cracked the door of the machine, and when she saw Gran's back was facing her, she made a beeline for the other contraption.

"I'm here," she said the second she closed the door.

"Do you want boxers or briefs?" Elizabeth asked.

Casey thought for a moment. "I'm not sure. Give me briefs to wear, and when you program in additional clothes, could you make me several pairs of each?"

Casey was pleased to see her outfits were like the ones she normally wore. At least some things stayed the same. She had to adjust her new member several times, because it felt uncomfortable when she first pulled up her jeans. Before she zipped her pants, Elizabeth gave her a strong warning to do this movement as carefully as possible.

"What do I look like?" she asked, when she placed the last of her necklaces around her neck, tucking them into her T-shirt.

"The same as you normally do, but slightly hairier and more masculine." She spoke to the ceiling. "Marah, could you display the wall mirror?"

The mirror materialized, and Casey gasped at her image. "Hairier? I look like Vashee."

"Stop dramatizing. You're a very handsome young man."

Studying her reflection in the mirror, Casey had to agree with her gran. As a man, she wasn't bad looking. Yet, all the scruffy facial hair had to go.

They entered Vasar Six together, and Elizabeth showed Casey her room so she could put away her things. Not near as big or fancy as her suite on Vasar Five, but still decent-sized. Her grandmother left her to unpack, instructing her to go straight to the operations deck once she finished.

Chasel appeared the second Elizabeth left to show Casey how to operate the controls to her hidden dresser and closets. Next, she explained the different computerized items in her side-office and bathroom and how each of the components worked.

The bathroom came fully equipped with highly advanced fixtures and accessories. Casey, with Chasel's guidance, programmed into the monitor parallel to the Belfont Originator which areas of her face she wanted clean-shaven. Before she knew it, her mustache and beard were gone. Once she felt comfortable with her surroundings, she thanked Chasel and headed several floors up to the operations deck.

"Wow, if I didn't know you were Casey, and if you were a Blunion, I'd be all over you," Parrow said with a snicker in his apparent attempt at humor.

"Parrow, even as a man, I have taste." Casey retorted, followed by hearty laughter from Eva and Elizabeth.

"Just fly the ship," Parrow said with a slight grin.

Eva was still giggling when Casey powered up the vessel. "Where's Vashee?" Casey asked Eva, as she prepared the ship for flight.

"I have her in a secured area until we finish the takeoff procedure," Eva said.

Satisfied, Casey opened the inner and outer doors. She slowly piloted the ship out, closed the doors behind them once they were clear, and re-materialized the barn.

"Nice job, Casey. This time you're going to use the long-range plotter. You can enter the coordinates as I call them out."

Casey activated the plotter, and Eva began reading off a series of numbers and letters. Next, Casey checked their path against the substance detection map.

"What's this reddish-orange dot?" Casey asked, pointing to a flashing spot on the monitor.

"*Teratopton*, a supermassive black hole two galaxies away from Couhl Tabarr. We go through a galaxy adjacent to it. If you like, we can make a detour on our return trip to see it up close."

"That'd be great. I've always been fascinated by the concept of a black hole."

"They're beautiful," Eva said. She double-checked the entry of the coordinates and the view of the detection map before giving Casey the signal to begin Crogonic ignition.

Casey braced herself as she pushed the last button in the sequence. She experienced no jerking movement, or any movement, other than what was on the screen displaying the outside of the vessel. The view was pleasantly surprising. Objects blurred, casting colorful rays of bright light in all directions. On the long-range visuals, images weren't distorted, but glided swiftly by, like the soaring scenery seen from inside a speeding car.

"Once you're in Crogonic travel, the ship virtually flies itself. You only need to keep an eye on the ship's status, and watch the monitors to make sure nothing changes. The long-range screen on your left gives a clear depiction of what is ahead of us," Eva informed. "The screen on your right shows what's behind us. We have many more views, but let's stick with these two for now."

Her grandmother touched an object resembling a planet on the left monitor, and the full image, with a detailed list of information, appeared on the main display. "This way you can examine an item close up,"

Elizabeth said before she rose from her chair. "Marah, can you tell Hanna it's safe to let Vashee out?"

"Yes, Elizabeth Malanight."

Elizabeth gave her body a full stretch. "I believe it's time for me to call it a week. Does anyone need anything from me before I turn in?" When everyone said or motioned no, Elizabeth placed a kiss on Casey's cheek and headed off to the serenity of her bed.

Once Elizabeth departed, Parrow sat in the empty chair next to Casey. "You're not bad at flying, Casey. I'm quite impressed." He followed his compliment with a firm pat on her back.

"Why, thank you, Mister Parrow." She gave him a playful wink.

Vashee showed up several minutes later, telling Casey everything she had done over the last few days while Casey was in class.

"How did you know it was me?" Casey asked.

Vashee settled herself beside Casey's feet. *"I felt your soul. I assume you'd be able to do the same if I had a different appearance."* Vashee yawned, looking as tired as Casey felt.

"Are you ready for bed?"

"Yes," Vashee said.

Casey relinquished her workstation to Eva before bidding her and Parrow a goodnight.

When Casey awoke fifteen hours later, Vashee wasn't in the room. She rubbed her eyes, but even after blinking, the grayish vision of the room didn't change. "Chasel, is there something wrong with the lights?" She couldn't wait until she was out of puberty and only sleeping this long once a week, instead of two to three times a week.

"I don't believe so, Casey. Would you like them on so you can check for yourself?"

Casey sat straight up. Her room was encased in a dimly lit gray light. "The lights aren't on?" Casey asked, feeling an excited tingle.

"No, Casey. Do you want them on?"

Casey scanned the room one last time. "Yes, please."

When the brightness of the light flipped on, Casey's vision adjusted. For a split second, all was bright white before her room drifted into normal clarity. "Could you please switch them off again?" The lights switched off, changing her vision into the grayish glow. She had Chasel flip the lights off and on several more times before she accepted the truth—her eyes had gained the gift of night vision.

Casey leapt from the bed, excited to tell Gran about her new discovery. She froze when her feet touched the floor. The top part of her pajama pants revealed the unpleasant outline of an erection.

Stealing a pillow off the bed, Casey used it to hide her midsection, and she hurried to the bathroom. After emptying her bladder, she was happy to discover this part of her softened to a size more manageable to conceal.

Her shower took several minutes longer than usual since she had to talk herself through washing the extra body part. She finished her hygiene care, including re-shaving parts of her face, and went in search of her grandmother. Striding through the corridor, Casey realized how much she enjoyed the smell of her aftershave. After thinking about it more closely, she decided she didn't mind her extra appendage either. If this hunk of male flesh between her legs made life easier when she traveled in the past, adapting to the alteration was worth the effort.

She found Gran and Vashee at the main controls, her grandmother sitting in the center chair, and Vashee lying on the floor next to her. After helping herself to a soothing morning coffee and a bowl of cereal from the deck's Belfont Originator, Casey sat and told her grandmother the news of her night vision and repeated the information to Vashee in her head.

"That's wonderful," Elizabeth said. "Oh, I've something to show you as well."

"*Vashee, I—*" Elizabeth conveyed without speaking, but after a full minute of waiting, nothing followed. "Sorry, I'm still learning. I can understand more of what she says to me though."

Casey was thrilled for her gran. "Did you hear what I said to Vashee when I told her about my ability?" Casey asked.

Elizabeth nodded after checking the monitors. "Some of it, but the end trailed off."

Casey finished her meal and offered to relieve her grandmother from the controls, so she and Vashee could find Eva and practice communicating. Grateful for the opportunity, Elizabeth did her best to explain this idea to Vashee, who happily agreed once Casey filled in the missing gaps to Elizabeth's offer.

Casey remained at the controls for the next four hours, studying the different objects and planets they passed. Fayrel came in halfway through her watch with dark circles under his eyes. He told Casey he had to set up the medical wing, made a list of the supplies he needed to purchase on Vasar, and helped Hanna repair one of the rechargeable weapons on the starboard side of the ship.

"Is it like the RRD?" Casey asked, since she hadn't gone over the heavy assault weapons in Hanna's class yet.

"Yes, mostly," he sluggishly said while typing commands on the monitor. A picture and description of the weapon appeared before her. "Do you see the similarities? The size of the machine and the damage it inflicts is more profound, but the function is the same."

Casey read through the information, but she stopped when she remembered the mounds of homework sitting in her quarters, untouched. "Damn!" She swiveled her chair to Fayrel. "Could you watch the station? I need to go to my room and get my satchel."

"Sure, Casey. Your academics are top priority."

The moment he focused on the screen, she rushed off yelling, "Thank you," over her shoulder.

She had her bag in hand and hurried as fast as she could to relieve the overworked Fayrel. Several team members came in to replace her throughout the day, but Casey waved them off, explaining she was fine and had to do her work anyway. When Hanna and Parrow entered, they ordered dinner, which the three ate together. Parrow told Casey he was going to return later and steal her for a game of wallball in the ship's simulation room.

"What's wallball?" she asked, sniffing the mound of yellow glop in her bowl. It smelled better than it looked.

"It's another game I'll kick your butt on," he said, shoving a full pastry into his mouth.

Casey winced at the jelly trailing down Parrow's chin. She glanced at Hanna, who held her own look of disgust. "I've tried teaching him better manners, but his father got a hold of him early on."

Parrow took off the second he finished eating, telling Casey he would explain the game once they were in the simulator. Hanna stayed with Casey on watch, and Casey poured herself into her studies. After thirty minutes had gone by, Hanna finally asked her why she had half of her homework laid out in a separate pile.

"I don't quite understand these assignments. I'll save them for later when Chasel can help me."

Hanna grabbed the computer pad on top of the stack. "What the hell is this?" she demanded several minutes later.

The sudden outburst nearly brought Casey out of her chair. Casey instantly searched the monitors on the desk for danger. Realizing Hanna hadn't seen something abnormal or threatening on the screen, but was referring to Casey's homework assignment, she relaxed.

"Why is he going over this material with you? You won't learn at least half of this until your first year of the Academy."

"Not sure," Casey replied, and Hanna scrutinized the rest of her homework. "Unbelievable. I know what that nasty program is doing. He's trying to get you to fail his class, so you won't be able to take his preliminary exams."

"Whatever his reason, I've got to do the work, and I will take and pass the test."

Hanna nicked another assignment. "Ridiculous. You shouldn't be going through this." She vehemently shook her head. "I'll speak to Elizabeth. She'll take care of it."

"I'd rather keep my nose down, do the assignments, and finish his class with no added stress between him and me." Casey gave Hanna a reassuring smile. "The worst that'll come from this homework is I'll be better prepared for the Academy."

Hanna wasn't as optimistic. She replaced the computer pads on the pile set aside for Chasel's tutelage. "Fine, but if Zeckner makes it any harder for you, or if he gets out of line, you must promise you'll let me know."

Casey finished over half of her homework by the time Parrow arrived. Following his brisk pace, Casey was soon three levels down on the opposite end of the ship from the operations deck. They entered a room containing a bathroom on one side, a changing room on the other, and a door straight ahead.

"I've laid out your clothes in the changing room. I'll head into the bathroom to get ready." He grinned from ear to ear. "Meet you out here when you're done."

Her outfit was bright red and resembled a combination of a football and fencing uniform. The major difference was the padded pants went to directly below the knees with a built-in protective cup between her legs, and the shoulder padding wasn't as bulky. The ensemble ended with a red helmet and a face shield with a light tint. Instead of putting it on, Casey carried it with her.

"Don't you look snazzy," Parrow said, sitting on a bench with his similar, sky-blue outfit.

"I feel like a futuristic gladiator."

He snatched his helmet and stood. "That's a fitting portrayal for the players in this game." He was slightly taller than Casey, but not as broad in the upper body as her male replica.

He directed her through the door of the simulation room, roughly half the width and length of a football field with artificial turf covering the entire floor. "I programmed this room to the required one-hundred-twenty-feet long by fifty feet wide, with a height of twenty-five feet. You see those three colored stripes running along the turf width-ways?"

"Yes."

"The red line directly in the center is the midway line, and the two bright yellow lines on each end of the court are the throw lines. They are exactly ten feet away from the back walls.

"They have actual grass in most of the official stadiums, but they're also twice the size. I designed this one for a team of one to three players, where on an official field, a team has eight players."

Casey inspected the thin mats which covered both sidewalls, running the full length of the room and stopping halfway up from the distance of the floor to the ceiling. She noticed how each of the two narrower back walls held seven different-sized circular openings.

"What's with those holes?" She finally asked.

"Those are the score walls," Parrow said. "The two topmost holes encircled with red paint are nineteen feet off the floor, and evenly spaced along the wall."

Casey guessed those openings to be about the size of a normal softball. The area of the wall below the red holes had protruding grips, like the ones Casey used when indoor rock climbing. They ran a few feet above the ground, upward almost to the actual holes. There were three other holes, twice the size of the top ones, also in a line equally apart from one another.

"The holes with the blue outlines around them are ten feet off the floor, slightly larger but not as wide as those purple holes which are five feet off the floor," Parrow said.

The embedded electronic scoreboard on the topmost center of each of these walls was solid black, fancier than what they used at her high school's basketball games. Parrow walked over to the corner, where he removed something round from an opening to the right. Casey noticed a similar opening on the opposite side of the room, past the midway line.

"Since we're playing a two-player game, some rules, like passing and blocking, will not apply." He tossed her a firm, silver ball. It felt like metal, yet also rubbery.

"The object of the two-player game is to go two twenty-minute rounds, and the person with the highest number of points wins. The two top holes are worth five points, the middle holes are two points, and the bottom are worth one point." He pointed to the yellow lines on the floor. "A part of your body must touch the throw line in order to toss the ball into the holes. You can throw any way you like at the top two sets of holes, but the wide bottom ones must be underhand. You can climb up and place the ball in, but it'll leave you exposed to your opponent."

He pointed to each end of the field. "You'll start on one end, and I on the other. Since you're on offense, you'll extract a ball and rush to the other end. That's your score wall. I can use any means in which to stop you, other than biting or striking the helmet. Most fans look down at players who resort to kicking and punching below the waistline, especially in the knees or gonads. They see this as playing dirty, and so do I."

"If you're tackled or fall to the ground, but remain in possession of the ball, we start over with you still on offense. You only get three chances to score this way, so don't go down."

"What if I score on the first try? Do I keep the ball?"

"No. I'll go to offense. If I take the ball from you and score on your offense, I'll still go to offense. You ready to try?"

"I believe so. Whatever I'm not sure of, I'll figure it out as we play."

"Sounds good. Put your helmet on, and after I start the clock, you'll go first."

Casey fastened the helmet onto her head, lowered the face shield, and watched him program something on a monitor by the door. Once the clock started, Parrow secured his own helmet, and positioned himself at a spot on the field across from her.

Holding the ball in a firm grip, Casey began running toward the other side. After crossing the midline, Parrow advanced toward her. He was ten feet away when Casey readied herself, tucking the ball under her arm like a football.

Parrow sprang with his arms out, preparing to slam directly into her, when Casey sidestepped, and ended in a complete spin to the left. He came up short, rolling headfirst onto his feet. Casey sprinted straight for the corner of the arena. She jumped onto the sidewall, and pushed herself off, using her momentum to soar toward the first of the middle holes. She slammed the ball into the opening and adjusted her body, hitting the ground in a roll of her own.

"Woman, that was outstanding," Parrow shouted, pulling his helmet off. "What was that?"

She took a few seconds to catch her breath. "Part football, part basketball, but mostly talent," she answered, displaying a cocky grin.

He beamed from ear to ear and ran over, slapping her hard between the shoulders. "I want to see how well you do on defense." He pointed to the other side of the field. "Get ready and I'll come to you."

She ran the full length of the field, pivoted, and prepared herself for his approach. The first two tackles were easy, but she had to sprint after him on the third, bringing him down right before he hit the throw line.

"For the love of small Blunions everywhere, you've got to be kidding me," he roared, taking off his helmet and throwing it to the ground. At first, Casey thought she had finally damaged his ego to the point of anger, and she readied herself for a brawl. It didn't take her long to realize his anger was actually excitement. He bounced his way to her, like a boy who had won his first little-league ball game.

"You're a natural."

"Okay, I don't get it. I'm kicking your butt. Why aren't you pissed?" she asked, somewhat upset he wasn't.

He blinked, stunned. "My dear, deprived Casey," he said, placing his arm around her shoulder and walking with her around the field. "Because it's wallball. I know you've led a sheltered life, so I won't take it personally." He eyed her tenderly, almost to the point of mocking. "Every known species plays wallball throughout our Universal Region. There are other games, but they're nowhere as distinguished as wallball."

Casey stared at him, confused.

"All right, look, Casey. I play against Mom and Dad all the time with someone from the team, or with a computer-generated player, and I'm always getting my butt beat." He gave her a mischievous grin. "I now have a partner who'll help me humiliate my parents as they have humiliated me." He raised his eyebrows. "Not to mention, the way you play, you'll easily be able to join the team at the Academy."

"Why would I want to?"

"Because you like sports and are extremely competitive. You're almost as competitive as a Blunion. Plus, you'll be extremely popular. Be able to attract any woman—I mean any person you want."

His smirk suggested his slip of the tongue was no accident. She changed the subject. "Whatever. Are we going to finish playing?"

He shook his head. "Heck, no. We're going to run drills and work our butts off on different moves to get you ready, so when we challenge Mom and Dad, we'll be unstoppable."

Chapter Eight

Earth Date: 14th October 2042
Vasar One

The rest of the trip consisted primarily of wallball with Parrow, duties intertwined with homework, and studying with Chasel. Casey had over two-thirds of her homework done before the start of the last day of travel and was planning to finish the rest on the return trip to Earth. This would give her a full week on Vasar One to take in the sights.

Parrow started playing practical jokes on Casey by the second day of the trip. First, filling her bottle of aftershave with a rubbing solution used to treat Gaminite herpes. The burning pain wasn't as bad as the irritated rash that followed. Next, he filled her evening slippers with Hanna's leftover banana pudding. Vashee had licked most of the pudding out of Casey's footwear before Casey tossed them in the cleaning module for laundering.

Casey began her retaliation that evening. Her first payback was the shaving cream incident from her vision before they left Earth. The second was affixing him to a chair in the ship's dining hall with super-strong, quick-acting, bonding cement Eva had given her from the engineering supply room.

It almost backfired when Fayrel moved to sit in the chair minutes before Parrow entered for breakfast. Casey's flailing body slid halfway across the table in her successful attempt at stopping him. Eva and Vashee had a good laugh at Casey's thrashing awkwardness, and Fayrel left the dining hall agitated. The slight hiccup had been worth it. Foulmouthed Parrow had to cut the butt of his pants off the chair before heading to his living quarters to change.

Three days later, Parrow had done nothing else to Casey. She knew it was only a matter of time. She was sitting with Eva on watch at the control station when Elizabeth came in and handed the Kan a computerized notepad.

"I finished the list of the supplies we'll need. Parrow will go with you and Hanna to the city once we're settled."

"Is Fayrel's list included?" Eva asked.

"No, you know him. He insists on getting his own supplies," Elizabeth said.

Eva placed the list in her side cargo pocket.

"Can I go with them?" Casey asked, hopeful. The thought of shopping on a strange new planet actually sounded exciting.

"I don't mind if you don't," Eva told Elizabeth.

This proposal didn't thrill her gran. "I'm not sure that's such a good idea. I think it would be best for you to remain under the security of the estate."

"Parrow and Hanna will be there. Plus, looking like this, what could go wrong?"

"I promise we'll keep a close eye on her. You have my word." The look on Eva's face was brimming with sincerity.

Elizabeth paused, thinking. "Let me run the idea by Hanna and Parrow, but I guess that'll be fine." She sternly spoke to Casey. "But only if you promise me you won't wander off on your own."

Feeling like a three-year-old, Casey nodded. She glowered at the computer so Gran couldn't see her building annoyance. She was growing tired of all the coddling. She had lived in a vast metropolis for several years with no handholding, so why did her gran feel the need to do it now?

"She means well," Eva said, after Elizabeth left the room.

"I'm not a child."

"She knows that." Eva's warm gaze fixed sadly on Casey. "When your mother died, a piece of your grandmother died as well. She was empty of all emotions for years. Her love for you helped her through that difficult time. In a way, she's still recovering. I can see it in her eyes. When you left for college, then moved to New York, she had a tough time without you, but she knew you needed to mature on your own. We all do at a certain point in life."

Casey rubbed her awkward man hands together. "Maybe I should skip the shopping."

"I won't have it. It'll be good for you, and good for her. She needs to relearn how to let go, to have confidence in you, and to allow fate to run its course."

The last few hours of the trip, Elizabeth assembled the team on the operations deck to discuss security measures and the itinerary for the entire week. "We'll be heading straight to the palace to go before the queen once we land," Elizabeth said.

"Are we flying or teleporting to the palace?" The question came from Hanna. Parrow's mother was thoroughly dissecting the schedule. Casey was suddenly struck with the certainty that with Barick on Earth, Hanna was now in charge of the team's security.

"We'll teleport. You and Eva will go first, and once it's clear, the rest will follow, leaving Parrow and Casey as the last two through. Hanna tapped fervently on her computerized pad while verbally giving her approval.

"I want as little time for Casey in the open as possible on this first day." Elizabeth stared at Casey. "You're scheduled to go out on the supply run tomorrow. I spoke with Queen Ann last night, and she approved of the idea, although she insists we take two additional security personnel from her team. Hanna, you're in charge. If anything feels out of sorts, bring everyone back to the estate at once."

Casey felt a sudden rise of excitement. She tried imagining what this outing on Vasar One would be like. The thrill of moving through shopping centers full of extraterrestrial life-forms was beyond imaginable. She missed most of the meeting that followed, barely catching the end of a conversation regarding Fayrel's daughter, Tanille.

"Yes, once Tanille finishes, she'll meet me at the estate," Fayrel said to Elizabeth.

Crap. Casey turned her full attention to the meeting, worried she might have missed a vital bit of information.

"Good," Elizabeth replied. Her gran addressed the group one final time. "Casey's male name will be Keavan, who is a new member of my team. His job is security, and he was assigned on our last trip to Vasar One."

When the meeting was over, Casey packed her bags and accompanied Vashee to engineering. She opened the reinforced cage, which Eva had secured to the floor. The inside was composed of thick padding on all sides.

Vashee assured her the cage was comfortable. Casey waited until Vashee was all the way in before fastening the latch and saying her goodbyes.

By the time she arrived on the operations deck, the rest of the team was fastened in and ready for the final approach. Eva motioned her to the front, seating Casey between her and Hanna. Once Casey activated her safety straps, Hanna passed her an earpiece.

"We'll be coming out of Crogonic travel in less than five minutes." Eva pointed to the monitor. "Bring up the visuals on the side screens."

Casey did as Eva instructed, while noticing in the long-range imagery the outline of several celestial spheres, each labeled with their planetary names. "Vasar Three is more beautiful than the videos from class," Casey said, studying the reddish-purple planet.

"Yes, and it's twice the size of Earth. The Academy's located there."

Casey nodded. She had gone through this part of the Universal Region in her classes with Program Intelligence Vespa. They had talked extensively about the composition of the Vasar Solar System and about all four planets, including the many cities, businesses, planetary wonders, and so forth encompassing each harmonious globe.

Vasar One was bluish green and five times the size of Earth. The entire planet was high-value property. The palace, Assembly, several prospering businesses, and the upper-class citizens lived there. The second planet, Vasar Two, consisted more of lush, grassy lands. From space, it almost mimicked Vasar One. Yet, the color was two shades greener and the size four times that of Earth. A good part of the upper-middle-class lived on it, along with many of the agricultural businesses. The reddish-purple color of Vasar Three was more breathtaking from space than Casey had imagined it would be. Twice the size of Earth, the planet supported everything from business to the normal working class. The Academy, several of the other academic institutions, and multiple scientific facilities were also here.

Casey pulled up the last image of the planets, Vasar Four. It almost mirrored Earth, except the rich colors were bright and crisp without all the pollution Earth offered, and it was slightly larger. Vasar Four held all classes of residences and businesses. Two of the major cities, though, focused primarily on gambling and the adult nightlife. The way Parrow talked, this planet was his favorite by far.

Each planet had its own legal system which answered directly to the queen. There were no prisons or jails on any. The crime rate was exceptionally low, not only in this solar system, but throughout the Universal Region. The unfortunate souls who committed a punishable crime found themselves immediately moved to the Naphia Solar System, where they housed the Universal Region's correctional institutions. Once there, they would stand trial. If found guilty, they'd be placed in the prison best suited for their punishment.

Casey had scarcely begun her lessons on the Naphia Solar System before this trip, so she knew little about the judicial system or what types of punishments the criminals faced during their sentence. What she'd learned so far was the planets in that solar system were dreary and unwelcoming, unlike any of the other solar systems in the Universal Region. But also rich in rare minerals.

"Vasar Six, this is tower five. We have you locked in. Please enter your clearance before beginning your approach."

The sound of the man's voice brought Casey to the present. They had come out of Crogonic travel, and Eva was entering a lengthy code into the keypad. Casey's eyes widened when she saw the view ahead. She stared at the miniature images of Vasar One and Two in the distance and the various sized and shaped ships clouding the area. Space around the Vasar planets was busier than she'd expected.

"What is all this? Is it normally this eventful?" Casey asked Hanna.

"Most are security ships. With the approaching war, our forces have more than tripled in case of an unexpected attack."

Casey observed the massive, corkscrew-shaped vessels patrolling outside this congested area. They looked powerful, strategically positioned, and gave her an overabundant feeling of safety. These impressive ships, even at this distance, made their vessel look puny by comparison.

"Vasar Six, you're clear to proceed. Welcome home." The man's voice sounded eager, or better yet proud, to be admitting a royal vessel into the protected area.

"Thank you, tower five. We're starting our approach." Eva directed Casey to switch to manual controls and take them in.

Vasar Six's entry into the circular opening of the planet's security force field was flawless, though Casey kept reminding herself to breathe. Eva directed her where to go, and Casey had to work on focusing her eyes forward, instead of on the images and terrain below. The undertaking was challenging. The futuristic allure of the mammoth-sized cities they passed made New York City look like an American Midwest farming town. All held uniquely erected skyscrapers and high-rises spanning the horizons, with architectural craftsmanship too beautiful to be true.

The plant life beyond the metropolises was colorful and more luscious than Earth. The flora blended in delightfully to the clear, bright blue sky with purple splashes of color scattered throughout. Even the ample bodies of water they passed were breathtaking, almost alluring enough to make Casey want to dive into their clear blue depths. They soared over several impressive estates, each one so vast, Casey expected to get the direction to land.

They flew for over thirty minutes, passing various sized cities and mansions before Eva finally spoke. "The Malanight Estate is directly over this next mountain range."

There were no words to describe what Casey felt the moment they passed the slopes of the rocky peaks, and her eyes took in the substantial outline of the structures before her. The Malanight Estate was over five times the size of the Malanight Castle on Earth with various and unusual types of trees and plant life enriching the wide-open, grass-covered valley. The buildings held wonderfully detailed carvings, noticeable from their distance, giving it a warm, serene look. The primary structures of each of the buildings were constructed out of a purplish-red stone, virtually matching the color of Vasar Three. The fawn-colored trimming on these same buildings glittered against the blue sky, emphasizing their silhouette alongside the surrounding foliage.

Far into the distance was the beginning of a second mountain range, stretching out on both sides as far as Casey could see. A lake twice as large and more stunning than Moraine Lake lay between the estate and the mountains. There were no fences, no barriers, or no markings of any kind to show where their property ended and their neighbor's land began.

Hanna looked over at her, as if reading her mind. "Everything you see is only a diminutive part of the Malanight Estate." Casey glanced at Hanna, then ahead of her, uncomprehending of how immense that area was.

"The landing pad is on the other side of the main house," Eva said, pointing to the right.

Casey steered the vessel toward that direction. The landing pad was the size of a small airport on Earth. She dropped the landing supports, and before long, Casey had settled the vessel and powered down the controls.

Hanna turned to her as proud as any mother could be. "Good job, Casey. Like with Eva here, you're a natural."

The team began unloading the ship, and Casey went to take Vashee out of her enclosure. Before departing, Hanna handed Casey a silky wallet, two metal markers resembling thick gold and silver credit cards, and a holster with an RLP weapon housed inside. "You'll carry these anytime you leave the estate. This gold card gives you access to anywhere in the Universal Region. Don't lose it. This silver card is a license which will cover you for any weapon and vehicle you use. No one may operate ground or air transportation or carry firearms without it."

Casey placed the two cards into the wallet. She secured the holster to her belt while watching seven figures dressed in long, extravagant garments approach from one of the entryways at the rear of the mansion. The colors of their clothing were a variety of earth tones, except for the man out in front, who wore a deep purple, suit-like outfit under his maroon-colored robe. Casey's heart raced. She was getting ready to meet her great-great-great-grandparents for the first time.

A man in a maroon robe threw his muscular arms wide around Elizabeth, embracing her in a full hug before greeting the rest of the team. Finally stopping in front of Casey, he blinked away his tears. "It's been too long," he said, leaning in and pulling the male Casey into his arms. "I remember the last time I saw you. On our last trip to Earth twenty-two years ago."

Not having the memory, yet feeling the powerful tug of familiarity, Casey eagerly returned his hug.

"David, stop hogging our granddaughter." Ashonda's tone was thick with humor, and she brushed him away, giving Casey an embrace of her own. "I'm so happy you're safe, my little Casmire."

The last time someone had called her by her birth name was twelve years ago, and it had been her mother. Parrow stifled a laugh at the name. She cringed, knowing she would never live this down.

"She looks like me," David said with pride in his voice.

"That's because she's a man. By her photos and those eyes, I can assure you, she takes more after my side of the family than yours."

Elizabeth smiled. "Actually, I've always thought you both held similar features, except one more feminine than the other, of course."

"Beth, it's not polite to call your great-grandfather feminine, even if he is."

Everyone laughed at Ashonda's joke, and David was the one who cackled the loudest. Casey was tickled by their playful bantering. *These people are definitely my family*, she thought, as Gran introduced her and Vashee to the rest of Ashonda's team.

They discussed how seeing a black panther roaming the streets of Vasar One would attract too much attention to their group. Therefore, they decided it best for Vashee to remain on the property. The queen and head of council were to meet up with them later to discuss the matter of Casey and Vashee over a meal David and Hanna would prepare. Ashonda instructed Casey to tell Vashee to enjoy herself within the boundaries of the estate, but to return in ten hours so she could experience the outcome of David and Hanna's wonderful cooking skills. After bidding an excited farewell to Casey, Vashee pounced off and in no time was soaring over the plant life of the mighty valley in long, full leaps.

"Not to worry, my darling, Casey," David said, throwing an arm around her. They watched the oversized panther enjoy the feel of rolling in the grass by the lake. "I'm sure the head of council will allow Vashee to remain with your team."

"I apologize for ending your time together," Elizabeth's voice cut in, "but we need to go. We have an appointment to keep."

The members of Ashonda's team moved the visitors' belongings into the mansion. Ashonda and David followed to make sure the rooms were properly prepared by the time they returned. Hanna took their team to a well-built structure off to the side of the main building. It housed the estate's teleportation chambers.

After programming the desired destination into the system, Hanna and Eva stood on two separate pads and within a flash, both vanished. Five long minutes later, a red diamond on Elizabeth's personal computer blinked, and once she pushed it, Hanna's voice called out, telling her all was clear. Elizabeth and Fayrel were the next two who teleported out.

After they left, Parrow shot Casey a sarcastic grin. "Casmire? Are you for real? You have the most girly name I've ever heard."

Casey blushed and was about to snap her retort when a yellow diamond on Parrow's communicator blinked. Holding his grin, he pressed the device before she could respond.

They materialized next to a stone fountain constructed of the same material as the buildings on the Malanight Estate. Casey noticed a gold pathway leading upward to an impressive *terropen* and gold fortress. "Is the gold from Earth?" she asked.

"No, it's Naphia gold," Eva said, as they made their way up to the guard post with the others. "The prisoners there mine many elements, including Naphia gold and *terropen*."

Once cleared, they proceeded along the gold path surrounded by a colorful and unusual array of flora. "Don't get too close to those black and yellow ones," Fayrel said, directing Casey to the center of the wide path. "Their bite is extremely toxic."

Eva said, "They'll only bite if you try to pick them, which I might add is a punishable offense on palace land."

Casey laughed. She had no intention of either touching or taking a flower, especially one that bit.

After climbing the stairs, an ecstatic, blusterous man greeted them at the doors. "Elizabeth, my dear woman, we've been expecting you." He offered her his arm and motioned for the rest to follow.

"He's the palace advisor," Eva whispered to Casey.

Parrow softly said, "Yes, and he's only sucking up to your grandmother because he likes his job, and she's the next in line."

Hanna threw him a displeased glare.

"I was very sorry to hear about your granddaughter…umm—"

"Casey," Elizabeth grumbled, and Parrow tossed Casey an "I told you so" smirk.

"Oh, yes, yes, of course…Casey. Sorry, I've been working nonstop here. Pretty tired these days. Not that I mind. Work is good for the soul—that's my motto."

He lifted his arm when they came to a set of beautifully etched golden doors. "Ah, here we are." He snapped his fingers like a man who demanded respect, and the double doors opened slowly toward them in the simple manner one would find on Earth. Casey rather liked this. It gave the palace a more traditional feel.

They entered a vast room with a black marble floor and white marble pillars. Gold and bronze statues and fountains lined the outer walls, and exotic colorful plants next to each pillar were housed in extravagantly decorated pots. The ceilings were high, at least twenty feet from what Casey could tell, with elaborate paintings and detailed tapestries throughout the area.

The palace advisor guided Elizabeth into this grand room toward six golden thrones, situated side by side at the far end of the room next to the top of red-carpeted stairs. Two women sat on the two center thrones. They were holding hands and smiling joyfully at the approaching group. Dozens of flowers and gifts sat upon the last throne, and a great deal more covered the surrounding floor.

"Queen Annabel, I'm pleased to announce your granddaughter, the future Queen of the Universal Region. May I present, Elizabeth Malanight." He said the name in a loud, theatrical voice which echoed throughout the throne room. "Oh yes, and also her team from Earth," he waved a hand backward, not bothering to look at the rest of them.

Casey half-choked down a laugh, causing Queen Ann to focus swiftly on her. "That'll be all," Ann said, not taking her eyes off Casey.

He paused for a moment before bowing low and hurrying from the chamber.

"Secure the room," Ann said aloud.

"Yes, your Majesty." The male voice of the Program Intelligence sounded parallel to Jasper but with a pleasant tone.

Both Ann and Bilana stood, making their way to embrace Elizabeth. Ann's eyes sparkled, as she took a step away to inspect her granddaughter. "You're as stunning as ever."

Elizabeth smiled warmly. "Thank you, and before you ask, no, we haven't destroyed your castle, but it's not because Parrow and Casey haven't been trying."

At the sound of Casey's name, Ann's focus returned, and she made her way to where Casey stood. "It broke my heart these many years to never look upon you with my own eyes," she said, holding onto Casey's arms.

Casey instantly felt a deep connection to her great-great-grandmother, Ann. Not only as one relative to another, but it felt as if someone had used the same mold to create them both. A spiritual kinship. A portion of what she experienced being in Vashee's presence for the first time.

"When your mother died, I wanted so much to be with you and Elizabeth. Unfortunately, my place is here, as you will one day grow to realize." She moved with Casey to the last throne laden with presents. "The Malanight legacy is both an honor and a curse," she said, directing Casey's eyes to the golden engraved headpiece on the backrest. *Casmire Malanight.* Casey stared for several seconds, before truly grasping the magnitude of her name engraved upon a royal seat in this grand hall.

Before Casey asked, Ann spoke. "Those gifts are but a scarce few of the offerings our people have left for you. They are still in mourning over your death, and many come daily to pay their respects and share in our grief."

Ann guided Casey along the line of thrones. "Your name will move to the left, as will your daughter and her daughter's daughter."

The next name was Elizabeth Malanight. The two middle chairs were Annabel Malanight and Bilana Savel. The last two, ending the line of golden seats, were Ashonda Malanight and David Titron.

"Now, let me introduce you to my wife before she gives me one of her long lectures later," Ann whispered, sounding highly amused.

They waited while Bilana fussed over Elizabeth between hugs. "You're much too skinny. Your eyes look sunken and drained. Are you getting enough to eat? You're not sleeping at all, are you?" She stopped to take a breath and embrace Elizabeth again, as if poor skinny exhausted Elizabeth were about to drop dead on the spot.

"Bilana," Ann said, "stop pestering her or else you will make her sick."

Bilana jerked to her wife, offended. "Can I not worry about my granddaughter?" She glanced at Elizabeth as her eyes watered.

Elizabeth reached out and gave Bilana another hug. "I promise I'll eat more and make it a point to get plenty of rest."

Bilana dotted at the corner of her eyes with a silk handkerchief. "That's all I'm asking." She sucked in a lungful of air to get herself under control. "Look at me. I'm a blubbering mess. I promise, no more crying."

Ann lightly nudged Casey before throwing her a mischievous wink. "Bilana, I'd like you to meet your great-great-granddaughter, Casey."

"Casey? My Valishima's little girl?" Without waiting for a response, Bilana threw her sob-shaking arms tightly around Casey's neck.

Shocked, Casey stood still, patting the hysterical woman gently with her pair of clumsy man hands. After Bilana finally settled, she spent the next several minutes asking about Casey's life since she'd been at the castle and about the relationship she'd developed with Vashee. The sincerity of love Bilana held for Casey and Elizabeth was awe-inspiring.

"How has Casey's death affected the region?" Elizabeth finally asked.

"Worse than we expected," Ann said. "Most of the region is still in mourning over the loss of their future queen, and some are insisting we bring you and your team home for additional protection."

Elizabeth waved this off. "We already expected this. What of the council?" she asked, brow slightly raised.

"They're worried about the future of the government. No one has mentioned it yet in conference, but I believe there's talk about sole council rule," Ann said with a heavy sigh. "The head of council and I can only do so much. If it comes down to it, we might have to bring Casey out of hiding and move her here to Vasar One for protection, at least until she produces an heir."

"Sole council rule must never be an option." Elizabeth wasn't only surprised, she was upset. "The consequences would be devastating. Look at our history. This cannot, and must not, happen."

Ann focused her attention on Casey. "What do you think, Casey?"

Casey stared at Queen Ann, who was waiting patiently for her to consider the question. Casey began to pace. "I'm sorry. I have a hard time sitting still when I'm nervous or in deep thought. Right now, I'm going through a little of both."

Ann laughed. "I used to do the same thing. At least I did until my wife finally broke me of the habit. Please, we're family. There's nothing you can say or do to offend us. Don't hold in your feelings, Casey. I promise your opinion matters."

Casey peered over at Eva, who gave her an encouraging nod. "I've not been too keen on the idea of having my death staged. I understand it's for my protection, and for the welfare of our people. Yet, if our people and our family line is hurt because of it, then I believe we should make my survival public."

Elizabeth pinched her lips together with frustration, and Ann motioned for Casey to continue.

Casey paused, choosing her words. "I'm meant to be an overseer. I sense it with every part of me. It's like a deep desire to protect. It's hard to explain." Casey broke off feeling suddenly childish. Embarrassed.

Ann was as kind as she was encouraging. "I understand you more than you realize. Please go on."

Relieved, Casey said, "I would prefer to remain on Earth to continue my training. As for my staged death, to be truthful, I feel like a coward."

Casey faced her gran. "We're supposed to inspire our people, are we not?"

"Your safety is of the utmost importance." Elizabeth straightened, as if realizing where the conversation was heading.

"How are we to tell our people to stand and fight, and possibly die for the good of the region, when their future queen can't even do this? What kind of leadership is that?" Casey asked.

"It's the smart kind,." Elizabeth snapped. "You're young. You don't understand the importance of your life."

Young? Yes, but she wasn't a child. Casey was tired of Gran treating her like an adolescent. She'd worked hard in school and during her time on the police force with no help from anyone but her own determination. This backtracking in adulthood was absurd. "We'd do better if we lead by example. Show our people we have strength and refuse to cower because of fear. I feel this will help inspire them, and they'll be more compelled to fight when it's time."

"Do you want to die?" Elizabeth asked, her voice sharp with anger.

"No, but I'm not afraid of it."

"You're overconfident, believing you're invincible."

"No, I'm relying on fate. If I'm going to die, I want to do it with pride and dignity, not shame and deceit."

Ann held up her hand, preventing Elizabeth or Casey from continuing. "Unfortunately, you're both right. I truly understand what you're going through, Casey, but your safety is more important than you realize." Ann narrowed her eyes at Elizabeth. "It would do you some good to place yourself in Casey's shoes. I don't believe you understand what she's given up because of our decision."

Elizabeth held her ground for several seconds until finally her shoulders relaxed. "I'm sorry, Casey. I guess I became so focused on keeping you safe, I didn't consider how this would make you feel."

This sudden change in Gran was both unexpected and welcoming, but it also made Casey feel guilty for losing her patience. "I know you're worried about me, and I love you for it. I'm sorry I lost my temper."

As Elizabeth wrapped Casey into a tender embrace, Ann turned to Bilana and said, loud enough for all to hear, "Nothing like having a nice quiet week with the relatives, is there, sweetie?"

After Casey and Elizabeth talked through every tiny issue troubling them, Ann ordered the group a lavish lunch in the larger of the two dining rooms, where Ann and Bilana finished filling in the team on the news of the region. Parrow, under the strict watchful eyes of his mother, ate his meal with the refinement of a proper palace guest.

Chapter Nine

The New Healer

"Grandmother Ashonda's waiting outside to take you on a tour of the estate once we're finished here," Elizabeth said to Casey, who had just stepped into the DNA Modifier.

Unable to reply, Casey braced herself to the pain, and focused her mind onto the misty vapors sliding down in tiny droplets on the wall in front of her. Once the torture device powered down and she stepped out, she gradually exhaled, happy to be back to her old self again. After a refreshing shower, Casey met up with Ashonda outside the doorway of her bedroom.

"I knew it." Ashonda said. "You *do* resemble my side of the family."

Casey laughed.

Ashonda took her by the arm. "There's so much to see, Casey. So many things for you to do, and I'm not simply talking about here at the estate, but in our Universal Region. I'm so happy you'll be going through the Academy these next few years. In a way, I'll have you all to myself. Whether you live in the dorms or stay here on the estate, I'll take care of all the arrangements for you. But since that's still many months away, I'll try to contain my excitement long enough to give you a proper tour."

Ashonda steered her through the vast hallway. "Let's say we start on the top floor and work our way down."

The extensive tour of all five floors of the Malanight Estate took several hours to get through. The extravagance each room held in this main building, with their many tranquil colors, tempered air, and pleasant furnishings, provided Casey with so many breathtaking objects to see and touch. By the time they made their way to the main level, Casey was in awe. When they passed the kitchen, Ashonda cracked the door enough so they could peek in to see how diligently David, Hanna, and Eva were working on the banquet-sized meal.

"Why are they cooking the food instead of using the Belfont Originator?" Casey whispered. She watched as Eva did her best to lend a hand and try to pick up some much-needed tips in the art of cooking, but to Casey, she appeared uncomfortable and out of place compared to David and Hanna's boisterous energy. Casey felt sorry for the Kan.

"It's a family tradition. David and Hanna always prepare the first meal when our family gets together, and those who choose to help jump right in and assist." Ashonda said, "Though, I'm not sure what Eva is doing with the dessert. I think that's the dessert." Ashonda's head shook in disbelief. "We still have this floor to finish. We better get to it and leave them to their work."

Ashonda directed her along a quaint hall. "Another Malanight tradition is you pick one room of the estate to decorate in your own taste and design," Ashonda said as they went from room to room. "Elizabeth is close to finishing her room, and after you graduate from the Academy, you'll need to start."

Casey gave her a sheepish grin. "I have no talent in decorating. It might be best for the grandness of this estate if we have someone else do it for me."

"Nonsense. I'm sure your room will look nice. Do what Elizabeth has done. Take your time and let it come to you."

Casey wondered if she could make a room look respectable in an old west design. Maybe give it a John Wayne theme. Casey inwardly grinned.

Ashonda was right though. Gran's room was very grand in its Roman design, but she still had an entire corner left to do. Casey's favorite two rooms were Ann's fifteenth century English charm, which resembled the Malanight Castle on Earth, and Ashonda's room, which was the main living space everyone normally gathered in. It emanated the same soothing appeal as the upper floors of the estate.

The waterfalls which ran from the ceiling into the top of the half walls gave the occupants a relaxing retreat, separating a well-designed seating area from the rest of the space. The two outer walls glided upward, opening the high ceiling to incredible views of the outside and bringing in the beauty of an enjoyable surrounding landscape. A breathtaking combination stone pond and waterfall sat near the rear of the room. The marble foundation and purplish-red stone walls brought the dark blue water up four feet from the ground.

"What's this stone?" Casey asked, feeling the outer, hard surface of the fountain.

"That's *crymonone*, a stone found throughout our solar system. It's abundant on Vasar Three, but you can find it on every planet."

"Why does the water ripple like this?" Casey asked, trying to get a clearer look into the swirling, shadowy depths.

Ashonda stood next to Casey. "Havan, please activate the tank lights."

Casey gasped when the glow from the bottom of the water revealed a corpulent, bright-red underwater creature swimming lazily around. Its body resembled a walrus, but instead of tusks, there were thick tentacles protruding from each side of its mouth. The animal had a flat pig-like nose and a strip of bright yellow fur running down the length of its back, with another yellow patch directly on the top of its head.

"He's a snifferniffel. They're very protective of their home, so please watch your hands around the edges of the tank."

"Do they bite?"

"No, but do you see those long, sharp tentacles?"

Casey nodded, not liking the way Ashonda clearly pronounced the word sharp in her sentence.

"If he feels threatened, he'll use those to defend himself. They're filled with an acid which is released as soon as the tentacles penetrate its target."

"If he's dangerous, why do you keep him?"

"He's very gentle. You only need to respect his space. Like I said, he'll only attack if he feels threatened. The weapons we attack with are more dangerous than his, and we, like him, attack only when we feel we're in danger." Ashonda pivoted away to continue the last of the tour.

"Is the pain in my mouth not enough? Now, I must endure this stinging of my eyes. For Blondon's sake, you creatures are bad mannered."

"What did you say?" Casey asked, confused by what Ashonda meant.

"Pardon me?" Ashonda spun, appearing as confused as Casey. "I didn't say a word. Do you feel all right?"

Suddenly, Casey squinted into the tank's deep waters. *"Did you say something?"* Casey thought.

"Oh, they can speak now. Splendid. First, I must amuse them with my appearance, and now I'll be expected to entertain them with conversation."

"No, I'm sorry. I didn't mean to bother you," Casey mentally said. She twisted her upper body to Ashonda. "Can you turn the lights off in his tank?"

Ashonda seemed puzzled by the request, but she did as Casey wished.

"Is that better?" Casey asked when the lights switched off.

"Why yes, and thank you." There was a slight pause before the snifferniffel said, *"I didn't mean to be so rude, but I've been in pain for quite a while now."*

"What pain? Is there something I can do to help?"

"Casey, is anything wrong? Why don't you sit down and rest? We've been walking around for hours."

"Could you please get Eva for me? I need someone better trained at dealing with animals."

Ashonda looked worried but turned to fetch the Kan from the kitchen.

"I'm ashamed to say that several weeks ago, in an improper haste, I devoured my food in three monstrous bites. My disgraceful performance has left a bone from my meal wedged between my teeth."

"If you can come up to the top and let me see it, maybe I can pull it out."

A few moments later, the snifferniffel emerged from the top of the tank, a tentacle swaying out on each side of Casey. It opened its wide mouth, revealing a full set of teeth.

Casey looked from its hazy eyes to the tentacles. *"You're not planning on poking me, are you?"*

"My dear, I'm no monster." He sounded offended.

"I'm sorry," she said. *"Oh, I see the bone. It's in there good, and your gum has pus, probably due to an infection."*

"Casey, are you mad? Step away from there at once," Ashonda shouted, followed by the sound of several running footsteps.

Casey held up a hand. "I'm fine. I need Eva and a pair of pliers if you have them." She didn't take her eyes off the oozing gumline. "Oh, and something for infection as well."

"Casey, I'm here."

Casey did a double-take at the sight of the messy-faced Kan approaching. Eva's hair, which was earlier in a pinned-up bun, was now swaying wildly about with half of the bundle drooping, covering part of her dirty face.

"What do you have smeared on your face? It looks like mustard."

"My dessert exploded. Let's not talk about it."

"I'd like you to meet Eva. She's a Kan, and she'll know more of what to do to help you."

"Nice to meet you, Eva. I'm Burtis."

Burtis explained the problem. When he was finished, he stretched out his mouth to show Eva the bone. Without another word, Eva opened a link on her communicator and gave Fayrel a list of items she needed from his medical supplies, while Burtis went down for a needed dip inside the tank.

Ashonda, followed by most of the remaining occupants in the house, returned with a gadget resembling pliers. They waited for Fayrel before extracting the bone out, giving Eva time to explain to everyone what was going on, and she translated information between Burtis and the others.

"The lights hurt his eyes?" David asked, sighing regretfully. "I've sometimes left them on for days thinking he liked it. Could you tell him I'm sorry?"

Eva conveyed this and gave Ashonda a list of his favorite foods.

Casey spoke to Eva in her head, *"Isn't Grandfather David half Kan?"*

"Yes, but he doesn't possess this gift of communication out of choice." Eva stared at her hands. *"Our people were unwelcoming to him and his mother, so he rejects any connections he has to them."*

Casey glimpsed at her grandfather, then asked Eva, *"Is it because his mother was Human?"*

"I believe so, but he refuses to talk about it." Her expression was full of compassion and even a little hope. *"You're his family. Maybe one day he'll explain this to you."*

Burtis made a noise, as if clearing his throat. *"If it's not too much trouble, can you see if they can find me a companion? This tank is more than big enough, and it gets awfully lonely down here from time to time."*

After Casey told Ashonda what Burtis asked, Ashonda hurried off to see what she could do.

"She's working on it," Eva said once Burtis returned from another of his plunges.

When Fayrel showed up out of breath from clearly running, Eva, with Fayrel's help, removed the bone and doctored Burtis's infection. Fayrel handed Eva the antibiotics for this type of animal.

Ashonda returned with the good news that she had located another sniferniffel and they would deliver her sometime next week.

"I truly appreciate what you both have done for me," Burtis told Casey and Eva. *"I shall never forget it."*

Casey stayed with Burtis when the rest left. They conversed for some time. Casey stretching out on the sofa, and Burtis swam around in the depths of his tank. Over an hour into their discussion, the excited chatter of voices coming from the next room brought Casey casually to her feet.

One of the centered, half-wall waterfalls was partially blocking her view of the door into the room. She moved over when she recognized Fayrel's male voice, but the female voice she couldn't identify. They were laughing but were talking too fast to make out any of the conversation. The door opened, and Fayrel walked in with a young woman on his arm. Curious, Casey shifted slightly more to the left, glimpsing the woman's young, soft features, while the sound of her voice captivated Casey's full attention. The woman pointed to a picture by the entrance. She and Fayrel strolled over for a closer inspection. This movement blocked Casey's view from one of the tall marble pillars. Intrigued, Casey stepped farther to the left. Her muscles tightened when the woman came into view. Everything about her was familiar.

"So when do I get to meet Casey?" she asked, turning to Fayrel.

From this angle, Casey had a clear visual of the woman's eyes. They were mesmerizing, with a gentleness, or better yet, a high level of compassion, that instantly overwhelmed Casey. A strange burning thirst swelled in her chest and slithered its way throughout her entire body. The sensation was scary and inviting at the same time. Lust, hunger, desire, all bordering on the verge of madness. She closed her eyes tight, taking in gulps of air. *What the hell?* she thought, fighting to remain in control.

"She's in the back, communicating with Burtis."

The woman sounded surprised. "Burtis? Is he also a member of our team?"

The recognition of whom this woman was hit Casey with a strength of heart-pounding excitement. This gorgeous creature was Tanille, Fayrel's daughter, her healer. The woman they were taking with them to Earth. Casey kept her eyes closed, trying to regain control of her senses. Whatever was vexing her, she needed to snap out of it. And fast.

An unexpected craving struck Casey with staggering force, starting in her stomach and ending with a throbbing ache forming between her legs. She fought with everything she had to stifle her moan. Taking several deep breaths, she mouthed a silent prayer to every known deity she could think of, God, Jehovah, Allah, even Zeus, until Casey finally got herself mentally and physically together.

"No, he's a snifferniffel. He lives in a tank in the back." He pointed, sending Tanille's gaze toward Casey. With the embarrassed feeling of having been caught peeping into Tanille's bedroom window, Casey pivoted to the side. The distinct feel of falling and of unexpected wetness instantly vanished when a sharp pain struck her head, spinning her world into total darkness.

Neither the excruciating ache in her head, nor the feel of her wet clothes clinging to her chilled body were what brought light into Casey's eyes. Hearing the soft, concerned sound of Tanille's voice made her stir. "Casey, can you hear me? Don't move. My father went to get his bag." She bent in low and examined each of Casey's eyes with a sharp blast of light.

"What happened?" Casey asked, blinking. Once the light vanished, Casey peered up into the hazel eyes of the most beautiful being in the cosmos. She fought, trying hard not to pass out from the pain.

Tanille calmly answered, "You fell into the snifferniffel tank and struck your head on the way down. Amazingly enough, the animal brought you up. Father and I pulled you out. Father stopped much of the bleeding, and I gave you mouth-to-mouth resuscitation." Casey noticed how Tanille's entire face brightened when she smiled. "So here we are."

Casey visualized Tanille's mouth on her own, and she moved her hand up to touch her own lips. As soon as her fingers brushed them, she realized what she was doing, and played it off by gliding her hand up to the pain in her head. "What did I hit?" she asked, moving to sit up. She had expected to feel an egg-shaped bump, but touched the outline of an open gash.

Tanille gently pressed her down while grabbing Casey's blood-covered hand and clutching it into her own. Tanille's touch was as gentle as the look on her face, and Casey's heart beat rapidly. She had to force the air from her lungs as they gazed into each other's eyes. "The rock in the tank."

It took a moment to comprehend Tanille's answer.

"This should do it," Fayrel said, entering the room.

The two women broke eye contact when Fayrel lowered himself to Casey's other side. He placed a cold, hard item on top of her wound while Tanille continued to hold her hand. "This will sting, but it'll instantly seal the gash."

Casey remained unmoving, allowing the apparatus to do its job.

Fayrel clicked a few buttons, intensifying the discomfort. "You're handling the pain well."

Casey bit the inside of her cheek. She knew her moment of fortitude had nothing to do with having a high pain tolerance, but more of not wanting to look like a baby in front of Tanille. "It's nothing compared to the DNA Modifier," Casey finally said, forcing out a trembling exhale.

"All finished." Fayrel replaced the contraption in his bag. He handed Casey two familiar-looking pills before turning to Tanille. "Can you go into the kitchen and get Casey a glass of water, please?"

Tanille left briefly, returning with the water in time to help Fayrel get Casey to her feet. They led her to the couch. Casey had to fight off the dizzy sensation as she swallowed the pills.

"Stay with her until it's time to eat. I want to make sure those pills take effect before she goes off on her own."

Casey's heart leapt. The idea of spending time with Tanille was electrifying. She glanced over, wanting to steal another peek of Tanille's amazing eyes, only to realize Tanille was staring directly at her. Casey tried to look away but couldn't. Some unknown force prevented this simple movement. The nervousness building in her stomach was intense, almost to the point of distraction.

"That way—" The sound of Fayrel's voice broke the contact between the two. Casey glimpsed away, embarrassed "—it'll give you both some time to get to know each other," he finished, and made his way from the room.

They sat there for several moments, not speaking, until finally Casey got up enough courage to end the awkwardness. "So you're my new healer?" If Casey could've kicked herself in the ass, she would have for asking such a lame, obvious question.

"Yes, well, if you want me—as a healer, I mean." Tanille's voice wavered.

Several additional moments of uneasy silence followed. Casey's nervous laughter brought Tanille to face her, puzzled. "I'm sorry, but I feel like a complete moron."

Tanille studied her closely. "What do you mean?"

"I don't know. I guess I don't normally have such a hard time speaking to people."

Tanille's eyes flickered. "Neither do I," she said, appearing uncomfortable.

"Can we start over?"

Tanille's features relaxed, and she brought her hand up to Casey. "I'm Tanille, your team's healer."

"I'm Casey, the person you'll be healing often." She gently shook Tanille's hand. Her skin was soft, warm to the touch. "These last several months I've been extremely prone to injuries."

Tanille gave Casey an amused grin. "Yes, Father told me. He's been carrying around extra supplies just in case."

Casey felt the heat as her face flushed. "That's comforting to know." Casey stood, trying her best to appear unaffected. "I need to look for Vashee. Would you care to join me?"

Tanille's eyes brightened. "That would be wonderful." She took a step back and inspected Casey fully. She veered her eyes away. "You may want to change first."

Casey inspected her wet clothes. Her shirt was clinging to her shapely chest. Two protruding nipples revealed the evidence of her unfamiliar arousal. Her face turned a brighter shade of red and she yanked her shirt away from her body. "I guess I'd better."

Before they left the room, Casey headed to Burtis's tank. *"Thanks for saving my life,"* she said. Within seconds, Burtis's head arose from the depths of the water. He gave her a long lash wink and sank back into the abyss. *"Anytime, young Malanight."*

Casey's attempt at a fast shower turned into a drawn-out disaster. Her excitement to spend time with Tanille was making her forget the basics. Once she had to exit the shower while dripping wet to retrieve her body soap, and her next blunder was when she finally finished scrubbing her body and turned off the water. Halfway through drying herself, she realized her hair was still plastered with conditioner. "Twenty-four years old and I'm *now* turning into a nervous pubescent. Get a grip," she scolded herself as she reentered the shower.

While Casey dressed, images of Tanille lingered in her thoughts. Had they met before? Perhaps years ago, when Casey was young. She knew the answer was no, but she couldn't shake the belief they knew each other.

She spent more time than usual fixing her hair, wanting it to be perfect for their walk together. Before exiting the bathroom, she noticed her shirt was on backward. "If you'd get Tanille out of your head for five minutes, you'd be finished by now. Seriously, get a hold of yourself," she protested to her reflection in the mirror. Irritated, she fixed her shirt.

Tanille was waiting for her in the sitting room next to her bedroom.

"You look nice," Tanille said.

Casey felt her face lightly flush, but she stayed focused, not losing a beat. "Thank you." She motioned to the door. "Ready?"

They made their way outside, passing Vasar Six before strolling through the rolling green landscape circling the estate. They walked for quite a while, switching between various topics, engaging freely in conversation with one another. Tanille was easy to talk to. She was intelligent and remarkably high-spirited. They told each other about the life they had led up to this point. Casey explained to Tanille what the Malanight Castle on Earth was like. She described the trip in time to ancient Rome, the fight in the arena with the lions, and of how Vashee had adapted easily to her new life with the team.

"What have you been doing since you left the Academy?" Casey asked, bending to feel the softness of the grass brushing between her fingers. She was having a hard time keeping her eyes off Tanille. Any distraction was welcoming.

Tanille's voice was as light as a leaf twirling in the wind. "I volunteered at a children's domicile on Vasar Three. The work was extremely rewarding, but heartbreaking at the same time."

Casey brought her gaze over to Tanille when she stood. "Volunteering to help children. You're an impressive person. I wish we had more selfless people like you on Earth. Humanity would be better off for it."

"It doesn't compare to you being a detective in New York City," Tanille said, taking a step closer to Casey.

Casey laughed nervously. "They paid me for my work, and most of the time I was around murderers and felons, not deprived children."

"You risked your life to help those who needed you." She took another step closer. "You put your life on the line for the safety of people you didn't even know. That is honorable."

"You make it sound nobler than it was, but I did enjoy it." Casey was finding it hard to focus. It might have been wishful thinking, but she swore Tanille was coming on to her.

When Tanille's lips parted in a wide smile, a shiver of longing shot through Casey's entire body. Tanille was a good four inches shorter than she was. Yet, the tender look in her eyes, mixed with her confident personality, easily made up for the difference in height. The makings of another cramp formed in Casey's midsection. She glared away.

"You can speak with animals. How remarkable is that?"

"Not very when you consider Blunions can shape-shift into animals."

"You don't take compliments well," Tanille said, reaching out and squeezing Casey's forearm.

Casey sheepishly grinned. "That's one of my many shortfalls." She kept her eyes fixed on a movement over fifty feet from the edge of the lake. Tanille was definitely flirting. The cramping was fading, but a sharp hunger was taking its place. She couldn't believe how assertive Tanille was or how unruly her own body felt. Casey always had some control of every situation until now, except for her staged death. Tanille easily had the upper hand.

"And your others would be?" The expression on Tanille's face when Casey peered back was intense.

Casey glimpsed at her personal computer, attempting to add humor to the awkward discussion. "How long do we have?"

Tanille's laughter brought Casey to the present. "Oh, it can't be that bad," she said, moving directly beside her.

Casey's mouth turned as dry as the Sahara Desert on the hottest day of the year. She fought with herself to act normal, casual, but the early stages of a mighty war waged inside. She desired this woman, and Tanille obviously wanted her. Yet she didn't want to rush this. Not her very first attraction. Plus, she didn't like being placed in a situation which left her feeling so vulnerable.

Casey bent over and picked a blade of grass. She stood and casually took a few steps away. She hoped the move was as smooth in reality as she pictured it in her mind. "Ask Parrow. He would disagree with you."

Tanille bit on her lower lip, and Casey did her best not to gawk. "You've mentioned Parrow often. You and he are close?"

Casey dramatically exhaled. "He's a pain in my backside that won't go away." She could tell Tanille didn't realize she was only kidding. She added with honesty, "He's a loyal friend."

Casey spotted a flash out of the corner of her eye, which was followed by a slight vibration on her wrist. Her communicator was blinking. Tanille had a matching one, which was also illuminating a flashing red diamond.

Fayrel was on Tanille's, telling her they were ready to serve dinner, and Eva was relaying the same information to Casey. When Casey told Eva they were still searching for Vashee, Eva let her know Vashee had been in the kitchen with them for the last thirty minutes, helping them clean up. Casey remembered Vashee's idea of cleaning when the panther ate the pudding out of her slippers. She rolled her eyes before ending the link.

She and Tanille talked the entire way back, strolling slightly slower than earlier. "Father's taking me shopping for medical supplies tomorrow. Would you like to come?"

Casey's sudden burst of enthusiasm changed into regret. "I can't. I'm helping Eva with the supply list for the rest of their team. I'd get out of it if I could, but she has a pretty long list."

"Do you need help?" Tanille asked, sounding hopeful.

Casey tried to hide her excitement as much as she could. "Sure, that'd be great. What about your father? I know he was looking forward to seeing you."

Tanille waved the question off. "I'm sure he'll be fine with it. He wants me to become more familiar with you…I mean, with my entire team."

When they entered the kitchen, Vashee was pulling her head out of a generously licked crystal bowl. Casey laughed at the pink-colored food all over Vashee's black face.

"I've missed you, Casey." Vashee made a move to jump on her, but Casey held up a hand, laughing. She ambled over, took the towel Eva held out, and cleaned the mess off the high-spirited panther. When she was

working on the last of the sweet-smelling substance, Vashee snatched the end of the towel with her teeth, deciding on a game of tug-a-war.

"I'm almost done," Casey insisted, and tried taking the towel away from the panther. Without warning, Vashee whipped her head sharply to the left, knocking Casey off balance and sending her crashing straight to the floor.

Vashee plopped her butt down on Casey's back. She started shaking the towel in her mouth victoriously. Casey was laughing too hard to free herself, so she remained there with the amused giggles of Eva and Tanille off to the side.

"She's so beautiful," Tanille said.

At hearing this new person, Vashee slowly climbed off. She kept the slightly torn cloth in her mouth and sat next to Casey, who rolled over onto her back. *"She's lovely. Is this woman the healer Eva told me about?"*

"Yes," Casey said, climbing to her feet.

"She says you're pretty." Eva relayed the compliment to Tanille.

Tanille blushed and slightly bowed her head to the panther. "Tell her I think she's beautiful."

Eva gave Vashee Tanille's message as she retrieved the bowl from the floor.

Vashee's apparent way of saying thank you was to rub her body up against Tanille's hip. *"She's your mate?"* Vashee asked.

Casey shifted uncomfortably, surprised by Vashee's question. *"No, why would you think so?"*

"You're both giving off a smell which is common before or during the mating process."

Casey's jaw fell, her cheeks blushed, and she shot Eva an embarrassed glance. Eva quickly spun away, almost dropping the bowl to the floor.

"Have I done something wrong?"

Casey coughed, her throat instantly dry. *"No, you didn't do anything wrong, but you must have smelled something else. Maybe a scent we carried in from outside during our walk."*

Vashee tilted her head in confusion. *"Yes, maybe I did,"* she finally answered. Her tone didn't sound convincing, and neither did the look in her doubtful eyes.

"What did she say?" Tanille asked.

Casey wasn't sure how to respond, so she lied. "She said she's ready to eat."

Eva snorted out a fleeting giggle, then busied herself with disposing of the bowl. This caused Tanille to stare at Casey, worried. "Seriously, what did she say?"

"You don't want to know."

"Yes, I do. We're on the same team together. What she thinks is important to me."

"I'm going to serve the meal," Eva blurted out, and seized the closest dish. She left the kitchen before anyone could stop her.

Tanille's worry intensified. "We need to start off developing a trust with one another. Please, don't keep this from me."

Casey tried hard to swallow, but nothing would go down. Her heart raced faster, and her chest felt tight, like her ribs were shrinking. She turned, avoiding Tanille's eyes. The light touch on her arm brought Casey slowly around.

"Does she not like me?"

Casey shook her head. "No, she does. It's rather personal."

"Is it about me?"

"Partially, but it's…umm, it's embarrassing to say."

Tanille gave Casey arm a tender squeeze. "Please tell me. I'm sure we can work through anything."

Casey inhaled as much air as she could. She released a jittery laugh, trying to play off her uneasiness. "She said we have a certain smell. An odor which suggests we want to, um…" She took another long breath. "That we want to mate." Feeling humiliated for saying the words out loud, Casey forced out an odd sounding snicker. "I told her she was wrong. You know, she picked up a scent from our walk."

Casey went to the Originator, got herself a healthy glass of water, and after knocking it down in one round, she pivoted to Tanille. "She's a primitive animal, so don't take it the wrong way. She doesn't know or understand everything about us yet." Her words sounded as lame as they felt when she spoke them. She concentrated on the way Vashee was chewing on the towel.

"She detected it from both of us?" Tanille asked.

Casey froze. Neither Tanille's voice nor facial expression contained any note of humor or denial. Casey spun to the Originator and guzzled another glass of water. *I'm in trouble*, she thought. Casey didn't know what to do or say. Before she got up the courage to face the issue, the door slid open, bringing Ann, her engaging wife Bilana, and Elizabeth into the room.

"I don't remember the last time we had an actual home-cooked meal," Bilana said, delighted.

"We had one the last time Elizabeth was here," Ann replied.

"Oh, you're right. Eva almost burned the kitchen down."

The three guffawed at one another, but Ann instantly fell silent, looking anxiously at the two women in the kitchen with their backs to each other. "Elizabeth, why don't you and Bilana help Tanille take these dishes out." She surveyed her two companions, who continued their talk as they each took a dish. Tanille snuck a glance at Casey before grabbing the last dish and rushing off.

"So, how's my granddaughter? I heard about your little swim today. I thought I was clumsy, but you, by far, have outdone me."

Casey stared at Ann, unsure of what to say.

With a look of worry, Ann went to Casey. "My dear, what's the matter? Are you hurt? Fayrel said you did quite a number on your head."

"No, my head's fine. Dealing with some personal issues is all."

"You know, if you and Tanille are not working out, we can have her replaced."

Casey shook her head and told Vashee to go get some food. The panther was up and out the door within seconds. "It's not that we're not getting along. Actually, it's the opposite. It looks as if we're getting along *too well.*" Casey all but whispered the last two words.

"Really?" Ann didn't act startled by the news, but relieved. Maybe even a bit thrilled. "Tanille's extremely attractive, and exceptionally good at what she does. Did you know she's been volunteering—"

"Volunteering at a children's home, yes, We talked for quite a while." Casey's shoulders dropped and she sighed. She told Ann about what Vashee said, and about her and Tanille's brief conversation.

There were no grandmother warnings about leaping without looking, or not to rush into anything until they had time to truly get to know one another. Instead, Ann's response threw Casey for a loop. "That's pretty awkward, but also, it'll be one of those fun stories you'll share with your grandchildren when they ask."

Stunned, Casey blurted, "Grandchildren, we just met!"

"Ah, so that's what's bothering you. The cautious, untrusting slice of our DNA profile. Unfortunately for me, that was also the most difficult weakness I had to work through. Being raised on a planet where the inhabitants struggle with relationships, I can understand your reservations."

"I'm not following."

"Most Trysals instantly connect with a soul destined for them. First, they copulate, then unite and are with them for the rest of their days."

"Are you telling me they have sex and get married right after they meet? No dating, getting better acquainted, nothing?"

"My dear, sweet Casey. You must realize we're genetically part of an advanced race. We're talking about millions of years of evolution, perfection, and yes—even DNA modification. There's very little divorce, adultery is almost unheard of, and every being is seen as equals. There's no sexism, racism, or any other phobias that plague some of the younger planets like Earth."

"Still, how can an advanced society consider instant relationships rational?"

"Look at it this way. As a society, we don't have all the stressors humans bring into relationships. We live on worlds free of internal conflicts. We do not battle with poverty or world hunger. Our crime rate is virtually absent. And we are advanced in medicine to the point where many of the physical and mental health issues humans face are nonexistent. Humans also lack a level of self-confidence due to all the stipulations and prejudicial beliefs sickening their planet.

Casey stood in silence, unsure of how to structure a decent retort.

Ann studied Casey for a short time before asking her question. "How did you feel when you met her?"

Casey remained unmoving, her brain overwhelmed. Finally, she gave in. "Excited, captivated, aroused, wildly out of control, and I'm not sure how to describe the rest."

"Did you encounter a sense of familiarity, like you've met her before?"

Casey was beside herself. "How did you know?"

Ann looked ecstatic. "My dear, I believe your soul has found its mate. Not every Trysal discovers this connection, but most do." She held up her hand to the obvious protest building in Casey. "We call it a union of the souls, but many Trysals see it as a reunion. You can deny your inner feelings all you want, but please, for your sake, hear me out." She placed her hand on Casey's shoulder for her full attention. "I will not go into much of this, because I feel religion is something each individual should decide for themselves, but you will learn that although there are many faiths within our region, most share common beliefs. On the question of did we exist before being born of the flesh, many theologians, including key scientists throughout our history, believe we once lived as celestial beings before our creator sent us to experience a mortal existence. And each of us were mated with a soul we were destined to be with for all eternity.

"Whether this theory is true or not, we cannot be sure. Only our creator knows for certain. What we do know is there is a pull we each have for the soul of another, and it's exactly like how you described your encounter with Tanille.

"Even some humans have reunited with their eternal mates. They've labeled these relationships as soulmates or twin flames."

The door slid open, and Elizabeth walked in. "The head of council—" She came up short when she saw Ann and Casey. "Is everything all right?"

Casey was too overwhelmed by Grandmother Ann's talk to speak.

"Casey is having a hard time swallowing a major pill," Ann said.

"I don't understand."

"Our granddaughter is in love."

Elizabeth gasped, and Casey redirected her numbness into anger. "I'm not in love. I'm just…hungry!" Casey stormed out of the kitchen. She stopped on the other side of the door to get her anger under control. Her grandmothers were talking loud enough she was concerned the others might hear.

"Ah, to be young and emotional again. How I miss puberty," Ann said.

"Who's she uniting with?"

"It's Tanille, and I have to admit, our granddaughter has wonderful taste."

Agitated, Casey peeked through the crack along the side of the door as Elizabeth clapped her hands together in astonishment. "That's fantastic news. Is she experiencing a reunion with Tanille's soul as you had with Grandmother Bilana? Does Tanille feel the same way? We need to let Fayrel know."

Ann held up her hand, laughing. "Hold on, Elizabeth. Yes, I believe their souls are connected, but Casey's having some issues working around this love at first sight thing."

"Oh, well…what did you tell her? Maybe I should go talk to her. My, Tanille is such a wonderful Trysal. You're right, Casey has excellent taste."

Casey could take no more. She made her way into the dining room and avoided Tanille completely. Hanna steered her away from Parrow and started introductions with the new arrivals.

By the time Ann and Elizabeth entered, the head of council was shaking Casey's hand briskly, his enthusiasm joyful. "A pleasure to finally meet you, Casey Malanight. And where's your panther, your soul-link, Vashee? I believe that's her name." He glanced over toward Ann, who reaffirmed he had the name right. "Ah, yes, Vashee. Is she here?"

Eva gestured with a dip of her head. "She's right behind you."

He jumped when he turned. "She won't attack, will she?" he asked.

"No, sir, she'll not attack you," Eva said politely.

He examined Eva, then the panther. "You're a pretty little thing." He briefly touched her fur, but withdrew his hand as if he'd scalded himself.

"Vashee, this man is Senior Paraney. He's the head of council. He'll be the one deciding if you may remain with us," Eva said.

Vashee went up to Paraney and licked his hand. Next, she rubbed her body against his long, dark-green robes.

Although her jumbled brain was still trying to process her talk with Ann, Casey couldn't help but laugh. *"All right, you've sucked up to him enough. Go finish your meal."*

The decision of Vashee remaining with Casey had gone better than expected. Senior Paraney not only insisted Vashee stay with the team, but he also suggested, for extra security, Vashee should accompany Casey once she started classes at the Academy.

"Will they allow it?" Elizabeth asked. "I've never heard of an animal ever living on the campus grounds before."

"Senior Paraney and I will get it all worked out," said Ann. "All you need to worry about is keeping Casey and Vashee safe and out of trouble."

Casey had a hard time concentrating on her food. Grandmother Ann's talk regarding her feelings for Tanille kept resurfacing in her mind and sitting across from Tanille didn't help Casey's appetite. Every time she thought about the conversation, her eyes would drift up to gawk over at the captivating woman. This usually ended with Tanille's gaze landing on hers, followed either by a haphazard gasp escaping Casey's lungs or her nervous hand knocking over a drink or dropping a utensil to the ground, to clang loudly for those seated in the vicinity to hear.

Unfortunately, no matter what she tried, Casey couldn't keep herself from staring. She watched as Tanille took another bite of food, letting the fork linger a little too long on her lips. Casey's mouth parted, her own bite of food left forgotten on her partially raised fork. Tanille's skin appeared so soft, so perfect, that Casey wondered if her flesh was the same throughout the rest of her body.

Crap! Stop this! Casey's mind scolded her inner desires.

Unable to resist, all sanity of logic gone, her gaze followed the curve of Tanille's neck slowly down, tracing every detail as if her life depended on it. Casey's mouth watered, her cravings burned, hungry for a small taste of Tanille's delicate flesh on the tip of her tongue. Moving slowly lower with her eyes, over Tanille's collarbone, down to where her silky white blouse parted, revealing a glimpse—

"Casey, did you hear Senior Paraney?"

Casey snapped out of her daze, looking up into the amused eyes of Tanille. Startled, she half jumped, banging the corner of the table with her hand, which sent a loud clatter throughout the room.

"Excuse…" her word came out dry, two tones higher than normal. Casey cleared her throat, rubbed the pain from her hand, and scanned those seated around the table, unsure of who was talking to her. "Excuse me," Casey repeated, hotter in the face than she had ever been in her life.

Thankfully, the abundance of food, along with multiple displays of floral and bulky, mood-setting objects of eloquent décor, lined the surface of the long table, shielding Casey from over half of the dinner-guests, including the head of council.

"Senior Paraney wants to know what you think about Parrow and Tanille, the new members of your team," Ann said.

Casey made a grab for her water, almost knocking it over, but Tanille calmly reached across, keeping the glass from tipping. She stroked Casey's hand with her finger before she pulled away.

Casey's heart skipped a beat, and a jagged cramp hit her hard in the stomach. Taking a steadying breath, Casey downed half of her water. Again, she cleared her throat. "They're fine."

Ann shook her head before peering to the other end of the table. "She's very pleased they're a part of her team, and she hopes to find others even half as talented."

"Splendid, that's splendid," Senior Paraney's deep male voice answered in return.

After dinner, Casey tried her best throughout the gathering to avoid looking at Tanille. The visual evading proved to be a bit of a chore, so when she had the chance, she snuck to the back where Burtis was swimming in his tank. She was safe, unnoticed by anyone, or so she thought.

"I have the strangest feeling you're avoiding me."

Casey froze at the mere sound of Tanille's voice. She felt her heart pound wildly in her chest while fervently vacillating between wanting to lunge at the tantalizing creature or run for her life. Deciding either would be in poor form, Casey managed a nervous smile, followed by an odd sounding giggle. "Don't be ridiculous. I only needed some air. It's stuffy in there."

Tanille stepped toward Casey. "I figured I was wrong. You're harder to read than most Trysals. I assume it's because of your family's uniqueness." Tanille overpowered Casey with an alluring gaze. "I never thought I'd be the one to do this, especially after hearing how assertive you are in about everything else you do, but here goes."

The hairs on Casey's arms rose when Tanille moved directly in front of her, followed by the distinct feel of goose bumps trailing down her spine.

"If you would have me, I choose to spend all eternity with you." Tanille said with a tender smile.

Casey was positive her heart completely stopped beating all together. "Ex…excuse me?" she choked out the words.

Tanille continued forward in her confessions of the heart as if she knew what Casey was thinking. "Don't worry, Casey, I've never mated with anyone before you. I'm untouched by others."

Dumbfounded, Casey's mind went blank. Her hands not only began to sweat, but they also shook, so she stuffed them in the front pockets of her jeans. "I'm not sure how to take that."

"I've never felt this either," Tanille said. "I knew, even before we met, my soul was connected with yours."

"I'm not following." Casey felt more confused with each word Tanille uttered.

"I was starting my last year at the Academy when I accepted this position. Queen Ann gave me a detailed profile on you and your life, including your childhood history. As I read through your file, while looking at your pictures, I knew our souls were joined for eternity," she said. "I had to stop looking at your pictures because the desires I had for you became too overwhelming. When I met you today in person, it all came rushing back. The power your soul has over mine, the beauty, the love."

"You wanted to be with me because of my pictures?"

"Not only your pictures, but your eyes in those pictures. The soul behind them moved me in ways I've only read about but never experienced before."

Casey opened her mouth, but her words were lost.

"I'm in love with you." Tanille placed her hand on Casey's cheek.

"But we just met."

Tanille's eyes snapped to surprise, then melted into anguish. "You don't feel the same way?" Her hand dropped to her side.

"Like I said, we just met," Casey repeated. "I mean, something like this takes time." This made no sense. How could a species as advanced as this one make these kinds of life-changing decisions in one day? It felt reckless on so many levels. Even if this soul thing was real.

Tanille steered her eyes sadly to the floor. "I'm sorry. I thought this would be different. I feel affection for you, and I thought you felt the same." Casey's heart sank at the intense, hurtful expression on Tanille's face. "Please accept my apologies. I will not bring this up again."

She turned to leave, but Casey took hold of her arm, stopping her. "Look, I…" Casey frowned, unsure how to make this better. "You don't need to go."

"I cannot stay. I must have some time of my own to work through this." Her eyes remained on Casey's, unmoving. "Please, let me go." She shook off Casey's gentle grip and hurried from the room.

Casey turned, feeling more confused than ever. *What happened? What did I do?*

"Not wanting to interrupt your internal quarrel, but to answer your mental question, I would say you let your future better half leave." Ann sauntered into the room and motioned Casey to join her on the couch.

"I didn't tell her I didn't want her. I only said, hell, I don't remember what I said."

"She probably took your hesitation as a rejection." Ann brought her hand up and gently raised Casey's lowering head. "I understand it's hard for you to accept your feelings, but you need to trust yourself enough to let go."

"I didn't want to rush into anything."

"No, you don't want to feel the way you do. I've been in your shoes." Ann wrapped her arms around Casey. "You need to stop resisting and give in to your emotions. No worries, no limits, Casey. Live your life to the fullest."

When Casey didn't respond, Ann sighed. "Casey, you're part human. Tanille's smart, so go explain this to her. Be honest with your feelings and come up with something you'll both be comfortable with."

Casey allowed her mind to linger over what Ann was saying. Why was she pushing away what every part of her wanted? Finally, Casey returned Ann's hug. "If anyone asks for me, tell them I'll be back."

"Where are you going?"

Casey headed straight for the exit. "To find Tanille. You're right, I'm sure there's got to be a middle ground here."

Casey barely managed to make it out of the room without someone from the group noticing her. She rushed to Tanille's bedroom. After she received no answer from the constant knocking, Casey made her way outside, sensing Tanille was taking another walk. She took the same path they had trekked over earlier, this time with a heavy heart at the thought of the hurt she'd caused the Trysal. She didn't care how different a shade of blue the sky had turned or notice that there had been no evening since their arrival. All she cared about was finding Tanille.

Her pace quickened from a brisk hike into a fast run as the image of Tanille's hurt eyes played in her mind. Squinting, she noticed a figure moving toward her at a moderate pace. Once she was certain the person was Tanille and not a patrolling guard, Casey slowed to a swift walk.

Both women stopped several feet away from each other.

"I was a moron for letting you leave."

Tanille shook her head with assertion. "No, I shouldn't have left the way I did. I just saw it all so differently."

Casey stepped closer. "You caught me off guard. Can we try this one more time?"

Tanille followed her defeated smile with a slight nod. "I should have asked you how a union is performed on Earth. After all, you are part human. You were even raised human. These human customs must signify a great deal to you. I'm sorry. I didn't consider this part of you when we met, and I apologize." Tanille smiled, looking as if she understood everything more clearly now. "What is the Earth custom for uniting with someone? They didn't mention this process in our classes at the Academy."

Casey fought the urge to laugh at hearing the word human so much in less than a minute. "Normally, when you find someone you want to get to know better, you go out on a date, like to the movies, out for dinner or to some other public place."

Tanille's eyebrows rose. "Sounds reasonable. What happens next?"

"If you like each other, you continue to date until you decide if you want to progress to the next step or move on."

"What's the next step?"

"It depends on the couple involved. They may decide to move in together, or possibly get married."

Tanille seemed slightly uncertain by Casey's description of Earth unions. "What did you mean by moving on?"

"If they don't get along, they part ways until they meet another person they'd rather be with."

"Humans will mate with more than one individual?"

"Oh, yes. Humans join with different people all the time. There was this one man on the force named Eddie. We called him 'Fast Eddie' because he would date several women at once."

"How barbaric. I cannot believe humans mate so, so carelessly. It's…"

Casey shuffled her feet, feeling small-minded for finding the idea amusing. She was not about to tell Tanille that in many countries, a man having more than one wife was customary. Legal by both law and different religions.

Tanille studied her nervously. "How many humans have you joined with?"

"Oh, I haven't." Casey said. "I've never connected with anyone. Physically or emotionally." Her words brought a look of relief to Tanille's eyes.

Suddenly, the recollection of the night in her dorm room popped into her head. Tanille's look of relief changed to worry when Casey skewed her face.

"I had one insignificant experience in college." Casey took in a deep breath and slowly let it out. "With my roommate. She came in tipsy one night from one of her normal weekend parties. She'd made advances toward me in the past, but this time, instead of turning her down, I gave it a try." Casey's chest felt heavy, and she could no longer keep eye contact with Tanille. "At the time, I thought I had something wrong with me because I was one of the few, if not the only, virgins in my dorm. I figured I'd see if this would, you know, jumpstart my libido."

"Did it?"

"No. the experience actually had the opposite effect. We only made out—"

"Made out?"

"You know, we kissed and felt around some." Casey was feeling like a sleazy pervert. "I got nauseated when my hand moved under her shirt, so I ended it." She wasn't sure why, but she felt like she had cheated on Tanille.

The touch to her cheek was softer than before, as Tanille's hands guided her head downward. Casey was unprepared for the feel of Tanille's lips on her own when they gently pressed together. The contact sent a hormonal current throughout her entire body.

Her senses heightened, and without realizing what she was doing, she pulled Tanille's body against her. Every part of her burst with excitement. Her lips moved against Tanille's, slow and steady at first, until something deep inside her awoke, bringing with it an appetite far greater than she could've dared to imagine. A hunger bordering on madness. Her vision fogged, and every muscle in her body swelled to the fullest. She felt strong. Powerful. The desire to take Tanille where they stood was so raw, so animalistic, that fear gripped her.

You need to stop, Casey's mind shouted, yet her lust was great, driving her hands forward, yanking Tanille's blouse upward, untucking it from the depths of her slacks. Her hands searched underneath the freed fabric, gripping upward until she forced herself to end the pursuit. Her mind felt as if she'd consumed a drug that made her equilibrium spin wildly out of control. Her heart pounded dangerously fast, and the area between her legs was vigorously throbbing, as if awakened for the first time. Her breathing came in small gasps, and she closed her eyes to steady herself.

"Why did you stop?" Tanille's voice was thick with desire, matching Casey's own.

"I had to. If we continue, I won't be able to control myself."

The need in Tanille's eyes swelled at Casey's words. "Then don't." The next kiss was more passionate than the first, the craving greater, bringing with it an unyielding drive deep inside Casey's body.

"I've dreamed about this moment for so long," Tanille whispered, as Casey's lips moved to Tanille's neck, nuzzling the warm flesh with her tongue, teeth, lips.

Casey's body tensed. Her lips stopped moving.

"Casey, is everything all right?" Tanille asked.

Casey was unsure what to say. Was she ready for this?

"Casey?"

"I'm sorry," Casey murmured. "Would you mind if we take this slow? I don't mean that I don't want this to happen, just not at this moment." Casey's words said one thing, yet her lust screamed at her to take the woman right here, right now.

Tanille reluctantly nodded. Casey's heart sank at the regret in the Trysal's eyes. "Would you like to head to the house?" she asked.

"Yes, please," Casey said.

They strolled along in silence for a good minute while Casey racked her brain for anything worth saying to break the awkward tension. Finally, a thought crossed her mind. "What's it like for Trysals to date?"

Tanille didn't answer right away. When she did, her words sounded uncertain. "I understand you're not a full Trysal. So, what I tell you won't pertain to us. Our situation is different. I realize that now, and this doesn't bother me."

Casey studied Tanille, unsure of what she was getting at. Tanille grabbed Casey's arm to stop their movement. "All I'm saying is the customary Trysal relationship, like the relationships on Earth, will be different for us. I want to give myself to you when you're ready, but I don't want you to feel our experience would be life-altering."

Casey frowned. "Maybe you should tell me."

Taking Casey by the hand, Tanille continued their walk as she spoke. "We don't date. It's not that we don't go out and do things together, we do. We normally do this after we unite with each other. When you connect with your eternal partner, you usually join together and go through a union ceremony."

"Join together?"

"You mate with your partner."

"You have sex and get married? Sounds a lot like Earth."

"Yes, but we only have one mate before we marry."

A thought sprang up. "What if you have sex with someone, but you end up mating with someone else?"

"It would be harder for one to mate again. I mean, don't get me wrong, we do have individuals who are promiscuous, but they're labeled as *tenliltes*. I believe this means slut on Earth."

"Many humans I know would consider that a compliment."

Tanille stopped. "Not for us. We believe this to be very improper. From a medical standpoint alone, this type of careless act increases the chance of terrible diseases and unwanted children."

Casey felt as if a one-ton truck came from out of nowhere and struck her head on. "So, if we slept together and didn't unite, you'd be labeled a *tenlilte*?" Her heart sank.

"Like I said before, our relationship is unique."

"But it wouldn't change how your own people would see you."

Tanille lifted her chin defiantly. "I don't care. I'm an adult. This choice is mine to make."

"I do care, and it's also mine."

Tanille wrapped her arms around Casey. "I want to give myself to you. I know what could happen, but my heart tells me it's right."

The idea of Tanille giving herself to some other woman, or man, played in the back of Casey's mind. The thought turned her blood ice cold. She had never felt jealousy before, and she didn't like it.

"What is it?"

Casey brushed the thought away. "What do you mean?"

"You seem upset." Tanille's voice was tender, as she touched her hand to Casey's cheek.

"I'm not sure if I like the idea of you mating with someone else," Casey finally said, and realized how childish she sounded.

Tanille's eyes glistened. "That's one thing you'll never have to worry about." She drew Casey's head closer and kissed her fully, sending a fresh wave of excitement coursing through Casey's body. "I need you."

The moment Casey's tongue parted Tanille's lips, the personal computer on Casey's arm vibrated. "Crap!"

Chapter Ten

The Trip Home

Tanille watched Casey press the flashing red diamond on her wrist.

Elizabeth's voice came on, sounding worried. "Casey, are you and Tanille all right?"

"Yes, we're on our way in."

A slight pause. "We're getting ready to open some Blunion Ale, and Senior Paraney was wondering where you both had gone."

"We'll be there in ten minutes," Casey said. She pressed the diamond to end the connection before continuing their discussion. "If it's okay with you, I'd like to start with dating and go from there."

Tanille's heart sank, but she held in her disappointment. "What exactly do we do during this dating period? I mean, will this relationship be exclusive?" she asked, recalling what Casey said regarding Fast Eddie.

"I'd like to keep it that way, if you're fine with it."

"Oh, definitely." Tanille's spirits lifted. She wasn't sure why she'd been so worried. After all, with the way Casey had acted around her since they met, she didn't believe it would take longer than two, three days tops, before Casey proposed. "I guess we'd better go."

They kept a hurried pace to the main house, entering the gathering through the side door.

"See there, sometimes the healer needs to be healed," Fayrel said. Senior Paraney roared with laughter and downed the last half of his drink.

"Ah, here they are." Senior Paraney beamed toward them as they entered the room, while one of his staff refilled Paraney's glass with yellow liquid. Tanille guessed it was the Blunion Ale, and he was already showing signs of inebriation.

"Where've you two been?" Bilana asked.

"I needed some fresh air, and Casey joined me," Tanille said. She sat next to her father.

When Casey took a seat between her and Queen Ann, Tanille's heart fluttered. Casey's body was less than six inches away. She could feel the warmth radiate from Casey's arm onto hers. Her hand was so close. Should she take it? She'd best not. Casey may not be ready to make this dating thing public.

"Is Gran upset?" Tanille overheard Casey whisper to Queen Ann.

Ann gave a little snicker. "She's secretly planning your and Tanille's union ceremony. I've tried to calm her, but you know how she is when she gets an idea stuck in her head."

Tanille's mind soared with delight. The news that Casey's family liked her well enough to be accepting of a union made so many worries fade away. She was debating whether she should slide closer to Casey or wait to see if Casey moved closer to her when she heard someone mention Casey's name from across the room.

"No, Casey's outstanding at wallball. I bet she and I could beat all three of you in a match." Parrow's announcement was extremely loud, probably due to the speed at which he was consuming the potent beverage.

"Wallball? Which one of you is good at wallball?" Senior Paraney asked, thrilled.

"Casey is, sir. I was explaining how she has a natural talent at sports and is exceptional at wallball."

"You don't say?" He beamed at Casey and motioned for one of his men to fetch her a glass of ale.

Good, Tanille thought, Blunion Ale had a way of bringing out honest feelings in thirsty souls, especially if one was unaccustomed to the beverage. Maybe this would help Casey with whatever was keeping her from mating.

"I'm a huge fan of wallball. I used to play in my younger days. Even played at the Academy. I wasn't one of the primary starters though."

Tanille watched Casey thank the man for her drink before shifting uncomfortably in her seat, as if she wished the conversation would deviate off her and on to someone else. Tanille smiled. Not only was Casey out of this universe gorgeous, with impressive muscles to boot, she had an endearing personality, which was rare to find in many of the upper-class circles.

She briefly closed her eyes when she felt a feverish ache flare between her crossed legs. She needed to stay focused on the group discussion until her excitement was more under control.

"We should get a game going the next time we come to Vasar," Parrow said.

"My dear fellow, what a splendid idea. You two can compete against two of my officers. Casey will have to disguise herself, of course." Paraney gave the room a high look of importance while stating the obvious.

"Are you not drinking?" Casey asked.

Tanille shook her head. "I don't care for alcohol. It's not the taste but the effects of the liquor. I'd rather enjoy life through natural means."

"I agree." Casey lowered her glass.

Tanille panicked, realizing what she'd done. "I don't mean for you not to drink. What I mean is, you should experience new things, and I must admit, Blunion Ale is quite good. You should try it."

"I guess a taste won't hurt."

Tanille held her breath as Casey brought the salty-sweet Blunion Ale up to her lips and sipped. Before long, Casey had downed two tall glasses and was working on a third when she loudly announced a great need to use the restroom.

Ann laughed, steadying Casey as she wobbled to her feet. "I take it you don't drink, do you?"

"Not really. Parrow got me drunk two weeks ago, but other than that, a glass of wine on rare occasions is normally my limit."

"We're lightweights," Elizabeth added, licking her lips. She motioned for another glass. "However, the drinks on Earth are not nearly as tasty either."

Parrow stood and swayed. "Do you need me to take you, Casey?"

"I've got her." Tanille was fast to her feet, stabilizing Casey before Parrow moved. She walked with Casey from the room and down the hall.

Once they were at the bathroom door, Casey braced herself against the barrier. "I could've made it here alone."

Mentally Tanille blurted out, *Not likely*, but verbally she agreed. "Yes, but I have to ask you a question. It can wait until you've finished."

Casey dipped her head in a bidding gesture before stumbling her way into the bathroom. The drunken politeness aroused Tanille even more. When Casey returned, Tanille asked, "What do you think of me?"

"What do you mean?"

"Do you find me attractive?"

Not missing a beat, Casey said, "I've never seen anyone more beautiful."

Tanille's stomach fluttered at the honesty in Casey's eyes. The Blunion Ale was definitely working. She decided to probe further. "Could you see us together?"

Casey snickered herself into a hiccup. The slight bout of laughter caused her body to sway. She leaned her back against the wall. "I thought you already knew the answer. Tanille, you're the only person I've ever had feelings for. I know in my heart we were made for each other."

Tanille's eyes sparkled with excitement.

Casey raised her brow, in a drunken form of self-assurance. "Are you asking these questions because you're crazy about me?" She grabbed Tanille's arm and pulled her easily in. Casey's strength was heart-stopping. She lowered her lips to Tanille's neck, nibbling, tasting, sucking.

Tanille's lust exploded and her knees wobbled. Her body was more than ready to mate. "What time is that man leaving?" Tanille whispered, tilting her head to expose more of her neck to feed Casey's hunger.

"I'm not sure, but I hope it's soon."

"After he leaves, will you come to my bedroom?"

Casey's nod sent Tanille's appetite soaring with heated anticipation.

Tanille worked hard at keeping Casey's drinks minimal throughout the rest of the gathering, but Senior Paraney was constantly making sure Casey's glass was properly full. He did the same for Elizabeth, and by the time he left, both women were too drunk to make it to their rooms on their own.

Ann and Tanille escorted Casey to her quarters, while Fayrel and Hanna carried Elizabeth, who passed out on the couch minutes before their guest left. Casey was extremely unstable but swayed the entire way with minor help. By the time they hit the bedroom, Casey told Ann she and Tanille were going to be married one day soon, and that she was madly in love with her. Ann kept saying congratulations, while she and Tanille exchanged amused smirks with one another. Casey passed out the instant she hit the bed.

"Do you need help with changing her?" Ann asked.

"No, I believe I can manage, and I wouldn't mention the marriage thing to anyone quite yet. We're only in a dating period. Whatever that means."

Ann gave Tanille a warm embrace. "Give her time. I guarantee she'll be worth the wait. If you need any advice, ask Bilana. I put her through the same thing you're experiencing with this one. Though I proposed to her right after we mated. Took three whole days." Ann waved a finger in Casey's direction. "Are you sure you don't need help with her?"

Tanille shook her head. "I'll be fine, thanks."

Once Ann left the room, Tanille searched through the wardrobe database for Casey's nightclothes. A laugh caught in her throat when several colorfully animated pajama bottoms and matching tank tops appeared on the screen. She didn't assume Casey would sleep in anything feminine, with delicate lace or pink ribbons, but she wasn't expecting this either. She picked out a black pair of bottoms with bright-red dancing chili peppers wearing oversized sombreros and a bright-red matching tank top. Tanille held up the outfit, giggling.

She returned to the side of the bed and bent to remove Casey's shirt. She straightened, suddenly hesitant, and squinted from Casey to the clothes. This felt wrong. Tanille turned and headed out of the room to locate Ann with the clothes clutched in her hand. She found her with Bilana, Eva, and Ashonda. She wasn't sure, but she could've sworn she heard Ashonda use the word union.

"Oh, good lord, what are those?" Ashonda asked.

"Casey's nightwear," Tanille said. "She has a bunch of different types in her wardrobe."

"Those are quite popular on Earth with the males," Eva said. "My favorite is the florescent orange set with sexy written all over them." She paused. "Casey wears them sometimes to class after she's pulled an all-nighter with her studies."

"Do you need some help?" Ann asked, giving Tanille a sympathetic look.

Tanille nodded, then whispered, "I don't feel right changing her alone. We're not married—I'm not quite sure what we—yes, could you please give me a hand?" She finished, turning slightly red.

Ann's smile widened as she followed Tanille from the room.

The typical pounding of the head or wave of nausea associated with excessive drinking, or the imbibing her and Parrow did a couple weeks ago, wasn't present to Casey's good fortune. She awoke, feeling as splendid as she would on any normal day. If not better, because within the last few hours, something inside her erupted, bringing with it a clarity she'd never experienced before. Her fears and doubts vanished, leaving a new, unrestrained Casey in their place. Her cherished life felt more meaningful now that she realized she was, in fact, deeply in love. Her head was peacefully clear, and the worries she carried earlier were nothing more than a fleeting memory, easily forgotten.

She opted for a morning jog around the property before her shower and breakfast. This would give her time alone to decide how to express her feelings to Tanille without sounding like an idiot. After having Chasel show her how to operate the control panel on her wardrobe, she changed into her running outfit and crept outside before anyone spotted her.

The air was crisp, with an orange and bluish haze filling the sky above the mountains, and two separate moons hanging on each end of the horizon. One was small, like a basketball perched in the vast view of the heavens, which glowed bright-white with a bluish ring encircling its richness. The other was twice the size and shimmered a magnificent sea-green. She ran for over an hour before deciding to return to the main residence. The view of the sky during the sprint back was just as impressive, displaying one of Vasar's two bright suns and a colorful image of Vasar Two directly beneath it. The buildings of the estate, with such an extraordinary backdrop, was more dreamlike than ever. Casey quickened her pace. This life was truly blessed.

After arriving at the mansion, out of breath, yet feeling physically and mentally revived, Casey took a massaging shower, following it with a shave to her legs and underarms before changing. She headed into the kitchen for some much needed sustenance to refuel her spent calories. On the Belfont Originator, she ordered a traditional Earth breakfast, complete with a side dish of biscuits smothered in sausage gravy, and an extra-large creamy sweet coffee. She took her food and drink out to one of the covered terraces overlooking the lake, to enjoy the view of the animated sky and the breezy green fields.

As she ate, Casey racked her brain with the best way to tell Tanille how she felt. Should she be chivalrous, funny, daring? Romantic was too cliché for Casey. She also knew she wasn't one to take a knee as an orchestra played symphonies of love in the background. Rose dangling from teeth. Nope, not her. Her mind cringed at the thought.

Image after image of different scenarios played out, jumbling her brain with farfetched scenarios, and each one ending more absurd than the last. She finally decided to keep it simple. She would go up to Tanille, take her in her arms, and say what her soul was aching to convey—Tanille, I love you.

Satisfied by her decision, she finished her food, downed the last of her coffee, and stretched herself against the backrest of her seat, closing her eyes to the tranquility of the moment. She was completely relaxed, feeling for the first time in her adult life she was taking an overdue vacation.

"You look comfortable."

Not opening her eyes, Casey grinned at the sound of Tanille's voice. "You could say that."

"Mind if I join you?"

Casey cracked her eyelids and took in the splendor of Tanille. She sat up and without thinking, guided her onto her lap. "I love you, Tanille."

The stunned look on Tanille's face was priceless. "Exactly how much did you drink?" she asked.

"I'm not drunk. I've had an epiphany, and everything is crystal clear. I know we've only known each other for a handful of hours, but I truly am in love with you. I'm not sure if I'm ready to get married—"

Before Casey could say more, Tanille flung her arms around her neck and kissed her fully on the lips. "I love you too," Tanille said. "I'll wait as long as you need."

Tanille's lips were so tender. This time, when Casey's stomach fluttered with excitement, she experienced no reservations like before. "Thank you for understanding, and for putting me to bed. I wasn't planning on drinking so much."

"Queen Ann helped me. I didn't want to cross any boundaries while you were inebriated." She wrapped her arms tighter around Casey's neck.

"It's refreshing to know you're as admirable as you are beautiful. If the roles were reversed, I'm sure I would've stared at your nakedness the entire time."

Tanille laughed. "Oh, I didn't say I didn't look. I simply said Queen Ann helped. I assure you, every time she turned her back, I snatched an eyeful."

"Well?"

"Well, what?"

Casey dramatically sighed, and she arched her eyebrows. "What did you think?"

"Oh, of your body?" Tanille's voice was light, playful. "Let's see…on the whole, not bad. After all, you have a nice tan complexion, and toned, athletic legs." Tanille softly traced her fingers over Casey's exposed bicep. "Your back is strong, and your stomach's tight. Still, you're slightly too muscular for my taste."

Casey saw the lust in Tanille's eyes, and her own cravings rocketed to life. "Fine, I can stop working out. Might become stressed and crotchety, but whatever will make you happy."

Tanille waved a dainty hand in the air. Her voice came out slightly breathless. "Don't worry. I'll adapt."

With a warm throbbing forming between her thighs, Casey claimed a feverish kiss, one she wished could last a lifetime. "Going forward, I give you permission to undress me any time you want, no matter how drunk I am," she murmured before their lips reconnected.

"And we worried they wouldn't get along." The sound of Ann's amused voice brought the two apart, and Tanille sprang from Casey's lap. As soon as Casey realized Elizabeth accompanied Ann, she jumped to her feet, feeling like she was doing something sinfully inappropriate.

"Please sit. There are several things we need to discuss," Elizabeth said, her tone matter-of-fact.

Casey cast a worried glimpse to Ann, as she and Tanille did as her gran instructed. Tanille sat in the chair beside her, then reached out under the table, giving Casey's hand a reassuring squeeze.

"First off, if you haven't already, you both must inform Fayrel of your relationship. Not only is he a good friend, but he's also Tanille's father. The longer you keep him oblivious to this relationship, the sooner this will become an insult to him and his good name. Now, as far as this relationship goes, Ann has informed me you're considering this a trial period." She looked from one to the other. Her disappointment was clear. "I would like to know why Fayrel and I aren't planning your union ceremony and whose idea was it to minimize such a perfect bond?"

Tanille was getting ready to speak, but Casey tapped a finger on Tanille's knuckle to dissuade her. "The decision was mine. I didn't want us to rush into anything."

"No, the decision was both of ours," Tanille insisted, avoiding Ann's eyes.

Elizabeth studied Tanille doubtfully. Casey's gran knew better. "That's fine, and I do support you both with your decision." She gave Casey a solid glare. "I don't know what has happened physically between the two of you, and I don't want to know. I must insist, however, that from this point on, you abstain from the physical component of your relationship. Until you decide if you're right for each other."

"Now, Elizabeth, I don't think—"

Elizabeth waved off Ann's feeble attempt at a protest. "If this trial is in place to determine their compatibility, I don't want physical emotion to get in the way." She narrowed her eyes only at Casey. "I'm sorry, but you can't have your cake and eat it too." Elizabeth straightened in her chair, peering at the unhappy couple. "If you cannot respect my request, I must insist you both go explain this to Fayrel. Enlighten him on why his daughter is good enough for mating, but not marriage."

Casey jumped to her feet, suddenly upset by what Elizabeth was implying.

Tanille gently touched Casey's arm. "Whether or not my father consents, this relationship is between Casey and me. We are adults and as with any relationship, we take responsibility for the potential outcome."

Casey's mind turned to their discussion during last night's walk and the word Tanille used. *Tenlilte.* Her anger dissolved, and she retook her seat with her shoulders slumped. "You're right, Gran," she said. She felt Tanille's grip tighten, but Casey ignored it. She wasn't ready to see the disappointment in Tanille's eyes.

Elizabeth's persona softened. "You'll respect my wishes?"

Casey nodded, with a heavy, empty feeling troubling her heart.

"Good, now you must both go get ready. Eva and the rest of the group will be eager to leave here soon to pick up supplies, and Casey still needs to go through the DNA Modifier."

Once Casey and Tanille left, Elizabeth turned to Ann with a mischievous grin. "Do you think that did it?"

"Hmmm, let's see. Not only is Casey deeply attracted to Tanille, but she's also going through puberty. With her enhanced sex drive, I give her two days at the most."

Elizabeth raised her brow. "Really, that long?"

They exchanged a cheeky smirk and guffawed to one another, both enjoying their well-thought-out plan.

By the time the male Casey came out of the DNA Modifier, she was already rethinking her resolve on not rushing into marriage. She loved Tanille, of this she was certain, but was she ready for this type of commitment? She weighed the pros and cons while she dressed. The pros didn't seem to hold the strength they had when first electing to take their relationship slowly, and now she doubted every single reason she had for waiting.

"Are you about finished?" Parrow entered with Vashee, who had come in to wish them a safe trip.

They exited through the rear of the estate to wait for the others. Vashee said her goodbyes before heading off to explore more of the land. Parrow explained to Casey, even though they were still in the first day on Vasar, the team went by Earth time so they wouldn't be off schedule when they arrived home.

Eva and Tanille were the last to arrive. Tanille was wearing a short tight outfit, showing off her trim yet curvy backside. Swallowing hard, Casey's gaze moved along the bustline of the black silk blouse, revealing the shapes underneath. Casey's heartbeat quickened and her man-member pressed against her pants. Realizing she had the outline of an erection, she untucked her shirt and let it hang, concealing her arousal.

Casey redirected her attention away from the approaching Trysal and instead focused on the colors of the sky. The more she tried to suppress her mind from mentally conjuring up visions of what lay hidden underneath Tanille's clothes, the easier the erotic images of a naked Tanille took flight. This soared Casey's sexual cravings to new heights, and her appendage into a hardening state of discomfort.

"Casey, is everything all right?" Tanille asked.

"Are the nights here as beautiful as the days?" Casey cringed at asking such a lame question.

"Breathtaking, but that's not what's on your mind." Tanille's hand brushed against Casey's cheek until their eyes met. "What's going on? Is this about us? Are you having doubts?"

Casey spotted Tanille's worry. "No, this isn't about me falling out of love with you. I have no doubts, only a minor issue." She shyly gestured to her own waistline. "When I saw you—" Feeling embarrassed, Casey reworded her explanation to short-and-sweet. "You excite me, and my body's reacting."

Tanille's eyes dipped downward, her tight lips trying unsuccessfully to wrestle away a grin. "Oh, I see."

Eva addressed the group of shoppers and guards, ordering them all to follow her to the estate's transportation warehouse where the team's transporter sat. The first half of the hovering vehicle was for passengers, and the rest of the open space was for equipment and supplies unfit for teleportation. There were two rows of rear seating and two main chairs in the front where Hanna and Eva sat.

Eva powered up the engines while everyone filed in. Casey and Tanille were the last to enter with only one seat left. Tanille gladly volunteered to sit on Casey's lap. "Nice whiskers," she said, placing her arm around Casey's neck to get more comfortable.

Casey reached up and touched the stubble on her face. "Sorry, I didn't have time to shave after coming out of the modifier."

Tanille tenderly ran her fingers along Casey's chin. "I like them. Makes you look rugged, wildly handsome."

"They feel scratchy and grow so fast I have to shave twice a day."

Tanille leaned over and whispered in Casey's ear. "Your facial hair isn't the only thing growing."

Casey blushed when she realized what Tanille meant. Tanille was right. The excitement she felt with Tanille seated on her lap caused her male extremity to rise further. The more this annoying appendage stiffened, the worse the confined discomfort of her jeans became.

"I'm so sorry. I've tried, but I can't make it go down."

Tanille brought her lips so close to Casey's ear, her warm breath teasing Casey's earlobe when she whispered, "If we stay behind, I can take care of that for you."

The thought excited Casey, making her harder. Regretfully, she shook her head no. "I promised Gran."

With a shrug, Tanille adjusted herself on Casey's lap. "You'll eventually cave." Again, she repositioned herself, but this time she shifted her butt slower, more intentional with her movements.

Casey groaned. "Please stop moving. The rubbing is making it worse."

"Oh, sorry."

Casey detected a hint of playfulness in Tanille's voice. She pushed it off, thinking instead of her problem. "How am I going to make it off this ship without the others noticing?"

"Try to think of something unpleasant."

"While you're on my lap? Sorry, not possible."

Casey's wasn't sure if Tanille picked up on the discomfort in her tone, but the Trysal's playfulness was replaced by concern. Tanille dug in her handbag and retrieved a container of assorted pills. She selected one that was drab-gray. "Take this. It's not the normal treatment used for this problem, but it should do the trick."

Casey did as Tanille instructed, and within several minutes, after dry swallowing the pill, Casey's firm body part softened.

"Thanks," Casey said. "I owe you one."

Tanille huffed. "Yes, but not for the pill."

As soon as Eva landed the ship, everyone exited to a row of teleporting chambers. They were in a holding area for ground vessels on a hillside overlooking the city. The city was breathtaking with buildings taller than Casey would have believed possible in a variety of shapes, designs, and colors.

Eva showed Casey how to program the destination into the holographic screen on the teleporting chamber, while several of the guards teleported ahead to make sure the area was free of danger. By the time Casey stepped through, most of their group had already departed, leaving Hanna and Parrow behind with Casey for protection.

One moment, Casey was standing in the chamber surrounded by rows of ships, landing pads, and grass, and a split second later she was in the shopping district of the city. It took her several seconds to get her bearings, but once she did, she was in awe.

The walkways were crowded, yet clean, unlike New York City. Gazing to the topmost levels of the buildings felt impossible without feeling as if she were about to fall over. As the group made their way through the buildings and clusters of people, Casey did her best not to stare at the different species she passed along the way. She wanted to learn more, to get a better feel for the beings who populated the Universal Region. After all, she would rule over this empire one day. Yet she didn't want to appear rude.

The inside of the first building was spectacular, with wall-to-wall computer screens as far as the eye could see. They displayed dimensional advertisements of the products they carried as well-dressed employees hustled about, trailing behind, or hurrying to assist one of the plentiful customers.

The group followed Eva to one of the empty monitors, and once she ran her right hand over the device and entered some information onto a touchscreen, a Program Intelligence materialized to help her with her many selections. The experience went faster than Casey expected. Eva scanned through the list of products, choosing the items and amounts they needed, paid for the purchase with a silver marker, and scheduled the items for delivery to the Malanight estate later in the day. After the transaction was complete, they went outside to the busy walkway.

Eva turned, handing Casey an identical flat silver marker. "With our tiring task out of the way, let's go shopping," she said, gesturing her hands out wide to the many stores and eateries. "That card will buy you whatever you want. But remember, any items you purchase must not leave the ship on Vasar Five because of the planetary secrecy laws."

Throughout the trip, Casey couldn't take her eyes off Tanille. The kindness she displayed when giving directions to an older female with bright yellow skin and gills on her neck dazzled Casey's soul. Tanille's affectionate personality captivated both Hanna and Eva in fun and illuminating chitchat, and Casey couldn't help but stare. Tanille's bright personality was like a magnet, drawing others in to marvel at such a wonderful creation. The most enticing creation Casey had ever met.

Over two hours into their outing, Casey realized the answer to her mental question from earlier. The thought of spending her life without this magnificent Trysal caused a pit of loneliness to emerge, which was all encompassing. She *was* ready to commit. Without waiting, she excused herself to find Parrow. "What do you get someone you want to marry?"

"Umm, union rings. They're like Earth wedding rings but…oh my God, you're in love with her! I knew it!"

"Ssshhh…keep your voice down, and please help me find one."

Parrow excitedly bounced on his heels before heading off to talk to his mother. When he returned, he was practically pulling Casey out of the store by her arm. "We're going next door. We'll take the guards outside with us."

The next store was as impressive as the last, with the first five floors designated for precious stones, jewels, and jewelry of all shapes and sizes. After Parrow finished communicating with one of the store's Program Intelligences, they went to the fifth floor. The program took them into a secured vault in the back, housing the pricier items, particularly the high-cost union rings.

"Wow, Gran would kill me for paying this much," Casey said, inspecting the price log.

"No, she'd kill you if you didn't. So choose anything you want, and don't worry about the price," said Parrow.

Casey moved around the vault, feeling uncomfortable. She was out of her element with the entire shopping thing. Plus, considering the significance behind the purchase she was preparing to make, she felt overwhelmed.

She searched for over an hour, with a frustrated Parrow doing his best to assist her before she finally found what she was looking for. The set of rings was on one of the last rows left unsearched, and more striking than she thought jewelry could be. Three fuchsia gems overlapping pale blue *terropen* bands stood out, as if calling to her, and once she held the jeweled rings in her hand, Casey knew these were the ones.

After paying a small fortune for the set of rings, the program instructed Casey to place them in the packaging slot by the monitor. With the rings boxed and shoved in her pocket, they left the building.

As Casey and Parrow waited outside with the guards for the women to finish with their shopping, Casey used the time to think about how she was going to ask Tanille such an important question. She was nervous and constantly fidgeted with the container in her pocket, afraid someone would steal it or the box would unexpectedly fall out.

"Crap!"

"What is it?" Parrow asked.

Casey brought her hands up to her face. "I don't know. Some type of bug flew right into my eye, and it hurts."

"Let me see, you big baby." He seized Casey's cheeks and forced open her reddening eye, none too gently.

"Can you be a little nicer? It feels like you're ripping my face off!"

"Do you want it out or not?" he snapped, apparently still frustrated after shopping so extensively for the rings.

Bags in hand, Tanille emerged from the building with Hanna and Eva directly in front. All three were laughing at how fast Parrow and Casey had left the store over an hour ago to wait outside with the guards. Apparently, milling around to people-watch was more exciting than clothes shopping.

Breath caught in her throat, Tanille froze in place. Less than fifty feet away, Casey was gazing into Parrow's eyes as he cradled her face gently in his hands. Tanille instantly turned away with a feeling of her very own heart perishing inside her chest. Destroyed by the one she loved. Was this the human part of Casey coming out?

When Eva asked what was wrong, Tanille couldn't speak for fear of crying. She kept her distance from Casey for the rest of the outing, which was cut short by Hanna and Eva once she told them she felt sick to her stomach. "Must have been something I ate," was all her depleted soul could come up with. The ride to the Malanight estate was unbearable, as she had no choice but to sit on Casey's lap.

"Are you okay?" Casey asked for the fifth time.

Tanille glared at a spot on the floor. "I don't feel well." She wanted to vomit but fought off the urge with every ounce of strength she possessed. She knew better. The fault was hers and hers alone. She allowed herself to fall for a woman whose genetic makeup was weak with temptation. She needed to see her father. She had to make sure.

Once they arrived and Eva powered down the transporter, Tanille left, and Casey headed to the DNA Modifier. She located her father, restocking the supplies on Vasar Six. Tanille took a deep breath and prayed. "Parrow and Casey get along well, don't they?"

He peered up, half in a daze from his computer pad. "Uh, Parrow and Casey, oh yes, they're hard to separate. Have been like that since they met."

Tanille squeezed the exam table with both hands, forcing herself to ask the next question. "Are they in…are they in love?"

"Hmmm, love, well yes, of course," he said, tapping rapidly on the monitor. "Love is eternal," he said, while punching in a long list of commands. "I'm sorry dear, what did you ask?" When he raised his eyes up from his work, he realized his daughter had left the room.

Tanille remained in her suite or with her father for the rest of the trip on Vasar One. At first, her excuse for avoiding Casey was because she felt ill. Then to spend time with her father. By the third day, there were no more excuses, only avoidance. Whenever Casey entered a room, Tanille refused to acknowledge her presence and promptly found a reason to leave.

"Did you give the ring to her yet?" Parrow impatiently prodded.

"I haven't been around her long enough to ask. I'm not sure what I did wrong, but it must've been bad."

Parrow gazed at his feet but didn't say a word.

After a minute of awkward silence, Casey grew tired of waiting. "What's on your mind?"

"I've been tossing around a thought. What if she changed her mind?"

Casey stared at him, as tears filled her eyes.

"I'm sure I'm wrong," he blurted out. "Please don't listen to me. You know my experience with love."

Casey turned away, feeling a sudden sharp ache in her chest. The pain in itself was staggering, but so was the truth behind Parrow's words. She'd come to the same conclusion herself, but she didn't have the courage to admit it until now.

Parrow touched her shoulder. "Look, let's open a bottle of Blunion Ale and get plastered together."

"It makes sense."

"No, it doesn't. I realized after saying it out loud, I'm way off base."

Casey reeled from his pity and wiped the moisture from her eyes. "She must have known I was next door buying union rings. Reality set in, and she wanted none of it."

"Okay, not good. Let me go get someone who can talk some sense into you."

Casey defiantly raised her chin, not listening to what Parrow was saying. "Fine, if she doesn't want to be with me, I'll be fine on my own. Hell, I was doing great before I met her." She slammed her fist on the dining room table and stood.

Without another word, she stormed off to her bedroom. She rushed over and threw open the drawer next to her bed, snatched the box containing the two rings, and angrily made her way over to the trash incinerator. Furiously opening the cover, she raised the box to throw it inside for swift destruction.

A vision of Tanille entered Casey's mind, along with a wave of heartbreaking emotions. Love, anger, regret. Casey slowly closed the lid to the incinerator and hugged the box tight with both hands. She slid onto the floor, where her body shook with each passing sob.

She remained on the floor for over an hour crying while thinking of the woman she'd lost. She swore to herself she would never let her heart love deeply again. When she finally had herself under control, Casey placed the box into the bottom of her bag and finished packing the rest of her things.

By the time Casey arrived at the loading dock, everyone was waiting outside by the ship to wish them a fond farewell, and Ann gave Casey the transmission code, instructing her to contact her whenever she needed to talk. She also stressed the importance of using her male name and appearance. Casey already told the concerned Eva she wasn't feeling well enough to pilot the ship, and after securing Vashee into her newly constructed seat on the operations deck, Casey went straight to her quarters to finish her homework assignments.

She was in there for the entire first day, with Chasel helping her. On the beginning of the second day, several hours after she finished her homework, Parrow came to get her for her watch on the operations deck.

"I take it you haven't spoken to her yet?"

Casey ignored the question, which felt heavy in a disapproving way.

"Look, go talk to her. You're sulking and extremely unpleasant to be around in this state."

"Then you should've sent a transmission instead of coming here to get me yourself," she snapped.

He grabbed her shoulder. "Casey, I care about you. I want to help."

She inhaled a deep breath and gradually released it. "I know you do. But please, I need more time."

Eva's eyes brightened the moment the two entered the operations deck. "I've set our course to go by *Teratopton*."

Casey ordered a coffee from the Originator.

"You remember, Casey. The black hole you wanted to see. We should reach it in a few days."

"Thanks," Casey said. She took the seat next to Eva. "I'm here to relieve you. Anything I should know?"

"Nope, all's quiet." Whether from her lack of excitement at seeing *Teratopton*, or her bleak mood being more obvious than Casey realized, she could sense Eva's probing eyes visually assessing her. "How are you feeling? I can stay up here a while longer if you need more rest."

"That's okay. I'm doing much better." Casey displayed a positive grin and held it until Eva toddled away with Parrow at her side. Several hours later Parrow returned to sit with her. They looked over the maps in silence, both exploring the vast space around them. Casey was getting ready to transfer the data of a planet from the long-range visuals to the screen on the desk, when a very minute object caught her eye.

"Hey, Parrow, what's this?"

He peered over after first downing the rest of his chocolate milk. "I'm not sure. See if you can pull it up on the monitor."

She did, but the image was still too far away for the computer to recognize it.

"Hmm, it's probably a meteor."

Casey shook her head. "No, it's going way too fast, and it looks to be traveling on our trajectory."

"No, it's not. See how it's hovering to the left," Parrow said.

"Parrow, it's going back and forth. Look closer. I think it's trying to throw us off, or maybe it's moving like that to keep us from identifying it."

"Okay, Dick Tracy, I'm going to get some of Mom's cake. Do you want any?"

Casey said, "Yes, please," and kept her eyes glued to the screen. As soon as he stepped away, she soared to her feet. "Damn!"

Parrow spun the moment Casey pressed the alert button, sending off sirens and flashing red and orange lights throughout the ship. "What the heck are you doing?" he asked, hurrying to the front desk.

She tuned out his protest while searching for the closest patrol squadron. By the time the personnel from the team were making their way onto the deck, Casey was already communicating with the head officer from patrol group Bravlon Seven.

"Parrow, what's going on?" Elizabeth asked, with the rest of the team gathering around.

"I haven't a clue," he replied, before pointing to the tiny spot on the screen. "Casey was observing this object, which I told her was probably a meteor. The next thing I know, she's freaking out."

"Bravlon Seven, this is Vasar Six. We need immediate assist at these coordinates." Casey typed in the numbers and letters.

"We copy, Vasar Six. We're on our way."

Eva placed in an earpiece. "Talk to me, Casey. What've you got."

"Watch this tiny formation here on the monitor. I'm positive it's Erule."

"Can you upload the data?"

"It's still too far, but it's advancing at a steady rate."

"We can't be sure what the dot is." Parrow retook his seat. "And Casey, the chances Erule ships could sneak this far inside our region is astronomical. You need to wait before requesting emergency assistance from the Universal Fleet."

"No, because if I'm right, once the ships get close enough to identify, it'll be too late."

Elizabeth stepped in closer and placed a hand on Casey's shoulder. "All right, tell us what you know."

"Look, watch the way the image distorts. See there, it's like the shape changes."

"So?" Parrow asked, leaning in closer to examine the tiny dot.

"So, there are multiple vessels," Hanna said. "Casey's right."

"Okay, there are at least two. What does that tell us?" Elizabeth did not take her eyes off the monitor.

Casey explained the importance to her grandmother as Eva operated the adjoining workstation. "In Barick's strategies class, I learned the Erules used this trap in the First Great War. They'd move like this to keep from being detected, and all in one fluid motion to hide their numbers."

"Flying so close to each other is a highly dangerous maneuver, one the Erules haven't used for many years." Fayrel sounded worried. "Especially in their newer vessels, it'd be damn near impossible."

Hanna was quick to respond. "As far as we know. We rarely encounter Erules until it's too late."

Positive these were enemy ships, Casey gestured to a slightly larger dot. "Now look at the very top of the silhouette. Do you see this blip? I think they're the Erule SRB Destroyers."

"How far away is the patrol you called in?" Eva was definitely troubled by Casey's belief. She punched in commands on the computer.

Casey searched for the information. "Three Crogons away."

"Change directions. I want you to head us straight for Bravlon Seven." Eva readied Vasar Six's weaponry. "Don't forget to check the substance detection map first."

"Do you think we'll make it?" Hanna asked.

"We're closer and faster. Of course, we'll make it," Fayrel said, holding tight to Tanille's hand.

Hanna turned to Fayrel and the others. "If Casey's right and they are SRB Destroyers, they have a highly charged engine which gives them a brief short-range boost, even after Crogonic travel is reached."

Casey bit her bottom lip in anger. How could she forget about Vashee? She asked Parrow, "Can you find Vashee and put her in her seat?"

At once, he darted from the room.

"If we make it through this unscathed, I'll see Barick gives you a good mark in his class," Hanna said.

Parrow returned a few minutes later, followed by Vashee. Eva instructed everyone to strap themselves into their seats. They all waited, eyes glued to the screen, as the dots grew steadily larger.

A vision flashed before Casey's eyes. She saw a beam of light fire at Vasar Six, hitting them to the left of the operations deck. The casualties were great, ending with the death of Hanna and Fayrel.

The touch from her grandmother brought her swiftly to the present. "What did you see?"

Casey gave her a painful grimace that spoke volumes. "Hanna, you and Fayrel need to move to seats closer to the back. Eva, as soon as they boost, steer us to the left as sharp as you can."

Casey spun toward Elizabeth. "I saw us take a critical hit. Hanna and Fayrel died."

Elizabeth pivoted to make sure the three switched seats and fastened themselves in. Suddenly, everything happened at once. Three deadly SRB destroyers sprang ahead straight at them. Eva veered the ship as Casey had instructed her to do, barely avoiding the velocity rocket.

Casey spotted a patrol of eight ships enter the area, going right for the Erule destroyers. The surrounding space filled with colorful blasts of light and exploding ships. Eva moved their vessel a safe distance away and the team silently watched. Within minutes, the fight was over. The only thing left of the enemy was bits and pieces of floating metal and charred debris.

"Copy, Commander, and thanks for your help," Eva said into her earpiece. "Two patrol ships will accompany us the rest of the way. Sorry, but we'll need to postpone your black hole excursion for another trip."

"That's fine," Casey said, no longer feeling overly excited about seeing it anyway.

Hanna and Fayrel thanked Casey once the team received the "all clear" from Eva. The same moment Parrow unhooked Vashee, Tanille departed the operations deck after sidestepping to avoid Casey. Straightening, Parrow wheeled to Fayrel. "Could you watch Casey's spot here? I think she needs to work off some of her stress. A quick game of wallball should do the trick."

"Yes, exercise is very therapeutic. Take all the time you need."

Parrow was the first to enter the arena after they suited up. Casey thought it odd how excited Parrow was acting over a game he knew he would lose. Yet, he was a Blunion, and stranger things excited him, so she pushed it from her mind. He strolled over to the dispenser and withdrew one of the silver balls.

Casey put her helmet on the floor for a quick stretch. "I'm sorry I've been moody lately. I thought staying secluded would help me feel better. I guess I was wrong."

"I'm sorry too. I only hope you'll realize later I do this because I care about and want the best for you."

"Do what?" Casey asked.

She made out a flash of the silver streak from the ball a split second before the circular object impacted with her forehead, sending her world into complete darkness.

Casey awoke sometime later with a massive headache. She brought her hand up to her forehead, trying to recall exactly what happened. She sat straight up, realizing she was still in her wallball outfit, and her temper flared. "Parrow!"

"He left five minutes ago. I can call him back." Tanille's voice was angry, yet hushed.

Casey didn't say a word. She only sat on the exam table, peering motionless into Tanille's hazel eyes. She opened her mouth to speak, but nothing came out.

Tanille spun away and removed two pills from a dispenser. "I fixed the knot on your head, but you still need to take something for the pain." She handed the pills to Casey and went to get a glass of water.

"I love you." Casey wasn't sure why she said it, but it felt right.

Tanille reeled on her, enraged. "How can you speak of love? I don't believe you're capable of—" She stopped, took a deep breath, and twisted herself away from Casey.

Casey watched as the back of Tanille's body shook with either rage or tears. She felt confused, unsure of what to do or say to make this better. "Did I do something wrong?" she finally asked.

Tanille handed Casey the glass of water with tears streaming down her cheeks. "Please take your pills and go," she whispered.

Casey climbed off the table. Her heart ached, yet all her anger over what she had gone through these last several days was inflating. She grabbed Tanille by the arm. "I deserve a reason!"

"You deserve nothing from me. Now let me go!"

"Why are you acting like this? I love you!" Tanille's increase in tears extinguished Casey's anger as fast as it entered, and she pulled her into a firm embrace. "Please, talk to me," she begged.

"I refuse to share you with anyone."

Confused, Casey took a step backward. "What are you talking about?"

"You know what I'm talking about. Him…your lover. Oh, I'm sorry, I mean your friend!"

Casey was beside herself. "Are you referring to Parrow?"

Tanille jerked sideways, breaking Casey's grip. "Yes, Parrow. I saw you together when we were coming out of the store."

"This has all been about Parrow and me?" she asked, as painful emotions from the last several days resurfaced. "I had something in my eye. He was getting it out. Tanille, he's a Blunion."

Tanille pivoted sharply so her back was once again facing Casey. "Relationships with Blunions and Trysals have been known to exist. Plus, my father said you loved him."

"I do love him. He's my best friend. I already told you that." Casey inhaled slowly, attempting to control her anger. It didn't work. "Not to mention," Casey said, with a sharp edge to her voice. "Parrow's gay, and if you don't know what that means, he's only attracted to other males."

On the verge of losing control altogether, Casey stormed from the room.

As Casey entered the elevator to return to the operations deck, she tried her best to rid herself of her anger. Nothing worked. Even the shower she took after leaving the medical wing didn't help. Every time she cleared her mind, thoughts of the pain she'd experienced the last few days, along with the vision of Parrow hitting her on the head with the silver ball, kept popping up.

Oh, how she wanted to run into Parrow right at this moment. She balled her fist at the thought of his name. She needed to lash out at something, anything. Right now, he seemed to be her most satisfying choice.

She entered the operations deck with heavy disappointment. He was nowhere around. Probably hiding, Casey thought, sitting irritably in the chair on the other side of Eva.

"Is everything all right?" Fayrel asked with a frown.

"I'm fine. I got hit in the head with the wallball."

"Oh, goodness. Tanille's down in the medical wing if you need to see her."

"I did, and thanks. I'm fine." Casey kept her eyes on the screen and brooded.

"I'm off to the medical wing," Fayrel said. "Unless you need me to stay longer?"

Casey shook her head no, her mind racing angrily in two different directions. First, she wanted to beat the crap out of Parrow. Second, she felt torn, unsure of what to do regarding Tanille. Throughout the rest of her duty, Casey noticed how Eva frequently peeked her way. Eva didn't express any concerns or pound her with questions, and for this Casey was grateful. She knew she was unpleasant to be around, but until she vented, her anger had nowhere to go.

Once Hanna came up to relieve her, Casey headed straight for the simulation room. Chasel showed her how to design her own simulation program in their class together, and she'd done so to exercise in a personal workout room she created. Today she didn't select a running track. There were no weights or machines of any kind. She only programmed a single punching bag hanging in the middle of the matted room. She silently wished it came with Parrow's face plastered directly in the center.

After changing into some loose workout shorts and a tank top, Casey shoved on the boxing gloves and entered the room shoeless. She normally played hip-hop or alternative music when she worked out, but today, the hidden surround sound cranked out classic rock. She began throwing several hard punches, then after relaxing her mind and redirecting her anger onto the workout, Casey put everything she had into destroying the bag.

For over thirty minutes straight, she sent a combination of kicks and punches, one right after the other, directly into the bag. She wasn't planning on stopping until fatigue got the better of her. Which hopefully wouldn't be any time soon. The workout felt wonderful. To have something other than pent-up anger to focus on. A healthy approach to alleviating her troubled mind and body. Life and the problems plaguing her heart didn't seem as overwhelming, or her temper as out-of-control, since stepping foot inside this dimly lit room doused in red.

Over an hour had passed when the door behind her opened. "Man, you're really upset with me. The last time I saw you attack a bag like that, I was a dog, and you'd hit a dead end on your first murder case."

Casey paused briefly to look at him. After flinging one good scowl his way she continued to assault the bag. "What do you want?"

"Your form has improved since then, but you still need to learn to—"

"I forgive you, all right," she panted through clenched teeth. "I understand your intent, not your method. Can you please leave now? I'd like to be alone." She wiped hot sweat off her face with the back of her glove.

"Forgiveness would be nice, but I can tell you're not ready yet. I probably wouldn't be either."

"So why are you here?" she asked, not willing to break from her workout.

"Tanille came to see me."

Casey misjudged her high round kick and caught the bag wrong, throwing her slightly off balance. She recovered quickly enough, but instead of continuing her workout, she gave him her full attention.

"She told me what she'd thought about me and you. I explained to her how the idea was crazy and how you're like my little sister." He gestured toward the door before continuing. "She apologized like a zillion times, and she wanted to know if I'd seen you or knew where you might be."

Casey glowered from him to the door. "Stop music!" The loud rumbling beat, which echoed out around the room, fell silent on her command. She puffed out her chest with a steady intake of air. "Tell me she's not here."

He raised his eyebrows. "Okay, she's not here."

Casey spun, sending a hard hit into the center of the bag. "I don't want to see her. Tell her what you want, so long as she leaves."

"You don't have to talk to me, but I'm asking you to please listen."

Parrow and Casey both twirled toward Tanille, surprised she'd entered the room. No one spoke for over twenty awkward seconds until Casey squared her shoulders and pivoted to the bag. "Music on!" Her punches came harder than before, as a fresh wave of anger teetered on the edge of her losing control.

Tanille motioned for Parrow to follow her from the room. As soon as the door closed, silencing the loud, rhythmic thud, Parrow frowned at Tanille. "I'm sorry, Tanille. When Casey gets like this, it's best to let her be until it blows over. Remember, she's going through the change."

Tanille ordered an extra set of boxing gloves. "Could you help me put these on?"

"Don't even think about it. Casey's not only stronger but better trained than you." He waved away the gloves she was holding out to him.

"Do you honestly believe she'd hit me?"

Parrow considered the question. "Normally I'd say no, but she's also going through her adulthood transformation and is quite pissed at the both of us. Either way, I wouldn't bet money on her ability to control herself."

"I'll take my chances." She handed him the gloves.

His sigh was long and thick with worry. "I hope you know what you're doing."

By the time Tanille reentered the room, a new song was blaring out to an almost unbearable pitch. She treaded a few feet in before instructing the music to once again switch off. Casey ignored the simulator falling into silence and took her frustrations out on the bag.

Tanille felt awkward but held her ground. "I only have one thing to say, and I'll leave you alone."

"Music on," Casey shouted, throwing three quick jabs.

"Music off."

Casey spun and glared at Tanille. "I don't want to talk to you!"

"I know. You're angry and want to strike out." Tanille took a step closer. "So fight me if it'll make you feel better."

Casey opened her mouth to speak but said nothing. Tanille took two more steps and cleared her throat.

"Save it. I want to be left alone." Casey reeled away from Tanille. "Now if you don't mind…"

"I made a mistake. What will it take for you to forgive me?" Tanille watched as Casey closed herself and her feelings off and directed her pain and confusion into the bag once again.

Squaring her shoulders, Tanille marched over to stand beside Casey. "Fight me."

Casey started to swing at the bag as if she hadn't noticed Tanille.

"I said fight me!" Tanille shoved Casey with her gloved hands as hard as she could. Her efforts produced little movement.

"Leave me alone!"

"You want to hit something, so hit me!" Tanille raised her fists.

"First you assume I'm cheating on you, and when I tell you I'm not, you don't believe me. Now you have it in your head I'm actually capable of hitting you." She stood to her full height. "You don't think much of me, do you?"

"I was wrong. I can't take back my mistakes. If I could, I would."

"No, you can't, and I'm too busy for childish games."

Tanille made a move to push her again, but Casey deflected Tanille's hands, while using her right leg to sweep Tanille's legs out from under her. Both women fell to the floor, Casey landing on top of her.

"Leave me alone!" Casey's jaw clenched as she spoke, her face inches away. "You owe me nothing. What we had together is gone. Short-lived and I've found peace with it."

Tanille swiveled her head to the side. Her tears fell. "I was judging you for being human. I thought you were going to break my heart. I was mistaken—"

"Mistaken? Do you know what you did to me? I've never felt so much pain in my life." She tried to swallow away the lump building in her throat. "I refuse to let that happen again."

Tanille reached for her, but Casey pinned her arms to the floor. "You plan to shut off your feelings like shutting off a program?"

"Yes. And what I do is none of your business."

"I love you, Casey."

"Don't you dare! I'm over you!" Casey glared at Tanille's moist eyes. Her heart broke in the face of the Trysal's pain, bringing her own anger to subside. She wasn't sure if most of this anger was directed at Tanille or at herself for being so unforgiving.

"I love you. The distrust I felt will never happen again," Tanille whispered.

Casey moved off into a sitting position next to Tanille. "Please, leave. I can't go through this a second time."

Tanille slowly sat up. "The last thing I ever wanted was to hurt you. I'm deeply sorry. Please give me—give us another chance."

Casey covered her face with her gloved hands and cried. She hated showing weakness in the presence of others, but she couldn't control it. Tanille reached over and wrapped Casey's limp body in her arms, and within a few long moments, Casey's frame melted into her embrace.

"I love you, but I don't want to."

Tanille nodded slowly. "I understand, and I'm truly sorry."

Casey peered into Tanille's eyes. "I'd never cheat on you. I know it in my heart. The very thought of being with another makes me feel sick to my stomach."

Tanille pulled Casey in tightly and whispered in her ear. "I'll never mistrust you again." She pressed her lips onto Casey's forehead, then her cheek, and finally their lips touched. Casey didn't deny her as the brush of flesh evolved into a kiss. A heated connection that overflowed with both love and tenderness.

Chapter Eleven

Earth Date: 1st November 2042
Unforeseen Intruder

On the first day of November, fifteen days before Casey's twenty-fifth birthday, Vasar Six arrived on Earth. Casey spent the rest of the voyage with Tanille, where they grew closer to one another. To aid both women's needed connection, Parrow and Vashee entertained the other with wrestling matches and devoting their free time to the rest of the crew.

It took over an hour for the team to unload the ship, and another hour for Casey to go through the DNA Modifier. Afterward Casey introduced Tanille to Darren and Barick. They had not yet eaten, so Casey escorted Tanille to the kitchen with Vashee to enjoy her first Earth-prepared meal.

"What are you thinking?" Tanille asked between bites of granola cereal.

Casey smiled. "I was thinking about you."

Tanille raised her eyebrows. "Is it good or bad?"

Casey amusingly slanted her lips. "Well—" This resulted in a playful slap to her arm.

"You hit like a girl." Casey leaned across the table and kissed Tanille fully on the lips.

"It's nice to see you both are getting along. I'm not sure what happened between you two, but I'm glad it's finally passed." Elizabeth poured herself a bowl of cereal. "I take it Casey prepared this glorious meal."

Tanille stifled a laugh and Casey squinted. "Hey, I had to fetch everything from the pantry, the cabinets, and the refrigerator. I worked up a sweat."

"I know, sweetie, we take you for granted." Elizabeth shot her a brief smile before continuing with a more serious undertone. "Now, have you two set a union date or spoken to Fayrel?"

All at once, the pieces of the puzzle came together. Casey realized her grandmothers, Ann and Elizabeth, had concocted their abstinence lecture on Vasar to push her into marriage. How devious the women in her family were. This time, Casey was the one who faked a solemn front. "We actually haven't discussed marriage, but I assure you, you and Fayrel will be the first to know."

Elizabeth spoke plainly. "What about our agreement?"

"We're practicing abstinence, as per our agreement," Casey said, as her mind tangoed a tiny victory dance.

Elizabeth's fleeting look of surprise shot from Casey to Tanille, who nodded with a slight blush. "You're both fine with this?"

"We don't have a choice." Tanille sounded disappointed.

"I find it refreshing." Casey lied, but she was convincing enough to fool her grandmother. "You were right, Gran. We truly *are* getting to know one another." The agonizing truth, their abstinence, was becoming unbearable. The more she was around Tanille, the stronger her pains from self-denial grew.

"Wonderful to hear. I'm proud of you both." Elizabeth picked up her half-empty bowl. "I guess I'll leave you two to your breakfast, and don't forget your classes resume first thing tomorrow morning."

Casey saw the unsettled look in Gran's eyes when she headed to the door. The edge of her lip turned upward. She would bet good money Gran was on her way to send an urgent message to Grandmother Ann. Their Machiavellian plan was backfiring.

Tanille spoke softly once Elizabeth left the room. "Can I ask you a personal question?"

Casey rolled her eyes. "Personal questions are all we've been asking each other lately. I'm sure one more won't make a difference."

Tanille didn't meet Casey's eyes. "Don't you find me attractive? I only ask because this relationship has been extremely hard for me. Not that I've not enjoyed it, but I feel like I'm going crazy not being with you."

Casey laid her spoon in her bowl. "I find you extremely attractive. I've never in my life seen anyone as beautiful as you." She struggled with her next set of words. "Every time you talk, or even look at me, it sends a thrill throughout me that is maddening. I experience this raw surge driving me to the edge of sexually attacking you, then I get an excruciating pain in my midsection when I deny myself the pleasure."

Tanille appeared both stunned and pleased. Her words were barely above a whisper. "I need you. If you don't want to marry me, can we please go explain this relationship to my father?"

A wave of dread filled Casey, and she shook her head no. "I can't tell him that." Casey had already decided to ask Tanille to marry her by this evening, but she didn't want to give her surprise away. She arranged for Vashee to bring in the rings later that night, with the box tied with ribbon around her neck when they were alone in the bedroom. "Can we change the subject? I know this issue is important, but I need some more time."

They spent the rest of the day watching old John Wayne movies together in the theater room on the second floor of their wing.

"Before I leave for school, we'll have to travel in time and experience the Old West firsthand," Casey said, thrilled by how much Tanille was enjoying the shows.

"I would love that." Tanille's eyes sparkled with excitement. "To journey across America in a covered wagon." She clasped her hands together. "Can't you picture it? Me cooking stew over the campfire, and you riding a horse with guns strapped to your side."

Casey snorted and laughed at the same time. "Actually, I can. It's a good thing I have this opportunity to educate you properly on Earth culture, before Parrow and the others get ahold of you."

They remained in each other's arms until Casey excused herself. She needed to get everything ready for this evening. She found Vashee, and after thanking her repeatedly, she secured the box to her soul-link.

"I'm delighted I get to be a part of this."

"So am I." Casey threw her arms around the panther, feeling blessed in so many ways. Her life was truly falling into place.

She instructed Vashee to hide in the upstairs office and wait for her signal before entering the bedroom. After Vashee agreed, Casey returned to Tanille to finish the ending of the last movie.

Tanille smiled broadly. "I loved that one the most."

"Yes, Maureen O'Hara and The Duke mesh well together. That one's also my favorite. I really like the end when he spanks her butt with the coal scuttle shovel."

"You would."

"She deserved it with what she put him through."

"She found lipstick on his collar."

"She didn't know how it got there. She didn't ask. She assumed."

Tanille's eyes widened. "Was this supposed to be a learning experience for me?"

After a brief reflection of the similarities, Casey tilted her head. "She does sound a lot like you, doesn't she? Maybe we should watch it again."

Casey jumped backward, avoiding Tanille's playful slap to her arm. "I can tell you're going to be the violent one in our relationship." She pulled Tanille into a fervent kiss.

"I thought we were trying to avoid these intimate moments," Tanille whispered.

Casey enjoyed the warmth of Tanille's hand on her cheek. It made her feel closer, loved. She bent her head for another lingering kiss. "We are. I only needed a little dose of courage before we head upstairs."

Tanille peered longingly at Casey. "You're more courageous than most."

"Not at the moment."

Tanille's expression became one of concern. "Is everything all right?"

"I hope so. Ask me again in twenty minutes."

This didn't relieve Tanille's worried look, but Casey refused to divulge her surprise. She guided Tanille from the room and toward the stairs.

Suddenly, both of their personal computers vibrated and Chasel instantly materialized. "Casey, Barick activated the alert button on Vasar Five. You and Tanille need to head there at once."

With a heavy heart Casey thanked Chasel. *Of all days*, Casey's mind grumbled. She immediately ushered Tanille to the first floor, down the concealed stairs, and out through the passage to Vasar Five. After entering the ship, they made their way to the operations deck. The rest of the team was there when they hurried in, and both Hanna and Eva were at each of the PDRs, like before.

"It's a Velocity Capsule," Parrow whispered to both women. "It already got past two patrols and is hurling for a place in southern Texas."

"Why there?"

Parrow mouthed, "I have no idea," right as Hanna and Eva fired at the target.

"Damn it!" Hanna shouted. All eyes were now on the screen. The capsule had shifted direction directly after both women fired.

"Impossible," Eva insisted.

"I didn't think capsules could maneuver like that," Casey muttered to Parrow.

"They can't. Not until today," Parrow said. "They're not designed for directional operation. They're too compact for such technology. It's more like aiming a missile at a target and firing."

Barick said, loud enough for all to hear, "Whatever happened, it's now going to touch down on the outskirts of a small community fifty miles outside the Malanight border."

Elizabeth glared at Barick, then at the screen. She spun toward Eva. "Send out a message informing Universal Command of the situation. You'll stay here with Parrow and Casey." She motioned to the rest of the team. "The rest of us are going to Vasar Six."

Casey pivoted to Tanille, who wrapped her arms around her for a hurried embrace. "Be safe, I can't lose you," Casey said, as fear weighed heavily on her chest.

"I will." Tanille placed a gentle kiss on Casey's lips.

When they broke apart, Casey realized Fayrel was patiently waiting for Tanille, who blushed slightly at his curious assessment. Casey watched them exit the room before she went up front to sit with Eva and Parrow, behind the main control desk.

"Did you ask her yet?" questioned Parrow.

Eva peered over to Parrow. "Ask who what?"

Parrow's face glowed. "She's popping the question to Tanille."

Casey punched Parrow hard in the arm. To Eva she said, "Please don't tell anyone. I was getting ready to ask her when this happened."

An alarm sounded, and Casey saw "hangar outer doors opened," flashing in red on the screen. Her heart felt heavy with worry. How much training did Tanille have? Would she be with the group, or would they all separate, leaving her alone? Vulnerable.

Eva squeezed Casey's hand. "She'll be fine. They all will be. Plus, this'll be a good chance for her to gain some experience with planetary emergencies. It's only one capsule."

Casey calmly acknowledged Eva's reassurance, yet her insides felt out of control. She wished she could've gone to protect her, but her gran ordered her to remain behind to watch and wait. She hadn't even been able to give Tanille her engagement ring yet.

"Oh shit, I forgot Vashee!" Casey shot to her feet. "She's waiting for me in my upstairs office. She was going to surprise Tanille with the rings."

Parrow seized her arm. "You aren't leaving until the threat is clear."

"Like hell I'm not. Vashee is my soul-link, and I'm not about to abandon her."

Eva stood. "Grab some weapons and take Parrow. I can watch this until you return."

"What's going on between you and Casey?" Fayrel asked Tanille the second they boarded the ship.

Tanille peered over, meeting Elizabeth's gaze. Brief, but long enough of a connection for Fayrel to notice the exchange.

"Is someone going to enlighten me on the situation, or should I guess?" he asked, staring at both women.

Elizabeth sighed and motioned for Tanille to tell him. She started from the beginning, as Barick piloted the vessel out. Tanille explained about their connection when first meeting on Vasar One, continuing with the trouble they had during their time out shopping. After she filled him in on their present situation, Fayrel sat and stared uncertainly at her.

"I'm sorry we didn't tell you. I know we don't have the normal relationship you're accustomed to—"

Fayrel held up his hand to her and addressed Elizabeth. "Why didn't you tell me?"

Elizabeth shook her head. "I have no justifiable excuse. I truly am sorry for keeping their relationship from you."

Knowing Elizabeth didn't deserve to be blamed for a decision she and Casey made, Tanille interjected. "She wanted us to tell you, but we were waiting to see how everything turned out."

He crossed his arms and stared out of the closest porthole. After taking a moment to mull over the information, he asked, "Are you in love with her?"

"More than I could have believed possible."

"And does she feel the same?"

"Yes."

His attention went to Elizabeth. "What do you think of this relationship?"

"Not what I hoped for, but considering Casey has chosen so well, I can live with it. For the time being anyway." She directed the last part more toward Tanille than Fayrel.

He frowned slightly. "I suppose I feel the same, Elizabeth." Fayrel paused long enough to throw his daughter an intense stare. "It would be nice to help plan your ceremony soon, so please don't take too long."

Tanille let out a long, steady breath. She wasn't the one dragging her feet, but she wasn't about to let Casey take the blame either. "Yes, Father."

"CSF Virus detected." Barick's warning brought the three of them quickly back from their conversation.

"Can you tell how many casualties we have so far?" Fayrel asked. He stood and motioned for Tanille to join him.

As his fingers worked over the controls on the screen, Barick said, "I'm not sure, but I'll let you know."

"Set off the sleeping agent. We'll need to go in," Elizabeth instructed.

Fayrel and Tanille went to the medical wing, returning moments later with several prepacked kits. He motioned for her to vaccinate the crew while he double-checked their bags. Once completed, Elizabeth directed Barick to land.

Barick powered down Vasar Six, and rotated his seat from the main console. "So far, three humans are infected, and the virus is spreading."

Elizabeth took one of the medical kits. "Fayrel, Tanille, and I will work on treating those who are still alive. Darren, you and Hanna will neutralize and kill the virus. Barick, you locate the capsule and its occupant." She checked her weapon. "Set your communication for open channel, and report all you can. Safety of the team must come first. You all know what your mission is, so let's get moving."

The moment they teleported to the surface, they fanned off in their assigned directions, each wearing a bright-red medical jumper and mask to conceal their appearance. The ship was already undetectable to unwanted onlookers, tracking devices, and radars. If all went well, and they found the velocity capsule, its occupant, and the virus, there would be no proof an alien presence had ever breached this town.

Night was falling fast, and within fifteen minutes of entering the sleeping town, Tanille had already spotted her first three dead victims. She entered the second residence of a street containing single-story houses, and discovered a mother, father, and a little boy, no older than five, dead, face down at the dinner table. She tried everything she could to spark life but couldn't. They were gone.

Shaking, Tanille remained temporarily unsteady. She examined each of the deceased and purged the bodies and surrounding area of the virus.

She tended to the lifeless child last and found the simple task of pressing a button close to his pale lips extremely difficult to accomplish. Even with her training at the Academy, nothing could've prepared her for this. Her heart filled with sorrow, and she gasped silently for air.

She knew this virus to be deadly, extremely painful, and fast-acting. All the damage would be on the inside of the victims' bodies, leaving no trace of visual abnormalities to indicate something unnatural occurred. All she could do was close her watery eyes in prayer for the unfortunate family and continue on to help others who might still be alive.

The next house was the same, taking the life of an elderly woman and her two cats. At the fourth house, all four occupants and their two canines were unconscious but still alive. She treated them as fast as she could.

"Tanille, how's it going?" Fayrel sounded slightly worried.

Tanille pressed a red diamond on her personal computer. "I'm finishing up with my fourth home. So far, I have four dead humans and two felines. Four humans and two canines are recovering."

"All clear on this side of town," Elizabeth said.

Fayrel presented his report. "Same here. Looks like we caught the beginning stage."

The sound broke slightly when Hanna's voice came on. "We destroyed the remaining virus. We're going to do one last sweep before we head in."

Elizabeth said, "Fayrel, let's meet at Tanille's location, and we'll do what we can to make this appear like an unfortunate accident. Since we've localized the casualties to two homes, let's rig an explosion in the gas lines. Barick, how's it going?"

"I'm almost to the capsule, Elizabeth, but something about this landing doesn't feel right."

"Nothing about this feels right." Hanna's voice was insistent, and Tanille silently agreed. "Starting from how that capsule could change direction upon entry, to the inconsequential size of this outbreak." The communication went silent. "This attack was staged. I'm sure of it," Hanna said.

Tanille gazed at her personal computer and debated contacting Casey. The sound of Barick's voice made her jump. "I found the capsule. Its occupant has fled, but they left an electronic pad inside. It's damaged, but I might be able to tap into its memory core from the ship's computers."

"Take care of the capsule and meet us on the ship as soon as you can." Elizabeth sounded deeply vexed. Was she also thinking about Casey?

Tanille finished her examination, then impatiently waited for Elizabeth and her father to show. Once the three of them checked the remaining homes in the area, treated those contaminated, and made the deaths appear as a human-made accident, all three hurried to the ship. Tanille entered to a picture of Casey plastered on the main screen.

"I found this on the pad's core that I pulled from the capsule," Barick said. "We still haven't located the intruder?"

"No," Tanille muttered.

Elizabeth spun toward Hanna. "Contact Eva and let her know what's happening."

Before Vasar Six powered up, Hanna addressed Elizabeth with her finger pressed into her earpiece. "I'm getting no response."

"Barick, get us to the castle as fast as possible," Elizabeth ordered.

Tanille anxiously rushed to her seat.

"She's not here," Casey said, after doing another sweep through the top floor of her quarters. "Chasel, can you try to locate Vashee again?"

"I still do not detect her anywhere inside your team's quarters."

Parrow rushed into Casey's living room panting, as Casey repeated the call to Vashee telepathically. "Maybe she's in the main castle looking for the others," he said.

Chasel space off for a second before responding, "No, I don't pick her up there either. I'm also getting an unknown distortion that's preventing me from searching the surrounding grounds."

"Check your system and make sure it's working properly. Maybe there's a glitch or a corrupt file." Parrow turned to Casey. "We'll find her. Let's go check the main part of the castle."

Agreeing, Casey rushed with him across the archway. They started on the top floor together before splitting off to speed up the search.

Within the first ten minutes, Eva's voice rang out from Casey's personal computer. "There's a breach in the outer areas of the property, and I lost communication with Vasar Six. I want you both back here now!"

Casey pressed the diamond on the side of her Personal Computer. "Parrow, have you found Vashee yet?"

"No, but we need to do as Eva said. Where are you a—"

"Parrow? Parrow, are you there?" She waited, but no response came. "Eva, I've lost communication with Parrow. Can you try to reach him?" Again, she received no answer.

Before she could take another step, the lights in the castle switched off. Feeling her neck muscles tighten, she spun and searched both directions of the long grayish hall. She gripped the handle of her weapon. Thank God her gifts blessed her with the ability to see in the dark.

"Chasel, can you spot Parrow for me?" When Chasel didn't answer, Casey tried to reach Jasper, but her effort was met with only silence.

Moving her body out of the open and against the wall, Casey's heart pounded. She silently prayed for the safety of her companions, while her natural sense to protect those she loved pushed her steadily on. She tried to lock on to Parrow's vision, but she couldn't. She was too overwrought regarding his safety to make the connection.

As she reached the stairwell to the second floor, she caught movement out of the corner of her eye, sending her gaze outside the window. A massive dark figure moved in the moonlight, running toward the castle. She knew the mass wasn't Vashee. This form was moving on two legs. The bulk of the figure also suggested this being wasn't someone on the team. The shadowy silhouette veered to the left, showing off a thick spiky tail. Her eyes widened, and she held her breath. Erule. Could it be?

She ran the rest of the way down the stairs, taking two at a time, moving from one window to the next, monitoring her moving target. By the time she hit the main floor, the unknown creature dodged into cover in the shadows of a row of evergreen trees. Casey froze by the corner of the next window. She wasn't positive if the creature had spotted her observing its whereabouts. If so, it would know where she was. As she was deciding her best course of action, the creature darted from behind the grouping of trees and sprinted straight for the main door.

She broke into a full sprint. Unrefined adrenaline drove her on with no thought of what to do once she encountered this beast. For this thing was a beast, the worst kind. She knew it, could sense it. Part of her screamed out a warning to proceed with caution, yet the wiring connecting her fight-or-flight mechanism commanded her to fight. She moved swiftly, running in the same direction as fast as she could, unable to view her target any longer.

Once she reached the door, Casey halted at the sound of a thunderous scuffle on the other side. She could make out the distinct echoes of violent shouting and pounding of angry fists. Not daring to wait a moment longer, Casey burst from the main doors, a mixture of fear and fury rising inside her.

She saw Parrow go flying against the stone wall of the castle and the outline of a weapon pointing at the center of his belly. Parrow climbed to his feet and wobbled forward. Not having a clean shot with Parrow in the way, Casey sprang for the creature, knocking the stunned beast and weapon to the ground. She tumbled with it, losing her own weapon on impact.

The putrid smell of bodily waste filled her nose. Unable to resist the urge, she peered into his dark, hairy face. Her stomach turned. He looked more horrid than any creature she had yet encountered with ugly, dark red skin and sharp, pointy teeth. With the strength of a long, spiky tail and outstretched claws, he resembled a prehistoric alligator on two legs. One with a hollowed-out nose and a square jaw, which had a hint of a human resemblance. His eyes were a dark yellow and appeared to glow brighter as they studied her face. She scurried quickly to her feet.

"Casey, run. I'll take care of him," Parrow shouted.

"Casey Malanight?" the creature croaked. He pulled his lips back in a revolting sneer and stood, towering over her by a good two feet.

Casey sent all the strength in her body toward his hideous face. Her fist made contact, sending the creature backward with a high-pitched screech. Parrow knocked her to the side and rushed in. Never had she seen such anger come from her friend. He ripped and tore into the beast, like a starved mountain lion tearing into its prey.

The commotion of approaching people brought her head around toward the direction of the stables. She could barely make out her name from their far-off shouts, and she assumed they were instructing her to run. How could she when Parrow was fighting this monstrous creature? Casey turned in time to see the bleeding trespasser pick up a hefty rock and smash it into the side of Parrow's head.

She leapt forward, surprised to see her guard still fighting for her safety after a blow like that. The creature raised the rock again. She lunged in with another hard right across the beast's jaw. It stumbled sideways, tripped over its feet, and tumbled awkwardly to the ground.

"Damn it, will you run?!" demanded Parrow.

"You run. You're the one bleeding everywhere." She glanced over at the creature on the ground, startled to see an evil smile on his face. Her gaze dropped to his moving hand, and she noticed with frozen fear he was wearing a miniature monitor with a built-in keypad on his right arm. His fingers stroked frantically across the keypad, and she sprang upon him once more.

"He's sending a message," Casey shouted.

"Don't let him send it!" Parrow dived for the other side of the creature. A loud beep sounded. "Damn it!"

Parrow's protest brought an amused howl from the creature. The beast caught Parrow off guard with his elbow and kicked Casey hard on her knee. Its brute strength was astounding. She heard the painful *pop* that buckled her on the spot as horrific pain shot through her leg.

"Get your weapon and shoot him," Parrow shouted. Casey stumbled for her gun, but the beast also moved, reaching it seconds before her. Her knee gave out, bringing her once again to the ground.

"Parrow, get down," Casey screamed out as the creature rolled, aiming the weapon at Parrow's chest.

Life for Casey played out in slow motion. Like a sick, twisted joke from Father Time. Parrow pivoted to the creature and froze. He was too far away. Casey watched Parrow's eyes fall on hers, where they softened, as if saying farewell to a dear friend. Casey's heart ripped in two. She, like Parrow, lunged toward the enemy, both knowing it would be too late.

A brutal snarl reverberated throughout the black sky. The creature's head whipped to the side. A heart-stopping screech of a roar followed, bringing with it a pair of glowing eyes from the charging panther.

"Vashee!" The cavalry was here!

Vashee's muscular strides were long, and the distance between her and her target was closing fast.

Spinning his arm wildly around, the creature discharged two uncontrolled shots. Vashee stumbled slightly, before diving teeth first, straight into her enemy's throat. Vashee held on, as bright red blood poured out of a gaping wound on her side. Within seconds, Vashee's powerful jaws ended the life of the monster.

Casey remained on the ground, unable to move. Something wasn't right. Her mind raced a million miles a minute, trying to see what was directly in front of her. Obscurity melted into loss, then despair. As reality washed in, a fire spread through her insides so great, it felt like everything beneath her flesh was turning to mush. "No!" Casey cried in panic, her arm stretched out in need. "Vashee." This time, Casey all but whispered the word.

Forcing her three working limbs to function, Casey crawled forward, reaching the unmoving panther at the same time as Parrow. She yanked off her shirt, and covered the saturated spot on Vashee's injured chest, where the blast from the weapon had struck her.

"Casey, move!" Fayrel's voice sounded like a far-off murmur.

With Parrow's help, Tanille and Elizabeth removed Casey from Vashee's body. Casey didn't care that she was openly crying or bothered by the excruciating pain in her knee. Mentally and physically, she felt numb. Even the soft hands holding her up were surreal.

Casey watched Parrow stroke Vashee's head, while she spiritually told her soul-link repeatedly to "*hold on.*" She followed in a trance behind the group, leaning most of her weight on Elizabeth's and Tanille's shoulders, as the team moved Vashee and the dead creature through the castle to the medical area below.

"She's going to be all right," Tanille continually reassured her.

Casey's eyes didn't lift from the unresponsive cat positioned on a table close to her own until Fayrel programmed a barrier to separate the two beds. Her entire body shook, as Tanille and Elizabeth fought with her to remain on the table.

"Fayrel's going to do everything he can. You can't help her right now, Casey, so let Tanille fix your leg while we wait," Elizabeth pleaded in a motherly tone.

Tanille's soft hands guided Casey into a lying position on the table. The young healer ran a machine over her injured leg. "She has a shattered kneecap and the ligament's torn," she said to Elizabeth. "It'll take some time, but I can repair it."

"I'm fine. Please, I need to be with Vashee." Casey jerked her head up when Parrow exited the newly partitioned room.

He avoided Casey's eyes. "Your father's asking for your help."

Tanille nodded, squeezing Casey's arm before she left. Casey moved to sit up, but Elizabeth and Parrow coaxed her into remaining still.

"How's your head?" Elizabeth asked Parrow.

"I'll be okay," he said before squinting nervously toward Vashee's exam room.

Casey couldn't tell if his observing eyes held hope or loss. With a heavy heart, Casey twisted her head away as her tears quietly fell.

It felt like an eternity had gone by when the two healers finally emerged from the divided room.

Fayrel approached Casey. "Vashee's stable, but I'll need to keep her here for several days to make sure she heals properly and doesn't get an infection."

Casey was too overwhelmed to speak. She took several deep gulps of air to steady herself.

Tanille came over and wrapped the shaken Casey in her arms. "Your soul-link is as strong as you are."

"Parrow's head is injured," Casey told Fayrel once she thanked him and Tanille for saving Vashee.

"I'll work on Parrow. Tanille, you take care of Casey's leg." He moved to go but stopped and retrieved a box from his pocket. "Oh, Vashee had this tied around her neck. I assume it's yours." He handed it to Casey and took Parrow into another room. Before Parrow vanished from Casey's line of sight, he pointed at the box and covertly to Tanille.

Elizabeth asked, "What's all that about?"

Casey's fingers gripped the box. "I planned this to be different, Tanille, but I should've asked you several days ago."

Casey stood from the table on her good leg, ignoring both women's protests, and gazed affectionately into Tanille's eyes. She did this on her feet, since the thought of going down on her good knee made her injured leg hurt worse. "Tanille…" Casey opened the box. "Would you do me the honor of being my wife?"

The room became silent. Tanille herself was flabbergasted. She leaned in and whisper in Casey's ear, "You don't have to do this."

Casey whispered back, "But I want to."

Tanille threw her arms around Casey's neck.

Casey held her tight, ignoring the fresh jolts of pain.

Releasing Casey, Tanille anxiously inspected Casey's leg and gestured her onto the table. "I'm sorry. Did I hurt you?"

Casey waved it off. "Was that a yes?"

"Yes," Tanille said, her eyes gleaming with her reply. "I'd love to marry you, Casey Malanight. Today, tomorrow, a year from now. My heart is utterly yours."

Chapter Twelve

The Final Lessons

Hanna entered the medical wing as Tanille was finishing the repairs on Casey's leg. The procedure, to Casey's relief, wasn't painful and required no scalpels or cutting of any kind. Tanille conducted the repair with the use of a high-tech handheld contraption that groaned and hummed throughout the entire procedure.

Casey observed Hanna pull Elizabeth aside, where the two women conversed in the far corner, each whispering back and forth so no one else could hear. Hanna looked anxious and off-kilter, especially for her disciplined demeanor. Eventually, Hanna offered a diminutive bow and quickly exited the wing.

Elizabeth signaled for everyone's undivided attention. "As soon as these two are well enough to move, we'll need to hold a group meeting on the operations deck."

"Parrow's about finished," Fayrel said. He glanced curiously over at Tanille. "How's Casey's leg coming?"

"She's healing nicely. I'll need roughly five more minutes to finish repairing the damage."

"Good. I'll tell Hanna and Eva to expect you all shortly." Elizabeth walked over and gave Casey a brief hug, followed by a kiss on her forehead before leaving the room.

"She loves you very much," Tanille said. "When we brought you in, she was sick with worry."

"Were you worried about me?"

Tanille studied the holographic monitor with a relaxed expression. "I knew my woman could take care of herself." She gave a wink, leaned over the exam table, and placed a long kiss on Casey's lips. "To be honest, I was terrified," she murmured when they broke apart.

"I didn't realize the procedure for a busted knee was to perform mouth-to-mouth. Guess I'm unaccustomed to the new techniques they're teaching at the Academy these days," Fayrel said as he moved into the room and grabbed something from the closest cabinet.

Tanille blushed. She pushed a few buttons on the monitor, and the machine lifted from Casey's leg and disappeared inside a compartment in the ceiling. "She's all finished."

Fayrel inspected the screen, revealing a detailed image of the inside of Casey's joint. "Nice job," he said proudly. "I couldn't have done the procedure any better. Why don't you escort her to her room and help get her cleaned up. We'll meet you both for the gathering in about fifteen minutes. I want to make sure Vashee's stable before I leave here."

"Thank you again for saving her life," Casey said.

"Your panther has definitely earned my utmost respect after what she did here tonight." He left to finish with Parrow.

"Mine as well," Tanille said, helping Casey from the table.

Casey led the way up to her room on Vasar Five, which was located directly across from the elevators they exited. Her clothes here were identical in style to what she had hanging in her closet of the estate. Tanille scrunched her face as she searched through the items in the wardrobe's programming.

"Don't you have anything more flattering?"

"What do you mean?" Casey asked and made her way over to search through the images.

"You only have T-shirts and sweatshirts in here, and most are too big for you."

"Yeah, 'cause that's what I wear." Casey chose a black T-shirt with a picture of one of her favorite rock bands on the front.

Tanille's nose wrinkled at the pressed fabric in Casey's hand. "Please tell me you're planning on throwing that in the incinerator."

"What, this? It's a classic. I'm not sure how Gran found this for me, but I assure you, it's considered top fashion here on Earth." Casey quickly slipped the shirt over her head.

"There's a hole in the back."

"No, it's a rip, and they designed it this way."

"You have an exceptional body, Casey. Don't you want to show it off with something more fitting?"

Casey smiled. She cocked her eyebrow and searched through her wardrobe's database. "I don't know. Do I want to show off my body? Are you saying others might find it more appealing if I wore tighter clothes?"

Casey amusedly watched Tanille's expression go from confusion, to understanding, and lastly to apprehension. "On second thought, I do like that shirt. Maybe you should put one of those sweatshirts on over it." She reached for the monitor.

Casey laughed and wrapped Tanille in her arms. "I think the T-shirt's fine on its own." She placed a long kiss on Tanille's velvety lips.

"I wish we had time for more," Tanille said the second they broke apart.

Casey pressed the controls, closing each compartment. "So do I." She fought against the excitement coursing through her body. "We'd better head up there before they come looking for us."

Tanille and Casey made it to the operations deck right as Fayrel and Parrow entered. Parrow snatched Casey's hand and inspected her finger. "The ring looks good on you."

"It feels good," Casey said.

Eva came over, giving Casey and Tanille an affectionate hug. "Hanna told me the good news. I wish you both the absolute best."

"Thank you, Eva." Casey felt the shiny ring on her finger and Tanille's hand on her lower back. The gravity of the engagement was still sinking in. She was getting married. Casey never would have guessed she would one day fall head over heels in love.

"How was Vashee when you left?" she asked Fayrel.

"Splendid, and after a few days of rest, I'll allow her to return to her quarters in the castle."

"I can't thank you enough."

At a brisk stride, Elizabeth entered and directed everyone to take their seats. "Now that we're all here, we have some vital things to discuss. First and foremost, we deciphered the message the Erules received from their assassin." Worry lines spread along her gran's forehead. "A confirmation that Casey Malanight is still alive and living on Earth."

"Assassin?" Eva paused. "Are you saying the Erules staged an attack on a nearby town to locate and execute Casey? How did they suspect she was alive to begin with? This plan would be too risky to perform on a hunch."

"We're still looking into that. Hanna apprised Grandmother Ashonda of the situation. She is discreetly checking everyone on her team, including the head of council and his staff."

Parrow voiced his beliefs. "I don't think the Erule was actually trying to kill Casey."

"Parrow's right," Casey said. "That creature was dead set on killing Parrow when I would've been an easier target."

Elizabeth thought for a moment. "Either way, they know you're here, and once Grandmother Ashonda relays the message to Queen Ann, the Assembly and our people will be told of your existence."

"Should we move Casey to Vasar One?" Fayrel asked.

Elizabeth looked directly at her granddaughter, her expression soft, yet decided. "I believe we should leave the decision to Casey. I'm realizing she's old and capable enough to make her own choices. So unless anyone has any objections, I say we let her decide."

No matter how awkward it felt to have all eyes on her, her grandmother's words had touched her, fueling her with an inner strength. "You are all my family," she said. "I would rather remain here on Earth with all of you than return to Vasar. Until I leave for the Academy, anyway."

None objected, and several even expressed their approval with verbal praise.

Elizabeth raised her hand for silence. "It's settled. I'll do all I can to provide us with additional protection here and when we travel. As for the security breach, I'll let Hanna explain this."

Hanna stood and addressed the room. "First off, the capsule had a custom-built thruster pack attached, which was skillfully discharged at the exact moment needed to send the vessel close to the Malanight Estate, but far enough away to deploy us from the castle." She signaled to Eva. "We've also discovered somehow they've learned the defenses here at the castle and come up with ways to not only go around them but also disable our communications." She held up a device Casey recognized as the processer the intruder used to send off his message. "This had all the right codes programmed in to shut us down."

Barick stood, outraged. "Impossible. How could an enemy outside of our Universal Region have gotten top-secret codes?"

Darren did his best to calm the Blunion.

Hanna gave Darren a thankful nod before continuing. "We're not sure, but for the next few days, we'll need to work at constructing a better system. This time, I suggest we keep our defenses to ourselves. After all, if someone had the right cipher, they could've recovered the information from the security systems at the palace on Vasar One."

"These said security breaches are getting out of hand." Fayrel scowled. "Exactly how high up do these deceptions go, and what do they want with Casey, if not to kill her?"

Barick grunted. "Doesn't matter. They will never touch her. Not on my watch," he said. The anger on his face bordered along the same frenzy Casey witnessed on Parrow earlier in the evening. Their level of devotion for her and her family was moving.

"I understand how everyone feels. We need to push past this attack and focus on how to diminish our weaknesses. I agree with Hanna. We must strengthen our defenses. Until these issues get ironed out, we'll continue with normal operations." Elizabeth checked her personal computer. "Let's wait to start Casey's classes until the day after tomorrow. I'll inform her other teachers."

Once the meeting ended, Casey and Tanille stopped by to see Vashee before heading up to their wing of the castle for some needed privacy. Vashee was sleeping comfortably when Casey bent in to give her a kiss on her black fur. "I love you, Vashee. See you in a few days," she whispered softly.

"I'll take good care of her," replied Fayrel. "Now you two get some rest. Don't worry. Once things settle, Elizabeth and I will begin with planning the union ceremony."

"We don't plan our own wedding?" Casey asked Tanille once they were alone.

"It's customary for the families to do it. We'll help, but not much."

Casey shoved her hands deep in her pockets. "I refuse to wear a dress," she said.

Giggling, Tanille slid her arm inside Casey's. "Stop grumbling. Your grandmother won't make you wear anything you don't like."

Thinking back to the time when she was a teenager and her gran labored for close to a year to make Casey look and act more proper, Casey cringed. Not only did the bulk of their arguments revolve around Casey's disinterest in dresses, but makeup as well. "Clearly, you don't know Gran."

The moment the elevator doors slid shut, Tanille drew Casey in and kissed her with such passion that as they parted, Tanille moaned with pleasure. "I couldn't resist."

Grasping the fact she could finally have Tanille, Casey's mind soared with excitement. Her happy ending to the painfully played out nightmare of self-denial. "Could this elevator go any slower?"

Tanille pushed Casey up against the wall. "I'm not waiting," she murmured, and her hands moved to the button on Casey's jeans.

Tanille's assertiveness aroused every part of Casey. She grabbed Tanille by her wrists, whirled her around, and pressed her against the wall. She bent her head low and brushed her lips against Tanille's ear. "I guess someone forgot I used to be a cop," she said, her voice thick with desire.

Tanille melted into Casey's embrace. "I didn't forget."

The sound of the beep, seconds before the elevator doors opened, brought them quickly apart. Parrow and Eva stepped inside, deep in conversation. Eva was the first to notice the other two occupants. She glanced at them before nervously smiling at the floor.

Casey could tell Parrow was fighting to keep a straight face. "You guys want to watch a movie?"

"No," they both said at once.

"How about the three of us order some dinner? I don't know about you, but I'm starving."

"Not hungry," Casey muttered, knowing Parrow was trying his best to annoy her.

The elevator doors opened, and Casey nearly dragged Tanille from the enclosed space.

"Let's do a light workout. Casey, you haven't trained in the past few days. You'll turn flabby if you don't watch it," he shouted after her.

Thankfully, Eva pulled him back into the elevator. "I'm hungry and would love a movie," Casey heard Eva say right before the elevator door dinged shut.

The second they entered the office on the first floor, before the passage door closed all the way, Tanille pushed Casey onto the desk by the force of her kiss. The warmth of Tanille's tongue stroking against hers made her head spin. Tanille reached down and untucked Casey's T-shirt.

Closing her eyes to her desires, Casey covered Tanille's hands with her own. "Let's move upstairs. Knowing Parrow, he'll come up with some lame excuse to return and ruin our evening."

Flustered, Tanille reluctantly agreed. Casey hurried them through the office and toward the stairway. By the time they reached the third floor, Tanille had already unfastened the buttons on her shirt, and both had kicked off their shoes. Once they were inside, Casey locked the door and pivoted to Tanille. Their eyes met, as if for the first time. At that moment Casey knew she didn't only feel excitement and lust gripping her, but also fear. An inexperienced, first-time fear which prevented her from moving.

As if reading her mind, Tanille stepped closer and placed a loving hand on Casey's cheek. A touch Casey knew she would never tire of. "I know," Tanille whispered. "Believe me, I know. I feel it too." She kissed Casey gently on the lips. "We'll take this as slow as we need."

Casey gazed deeply into the eyes of the woman she loved. The eyes staring back overflowed with the same love, blanketing Casey with a calmness she had never felt before. Without thinking, Casey scooped Tanille into her arms and carried her over to the bed, neither breaking eye contact. "You are my everything," she whispered, laying Tanille on the bed. She crawled on top, with the touch of the woman beneath her awakening every nerve in her body.

Their next kiss did more than excite Casey. It consumed her. She didn't merely want to please Tanille—she needed to. She knew this woman was her foremost reason for existing. She slipped her hand underneath Tanille's parted blouse. The soft skin beneath her fingers felt like satin.

"I love you, Casey," Tanille gasped.

Casey unfastened Tanille's slacks and yanked them off. Her mind and body were both in need of sleep, yet, as her hands and mouth moved downward, touching, tasting, exploring, she refused to give in to her tiredness until after first taking what was hers.

Several hours later, Casey awoke to the feel of her jeans unzipping. "What are you doing?" She asked, groggily raising her head.

"It's my turn."

Casey leaned against the pillows, trying to clear the sleep from her mind. Tanille was attempting to pull her pants down over her hips when Casey seized both her arms and brought Tanille up to her. She half-croaked, half-laughed as she blinked a clear image of Tanille into her tired, hazy eyes. "No, but thanks anyway."

"What do you mean, no?"

"I'm fine. I don't need you to do that."

Tanille's stare was steadfast, her voice commanding. "I'm not doing this for you."

"Let's go back to sleep."

"Will you stop being so damn controlling in bed? It might've been sexy earlier, but now it's pissing me off. I have a right to your body as you have a right to mine. Now lay back and freaking enjoy it."

Casey's eyes widened. "I'm not controlling. I only wanted to please you."

Tanille released a slow, steady breath. "I know, and you pleased me very well, but I want all of you. Let go of the past and trust me. I promise your heart is safe with me. I'll never hurt you again."

Was she having issues with trust? Casey searched Tanille's eyes. They were so beautiful, especially with the way the light from the moon reflected in through the bedroom window and made them glow. Maybe Tanille was right, but even so, Casey knew she was safe and loved. She helped Tanille remove her jeans. "I love you."

"I know." Tanille straddled her nakedness onto Casey's hips. Her hand went around and unhooked Casey's bra. "I can't believe how beautiful you are," she whispered, taking Casey's nipple into her mouth.

The tingling sensation between her thighs heightened with every caress of Tanille's moist tongue.

Tanille lightly traced Casey's flesh with her fingertips before trailing her hand to the area between Casey's legs. Casey felt lightheaded, and within seconds, Tanille's fingers found what they were searching for.

A moan left Casey as Tanille stroked her fully through her wetness. "Do you want me inside you?"

Casey glanced up, her vision slightly blurred. "Yes," she murmured, her throat dry.

"Sorry, I didn't catch that."

"Yes."

"Yes, what?"

Casey sighed, frustrated. "Yes, I want you inside me." Her words didn't come out sounding as childish as she thought, and her tone was thick with desire.

The moment Tanille entered, Casey's world turned upside down. The need for release raged throughout her body and she moved her hips up to meet Tanille's thrusts.

Her body shook with pleasure, and she clutched so tight to her pillow, her knuckles ached. When her quivering stopped, she reached for her lover, but Tanille brushed her hands away.

"What are you doing?" she asked when Tanille's head slid beneath the sheets.

"Tasting you. Like you said to me an hour ago, I made the mess, so I should be the one to clean you up."

Tanille's tongue felt exhilarating. She massaged it slowly between Casey's legs. She didn't rush but guided each stroke with purpose. The thought of a lifetime sharing her bed with this woman brought a thrill to Casey unlike any she had experienced before. Her body climbed toward ecstasy once again. When she hit her peak, the release was quicker the second time and twice as powerful.

"I'm sorry," Casey finally said in between breaths.

Tanille brought her head out from beneath the sheets. "My love, what do you have to be sorry for?"

"For not trusting you. You have all of me."

"And you, me." Tanille lovingly placed tender kisses all over Casey's face. Within minutes, Casey fell into a peaceful sleep.

The following day, they made love in every room on the third floor of their quarters, stopping occasionally for some much-needed nourishment, only leaving her wing twice to go check on Vashee. Casey felt happy and grateful to be alive. She was like a child who won a lifetime supply of chocolates, and she couldn't stop smiling. She still fought Tanille against her own body being satisfied, but every so often, Casey would lose the fight, followed by another earth-shaking release. Not because of trust but because she loved the way Tanille tasted. She couldn't get enough. When the next night transitioned into the start of the busy morning, they showered and dressed together and ate a hearty breakfast before Casey began her classes.

It didn't take long for a day-to-day routine to set in, and over the next several days, Tanille and Vashee grew closer to one another. While Casey was in her classes, they went everywhere together. Both enjoyed taking long walks out in nature.

A week later, as Casey emerged onto the operations deck of Vasar Five to begin her overseer duties, everyone jumped out, wishing her a happy twenty-fifth birthday. She couldn't believe she'd forgotten such an important day in her life. Between her studies and spending as much time as she could with Tanille, it surprised Casey she even remembered to eat.

Hanna volunteered to do Casey's overseer duties, giving Elizabeth and Fayrel the opportunity to whisk the kids off to discuss their plans for the wedding.

"No, I'm not wearing a dress," Casey said for the last time.

"Honey, it's a robe, and I think you'll look splendid in it."

Casey turned toward Tanille for help, and Gran rolled her eyes in frustration. "I'm sorry, Casey, but jeans and a T-shirt will not be proper attire for this type of ceremony."

Tanille kept her voice subtle, her expression respectful. "As I recall, Queen Ann wore a glorious suit at her union. One elegant and tailored beautifully."

Casey raised her eyebrows. "I can wear a suit."

Elizabeth stood. "No, no, no. I've come up with this beautiful robe to go with Tanille's dress, which Fayrel designed himself."

Casey gazed pleadingly at Fayrel, who had backed himself into a corner the moment the Malanight women began bickering. He let out a tiny cough, then glanced toward Elizabeth, who now had her hands on her hips, her fingers drumming impatiently.

"Well…" he said, clearing his throat, "I watched the old viewings of the wedding, and Ann looked rather stunning in her outfit. I also read through the media coverage on the affair, and it mentioned several times how the citizens were quite fond of it."

"So everyone's against me?" Elizabeth threw up her hands.

Tanille shot Casey a sympathetic frown.

Realization struck Casey hard in the chest. Gran could not plan her own daughter's wedding, so her granddaughter's wedding was very important to her. Casey's shoulders dropped. She pivoted her body slowly toward Elizabeth and sighed. "If it means this much to you, I guess the dress—robe will be fine. How long do these things last anyway?" Casey asked Fayrel.

"Around ten to twelve hours, if you're lucky."

"No shi—I mean, really?"

"Like I said, that's if you're lucky," he repeated, unable to conceal his sudden bout of amusement.

Casey sat down in the closest chair, her stubbornness defeated. "If that's what you want, Gran, I'll be fine with it."

This time, Elizabeth was the one who sighed. She seated herself in a chair next to Casey. "I'm sorry. I guess I lost my head. It's your wedding, darling. If you want to wear a suit, then by all means…" She sighed again. "I'll design you a suit."

What was one day compared to the rest of her sneaker-wearing-life? "No, this wedding belongs to all of us." She squared her shoulders to show her grandmother she was certain of her decision. "I'll be proud to wear whatever you come up with."

Elizabeth squeezed Casey's hand. "Let me work on it. Maybe I can design an outfit we can both tolerate."

Casey agreed. She peered over at Fayrel. "Okay, next subject."

They talked for another full hour before Casey followed Tanille up the stairs. Every inch of her felt drained. Achy.

"I'm very proud of you," Tanille said, placing her arms around Casey the moment she closed the bedroom door.

"What for? Oh, it's because of the dress thing."

Tanille giggled. "Honey, it's a robe."

"If it looks like a dress, and fits like a dress, it's a dress."

"I'm proud of you either way. I promise, no matter what you wear or however painfully long the ceremony is, I'll make it up to you on our honeymoon."

"Why not start now?"

Undoing the top button on her blouse, Tanille ran her tongue seductively over her bottom lip.. "Maybe a little taste won't hurt."

They made love for over three hours that night, exploring each other's bodies in every way imaginable. The second Tanille fell asleep, Casey got up and headed straight toward her office to start on her overabundant stash of homework. Vashee entered within minutes and lay by Casey's feet. The hours drifted sluggishly by with Casey working feverishly over her assignments.

Several hours later Tanille came in to find the two soul-links fast asleep, Vashee in deep purring snores and Casey with her head hunched over her laptop. She woke both up and guided each onto the bed next to the other. Once she had the pair tucked in, Tanille returned to Casey's office to organize the mess Casey had left.

Over the next several weeks, Tanille made sure Casey got plenty of rest and her homework done before they were intimate with one another. At first, Casey protested this seemingly harsh treatment, but soon she realized Tanille's inhumane decision had pushed her along further in her classes. Within the next month and a half, Casey had tested out of nine of her fourteen testable classes. She still had all three of Zeckner's subjects, and Barick and Eva's class remaining.

Although the abilities training was for Casey's benefit only and not for the Academy, her gran told her she needed to continue to work on honing her gifts until she left for school. Once there, she would resume with Grandmother Ann during her two years living on Vasar. Her favorite was the moving of matter. Casey accidentally smashed her gran's antique desk into the wall of her office, so they continued with this class in the safety of the outdoors.

As she made her way to the last test in Eva and Barick's courses, Casey felt nervous, yet excited. They told her the previous day she was ready to test out in each of their classes. She was to first meet Eva in the hangar after she finished Zeckner's last class, where they would have a surprise waiting for her.

When she spotted Eva on the platform in the hangar, she noticed Vasar Six's landing pad stood empty. After they teleported onto Vasar Seven, Casey asked Eva, "Where's Vasar Six?"

Eva bubbled with excitement as she led them to the operations deck. She took the seat next to Casey. "That's your surprise. We're going to test your abilities in flying and also your in-flight combat and strategies course during the same exercise."

"How will this work?"

"Easy. You'll defend us as Barick tries to destroy our ship."

Casey wasn't sure if she heard Eva correctly. "Excuse me, did you say destroy our ship?"

Eva's eyes brightened. "Don't worry, Casey. We reconfigured both ships, along with their weapons, to simulate the real thing. If you do well, we'll both pass you. Of course, Barick's extremely skilled. We're not expecting you to win. But make a good show of it. Keep us alive as long as you can, and we'll allow you to take your exams at the Academy."

Casey smiled broadly and powered up the ship. "I've got this."

"That's the spirit," Eva said. "Be careful. Barick's a pro and is shrewd with his fighting techniques."

Confident with the controls and this exercise, Casey piloted the vessel out. Flying was becoming second nature. She was looking forward to trying the different vessels at the Academy. Eva often told her she was a natural. "A very gifted aviator," Eva once boasted to Elizabeth, and Casey was going to do all she could to live up to Eva's compliment.

The first thirty minutes were nothing more than routine flying, identical to their other classes together. Yet when their flight time drew closer to an hour, Casey started to get an uncomfortable feeling in the back of her mind. She was about to close her eyes to see if she could lock onto Barick's position when Eva spoke. "Nope. Elizabeth insisted you do this without your abilities, and we both agreed."

Casey opened her mouth to protest, but suddenly, the hairs on the scruff of her neck stood on end. She squinted around, searching for anything out of the ordinary. When her gaze fell to the right, a flicker in her peripheral caught her attention. She was positive she'd seen a figure of a mass dodge behind the moon. She grinned inwardly at herself, while shifting the ship downward in an abrupt jerk.

Eva gripped her computer pad tight against her chest as she peered around. "What is it?"

"Nothing. Only working on some of my maneuvers."

Eva focused on Casey, then skeptically at the wide view of deep space. Casey steered them to the opposite side of the moon, where she hovered briefly and waited.

Eva teasingly criticized their lack of movement. "I'm rating your grade on your flying skill, not your—"

The vessel came out of nowhere. Casey wrenched open their ship's boosters all the way and rolled hard to the left. She could tell by his veering Barick was as surprised as Eva was, and she used this to her advantage. Casey flipped the ship upward, and spun around to where they were right behind Vasar Six and closing in fast.

"Casey, I'd say you've passed my class with flying colors, no pun intended. Now let's go take down a Blunion," Eva eagerly shouted.

Eva leaned forward, as if this would make the ship go faster. Casey laughed at the excitement on Eva's face, bringing her to open the rest of the boosters.

"Don't let him move behind the Earth," Eva cried out. The Kan pounded a hand on the console, engrossed in the moment.

Suddenly, Casey froze. Her mind working through the situation like a computer, scanning the database, searching for the right program. Without warning, Casey brought the ship to a complete stop at an odd angle and powered down the primary controls.

"What happened?" Eva asked, inspecting the monitors on the panel.

"I'm being tested on strategy, right? We'll be out here all day if we try to chase him down. After all, he has the faster ship."

Eva sounded anxious as Barick's ship changed directions. "I'm not following," she said, apprehension etching itself into her composure.

Casey flashed Eva a cocky grin. "Have a little faith. Oh, and hold on tight to your computer pad."

The other ship grew closer and closer as the female voice of the computer announced the warning of the other ship's weapons charging. Casey peered over, giving Eva a reassuring wink. The instant Barick fired, Casey flipped on the controls, gunned the ship to full speed, released the countermeasures, and rolled to avoid the hit. She whipped their vessel toward Vasar Six and aimed her own simulated weapons. She sent two direct hits, holding her breath until the computer informed them Barick's ship had lost the match.

Eva cheered with gusto, patting Casey excitedly on the back. "Take us in, and if Barick complains about your little stunt, I'll deal with him."

Barick's reaction was the exact opposite. Not only did Barick congratulate her on her flying abilities, but he also gave her a high passing score in his class. He ran off to tell everyone about the wonderful flying maneuvers she'd used against him.

By the time Casey made it to her room that evening, Tanille was waiting for her on the bed wearing nothing but a black ball cap with bold printing on the top in bright-red lettering. *I live to fly.*

Casey dropped her bag in the chair beside the table. "I take it you heard."

"Who hasn't? Now strip and get in this bed so we can properly celebrate."

Chapter Thirteen

Earth Date: 12th January 2043
Distress Call

"It's all set," Elizabeth said as she entered the kitchen on the first floor of Casey's team's quarters, directing a brilliant smile to the Casey, Tanille, and Parrow, who were sitting at the table, deep in discussion.

"What's all set?" Parrow asked.

Casey noticed Fayrel's look of delight as he strolled in right behind Elizabeth, brushing off pronounced flakes of snow from his long fusain-colored coat. "The wedding, of course. What else have we been doing for the past two months?" Fayrel sat at the table beside Casey. "Go ahead. Tell them what the queen said."

Elizabeth paced with animation in front of the bay window. "We're leaving in three weeks to head to Vasar One. We've scheduled Casey's exams for the first day we arrive. Oh, and when we land, the citizens have requested your appearance at the palace to give praise." She stopped long enough to catch her breath. "Then on February twentieth we'll have the union ceremony. Queen Ann is sending us three members from her team to watch the overseer post here on Earth, which means we'll all be able to go."

Fayrel clapped Casey between the shoulders and smiled broadly at each of them. Casey tried her best to return the gesture. She failed. Parrow and Tanille didn't respond. At once, Fayrel and Elizabeth's joy faded. The three's melancholy moods were clearly not the reactions either expected.

Elizabeth sat down, as if she were preparing herself for a mess of bad news. "You two haven't changed your minds, have you?"

Fayrel held his breath when his concern bobbed from Tanille to Casey.

Casey spoke first. "Zeckner told me he doesn't believe I'm ready for the exams. He thinks I should wait until next year to be sure."

"Look at the assignments he gives her," Tanille shouted, throwing Casey's bag on the table with enough force Casey's elbows felt the thud.

Casey cringed, but she blew out a sigh of relief once she remembered her laptop was upstairs in her office. Tanille removed several computer pads, roughly tossing each on the surface of the high-polished oak.

"Most of this rubbish is so advanced she won't cover it at the Academy. I mean come on, Paramacriam physics, Trysalum genetics. The list goes on and on." She angrily shoved the pads back into the bag. "He even has her going every day to his classes since she's passed the rest. He's being a complete asshole!"

Fayrel about jumped out of his seat. "Tanille! Some words in the English language I would rather you not use, or learn, for that matter." He gave Parrow a disapproving look, and the Blunion shifted his gaze away.

"Sorry, Father," Tanille said, "but I'm calling it how I see it."

Tanille was no longer the only one outraged. Elizabeth stood from the table. "Why didn't you tell me about this sooner?"

Casey's mouth dropped open but no words came out. Gran's harsh tone wasn't only out of character, the rigid pitch was intimidating.

"Oh, never mind! I'll go deal with this myself!" Elizabeth stomped off toward the direction of the first-floor office.

The rest of the group leapt up from the table and followed. When Elizabeth entered the conference room, everyone waited outside, trying unsuccessfully to listen in at the door.

Several moments later, Elizabeth emerged, appearing as triumphant as ever. "Casey, Zeckner has seen the error of his ways, and he's going to give you your tests first thing in the morning. Chasel will oversee the tests and upload them into the system for grading."

Tanille and Parrow each exchanged a look of satisfaction with one another. Casey remained self-possessed.

"Tanille, I want you and Parrow to help Casey tonight with studying for Zeckner's tests. As soon as Casey passes, you'll both work on getting her ready for the Academy exams. Now, our temporary replacements will be here by the beginning of next week to get reacquainted with our system, and Fayrel and I have some last-minute details to work through with Queen Ann over the wedding." Elizabeth raised her head slightly, as if mentally checking to see if she covered everything. Finally, with a quick farewell, she and Fayrel left.

Tanille's eyes followed Elizabeth's exit with admiration. "I'm impressed."

Parrow radiated with pride. "So am I. She's going to make a wonderful queen someday."

The three stayed in the den most of the evening, going over what they thought Casey should study. "No, you don't need to know this," or "They won't cover that until your second year of the Academy," were words Parrow and Tanille stated repeatedly throughout the entire evening.

When Casey did finally fall asleep, her mind felt lost. She awoke several times, jumping from the bed, thinking she'd overslept. Once, she even had a horrific nightmare. It entailed her sitting on a metal chair in a cold dark room with her hands tied behind her back. Zeckner marked a big FAIL on her forehead using cherry red lipstick. Casey's spirit was worn out with stress when Tanille woke her the next morning.

"You look terrible, didn't you sleep well?"

"Define well," Casey said, as she rubbed her forehead. She inspected her hand for traces of lipstick.

Tanille grabbed a piping hot coffee from the Originator. "What are you doing?"

"I had a dreadful dream. It involved Zeckner and lipstick."

Tanille climbed into bed and placed a tender kiss on Casey's nose. "You'll do great. Here, drink some coffee. Afterward, I want you to take a shower. It'll make you feel better."

Tanille was right, and by the time Casey entered the classroom to take the test, Chasel was waiting for her with a freshly made iced soda. "I'm sure this'll help," she said.

Casey noticed Zeckner's displeased glower, but she didn't care. She hoped this would be the last time she would ever have to deal with the unpleasant program. She finished the test well under the time limit, and once Elizabeth received the grade, she told Casey the good news. In all three of his exams, Casey hadn't missed a single answer.

Casey was ecstatic. The first thing she wanted to do was take Tanille upstairs and make love. After that, nothing else mattered.

"We need to celebrate," Parrow said in good spirits the second Casey told him and Tanille about her test. Parrow threw Vashee a hunk of his sandwich.

Tanille rose from the kitchen table and headed to the Originator. "Sounds wonderful! I'll order us some food."

"I have a container of very aged Roman wine, which I've saved for an occasion such as this." Parrow beamed at both women. "I'll be right back." He hurried toward the stair and called out over his shoulder, "Oh, and we'll need to make another trip to Rome before you start at the Academy. I've got to restock."

Casey agreed and couldn't help but laugh as she watched him run upstairs to his suite with Vashee following close behind. "I was hoping for a little one-on-one time, but I guess it can wait." She stepped behind Tanille, wrapped her arms around her lover's waist, and pressed herself against Tanille's nicely curved backside.

"Please don't get me started. I'd hate to witness the disappointment in Parrow's eyes if we had to excuse ourselves for a few hours."

"He'd get over it," Casey murmured. She bent her head and nibbled on Tanille's soft neck.

"I've got it," Parrow shouted, running down the stairs.

Casey shifted away, but not before hearing Tanille say, "You'd better not get drunk this time."

Once the celebration was over, Casey had to assist Parrow into his bed. Vashee said she would watch over him, allowing both women to head up to their bedroom for a quiet celebration of their own.

"I think Vashee's really starting to like me."

Casey wasn't sure if Tanille's statement was a conviction, or if she was fishing for hopeful validation. "You and Parrow are all she talks about these days. So, yes, she's very fond of you," Casey said, lighting the bedroom fireplace.

"I wish I could communicate with her. There's so much I want to say or ask her when we're alone that whenever I eventually find you, your grandmother, or Eva, I've forgotten most of it."

"You should write it down." Casey stood. Tanille was watching her with longing eyes.

"Your beauty is captivating, Casey Malanight. Especially when the flame's light dances against your tall, athletic, mouthwatering figure." She shuddered with delight. "It's incredibly arousing."

Casey bit back her laughter. "You sure know how to flatter a girl."

"So where were we?" Tanille crooned. She ambled over and lifted off Casey's sweatshirt.

Casey turned Tanille around and brushed her hair from her shoulder. "We were right about here," Casey whispered, and caressed Tanille's neck with her mouth.

"Ah, that's right. It's all coming back to me now."

Once Vasar Six and Seven left the Milky Way, several patrol ships escorted them to Vasar One. Elizabeth, Hanna, and Fayrel were flying separately for the Couhl Tabarr Solar system in Vasar Six to collect the Hafite council members for the Assembly meeting. The Hafite officials said their ambassadorial vessel was on another mission, and they refused to travel in anything less fitting for their status as political representatives. The queen was planning on sending a ship from Vasar One, but Elizabeth offered since they would travel by their location anyway. Elizabeth arranged the pickup a few days before they departed and accepted the feast the Hafites insisted on holding in her honor. Vasar Seven continued to Vasar so Casey would make it on time for her entrance exams.

"The Hafites are only doing this because they want to show up under the escort of the future queen," Parrow said, clearly annoyed by the situation.

Eva agreed. "They're not stupid. This will make them look more favorable to the media."

Casey gazed out of the front porthole, watching Elizabeth's ship and one of the patrol ships depart from their group. She didn't like the idea of them leaving, but her grandmother promised repeatedly she would be in no danger. Her mind briefly relived the night Gran told Casey her mother had died. She'd experienced the worst pain ever. Casey tightened her fists and lowered her head. She couldn't lose Grandmother Elizabeth from her life as well. The thought was agonizing.

Tanille stroked the tightening muscles between Casey's shoulder blades. "She'll be fine, my love."

"Of course, they'll be fine." Eva raised her brow. "However, if you fail your entrance exams, you won't be when she returns. I suggest you three go back to studying."

On the day their vessel entered the Vasar Solar system, Casey felt more than ready to take her tests. They would be held at the Academy on Vasar Three in less than fifteen hours.

"Where are we going?" Casey asked Eva once she noticed they were not heading for the Malanight Estate.

"Didn't your grandmother tell you?"

"Tell me what?"

"The people are holding a ceremony in your honor. After all, you're the future queen, and they had presumed you to be dead. They want to meet you."

Casey was a bit unnerved. "I thought it would be after the tests."

Eva said, "It shouldn't take too long. I promise you won't be late."

Casey shifted uncomfortably. "Do I have to make a speech?"

"I'm afraid so." Eva sounded almost empathetic. "It'll be good practice for you, Casey. You'll need to get used to it."

Eva was wrong. Once they landed, the royal meet-and-greet took over thirteen hours. Casey was happy to see Grandmother Ann and Bilana were waiting for them on arrival and remained by Casey's side throughout the entire process. Casey did have to make a brief speech first, outside on the steps leading up to the palace. Once finished, they moved the ceremony inside.

Casey sat on her throne chair next to Ann, as citizens of the Universal Region, which comprised many species, came up one at a time. There were tens of thousands. Some cried, others shook her hand in enthusiasm, and all brought gifts.

The first to offer homage was a Gaminite official who oversaw an outer province at the edge of the Universal Boarder. Two of his guards placed a ruby-etched chest at her feet, which he said was crafted from the exquisite gems mined on one of his planets. Opening the lid, the guards revealed a magnificent egg-shaped sapphire diamond, twice the size of an ostrich egg, which rested on a bed of golden shavings that resembled a nest. Casey tried saying no to the offering, but Ann whispered how the people would look at this as an insult. Therefore, the vast pile of rare and valuable treasure steadily grew.

"What am I going to do with all of those gifts?" Casey asked as soon as they returned to Vasar Seven and were out of earshot of others.

Ann sat with her wife across from Casey. "Security will inspect each gift thoroughly before moving the treasure to the vault on the Malanight Estate until you decide."

"I didn't realize so many people would show up to see me." Casey activated her safety straps. She shifted in her seat, trying to find a comfortable position.

"You don't understand the love our people have for our family. There would've been more, but not everyone could make it through security in time. Most had waited there for days just to catch a glimpse of you."

Casey stopped fidgeting. The cushioned seat wasn't what was making her uncomfortable. "Why would they be bringing presents? I haven't done anything to earn such gifts."

"Casey, the Universal Region has prospered under our family's rule for many millennia. We provide our people with safety in a world free of poverty. This is their way of showing their love and appreciation. These offerings also help us see the region continues to thrive. We do not squander our riches but rather put them to good use for the welfare of everyone."

Casey peered out of the porthole at the multitude of faces, young and old, as the line of those she didn't have the time to receive stretched out for miles. This life of hers felt so overwhelming. She wasn't sure whether to be thankful or find some remote place far away to hide for the rest of her many years of life. She was grateful Ann and Bilana rode with them all the way to Vasar Three. With the way her nerves felt, Casey was finding it difficult to concentrate.

Parrow entered later, munching on a half-eaten sandwich. "After Casey passes her exams, I say we go out and celebrate."

"That'd be fun," Bilana agreed, delighted at the idea. She glanced at her wife with a sudden air of disappointment. "Wait, we have an engagement later. Damn!"

Ann patted her hand. "We'll tag along next time, I promise. You all should go though. I can send several of my men to accompany you."

Tanille placed her arm around Casey's waist, her eyes urging Casey to say yes. "Doesn't that sound wonderful?"

Eager to see what the nightlife on this side of the cosmos offered, and not wanting to disappoint Tanille or Parrow, Casey went along with the idea.

They arrived at the campus precisely on time, where Casey immediately met with a panel of seven instructors. The first few hours held one lengthy exam, which she performed on a holographic monitor. Several hands-on tests followed, including the last one, which was flying an expedition vessel in a simulator room.

She returned to meet with the members of the panel over five hours later. The panel had the results of all her graded tests. After the discussion was over, Casey found her group waiting for her anxiously in one of the Academy's lavish waiting rooms.

"How'd you do?" Tanille was the first to ask.

"I could've done better."

"You passed though, right?" Bilana nervously asked.

"Of course she passed. She's a Malanight after all," Eva said.

When Casey failed to respond, Ann placed a comforting hand on Casey's shoulder. "It's all right, Casey. You didn't have long to study, plus—"

"I made the second highest score on every test but flying, weapons, and combat," Casey said, unable to hold in her excitement any longer.

Tanille shrieked with delight, and Ann shoved Casey playfully for worrying them. Eva and Parrow's downcast spirits didn't improve.

"You're great at flying! One of the best, if not the best, I've seen," Eva said.

"What about her combat? Blunions trained her." Parrow puffed out his chest defiantly. "How many individuals actually have that luxury?"

"Don't worry," Casey said, grinning from ear to ear. "I received the highest on each of your classes and in weapons."

Parrow grumbled at Casey's wit, Eva clapped her hands together at the news, and Barick let out a long whistle. "Thank goodness. Hanna's been worrying for the last few weeks. I told her she'd done a good job training you, but you know how females are."

Darren laughed but fell silent when Eva glared at him.

"Time to celebrate!" Parrow announced, ushering everyone out the door.

Parrow and the four guards waited for over an hour for the two women to get ready for the club. Their lag was due to Tanille's built-up sexual frustration from a weeklong, all-study, no-sex postponement. Casey gladly helped her remedy her dilemma twice.

After Vashee said her farewells and bounced off to explore more of the estate, Casey and the other two headed to a club located on Vasar Three, which Parrow said the university students frequently populated. Casey wasn't sure what she expected alien nightlife to be like, but her imagination came nowhere close to being this grand. Everything about this so-called "club" was amazing. It encompassed over twenty immense floors of wall-to-wall entertainment. The lighting, music, and atmosphere were different anywhere in the building they went, with fancy bars and dance-stations throughout. Simulation chambers were where fantasies took hold, and the occasional screams drifted out from roller coasters Casey herself was too scared to try for fear of vomiting in front of Tanille.

"There's a swanky casino on the top two floors. Maybe later, when we're drunk enough, we can go," Parrow suggested before heading off to order the first round of drinks.

"How do they move like that?" Casey asked, eyeing the packed dance floor closest to them. "The way they grind their bodies together, it's sensual to the point of almost being pornographic."

"Maybe we should go to the casino instead."

Amused, Casey snorted at Tanille, who didn't appear thrilled by Casey's observations. She pulled Tanille into her arms. "I only have eyes for you."

Tanille gave a playful humph before taking the glass from Parrow. The beverage was a hazy blue and tasted refreshingly fruity. Casey downed it in minutes.

"Better watch out, Casey," Parrow warned. "That beverage might taste innocent, but it's not. They make drinks with actual alcohol. Not that 'Kool-Aid' crap they serve on Earth." He left to go get her another.

The sound of the music, along with the drink, moved Casey from the inside out. She'd never danced before, except in the privacy of her own home, but this beat was catchy, almost hypnotic. A distinct pulse of reggae and the unmistakable thunder of hip-hop combined with a futuristic dance blend and a subtle bass pumped through Casey's body as an irresistible harmonized mixture.

She watched in delight as couples of the same gender and even different species intermixed with one other. She saw no hate, no anger, and no judgment as all moved about, enjoying the carefree atmosphere of the club.

They finally found a spot close to the dance floor in a booth beside a simulation chamber. "Aren't you Casey Malanight?" a short woman holding two drinks asked the second Casey sat. "Yes, it's you! Hey, honey, come over here," she shouted toward the far corner, which brought over a woman in a tight purple and black elastic dress, identical to the one the drink woman was wearing.

"Look who I found." The woman who was talking appeared to be the dominant of the two, but as Casey glanced around, she noticed that few of the Trysal women here seemed very…athletic.

"Wow, you're kidding," her partner muttered, stunned.

"We need to let everyone know." The woman holding the drinks left with her partner before Casey or the other two could stop them.

"Here, drink this. It's going to get crazy in here." Parrow handed her the glass and motioned over to their guards.

Casey took a sip before turning to Tanille. "Is it me or do most of the female couples in here seem to all be kinda girly?"

Tanille smiled and motioned to the dance floor. "Most of the women in this club are Trysals, Casey. Trysals are more sophisticated, using mainly brain over brawn. Yes, you are more masculine than most, especially in this level of the club. This means you'll be a desirable item with several of these unattached women. Add future queen to that, and I'll have to keep a close eye on you."

Casey laughed at Tanille's coy squint, then gulped more than half of her drink. "Man, this tastes fantastic," she said, eyeing Tanille's nearly full glass. Tanille giggled and slid her drink slowly away from Casey. Casey playfully pouted.

"Everyone, I must have your attention," A loud voice reverberated from around the establishment, and at once, the music stopped. "Tonight is a special night. For of all the clubs in our universe, Craznides is blessed to welcome our very own Casey Malanight!"

The applause that followed was intense, as all eyes searched in every direction to locate their future queen.

"I need another drink," Casey said, wanting to slide underneath the table.

"I'll make them doubles." Parrow spoke to the guards, before beelining for the bar. When he returned, he had to shove his way through the crowd, as people began flocking around their booth. Thankfully, the guards enforced a five-foot clearance on all sides. "Maybe next time we'll use the DNA Modifier," he bellowed, so the other two could hear him over the noise.

"It'll die down. We only need to ride it out," Tanille shouted in Casey's ear.

"All right, everyone, let's give them some room. The future queen didn't come here to get trampled by a crowd of gawking patrons," said a burly man, who directed the onlookers away from their table. "I'm Blandon, the owner of this club. If you need anything, please, let me know." He waved over a woman in a tight red outfit. "My best bar mistress. Everything we offer is on me. Please enjoy yourselves." He bowed to Casey before leaving.

Parrow ordered another round of drinks and faced his companions. "You guys want to dance?"

"I'd love to," Tanille cried out, ogling Casey.

Casey gestured for the two of them to go. "I'll need to drink a great deal more to gain some false courage before making a fool of myself."

"You big baby. It's easy. Watch us and learn." Parrow took Tanille's hand and led her out to the middle of the packed floor.

Casey sipped on her drink, enjoying the view of Tanille and Parrow swaying enthusiastically to the beat of the music. Halfway through her next glass, she sat up straight in the seat. "Finally," Casey mumbled. "Another woman wearing pants."

A Trysal with short brown hair and dark blue eyes circulated around the room. Casey noticed how she, too, was taking pleasure in watching the patrons on the dance floor. She acted cocky, if not arrogant. Yet, Casey found it refreshing to see another woman who appeared to detest wearing a dress, almost as much as she did. Kindred spirits, one might say.

"Oh, she's going after someone," Casey muttered, sitting forward in her seat. Casey gazed at the dance floor, trying to figure out who this woman had her sights set on. The woman moved fluidly around the crowd and eventually fell into step right behind Tanille. With every beat of the music, she inched closer, and her eyes ogled lustfully over Tanille's body.

"Oh hell. I think not," Casey spat. She scooted herself from the booth and stood. She felt slightly tipsy as she made her way to the dance floor. The moment she reached the edge, the woman pulled Tanille to her, making the startled healer jump.

"She's spoken for," Casey heard Parrow say, and he dragged Tanille toward him.

Tanille spun, frowning at the woman. Her lips tightened when she noticed Casey approaching, looking none too pleased. Tanille moved forward, took Casey by the hand, and steered her to the other end of the dance floor, away from the woman.

"She's not worth it," Tanille said. She placed her hand on Casey's cheek to direct Casey's eyes to her own. "Please, let it go." She pressed her lips softly against Casey's mouth.

The thought of the other woman vanished, and they stood with lips together, eyes closed. Tanille brought her hands to Casey's hips. She moved a leg between Casey's, and soon both women swayed to the rhythm of the music.

"You know, in case you two were wondering, I don't enjoy dancing alone." The sound of Parrow's voice brought them apart.

Tanille giggled. She stepped from Casey so all three could dance together.

"You're not bad for a newbie," Parrow told Casey.

Tanille tossed Casey a flirty wink. "I think she's dancing wonderfully."

"If she farted, you'd think that was wonderful too." He rolled his eyes with a deep sigh. "New love is so…nauseating."

Casey laughed until she caught sight of the figure out of the corner of her eye. The woman from the dance floor was moving toward them. Casey pivoted to Tanille's side and stood her ground.

"I think maybe we should go to the casino for the rest of the night," Parrow said, glancing from Casey to the approaching woman.

"Good idea." Tanille reached over and gripped Casey's arm. "We're leaving."

Casey studied Tanille momentarily before finally relaxing her tense muscles and agreeing.

As they were about to exit the dance floor, a firm voice behind them spoke. "Care to dance?"

"No, thank you." Tanille called over her shoulder as she quickened her pace, dragging Casey along with her.

The woman persisted. "I would like to dance with you."

Casey removed Tanille's hold and spun. "She said no!"

"I wasn't talking to you." The woman glowered. "I don't care who you are. Being a Malanight doesn't make you better than me."

"No, but how you're acting at this moment does. For the last time, the answer's no."

The woman stepped in, taking a wide swing at Casey, who ducked easily to the side. Casey's fist landed with a jab to the woman's nose, hard enough of a hit to knock the woman off her feet and onto the floor. The music stopped, and the guards moved forward.

"Get her out of here!" Blandon shouted. From out of nowhere, two stout men came forward and picked up the nose-bleeding Trysal. They dragged her protesting body toward the exit. "I'm sorry, Ms. Malanight. She'll not enter my club ever again."

Tanille grabbed Casey's hand and removed her from the scene. "We're going home."

"We are not!" Parrow shouted. "You've both been at each other for months. Damn it, we're on Parrow time now! We're going upstairs to blow as much money as we can for the next few hours, and both of you are going to have a freaking good time!"

Knowing he was right, Casey and Tanille followed him and the guards to the casino. They took turns pointing out the many glitzy games to Casey before Parrow took off to try his luck at the tables. Casey stayed with Tanille, where they played several unusual-looking mechanized slots. Within an hour, Parrow swung by to show them the large stack of markers he'd won. Casey finished her eighth drink, and was about to order her ninth, when the surrounding room began to spin.

"I think we should go. She's not looking good," Parrow said, and with the help of Queen Ann's guards, they loaded Casey onto the ship and headed for the estate on Vasar One.

Casey passed out in her seat before they arrived back. Parrow carried Casey to bed, apologizing to Tanille for insisting they stay out so late.

"I guess Casey won't be going shopping with us," Eva said with a smirk when Parrow and Tanille entered the kitchen.

"I'll stay with her," Tanille said, ordering a coffee from the Originator.

"You'll do no such thing," David gave a brisk shake of his head. "Casey will be fine. The estate is impenetrable with a state-of-the-art security system and armed guards patrolling the property line. Plus, Vashee's roaming the grounds, so Casey's good and protected. All she needs to do is sleep it off."

Ashonda concurred with her husband. "Anyway, I have a shopping list Elizabeth sent me for your wedding."

Barick raised his eyebrows the moment Ashonda opened the list on her handheld computer pad. "That'll take us all day."

Eva studied the list. "We can break up into groups of two and get it knocked out in around five or six hours."

"That's what I was thinking," Ashonda said. "The sooner we go, the sooner we can come back and start preparing the family meal for when Elizabeth and the others arrive."

Once all had consented to the plan, Tanille returned to the bedroom and gave the snoring Casey a kiss goodbye. She wrote her a note on where they would be in the slim chance she woke up before they returned.

Casey awoke several hours later to a sharp tingle on her wrist. She squinted at her personal computer as the orange flashing diamond pulsated, signaling someone was sending her a message. Casey gently propped herself onto her elbow as her fingers rubbed at the throbbing ache radiating from her forehead. She pushed the button. A distorted image of Elizabeth appeared on her personal computer's holographic display. Abruptly, Casey sat up. Something in her gran's eyes was amiss, and within seconds, her grandmother's voice spoke out sharply.

"I'm Elizabeth Malanight. We're under attack! I repeat, we are under attack! Our location is two-seven-eight-four lightyears outside the Universal Region at coordinates S-C-six-eight-four-five-one-seven-nine."

"Gran, it's Casey!" As soon as she pushed the button and spoke, the feed vanished.

She felt numb with fear. Casey jumped from the bed and frantically searched for something to write on. She found a note in Tanille's handwriting, grabbed a pen from the drawer, and jotted the coordinates on the blank side. Once done, Casey flipped over the note and read.

"Crap!" she shouted, running through the house. She tried her personal computer, but no one responded. She didn't know how else to reach anyone. Thinking of Vashee, she touched her soul-binding necklace. *Vashee, where are you? Gran is in trouble.*

Casey couldn't understand why Vashee wasn't responding. She tried several times, but only silence answered her. Eva had told them the necklaces would help them communicate from far distances, but Vashee must be too far away, exploring the massive estate.

Unable to wait any longer, Casey threw on her shoes, wrote a note to the rest of the team, and ran out to the platform toward Vasar Seven. She yelled for Chasel, who instantly appeared. She swiftly explained to Chasel what was going on. The Program Intelligence helped her power on the ship, and they were up and heading out into space by the time Casey programmed in the location Elizabeth had sent in the message.

"It'll take us less than two hours to make it there," Chasel said, "But you do realize we'll be flying in dangerous territory. Outside the Universal Blockade."

"I don't care where it's located."

"Vasar Seven, this is Tower Seventeen. We do not have you scheduled to depart today. Could you please enter your code?" a woman's voice announced.

A new thought struck Casey, and she punched in the code. "Hello, I'm Casey Malanight. I've received a distress call from my grandmother, Elizabeth Malanight, at this location." She read off the coordinates and waited for someone to respond.

"We copy. Please stand by. We'll raise a military escort to accompany you."

Casey anxiously waited. Five agonizing minutes later she was still pacing the operations deck. She was on the verge of giving up hope for military help when the female voice came back on. "This is Tower Seventeen. I apologize for the delay. Most of our patrols are out on security because of the Assembly meeting tomorrow, but the escort should be ready within the hour."

Casey's temper blew. "We don't have that long. They might already be dead!" Casey's eyes teared at the thought of losing her grandmother.

She yanked out the earpiece, and slammed it down on the console. She quickly finished punching in the sequence for Crogonic travel. Next, she crosschecked her route with the substance detection map. Casey glanced toward Vasar One, then pushed the final button.

Chapter Fourteen

Earth Date: 3rd February 2043
The Unthinkable Plot

The shopping crew arrived at the estate with a full load and more scheduled for delivery later in the day. The atmosphere in the shuttle was boisterous. Everyone was thrilled about the upcoming event. Tanille was showing Darren what she'd bought for Casey when Eva's alarmed voice brought the engaging group to a dead halt. "Where's Vasar Seven?"

"Pardon me?" Ashonda asked, rotating in her seat.

"Vasar Seven's gone," Eva repeated.

Barick leaned over. "Impossible. The only one here with access to the ship was…Land us now!" The instant the craft settled, Barick was out and running for the house, with everyone following close behind.

"Casey!" Tanille yelled out, hurrying inside the main building.

Tanille heard Barick shout for Casey while he went from room to room, a terrified expression fixed on his face. She headed straight for their bedroom. The moment she entered, she saw the note sitting next to the unoccupied bed. Fear gripped her. She rushed forward and snatched the paper. On one side of the page was her note, explaining to Casey about their shopping excursion. The writing on the other side chilled her. The others were making their way into the bedroom right as she was heading out.

"What is it?" Ashonda whispered fearfully.

Tanille held out the note to Ashonda, who was standing with one hand pressed to her stomach. She grabbed the note and read it aloud. "Received a distress call from Gran. They're under attack. I couldn't reach anyone, so I'm going to go find them. Casey."

She crumpled the paper and clutched it to her chest. "David, see if you can get a hold of Elizabeth. I'll contact Ann." Ashonda exchanged a worried glance with Barick before exiting the room.

The second they entered the front part of the house, a deep rumbling noise outside caught their attention. "Casey!" Parrow bellowed, rushing to the rear exit. They all followed.

"It's Vasar Six," Ashonda said. "I need to tell David." She pivoted and was gone.

Elizabeth was the first one out of the aircraft. Her gaze went from Tanille's damp eyes to Barick's pale face. "Where's Casey?"

Eva anxiously filled her in. "Casey left a note saying you were in trouble and she was going to find you. Vasar Seven is gone."

Ashonda returned with David at her side. She spoke quickly, gripping firmly onto her husband. "Planetary Security alerted Queen Ann. Casey left here over an hour ago, saying she received a distress call from Elizabeth. They've tried to reach her several times but have been unsuccessful. They have the location she was heading to, and Fleet Four is ready to head out after her."

"What distress call?" Elizabeth asked.

Ashonda curtly said, "Ann didn't say. Elizabeth, we need to go after her."

"Darren, could you please take the diplomats from Couhl Tabarr over to the palace," Elizabeth pivoted, finishing her words over her shoulder as she headed for Vasar Six. "We're going up to meet the Fleet."

"I'm going as well," Parrow declared, followed by agreement from the rest of Elizabeth's team.

Fayrel reached for his daughter. "You should remain here."

"I can't. I have to be up there with Casey."

"I insist."

"My decision isn't open for discussion, Father." Tanille shook off his hand and sprinted after Parrow. Fayrel hurried close behind.

"We're halfway there," Chasel said.

"Thank you." Casey tried to lock on to her grandmother's signal, but she was too worried to make the connection.

"You should eat something. If you become weak, you'll be no good to anyone."

"You're right," Casey said, heading to the Originator. She programmed in a turkey sandwich and a glass of milk. Although she had no appetite, Casey finished almost half of her meal when Chasel announced she was picking up a signal from the long-range scanner. The images were still too far away for any visuals, so Casey waited.

"Warning! Vessel approaching the regional border! Warning! Vessel approaching the regional border!" the computer echoed, while casting red flashing lights throughout the ship.

Casey reached over and switched off the emergency program. She knew heading there alone wasn't safe, but the unthinkable image of Gran's lifeless body drove her on. She had to do something, even if it meant risking her own life.

What would her death do to Tanille? The thought was heartbreaking. She stood, pacing worriedly throughout the control room. "How long do we have?" she asked Chasel.

"Five and a half minutes. I'm picking up a visual, Casey."

Casey reached over, setting the long-range visual to show on the main screen. What she saw wasn't the image of a damaged Vasar Six, but three distinct mercenary vessels heading straight for her. It was a trap.

"Chasel! We need to turn the ship around."

"Casey, there are three more vessels closing in from behind."

Impossible. How did they slip behind undetected by Vasar Seven's warning system? Casey scanned the control panel, racking her brain for ideas. "Set a course for as far away from here as you can."

"I'm sorry, Casey, but we don't have time."

A powerless feeling rose in her stomach. Casey switched views on the screen before turning to Chasel. They were out of options. She flew them right into the middle of an ambush. The only thing to do was to make sure the ship's data was either safe or destroyed. "Chasel, I need you to store your program, along with everything from the primary system, into the backup drive."

"What are you planning, Casey?" Chasel asked. Her expression was grim.

"I'll be fine. I don't plan on dying today." Casey did her best to appear confident. "I need to make sure those bastards don't get hold of any vital information."

"Casey, make sure you stay alive," Chasel said. She vanished instantly from sight.

Casey guesstimated the lead ship was minutes from reaching her. Her heart pounded. She focused her attention on the information downloading on the monitor. The process was taking too long. "Hurry," she shouted, thumping the panel with her fist.

After the final download of information was completed, everything instantly powered off. Casey removed the drive from the control panel, and stashed it, along with her computer, ring, and both of her necklaces, behind one of the metal plates along the floor.

Loud thuds and clinks echoed, followed by the sound of hefty beings rushing toward her. How were they able to bypass every security measure and board Vasar Seven?

Knowing her freedom was dwindling down to mere seconds, she spun, dashed to the weapons panel, and programmed in a sheathed throwing dagger. Once she shoved it inside her sock, she grabbed an RLP and flipped off the safety switch. When she stood and turned toward the noise closing in behind her, a weapon fired, sending her into painful darkness.

Casey gazed into Tanille's eyes as her finger traced the outline of her lover's naked breast. The air was clear. Full of life. She breathed it in, greedily filling her lungs.

"I love you," Tanille whispered. Her hair lay in a sweeping wave amidst the fresh green grass on the hillside of the Malanight Estate.

"I know, but I think I've really screwed up this time."

"You didn't screw up. You've only hit a snag."

Casey peered upward to the blue sky, as a tear slid slowly along her right cheek.

"Hey, what's this?" Tanille's voice was soft and loving, and her fingers gently brushed away Casey's tear. "Crying would mean you've given up, and I know my woman. She's not a quitter."

The sound of her own laugh felt hollow in her ears. She leaned her naked body closer to Tanille, kissing her lips long and gently. "No, I won't quit. I'm only worried about what'll happen to you if I don't return. Do we have more than one soulmate?"

"No, my love, you're the one I've given my heart to, for now and forever." Tanille rolled out from under Casey and stood. She extended her hand, helping Casey to her feet. "Let's go for a swim. I'm sure the water will be perfect today."

They strolled to the clear body of water arm in arm. "I want you to tell me you love me," Tanille said, the moment they entered the tempered lake.

Casey grinned, enjoying the feel of the water as it engulfed her body. "I love you very much."

"Tell me you'll marry me."

Casey veered her eyes from her lover. The urge to cry swelled in her throat. The feel of Tanille's hand on her cheek brought her to take in a deep, shaky breath. "I'll do all I can."

Tanille stubbornly raised her chin to Casey. "Tell me you'll marry me."

Casey gave her a weak smile. "I will mar—"

Strong hands encircled Casey's legs and yanked her under the water. Kicking hard, she fought her way to the surface. Tanille was missing. Casey coughed out a mouthful of water, gasped and choked for air, while screaming out Tanille's name as best as she could. Her head was splitting in two. Something dragged her back into the depths of the water. This time longer than before. When she finally came up, Casey no longer saw a beautiful, warm sky, or smelled fresh green grass. Instead she was faced with the cold, dreary metal of a ship, followed by the stench of rotting flesh, mixed with engineering grease.

"She's awake, sir," croaked a rough voice somewhere close by.

Her clothes were tacky-wet, clinging to her chilled body, and on closer inspection, she noticed some type of nasty grime covered them. Her arms, legs, and chest were strapped to a metal slab, which teetered on the edge of a tank filled with filthy green water.

"Good. Dunk her again to make sure she stays awake."

Casey inhaled a mouthful of putrid air seconds before the upper half of the slab and her body was once again submerged. She was upside down and disoriented but pushed it all from her mind. Eyelids pressed tight, she concentrated on the rigid feel of the hard metal against her body. Two robust Erules flipped her from the water. This time, she locked eyes with her captors while trying to steady her breathing, so as not to appear frail.

"What abilities do you possess?"

She spit a rancid taste of decaying algae from her mouth and fought against the urge to cough. She thought about using her abilities to see if they truly only worked in the boundaries of the triangle, like her Gran said, but with five Erules in the room, attempting to use them could place her in more harm. So she bided her time and waited. "This looks like a lively crew," she said politely, holding her best smile. "What do I owe for the honor of this get together?"

"Dunk her again," the biggest of the five Erules shouted, outraged by her uncaring demeanor and cheerful comment.

This time when she emerged, she was breathing harder, which seemed to please the leader. "What are your abilities?" he growled.

"I'm afraid," Casey said, between mouthfuls of air, "your slime water has missed a spot behind my right ear. Do you think I might go in one more time?"

"Maybe you would like me to cut off that ear?" he sneered and extracted a rusty serrated knife from his belt.

Casey looked at the blade, then at the Erule. "I'm sorry to be such a complainer, but do you think I could get like a tetanus shot first, or maybe even two? You know, with lockjaw and all." Her head was freaking killing her. The pain pounded so hard she had a difficult time holding her grin.

"Silence!" Slobber flung from his mouth onto one of the creatures stabilizing Casey's metal slab. "You dare try to make a mockery of me. I'll have you carved apart a piece at a time."

"But sir, they ordered us not to kill her."

The leader exploded in a fit of rage and dove like a wild animal, straight for the Erule who spoke. He plunged his knife deep inside the smaller creature's chest and violently twisted it around. He yanked it swiftly out, only to plunge it in several more times. A dirty-green, blood-like substance flowed foully from the dying creature's wounds.

This new aroma of Erule death, mingling with the already decaying smell of the ship, made Casey's stomach lurch. She fought the urge to vomit, more than once, while working at remaining as casual as ever. The struggle was demanding.

Eventually, the creature ceased his stabbings once the lifeless figure lay motionless at his feet. He wiped the back of his hand across his ooze-splattered face in an unsuccessful attempt to clean off some of the gruesome droplets. "Did I say I was going to kill her?" He bellowed at the unmoving body, before glaring at Casey as if to demonstrate his dominance.

Casey stared from the dead Erule to the leader, then to the dead Erule. "The bastard didn't answer you. Are you going to let him get away with that? Stab him again!" she shouted.

The Erule lunged violently at Casey, plunging the knife in her right leg, striking the *xhemight*. She bit at her pain as he twisted the blade sharply before yanking it out. He turned to the shorter of his four mercenaries while he licked Casey's blood off his weapon. "Fix her."

The creature nodded and rushed over to clean and seal Casey's wound with what few items he had in his shabby little medical bag.

When he finished, the leader glared at Casey. "Say something else condescending. I dare you." He all but snarled the last part out.

Casey closed her thoughts to the pain. She looked straight at him with a forced smirk rolling across her lips. "Not to worry. I remembered I had a tetanus shot a year ago. You may carry on."

He waved a hand, motioning to the two Erules standing on opposite sides of her table. They each took turns beating her as she twitched helplessly against the restraints, arms stretched above her. She closed her eyes firmly while fighting with herself to dig in and receive every excruciating strike. The pounding went on for several minutes before their leader finally called them off.

"Which planets do you keep overseers on, other than your beloved Earth?"

Casey silently cringed at the anguish her body felt. Once again, her busted lips curved into a bloody smile directed at the leader. She felt swelling on the right side of her face, yet she remained defiantly silent.

"Do you know what we're planning on doing with you?" His eyes were sinister when he spoke.

Casey gave him a rebellious glare. "Kill me after a nice, long torture. So what? I say you untie me, and we have some fun with this before I go."

He produced a low, growling laugh. "The torture and the kill part are right, but you forgot the piece of the plan regarding the breeding."

Casey threw him a vacant stare. "Come again?"

His sneer wasn't only repulsive, it was evil. "We're going to take you home to a nice cozy bed and breed you to General Morsen, the Dayshire leader. With your abilities and the Dayshire strength added to your bloodline, we'll create the perfect military force to aid us with destroying your precious Universal Region once and for all." He smirked at Casey, apparently realizing he had finally gotten to her. "I'm hoping the rumors are correct and you piss out a girl," he said. "One I can snuggle up with on cold, lonely nights." His eyes held a sick, twisted glare, and he flashed a sharp toothy grin at Casey.

Casey felt a mixture of panic and rage at the sound of his words. She tried to focus on disengaging her restraints, but her emotions were too unsettled to think clearly. She tightened her lips and spoke in a threatening tone. "I'll get loose from here, and when I do, I'm going to kill you, and I swear it will not be pleasant."

He jumped at her again, not out of rage this time, but excitement. She could see it as clear as day. He brought his knife up, plunging it deep into her left shoulder where it went all the way through, before striking the metal table behind her with a loud ping. Casey laid her head against the metal surface and welcomed the anguish in.

Her laugh was loud, defiantly so. The creature removed the knife roughly from her body. He remained there for a moment, peering at her in disbelief, while holding up a hand to stop the other Erule from coming in to heal her injury. Casey visually inspected the bloody injury before she spoke. "Good shot, you missed my *xhemight* completely. If I were you, I'd give it another go. But remember, this next one could be your last."

He cocked his head in bewilderment before motioning for the other to seal her wound. "What are the codes to get your ship into Vasar?" He waited for her to respond, but she only smiled at him.

"Have her moved to the other side. Apparently, I need the special equipment to break this *tenlilte.*"

Once he left, the other creature instructed the two remaining guards to move Casey to the room across the hall. She felt the pain trying to infect its way into her mind, as they dragged her wet, injured body from the room. She fought it down, thinking of her family and those she loved. She felt renewed.

The second they dumped her crumpled body on the ground and busied themselves with rigging up a chain restraint, she focused her mind on the closest Erule. First, she tried to send him flying across the room, but his bulky form didn't budge. With a new wave of pressure building in her head, she forced her thoughts onto a table sitting in the room. She mentally willed it to smash into the mercenaries, but the damn thing remained fixed in place. She lowered her throbbing head to the cold metal grating and breathed through the pain.

Within ten minutes, the leader returned with two other personnel, both more hideous than he was. He directed them to place his items on the two tables before him while he focused on Casey. She was hanging by her wrists from the chain in the center of the cold, unfriendly room. He smiled and gave her a friendly nod before grabbing an item resembling a lime-green, glowing whip. He instructed his two recruits to leave him and the medical creature alone to resume the torture.

"This tool is one of my favorites," he said, flicking it straight out into the air, where it snapped inches away from Casey's face. "Do you know why?"

She gave him a comical yawn before replying, "I *really* don't care."

He grinned. "Oh, you will. You see, this little beauty burns open the flesh when it strikes. What truly makes it unique is the whip leaves a permanent scar which is untreatable, even by the so-called remarkable Trysal medicine." He shrugged. "Something in the chemical it's made of, but it matters not."

Casey's eyes held nothing but hatred for the creature. "You're planning on killing me anyway. Why would a mutilated body be a big worry to me now? Wow, my instructors were right. Erules are an unintelligent race." She paused. "I'm sorry. That was probably too big a word for you to comprehend. How about dim, brainless, or better yet, stupid?"

With a mighty force, he flipped the whip diagonally across her chest. The contact to her flesh burned with an agonizing ripping sensation.

"Damn it," she half yelled, while taking several needed breaths. "This shirt is one of my favorites." She forced a weak grin, while deep down, her agony threatened to spill out.

He sent it against her flesh repeatedly causing her body to spin helplessly on the chain. She refused to scream. The blistering weapon seared her back, chest, face, arms, and legs, scarring her body for the rest of her temporary life, both physically and mentally. This went on for over twenty lashes before he halted and motioned for his poor excuse of a healer to tend to his weakened prisoner.

"Now, this next item will be more for my benefit than yours. I'll have you hooked up to this for, let's say, an hour, and leave you to your grief, thus giving me time to go check our status on deck." He directed the healer to insert the four needles deep into Casey's arms and legs before he pivoted to leave. "Don't have too much fun while I'm gone," he said, as the door closed behind him.

Each of the needles dug into her flesh with searing pain. The instant Casey's blood seeped from the puncture sites, the healer greedily licked off the excess with his long, bumpy tongue, while making piggish grunting sounds. Once all the needles were in, he leered at her and exited the room.

Casey glanced wildly around for any means of escape. When her mind drifted to the clasp on the chain binding her wrists, hoping with all her might to snap it open, a powerful wave of electricity ripped through her body. It shook her on the chain with a force so great she thought it might actually break her loose. The torture lasted for what seemed like a lifetime before subsiding briefly for her to catch a raspy bit of breath, and starting back up again. Casey fought the darkness and instead concentrated on the connection between her and her grandmother.

Elizabeth jumped in her seat. "Casey?" she uttered. Her eyes closed tight with a look of confused pain etched on her face.

Each of the team members glanced over, unsure of what was going on. Hanna made a move to touch her arm, but Ashonda motioned for her not to interfere.

Elizabeth leaned forward in her chair and wrapped her arms firmly around her body. She closed her eyes tighter. "I know it hurts, but you need to hang on." Elizabeth let out a tiny cry. She mumbled Casey's name repeatedly while her entire body trembled.

Tanille's quivering hands covered her tear-filled eyes. *This can't be happening,* she thought, feeling more helpless than she ever had in her life.

Elizabeth took quick shallow breaths, as if she were preparing herself before the next wave of agony hit. "No, you can make it. Think of what we've learned together, and try to use your abilities to your advantage."

Elizabeth screamed out again. Eventually, she bit down hard on her bottom lip and shook her head. "Don't give up. I promise we're coming for you."

She opened her eyes and peered around the room. Tears fell. She focused on Tanille but swiftly glanced away, refusing to reveal what she had experienced.

Ashonda spoke with a low and soothing voice, sitting in the seat beside her. "Casey is alive?"

Elizabeth nodded.

"They have her?"

Elizabeth nodded again.

"What did you see, Elizabeth?"

Elizabeth's gaze returned to Tanille. Her hands and head both shook. "I can't—I can't say."

After taking in a deep breath, Tanille made her way over and bent next to Elizabeth. She reached out for her trembling hands. "Please, if Casey is in medical need, we have to be prepared in order to treat her." She paused. "I must know, Elizabeth. I need to know."

Elizabeth peered at Fayrel, who slowly urged her on, looking sick with grief himself. "She's in severe pain. I could feel it. She wanted it to be over, but I made her fight through the—" Elizabeth began to cry, unable to finish.

"What were they doing?" Ashonda asked.

Elizabeth took in gulps of air, fighting away the tears. "They have electric probes attached to her extremities, which are set to an alarming concentration. She's been savagely beaten, and I think they've lashed her with a Dayshire whip, but I'm not positive."

"Is that everything?" Fayrel asked when his daughter was unable to speak.

"I don't believe so, but I'm not sure."

Fayrel left the deck after informing Tanille he would prepare the medical wing for Casey. Tanille held on to Elizabeth as both women wept in each other's arms.

"We're approaching the Barrier," Eva said, inhaling a soft, steady breath. "The Fleet commander has issued an all-stop until we can get the approval to cross into Dayshire territory."

"Absurd," Barick roared with heightened anger.

Eva's response was filled with regret. "If we cross, we'll be instigating open war. The Assembly will need to be involved."

"Then let's instigate open war! They have a member of the royal family. This should be reason enough!" Barick was on his feet, anger flowing from every pore.

"We cannot be the ones to trigger this war. You know it as well as I," Darren said.

Ashonda stood. "I'm going to contact Ann. Maybe she can speed this up."

Elizabeth dried her eyes and gave Tanille's arm a squeeze. "I'll go with you," she told Ashonda and followed her out of the room.

Parrow went over and wrapped Tanille in his arms. "Casey will be fine. She's a very strong-willed woman."

Tanille's mind spun. Her body felt weak. "The Dayshire whip, Parrow. They used the Dayshire whip on her." She shook her head in disbelief. "And there's a reason we don't use electric probes on criminals. Few would survive, and there's no telling what else they've done or plan to do." Her body trembled with uncontrollable sobs. "How can she make it through that kind of torture, Parrow? How?"

Parrow forced their eyes to connect. "You must stay strong, Tanille, for Casey's sake. Stay strong for her."

Casey peered up into the blackness of the leader's eyes when he marched into the room. "I've missed you something awful," she mumbled, barely able to hold her head up.

"I must admit, being part human, you're tougher than I expected." He waved his hand at the healer, directing him to remove the probes.

Casey gritted her teeth as the subordinate roughly removed each probe. "Don't get soft on me. I still plan to kill you."

The leader ignored her comment. "What shall we do next?" He fumbled through his bag of goodies. "Ah, yes, this'll do nicely." He held up a long, bloodstained needle. The hollow needle was as wide as a beverage straw. "Let's see how red and tasty that Human blood of yours is."

He handed the needle to his healer, who quickly snatched it and pivoted with great enthusiasm toward Casey. He chose a vein on her right arm and roughly shoved the needle inside. Her blood instantly spilled out the other end, where the creature ravenously began to drink.

"We're not animals," the leader shouted. "Use a cup for Daynard's sake!" He tossed two large cups at the creature, who filled them.

Casey's body grew cold, signaling her death was finally approaching. She closed her eyes and prayed. She believed in God, and although she hadn't attended church since she left for college, she knew he was listening. She silently prayed for her loved ones to have long and happy lives. For the safety of humanity, and all those living inside the Universal Region.

The leader grew impatient. "If you let her die, I swear you shall experience a torture far greater than hers."

The second-rate healer placed the cups on the table and withdrew the needle. He gave Casey an injection on her forearm. He retrieved both cups and handed the fuller of the two over to his captain.

"Don't worry, young Malanight." The leader eyed the contents of his cup as he spoke and swallowed in anticipation. "That hasn't only stopped your bleeding, but it will quicken the production of blood inside your feeble body. You still have so many wonderful things left to enjoy."

"To her good health," the leader toasted, bringing a rasping sound of laughter from his subordinate.

The leader downed half his glass and smacked his lips together. "I would offer you a taste, Ms. Malanight, but your nectar is far too exquisite to share."

This procedure went on for several more rounds before he started with his next method of torture. He used a sharp knife, as filthy as the needle, and carved deeply into different parts of Casey's body.

She closed her eyes and pictured the first time she met Tanille. How beautiful she was standing with her father, gazing up at the picture on the wall. If she could only kiss her one last time, then this premature ending to her life would be endurable.

Relaxing her mind and body, Casey recalled the first time she placed her head between Tanille's slender legs and tasted her, breathing in her sweet smell. Her mind was seconds away from mentally tasting Tanille's tantalizing wetness as she envisioned her tongue stroking into the delicate nectar.

"Why are you smiling?"

The roar of the leader returned her reluctantly to reality. "Oh, am I not supposed to? I'm sorry. I'll stop. Please continue with what you were doing."

He growled with uncontrollable rage and drove the knife straight into her leg. Casey felt the tip break off the moment it struck against her *xhemight.* She could take no more and screamed out in pain, sending a grin to the Erule's lips.

"Do I have your attention now?"

Casey wasn't sure if the smug look on his ugly face or the exploding pain in her bleeding leg was what made her glare at the knife in the Erule's hand. She concentrated with every ounce of energy she could muster, which made her body feel ablaze with fever. The blood-soaked weapon in the leader's hand jerked straight up, and with enormous strength, plunged deeply into his thick throat.

Eyes wide with disbelief, the leader fell onto the floor, flailing in agony, clawing frantically at the handle of the knife with trembling hands. The smaller creature, stunned, stared from Casey to his dying leader. The instant the reality of the scene struck him, he made a mad rush for the door. Casey's eyes grew red with burning hatred. She lifted the table with her mind and sent it hurtling against the creature. Her aim was accurate, and she heard his neck crack under the impact. Next, she concentrated on the clasp around her wrists. Within seconds, both metal cuffs opened, sending her limp body to the floor in a painful heap beside the dying Erule.

Casey slowly sat up with a throbbing headache as she wiped off a stream of blood from under her nose. She crawled to the gurgling leader, reached over, and ripped the knife from his throat. He twitched slightly as she plunged the knife with all her might repeatedly into his chest. Within seconds of the last stab, the creature was dead.

Searching through his clothes for a weapon, Casey felt a square object in his left breast pocket. She yanked it roughly out. It resembled the computer backup drive she had used to store the vital information from her own ship's computer system. Casey pocketed it before continuing her search. Unable to find a firearm, she grabbed the knife sticking from the dead leader's chest before struggling to her feet.

Her entire body felt dangerously weak, and excruciating pain radiated with every movement. She staggered over to where the discarded medical bag lay. Tearing through it, she removed anything she could use for a temporary mend. Right as she finished, the door to the room slid open.

"Sir, we're approaching—" The dimwitted Erule stopped mid-stride. His eyes examined the bodies of his fallen comrades in frightened surprise. Before he could decide a course of action, a knife came soaring through the air, catching him above his left eye. His body fell with a thump backward onto the metal floor.

Casey could move slightly faster now. She made her way over and dragged the dead Erule fully inside. Stripping off his holster and sidearm, she fastened the setup around her waist. A tingling sensation in her right arm worried her. She tightened her fist and tried to shake more feeling into this part of her body. Without full use of her arm, hand-to-hand combat would be difficult, but firing the weapon would increase the likelihood of being caught or killed, and Casey was determined to make it out of this hellhole alive.

Casey closed her eyes and thought of Elizabeth. She wasn't sure if their previous connection had been real or not, but she had to try something to let the others know she was still alive.

"What do you mean they said not to go any farther?" Elizabeth glowered at the monitor. A tearful Queen Ann sat with her shoulders slumped on the other side of the screen.

"The Assembly said the Dayshire would consider this an act of war. Elizabeth, the delegates from Couhl Tabarr fought the hardest on this decision. They swayed the vote against further assistance."

Elizabeth froze, her mind working out the puzzle. "They're in on it."

Ann's eyes grew cold, her pupils fixed on the screen. "I've considered this, but without proof, it's too risky to bring accusations like this up before the Assembly."

"Look, they were the ones who set this up. I'm sure of it. They were the ones who originally asked me to come get them, and by doing so, it separated the team. Plus, they delayed us with the feast, so we wouldn't make it to Vasar until after Casey had left." Elizabeth spoke to the floor, her mind reeling to piece together the unknown. "But how did they get her to leave? Why would Casey think I was in trouble?"

"This doesn't matter now." Ashonda insisted. "We can worry about placing blame once Casey is safely home."

Elizabeth spun toward the monitor. "What if we only take our ship across the Barrier?"

Ann gave her a stern look. "No! That would not only be political suicide, but too dangerous for you and your crew. You know that area is swarming with Erule and Dayshire ships."

Elizabeth threw up her hands in frustration. "What do we do? Sit here and wait—" Her body went rigid.

"Elizabeth, what is it?" Ann asked, but Ashonda held up a hand to quiet her daughter.

Elizabeth closed her eyes. She watched Casey kill an Erule from behind, and kneel beside the creature.

Elizabeth's head jerked up as soon as she lost the connection. "Casey's alive and has freed herself somehow."

Ann leaned closer to the screen. "Casey's escaped?"

"No, she's still on their ship. I saw her kill one of them."

"If she's on the Erule ship, Casey's outside the area of the triangle. How's this possible?"

Appearing impatient, Ashonda hurriedly answered her daughter. "We're not sure. Call it a miracle if you like, but they've tapped into a connection between one another." She immediately asked Elizabeth her own question. "Were you able to see where she was? Do you think we can make it there in time?"

Elizabeth shook her head, yet Ann was the one who spoke. Loudly. "No, I'm sorry, Mother, but you'll stay inside the Universal Region. If you try to cross, I'll have no choice but to have you all arrested and brought straight here."

"I know, Ann. My statement was nothing more than a hypothetical slip of the tongue." Veering her head from the screen, and her daughter's probing eyes, Ashonda whispered to Elizabeth. "We should go tell the others."

"I'm not finished, Mother," Ann said.

"I'm sorry, dear. Could you repeat that?" With a gradual shift of her arm, Ashonda covertly reached for the controls.

Ann narrowed her eyes. "You heard me. Don't you dare touch—"

Ashonda flipped the switch, closing the connection.

Elizabeth's smile was warm as she helped her grandmother stand. "She's only doing what's right."

"I know." Ashonda's exhale was overly theatrical. "She still talks too much though. Was like that since she was little."

Elizabeth and Ashonda returned to the operations deck to inform the crew of the situation.

"This decision should be our choice," Barick shouted, banging his fist hard on the control desk.

Parrow was as outraged as his father. "They cross into our region all the time!"

"Right or wrong, the Assembly has already voted." Hanna stared directly at both her husband and her son. "We'll not go against their ruling unless it comes from the Fleet commander himself."

"Why is this decision left up to the Fleet commander?" Parrow demanded. "We're carrying members of the royal family with us. They have power over him."

David interjected. "Because he doesn't have blood ties to Casey. His decision wouldn't be made from emotion, but with the logic of a Universal commander."

After disengaging their ships comms, Eva removed her earpiece. "I know David and Hanna are right, but I'm not sure if I have the restraint to remain here much longer."

"We'll wait as instructed, whatever the outcome." Elizabeth gave her a stern glance before taking a seat next to Tanille.

Tanille's shoulders hung with the pain she carried. "Casey crossed into enemy territory alone to save the people she loves. It's not right for us to leave her to her own fate," Tanille muttered.

Elizabeth fought for strength. Her self-discipline was challenged by her own desire to defy those in power to save her granddaughter. "We have no other choice." Elizabeth took Tanille's hand as they waited.

Chapter Fifteen

Restricted Boundary

Casey stowed her last dead victim behind a cupboard in the ship's dining area. This room was as grimy as the rest of the vessel, and she was more than ready to be free of the stench. She made her way blindly around the ship, trying to find the passageway that would take her to her own vessel.

She knew the Erules were towing Vasar Seven because she saw a diagram of her attached ship on an image-monitor she passed. Unfortunately, time was not on her side. She'd already killed seven personnel. Soon they were bound to discover she'd escaped. If she could only find a sign, picture, anything to point her to the ship's hangar.

Hearing someone approaching from the far end of the room, Casey hurriedly made her way out into the corridor and continued with her search. She snuck into the next room for temporary seclusion to catch her breath. The moment the door behind her slid shut, she realized this room had to be the captain's quarters.

She scurried to the cluttered desk, hoping to locate some sort of map to help direct her with where she needed to go. Forcing open the drawers with her bloodied knife, she hastily searched through drawer after drawer, each as disorganized as the next. In the second to last drawer, she found a map, along with a shiny black container. A sloppy, "deliver to General Morsen" was etched on the top. Casey squinted, puzzled. This inscription wasn't some foreign enemy's handwriting she couldn't comprehend, but the familiar style of the Hafites. She found two more containers in the bottom drawer, and after retrieving a bag in a corner closet, she shoved each item deep inside.

Risking no more time, she studied the map. The writing was Erule, a language she hadn't learned yet. Fortunately, she understood the pictures and designs to some extent. Her heart raced in panic at how vast this ship was. She needed to make it onto her own ship, enter her destination, and have it ready to engage before anyone noticed she was no longer a prisoner. If the Erules discovered her escape before then, she knew she would be in a much worse predicament than before.

After several minutes of haphazard deciphering, she finally spotted an area which looked promising. She tucked the map in the bag and moved to leave.

Without warning, the door to the room gave a tiny beep, and Casey swiftly hit the floor. Damn! She slowly peered around the desk, trying to get a view of the unknown intruder. An Erule, much older than the others she'd encountered, entered. Instead of heading to the desk where Casey was hiding, he advanced toward the corner wall. Once there, he revealed a secret compartment hidden in the shadows, pressed a sequence of commands into a side panel, and caused a thick metal door to slide open.

As he was placing several items inside the murky opening, Casey sprang forward with her knife raised. She desired a fast kill, silent like the others. She was seconds away from thrusting her weapon straight into the weak spot on the base of his skull when her foot caught on one of the many obstacles littering the floor. She recovered, but not fast enough.

He pivoted wildly around and faced her. "You!" He brought his elbow up hard against the side of her swollen face, knocking her against a chair. "You should not be here." The strength and speed of this older creature surprised Casey. Yet she'd learned through her training, it takes more than brute strength to win a fight. He gripped her tightly in his bulky hands and lifted her high above his head. Right before he slammed her body to the ground, Casey laughed. He paused, peering upward, obviously puzzled by her reaction.

"You're a stupid bastard." Casey winked and swung her knife around hard, skillfully plunging the weapon into the back of his disfigured skull.

His body hung temporarily in the air, as if suspended by invisible strings, before falling in a heap with her landing painfully on top. She lay there, taking a few breaths, while silently wondering how much more her body could take. Every part of her hurt. Sharp pains, burning aches, slashed and mutilated flesh. She closed her eyes, trying with all her might to welcome it all in.

Once she made it to her feet, Casey lurched to the exposed compartment in the wall. She reached inside, emptying the entire contents of the compartment into her overstretched bag, along with the items the Erule had dropped on the floor. She heaved the bag over her shoulder where it rubbed painfully against the open wounds on her back, but she believed she didn't have much farther to go. She removed her firearm from its carrier and mentally prepared herself.

"Just a little longer," she whispered, hoping her luck held out. She exited the room and took the first left, scampering along the corridor. Inspecting the map, she stopped before a gray door smeared with grease and grime. She paused for two deep breaths before activating the door mechanism with her weapon ready.

To her good fortune, no one was in this loading bay. Nor did it look as if they had offloaded anything from her vessel. Surprised, she hurried to the steep access ramp leading to Vasar Seven. Her heart pounded as she forced her body up the incline. The middle of the ramp had groves and handles, but at this angle, and carrying the bag, the trek was proving extremely difficult to maneuver. When she finally got to the top, she raised the entry hatch in one try, but lifting the packed bag onto the floor of her ship took all the strength she had left. She closed and latched the hatch once she crawled in, then laid on the cool, clean floor for several raspy breaths.

"You're almost there," A voice inside her head yelled, forcing her instantly to her feet. Her head pounded as her eyes darted around for her grandmother. After a few seconds of searching, Casey figured she had only imagined the voice. This repeated illusion of Gran was the primary reason she had gotten this far. She took it for what she assumed the vision was—a hallucination brought on by her body's vulnerable state. It was enough.

She kept her gun raised in case any unexpected visitors were lurking about her ship. Entering the elevator, Casey went straight to the operations deck. After dropping the bag, she rushed to where she placed the ship's backup drive, her cherished Program Chasel, and her personal items. At first, her heart skipped a beat, but finally her fingers located the drive and her possessions, removing them from their undetected hiding place. Casey hurried to the console and plugged the drive into the system. Within moments, Chasel materialized, sending a fresh wave of hope coursing through her veins.

"I was so worried about you," Chasel said.

"Me too." Casey peeked over her shoulder, half expecting to see a handful of Erules rushing in to finish her off. "We need to hurry before they realize I'm gone."

Chasel agreed and instantly disappeared. Two seconds later, Casey watched as the upload of Vasar Seven's programming increased in speed. When Chasel returned, she sounded genuinely frightened. "It's done, Casey, but I've detected a life-form inside Elizabeth's chambers. An Erule."

Casey squeezed the butt of the weapon she still clutched in her hand. "Let me know if it moves."

"I will."

Casey started the program sequence for Crogonic travel, and checked it against the substance detection map. She spotted an asteroid field close to the Universal Region's border, so she set the destination to a location directly before that point in case something changed.

Once she entered the final sequence, Casey asked Chasel, "How do I detach us from the other ship?"

"There's a lever on the floor to the left of the hatch which must be released. I would do it from here, but they set it to manual detach only."

"I'll go deal with the intruder and detach us. Once I tell you to, activate Crogonic travel."

Chasel bowed her head and wished Casey luck.

The ship felt warm and friendly as she made her way below. She took extra care around the corners and kept a constant watch behind her while she moved. By the time she positioned herself in front of her grandmother's quarters, she was ready. The door slid open, bringing a horrid, half-awake Erule to roll over in the bed, surprised.

"I gave her those sheets for Christmas, you ugly fucker!" Casey squeezed off several bursts into the body of the unexpecting Erule. She brought her hand smartly up to her nose. She had to fight off the urge to gag. His grotesque stench was enough to make even the strongest Blunion sick. Casey shook her head at the smell. "Gran will not be happy," she muttered.

At the entry hatch, Casey located the lever. Right before she pulled it, a clink below her hand echoed. She lowered her head closer to the hatch. Heavy shuffling from multiple beings rushing up the ramp. Erules. If they opened the hatch, the ship wouldn't be able to leave.

Casey hurriedly flipped the lever over and shouted, "Launch, Chasel. Launch, now!"

Elizabeth sprang from her seat. "Casey's escaped. She's on her way back."

"Are you sure?" Eva asked.

"I'm positive," Elizabeth said. "She's on Vasar Seven in Crogonic travel and less than two hours away."

Eva rotated her seat to tell the Fleet commander to be ready for battle.

"She's badly hurt. I'm not sure how much strength she has left, but she'll make it."

"The medical wing's ready, Elizabeth," Fayrel said, holding Tanille in his arms.

Hanna asked Elizabeth, while bringing up the long-range visuals, "Can you tell how many ships are following her?"

"No, but I'm sure there's plenty."

Hanna motioned to her husband. "Barick, you'll need to help me operate weapons if things become dicey."

Out of nowhere, Eva argued into her communicator. Movement on the operations deck grew silent as all listened, trying to grasp what they could of the conversation.

Eva spun in her seat, her eyes blazing with fury. "The Fleet commander's been ordered to return to Vasar!"

Elizabeth was outraged. "On whose authority?" she demanded.

"He said the Assembly's."

As if in hearing her, a link from Queen Ann bleeped in.

"Answer that," Elizabeth shouted.

The second Eva opened the link, Ann's image popped on the screen. "Elizabeth, we have a problem."

"We've already heard! What in the hell is this? Never in our history has the Assembly treated the royal bloodline with such contempt."

"Elizabeth, listen to me. Whoever's behind Casey's abduction is using internal means to prevent Casey from returning home, at any cost."

"How so?"

"The Hafites called an emergency meeting the moment they stepped foot inside the Assembly. We never expected this would happen. Over half of the delegates didn't know about the meeting until it was too late. Many didn't arrive in time to cast their vote. The head of council and I scarcely made it there ourselves." Her expression was grave yet stern. "The Zelic and Floun diplomats joined with the Hafites, striking up fear of immediate war if the Fleet intervened. Their fear helped weigh the decision. I have no proof, but my guess is the Hafite delegates have switched sides. Maybe the Zelic and Floun delegates as well. At this point, I'm not sure who we can trust."

Ashonda was beside herself. "How is this possible? What right did they have to call a meeting?"

"Casey's in danger and a member of the royal family. Summoning an emergency meeting was within their right."

"Our ancestors enacted that law to aid and protect the royal family, not to place a royal descendant in further harm. Exactly how deep does this treachery go?"

"I'm not sure, but I'm on my way out to you with my team. We left as soon as the decision was final," Ann said.

Ashonda stood. "You are the queen. You're forbidden from leaving Vasar."

"I already have, Mother. I'm sorry, but it's gotten to the point where we need to take care of our own. We'll be there within the hour."

Elizabeth knew Grandmother Ashonda was right, but if they lost Casey, what hope of a future did the Universal Region have? "We'll wait until then, but please hurry."

Ann signaled to a member of her team, and the connection ended.

Elizabeth collapsed in an open seat, her mind mulling through the events of the last five hours. "What's going on?" Her voice was heavy with despair. "I can't believe the Assembly voted *not* to save Casey's life."

Hanna answered, "We're feeling the beginnings of the next Great War. We have many allies but will also lose ones we thought we could trust."

"The Zelics and the Flouns I'm not as concerned with," Barick said. "They're from outside the Regional Blockade and are newer to the Assembly. Neither has much of a military, but the power they now hold combined with the Hafites could prove a problem."

"The Hafites turned on us during the last Great War. Betrayal is nothing new for them." Eva's face skewed in disgust, as if saying the name Hafite had left an unpleasant taste in her mouth.

Barick leaned back in his chair and crossed his arms. "Yes, but they're near the center of the region, and their military is not as weak as it once was. They also have a stronger pull with several members of the Assembly."

Elizabeth understood each of their beliefs, but she wasn't completely convinced the Hafites as a whole would switch sides and join with the enemy. "I know many Hafites, and I can assure you they don't all lust for power. It's more of a problem for us to find the ones who are loyal to the Dayshire and replacing them in the Assembly."

"That's easier said than done," replied Ashonda. "Helping them get nominated is one thing, but they still need to be elected." Ashonda lowered her eyes in thought. "We might have enough of an influence on Vasar alone to persuade the vote. I can make a few inquiries. See how many of the Hafite citizens living among us are truly trustworthy."

Suddenly, Tanille stood. "I'm sick of listening to this! This may one day be important, but can you please concentrate on getting Casey safely home?" She stormed from the room.

Elizabeth waved down the flabbergasted Fayrel. She understood Tanille's worry and knew the young Trysal required a tender embrace, not a scholastic sermon. It'd be best if she handled this. When Elizabeth entered the corridor, Tanille was nowhere around. "Jasper, can you locate Tanille for me?"

"Most definitely. She sprinted to the elevators. I was going to scold her for her reckless pace, but she seemed pretty upset."

"Thank you, Jasper." Inside the elevator, Elizabeth asked, "Do you know where she's heading?"

"I'm not sure, but she exited two floors down. Do you want me to inform you when she reaches a destination?"

"No, I believe I know where she's going."

Once the elevator opened, Elizabeth took the first right to Casey's quarters. The second she entered, her heart broke. Tanille was lying on Casey's bed, crying. Her arms clung tight to random articles of Casey's clothes, cuddling them as she wept.

Elizabeth swallowed several times, working to remain poised. "I thought I'd find you here," she said.

Tanille's head popped up and her body sluggishly followed. She steadied herself before she spoke. "I'm sorry I lost my temper."

"No need to apologize."

Tanille wiped the tears from her eyes. "Casey is too wonderful of a woman to be yanked into a nightmare as horrifying as this." Tanille shifted to the edge of the bed. "Why did she leave by herself? What could she have been thinking?"

"I'm not sure." Elizabeth sat beside Tanille and cupped their hands together. "I wish life were easier. I wish the road ahead could be less challenging for us all, but this grief is only the beginning. I have a feeling what Queen Ann said about us needing to care for our own is more real than we know." She paused, peering at the wall display, which revealed the star-speckled blackness of deep space outside their ship. "When Casey makes it home, and after you two marry, you'll need to stay strong for each other, no matter what happens."

Tanille faced Elizabeth with red, puffy eyes. "What do you mean?"

"A war like this rips people apart. It has a way of making us feel alone. Vulnerable. Especially for leaders like us who hold the well-being of our citizens in our hands. We need to be strong, no matter what we encounter."

"Nothing could tear me away from Casey. Especially not an asinine war. I love her too much."

"And that love you have for one another will strengthen us in ways no weapons or abilities ever could. You'll see."

Tanille gave Elizabeth a hug. "I'm truly sorry I acted the way I did."

"Never apologize for worrying about your loved ones." Elizabeth stood, straightened the bedding, more from habit than responsibility, and held her hand out. "Now, shall we go check on the rest of the crew?"

As soon as they entered the operations deck, all eyes turned in their direction and Eva signaled to Elizabeth. "We're picking up a line of ships approaching from inside the Universal Region," Eva said, gesturing to the image on the main panel.

"Is the Fleet returning?" Elizabeth asked.

Eva shook her head. "No. I'm positive that's Queen Ann's vessel in front, but I'm still uncertain about the others."

"Open communications."

Within seconds, Ann's smiling face emerged on the holographic screen.

"Who's with you?" Elizabeth asked, trying to make out the additional vessels.

"Most of the delegates in the Assembly have sent out their own personal security ships to help us hold the line. Many are also having their militaries assembled. Our own Royal Military is also on standby. If this escalates into the beginnings of a war, we'll be ready."

"I guess we're not as alone as we believed ourselves to be." Ashonda grinned as her daughter's ship slowed from Crogonic travel.

"I count over fifty ships," Eva excitedly announced as the crew stood to marvel at the numbers.

Ann's carefree hand swayed on the monitor. "Maybe we should have this war out now and be done with it."

Elizabeth grinned. "Multiply the number of your ships times five thousand, and you have a deal."

"I guess we'd better wait," Ann said, smiling.

Eva swiveled her seat halfway around and addressed Elizabeth. "I'm picking up a signal from a ship on the long-range scanner. It's not on visual yet, but soon will be."

Casey rubbed ointment into one of her many open wounds. She was near exhaustion, and without the healer's security codes for key areas of the medical wing, her supplies were limited. Not a good thing, considering how dangerously low her vitals were. She tore off the wound sealant lid and shook the cannister.

Chasel's voice drifted out from hidden speakers. "Casey, I'm tracking unknown objects on the long-range scanner."

"How much time do we have until we come out of Crogonic travel?" Casey asked, limping to the elevators.

"Less than eight minutes."

Casey entered the operations deck, where Chasel had already loaded the images on the main screen. She inspected the readout on the control panel before analyzing the imagery. She couldn't tell if the mass of ships approaching were friend or foe. "How far behind are the Erule vessels?"

"Roughly two Crogons. They've added nine more ships to the chase, which brings their numbers to thirty-seven."

She squinted at the main screen. The last thing she wanted was to fly into more enemy ships, but she didn't know where else she could go with so little time to adjust. The minute her ship identified the lead vessel, her heart raced. "It's Vasar Six! Those must be Fleet ships behind them. I don't recognize the markings, but hey, there's a lot." She turned toward Chasel with a high-spirited laugh. Unfortunately, the building pressure in her chest sent a wave of uncontrollable hacks and coughs, followed by her spitting up an alarming amount of blood.

"I dislike your health status, Casey, and for the last hour, your temperature has been increasing. You're unwell."

Casey held up a hand to Chasel. "I know, but let's enjoy this bit of good news for a moment."

A light flashed on the panel overhead, informing Casey her ship was preparing to move out of Crogonic travel in less than a minute.

"Here we go, Chasel. If I should pass out, I want you to head for that mass of ships ahead."

As her ship slowed, Casey kept a watch on the vessels behind them. The Erule numbers had almost matched the Universal Fleet. Not a major concern in her eyes. She knew the training, skill, and vessels of the Universal Fleet were unsurpassed by any other species, even by the Royal Military. She powered up the short burst rockets, preparing to launch Vasar Seven safely forward.

As she was about to hit the button, the unexpected happened. She experienced a futuristic vision outside of the Universal Region, and past the boundaries of the triangle. Her holographic ghost-self stood inside the ship with her loved ones. Sounds of blasts and explosions vibrated the air as all anxiously viewed the main screen.

Eva maneuvered the vessel in and out of oncoming fire, as Vasar Six went head-to-head with three Erule vessels. "There's too many," Eva shouted. The same fear engulfing Eva overshadowed Casey. Her palms started to sweat.

"Barick, fire at the lead ship. I'll take the one on its left," Hanna yelled, throwing herself at her controls. They both destroyed their targets.

The moment Casey let out her trapped exhale, she saw it happen. The third ship came upward, spinning straight for them. The visual agony played out in slow motion. The firing of the other ship's weapons, the bewildered fear in her grandmother's eyes, and the last painful glimpse of Fayrel and Tanille as father and daughter held one another. A flash of the explosion sent Casey to her own time, her own ship, where she surged swiftly to her feet.

Chasel jumped in surprise. "What is it?"

Fighting off the urge to vomit, Casey shook her head. "If we draw the Erules over there, everyone on Vasar Six will die."

"Casey, what do we do?"

Casey disabled her plotted boost. "Do we have time to plot a new course?"

"No, I'm sorry. We can either stay here or go forward."

Casey shook her head. "I have a feeling either way, this will end badly for them," she said, and she forced her mind to push the upsetting vision as far away as she could.

She paced the area in front of the monitor. "There has to be something." Her eyes came up, and she focused her gaze out into the vastness of space. "That's it!" Casey felt a wave of hope.

"What is?"

Casey studied the lengthy cluster of asteroids drifting close by. "Please, let this work. How long until the Erule ships reach us?"

"It will be in thirty-two seconds."

"Thirty-two seconds," Casey whispered. Her heart ached, but she knew she was out of options. Her gaze landed on Chasel. "I need you to tell everyone I love them and let Tanille know I want her to live a long, happy life."

"What are you going to do?"

"What I have to. Thank you for all your help, Chasel. You've been a genuine friend."

"Fifteen seconds," Chasel said, her voice stricken with grief.

Casey focused on the asteroids. One of God's many marvels. Closing her eyes, she concentrated.

"Ten seconds."

She leaned in, relaxing her mind and body, and focused on the bulk of the vast field of spinning rock of various shapes and sizes. A slowly forming heat burned deep inside her brain.

"Five seconds."

Casey's body shook, followed by the violent rumbling of Vasar Seven. She held on to the desk as tight as she could.

"The Erules are behind us," Chasel said.

The massive group of asteroids beside them shifted direction. Boulders as big as mountains, some resembling oddly shaped planets of their own design, moved gradually at first, and one by one, they picked up speed. They raced by, plummeting straight into the massive gathering of ships behind Vasar Seven.

The entirety of Casey's body felt ablaze with fire. She gripped tighter, willing herself to stay on her feet while her mind worked its last, greatest miracle. Blood poured from her nose and ears, and she tightened her jaw against the exploding pain in her head.

"All ships have been destroyed," Chasel said a few minutes later, while she helplessly watched Casey's body fall lifelessly to the ground.

"It's Vasar Seven," Eva shouted, followed by the excited cheers of everyone on board. Elizabeth gave Tanille a joyous hug before embracing Grandmother Ashonda.

"She's slowing down, probably because of how close she came out by the asteroid field. I taught her that." Eva beamed proudly. "Soon, she'll boost to us."

Barick leaned over, kissing Hanna fully. The Blunion was too excited to protest such an unusual public display of affection from her husband.

"I'm picking up multiple Erule ships, so everyone had better strap in and get ready." They did as Eva suggested. Several moments passed before the Kan turned uneasily to Elizabeth. "Casey should have boosted to us by now."

"See if you can reach her on communications."

"I already have, but she isn't responding. The asteroid field could be interfering with comms."

Unfastening her restraints, Elizabeth rushed to the main computer console. "Casey…don't do it," she breathed, clutching her chest with both hands.

"Why is she not moving toward us?" Tanille asked, releasing her safety latch.

Elizabeth reached out and gently touched Casey's ship on the monitor. "Because she's seen our deaths." Elizabeth absorbed the pain of knowing she was going to lose her granddaughter. "She's sacrificing herself to save us."

Elizabeth's tears toppled on the surface of the monitor as Tanille screamed out in protest. "Stop her!"

Elizabeth gripped onto Eva's chair. "It's too late," she said, her voice trembling.

They all witnessed in silence as the asteroids changed course and headed for the gathering of ships appearing in waves behind Vasar Seven. The enemy had no time to react. Various sized rocks and boulders ripped through the vessels, destroying everything in their path. The explosions were massive, going from balls of flashing fire before dissipating, as stored oxygen burned away and left hunks of metal and debris shooting out in every direction. The moment the boulders obliterated the last of the ships, Vasar Seven navigated straight for them.

"She made it!" Tanille hysterically laughed and cried at the same time. "Casey made it!"

Eva addressed Elizabeth. "Chasel's on comms. She's flying the ship. She said Casey's on the ground. Her vitals are barely readable and she's not moving." The Kan lowered her eyes. "Her brain function—" Unable to go on, Eva whirled to her workstation.

Elizabeth motioned to Fayrel. "We'll board the ship and bring her to you. Do what you can."

He bowed his head in silence while dabbing at his eyes. He guided Tanille out of the room with him. "I want to give you something to help you sleep," he said.

"I'm fine, and so is Casey. If she were dead, I know I would feel it. Besides, you'll need my help with treating her."

The look he offered resembled pity. "If she makes it, the damage she's inflicted on her brain alone will be so great, she—"

"Don't you dare, Father." Tanille clenched her teeth. "Casey risked her life for us. You will show her your gratitude by not being so damn pessimistic."

He seemed at a loss for words. He opened his mouth, but suddenly closed it. Eventually, he agreed. They rode the elevator in silence, one eager to begin prep work, the other eye-bobbing worriedly from his daughter to the ground. The two worked at setting up for any situation they might have to deal with. They were ready and waiting by the time Barick and Parrow hurriedly carried Casey's limp body into the room.

"She has a slight pulse, but it's fading fast," Parrow said, looking directly at Tanille.

The moment she saw Casey's battered and bloody body, her neck-muscles tightened, and her eyes grew moist. She cleared her mind, willing herself to push past the ache of a lover and concentrate instead on the professionalism of a healer. She swiped the dampness from her eyes and motioned for them to position Casey on the newly prepared table.

The crew began filing in, one right after the other. Keeping clear of the table where both healers were working feverishly, everyone gathered toward the far corner in silent prayer. Not long after, Ann trotted in and joined them.

Tanille read through the monitor while her father guided the analysis machine over Casey's body. The list of injuries was extensive. The system arranged them on the screen from most critical to least life-threatening. The diagnosed outcome on the monitor read the chance for normal brain activity after surgery was virtually nonexistent.

Fayrel said, "She has major damage to the frontal and both temporal lobes, not to mention the rest of her body."

"She'll be fine." Worried over Casey's condition and irritated with her father's lack of faith, Tanille angrily rotated the damn screen out of her way. "Casey will pull through." She snatched several items from a nearby counter.

"Look at the damage, Tanille. Read what the—"

Tanille spun, piercing her father with a threatening set of eyes. "You can either help me or let me bring someone in here who will. Casey is my patient. I'm her healer."

"Tanille." Elizabeth's voice was grief stricken. "Casey wouldn't want to live out her life off machines."

Her father spoke over his shoulder as he programmed various drugs and their dosage into the Medications Originator. "Even if we stabilize her, the damage is too great for recovery, and you know it." Her father retrieved several injectors. "We can continue to manage her pain—"

No longer able to control her anger, Tanille snapped. "I don't believe this coming from either of you. You're her grandmother. How could you give up on her like this? And you, Father. You're talking about Casey. You know she's not a normal patient." Tanille shook her head fiercely. She had heard enough. She balled her fists, refusing to allow Casey's subconscious mind to be subjected to any more negativity. "I want this room cleared now," she demanded, throwing out her arm and motioning the group toward the door.

No one moved, bringing Parrow to square his shoulders. "You heard her. She said now!" He took a threatening step forward, preparing to lash out at anyone who defied him.

Ann held up a hand. "Everyone, please step outside and let Casey's team take care of her," she ordered. "I'll call if we need you."

"You also, Father."

Fayrel stared at Tanille tenderly before he followed Elizabeth from the room. Tanille watched him leave, feeling a wave of mixed emotions. Yes, studying the assessment monitors, any other healer would have agreed with him. If these findings were from another patient, she would herself. But this incredible being was Casey Malanight. A woman who descended from a phenomenal bloodline. Lineage with remarkable abilities advanced medicine couldn't explain. Casey was a truly unique miracle in so many ways. Whether she survived this or not, she deserved a fighting chance with all the help Tanille could offer.

Once the room was clear, Ann faced the two of them. "I did pretty well in my medical classes at the Academy. I can assist if you could use me."

"I would be appreciative of the extra set of hands," Tanille said gratefully. She took a moment to collect herself before visually inspecting Casey's body. Seeing the woman she loved in this state was beyond difficult. Casey's body, swollen, bloodied, and broken was borderline unrecognizable. Tanille wanted to scream, to lash out at those responsible. Make them feel a fraction of the pain her Casey had experienced.

A tender hand squeezed her arm. "We'll get through this together." Ann gestured with her head to Casey's unconscious body. "She's like me, a fighter."

Tanille breathed in steadily, blinking clarity into her eyes. After wiping away the remaining tears, she swiveled the monitor closer, and reassessed the situation. Mentally, she had to rewire her mind into seeing a patient lying on the table in need of medical attention and not Casey, the woman she loved. Eventually, a plan of action unfolded. She called for multiple instruments and high-powered devices, which the ship's computer provided. The area around the bed sprang to life, as medical gadgets and surgical mechanisms dropped from compartments in the ceiling or rose from sections under the floor.

Chasel showed up moments later and assisted the group as best she could. They started at the top of the long list of injuries and slogged their way down. Even Parrow aided Tanille by fetching requested items and diligently cleaning up the mess between procedures.

"How are the fluids? Do I need to program in a higher dose?" Chasel asked, visually inspecting Casey's mangled body.

"No, they're fine. Keep track of her vitals. If anything changes, let me know."

Parrow muttered, "I cannot believe how much blood she's lost." He gripped Casey's hand.

The three exchanged reassuring stares before Tanille said, "Parrow, I need you to hold this extremely still above her head. If you get tired, have Ann take—"

Red flashing lights and a high shrieking alarm rang throughout the room. Without hesitating, Tanille searched the screen. "Her heart stopped."

She punched in a few commands, and a separate machine lowered from the ceiling.

Ann and Parrow remained silent, out of the way, as Tanille worked over Casey to do everything she could to bring her back. She activated the cardiac machine and positioned the contraption over Casey. It covered her face and chest, giving off a humming vibration.

A computerized voice called out, "One minute."

Tanille entered a few more commands causing the machine to hum and vibrate louder. Glowering at the screen showing Casey's vitals, she held her breath and focused on the indicators, trying to mentally will them into rising. Over two minutes passed, and still no response came.

"Damn it, Casey, breathe," Tanille demanded, squeezing Casey's pale arm.

When the automated voice called out, "three minutes," Tanille spun, seizing a flat injector off a nearby stand. She touched the device to Casey's neck, injecting her with two full doses.

It took over four agonizing minutes before the alarm shut off, and Casey's heart began to beat at a semi-stable rhythm.

"Good job," Ann said in a weakened voice.

With shaking hands, Tanille slowly disengaged the cardiac machine. "Okay, let's keep going."

The rest of the long evening went by relatively smoothly, considering the degree of damage the Erules left for them. Casey's heart had stopped once more, but again Tanille brought her back. Four hours had passed before Tanille was finally able to order the removal of the equipment. "There's nothing more we can do."

"Is she going to be all right?"

Tanille peered briefly at Parrow, before giving Casey an injection in her right arm. "I just don't know. If her brain is functioning properly, this injection should bring her around momentarily."

"What if it doesn't?" Ann asked.

"I don't know." Tanille tried to ignore the constriction in her chest. She studied her computer, as she softly stroked Casey's hair.

They all waited while the minutes ticked steadily by with no signs of movement from Casey. A tear slid from Tanille's eye and down her cheek, and she defiantly wiped it off, refusing to accept what her own body was telling her. She watched Ann turn her eyes away, as if the empty pain inside the queen's chest grew too heavy to bear.

"Come on, Casey, you only need to open your eyes for a moment," Tanille finally pleaded, leaning her head down close to the unconscious woman.

When no response came, Tanille double-checked Casey's vitals as Ann and Parrow remained unmoving. She adjusted a few things on the machines before speaking slightly louder. "Look at me, Casey. Please…open your eyes and look at me."

Still, nothing. Her body lightly trembled when the agonizing truth sank in. She bent closer and placed a loving kiss on Casey's lips. "I'll love you always."

When she backed away, she gasped. Casey's eyelids were slightly parted, and her beautiful eyes were staring right at her. "Casey, can you hear me?"

Casey gave her a weak smile. "No," her voice was rough and barely audible. "But I can see you, and that's all I care about."

Tanille's sob was joyful, and her tears of happiness trickled onto Casey's neck. "It's not good to joke with your healer."

Parrow and Ann encircled each other in a heartfelt embrace.

"I know." Casey blinked slowly, as if this movement alone required all the strength she had. "I love you, baby. I'm tired though. Mind if I get some sleep before we make love?"

Tanille blushed but never broke eye contact. "Yes, darling, get some sleep. I'll be right here when you wake up."

Casey closed her eyes and drifted off.

Chapter Sixteen

Two Become One

"It's about time you joined us."

Casey jerked in surprise and blinked the sleep from her eyes. Seeing her grandmother sitting in a chair beside her bed, she instantly relaxed. "Is everyone safe?"

"Yes, dear, everyone is fine. Tanille could use a bit of rest and food, but she's about as stubborn as you are."

Casey's eyes swept the room. "Where is she?"

"She's checking to see if one of your tests has come in yet. She'll be upset she wasn't here when you woke. Poor child hasn't left your bedside since we arrived here a week ago."

"I've been asleep for a week?" Casey tried to sit up but decided against it. A sharp pain surged throughout her body, and her head throbbed.

"Yes, but considering what your body went through, a week isn't too much to ask." Elizabeth fidgeted with her hands. "Tanille was the one who saved your life, Casey. We didn't think you could survive the damage you sustained, but she never gave up on you."

"You saved me too. I heard your voice, urging me not to give up." Casey grimaced, staring at the far side of the room. "I know it sounds crazy since there's no way we could communicate while we were so far apart, and it must have been my mind's way of keeping me from giving up. Still, it kept me going. You keep me going." Casey looked back at her grandmother, surprised to see the tears in her eyes.

"That wasn't your mind playing tricks on you. I heard you across the galaxy. It's how we learned what had happened to you. I don't know how we were able to do it, but I did send you encouragement." A few tears escaped her eyes, rolling down her cheeks. "You were slipping away. I felt so helpless. We all did." She sniffed and huffed. "Except Tanille. She refused to believe you wouldn't make it back to us."

"Like you said, Gran, she's stubborn." She closed her eyes against the pain. "It feels like my chest and back are on fire."

Elizabeth stood, straightened Casey's blankets, and adjusted her pillows. "Yes, they said the pain will last for one, maybe two more weeks. The Erules intertwine Dayshire whips with *acidifora*. That's a very nasty chemical substance which affects you physically and mentally. It's illegal here in our region. Fortunately, much of it will heal, but you'll be left with some pretty nasty scars."

The torture on the Erule ship resurfaced, and Casey lifted her loose-fitting hospital top. She glared at the multiple bandages stuck to her body. They were clean, white, and abundant, covering most of her flesh. "How bad are the scars?"

Elizabeth went to the Belfont Originator by the door and retrieved a glass of water. "Eva caught a glimpse after we brought you in, and she turned completely white. For a moment, I was afraid she was going to pass out."

A mixture of fear and anger flooded Casey's mind and soul. The remembrance of the many lashings took hold, and she realized most of her body had permanent damage. Ignoring the pain, she removed the edging on one of the more significant bandages an inch above her bellybutton, which ran upward between her breasts.

"Casey, what are you doing?"

"I need to see it!" The profound desperation she heard in her own voice startled her. But she had to know.

"You must leave the dressings alone so they can heal." Elizabeth placed the glass on the nightstand with haste and did her best to calm her granddaughter. "You're being ridiculous, Casey. After everything you've been through, how can you worry about a few scars on your body?"

Casey blocked out what Elizabeth was saying. She lifted the white piece of fabric from her stomach. Her body turned hot. Her palms grew cold, sweaty. The injury was much worse than she thought it would be. Her jaw tightened as her eyes traced the wide, swollen gash, which snaked around darkened, scorched flesh. She stared at it for a few moments in disbelief before lowering her head onto the clean, fluffy pillows. Suddenly, time felt frozen. Her future became bleak.

Elizabeth shifted to leave. "Why don't I go get Tanille—"

"I don't want to see her." Casey's words were nothing more than a whisper. It felt as if a deep loneliness was emerging from her body, filling the room with despair.

"Why? She's your healer. She's also going to be—"

"What, my wife?" Casey snapped. Her heart felt torn. The Erules did their job well. She lowered her eyes and her voice. "How am I supposed to ask her to wake up to this every day? To make love to a body as horrid as this?" Casey raised her chin, adamant in her decision, even though her heart was filled with anguish over the life she had lost. "I don't want to see her."

"This depression you're feeling is a normal side effect. *Acidifora* either brings out major depression or uncontrollable rage from its victim. Sometimes both. Now, you rest. I'm going to go find Tanille—" Elizabeth spun around and gasped.

Casey followed her gaze. She quickly pulled the blankets up over her chest when Tanille shifted from the doorway.

"Thank you, Elizabeth. I can take it from here."

Elizabeth gathered her book and drink before departing from the room.

"Now, what were you saying about not wanting to marry me?" Tanille asked. She was carrying a container filled with a sweet-smelling liquid, which she placed on the table next to the bed.

Casey opened her mouth to speak but closed it before any words came out. Tanille raised her eyebrows, apparently waiting for an answer. After a few moments, Casey angled her head away.

She felt the bedding lift off her chest. She snatched the top fold and jerked it back to her. "What are you doing?" Casey demanded, glaring at Tanille.

"What does it look like? Taking care of your wounds. I'm your healer, or do you want to end that too?"

"It's not that I want to end anything. But look at me," she snapped.

Tanille gripped the sheets and yanked hard. "That's what I'm trying to fix," she said, pushing Casey's arms away. "Now lay back and quit being so damn difficult."

Casey stared at Tanille briefly with a set of hurt, watery eyes. Tanille ignored her as she removed the dressings, one at a time. "I've named them, you know," she said a few minutes later.

Casey peered rebelliously out the window. "Named what?"

"Your wounds. I've named them."

The irritation Casey felt changed to a mixture of disgust and confusion. "What are you talking about?"

Tanille shook her head. "If you want to know, tell me you love me."

"Do what?"

"Say you love me first, then I'll tell you."

"This is absurd."

"Yes, it is," Tanille said calmly, while placing the towel soaked in brown liquid on a large portion of Casey's frontal wounds.

The instant the damp cloth touched Casey, a soothing relief ran throughout the wound, the despair fueling her mood slowly dissipated, and life began to, once again, hold meaning past her despondency. "That feels better," she finally muttered.

"Yes, one of our most distinguished healers discovered it while I was in school. Not only will it help you heal faster, but it should also keep most of these gashes from scarring." Tanille paused, as if choosing her words carefully. "I'm sorry, but I hope some of these will not disappear."

Casey wasn't sure how to respond. "Why?"

"Not until you tell me you love me."

Casey rolled her eyes. "You know I do."

"That was very touching."

Casey sighed heavily, feeling emotionally drained. "I love you very much. I'll always love you."

"This one I've named Elizabeth," Tanille said, pointing to the largest scar on Casey's chest. "It's the biggest, and you received it on your quest to save her." She placed the rag on the gash above Casey's left breast. "This one I named after me. One, because it's the wound closest to your heart, and two, because you almost died to save me."

Tanille bent and gently kissed the area above the wound. Casey had to fight off the lump in her throat.

"This one here on your side is Parrow, because it resembles the Blunion mark he has under his eye. Also, because—"

"Let me guess, because I almost died to save him?" Casey grumbled.

"Oh, someone's catching on." As she treated each of Casey's wounds, Tanille shared the names she had given them, including the ones on Casey's back. Once she finished and redressed the wounds, she assisted Casey into a comfortable position on the bed, pulled the blankets up, and gently tucked her in.

"I'm sorry," Casey said, feeling ashamed and a little foolish for how she had acted earlier.

"Your grandmother was right. These waves of hopelessness will come and go until the rest of the *acidifora* leaves your bloodstream. We'll need to keep a close eye on you until it passes. What worries me, though, is this chemical causes depression, yes, but it also heightens your stressors. Leaving me to believe you actually *do* have issues with these scars."

"I overreacted. I'm not saying I'm pleased about these wounds, but I know it could have been much worse. I actually shouldn't be alive right now."

Tanille's eyes held nothing but compassion. She motioned to the bandages. "I love your strength, Casey Malanight. It's one of your many qualities I find attractive. These 'battle wounds' add to it." Tanille traced her finger along Casey collarbone. "Makes you look dashing and full of raw power. Not to mention the story they'll one day hold for our child."

Casey knew Tanille was treating more than her physical wounds. Her spirit was also mending. "You're somewhat of a freak, but I still love you."

"Thank you."

Without warning, the door slid open, and Queen Ann came rushing in, heading straight for the bed. "What is this Elizabeth was saying about you not wanting to get married?" She shook a finger inches away from Casey's face.

"Ann," Tanille began, but the outraged queen was hearing none of it.

"Do you realize what Tanille has been through? What she's done?" She waved an uncaring hand over Casey's body. "What, because of some insignificant scarring? For heaven's sake, Casey, will you stop being so damn insecure about trivial crap, and get on with your life!"

Casey knew her great-grandmother had every right to be upset. "I had a weak moment. I told Tanille I was sorry, and thankfully, she forgave me."

Ann opened her mouth to argue, but closed it tight. She carefully studied one woman, then the other. Satisfied, she gestured from Casey to Tanille. "So…she's talked some sense into you."

"She has," Casey said.

Ann gave her a threatening look. "What about the wedding?"

Casey smiled at Tanille. "I'm more than ready. If you'll still have me?"

Tanille's lips curved playfully upward. "You might sway me," she said seductively. "However, it'll take some heavy persuading."

"Yes, well—I'll let Casey get to it." With an air of amusement, Ann kissed Casey on the cheek before saying her goodbyes.

Casey guffawed at Tanille the moment Ann left. "My brazen sense of humor must be rubbing off on you."

"Who said I was joking?"

Casey stopped laughing. She squinted from Tanille to the door. "What? Do you mean here? Now? What if someone comes in?"

Tanille gave Casey a flirtatious wink before strolling over to the monitor and pushing several commands into the system. On her return to Casey's bedside, she undid the buttons on her blouse. "The hormones released will help improve your depression."

Casey found it difficult to swallow. "You're not playing, are you?"

Tanille said nothing as the light fabric covering the top half of her body fell in a sweeping motion to the floor, revealing a black see-through bra.

"Can I—I mean, am I healthy enough?"

Tanille placed a finger over Casey's lips to prevent her from talking. She reached behind her back with her other hand, unfastening her bra. It, too, fell to the floor. Climbing in under the covers beside Casey, she leaned in, nibbling along Casey's neck. "Don't worry, my love. I'm your healer. Your physical and mental health are in loving hands. I'll labor vigorously to care for you. All night if I have to."

Casey pressed her lips against Tanille's. She could tell Tanille's body had missed the feel of her touch. She pulled her closer, savoring the taste. "I'm feeling better by the second."

If it weren't for Tanille's honed reflexes, Casey would have fallen off the bed twice. Once backward during the first in-depth "healing" session, when Casey became tangled in the sheets while making her way slowly down Tanille's body. The second was when Tanille's knee brushed against one of Casey's sores by accident, and Casey had jerked sideways, losing her balance. Several hours later, thanks to her healer, Casey was in a much better mood and still in one piece.

Casey inhaled deeply as Tanille slipped on her navy-blue slacks. "You realize there's a distinct aroma of our passion in here."

Tanille grinned. "Is that a bad thing?" She placed a kiss on Casey's lips.

"It will be if Grandmother Elizabeth walks in, or worse, your father."

"I'll take care of it," Tanille said, searching the floor around the bed. "Have you seen my bra?"

"I'm not sure. Have you decided to marry me yet?"

Tanille huffed. "May I please have my bra?"

"Yes, after you give me an answer."

Tanille gazed at the ceiling in humorous thought. "There's a slight probability." She narrowed her eyes at Casey. "It might take a little more persuasion. After all, I'm not totally convinced you genuinely want me."

"You're not being very nice."

The entrance to the room made a clicking sound, startling both women. They froze, staring apprehensively toward the door.

"Tanille, is everything all right?" Fayrel's voice echoed out from the other side of the room.

"Give me my bra," Tanille whispered, hastily fixing her after-sex hairdo.

"I'm trying." Casey felt under her pillow, then lifted the covers. "It must have fallen."

"Tanille, Casey, are you two all right?" Elizabeth's muffled voice shouted. She pounded smartly on the door.

"Never mind. Straighten the bedding, and for heaven's sake, look relaxed," Tanille said, throwing her arms into her blouse and hastily buttoning it.

"What about the sex scent?" Casey muttered when Tanille ran toward the door.

"Oh, right!" Tanille punched some commands into the keypad, and the sound system blared out a lively tune. "Crap!" She pushed more buttons, sending the room back into silence.

"Let's come back later." Casey heard Ann say, but Elizabeth continued to call out for someone to answer.

On Tanille's next entry into the computerized system, a fog of floral fragrance blew from barely visible holes along the ceiling and walls.

"That's too much. Switch it off!"

"I'm trying! And your impatient tone isn't helping."

The cloud of smoke ceased, and Tanille waved her arms in the air to fan away part of the overpowering scent.

"That's not working. Just open the door."

Elizabeth and Fayrel practically fell into the room when the door slid open.

"What's wrong? Why was the door locked?" Elizabeth wrinkled her nose. "And who bathed in a pool of lisnac flowers?"

"I've missed you, Gran," Casey said, holding out her arms to Elizabeth.

"Oh, I've missed you too." Elizabeth's eyes softened, and she hurried over for a warm embrace. Right before her arms encircled Casey, Elizabeth straightened, and her features crumpled with curiosity. She reached over and snatched a black bra from the crevice by the headboard. She held it up, as if she'd never in her life seen such a contraption.

"Ah, good. You found it," Ann said, a little too loudly. She sauntered over and nicked the article of clothing from Elizabeth. "I've been looking everywhere for it." She shoved it into the front pocket of her coat.

Dumbfounded, Elizabeth asked, "Why was your bra in Casey's room?"

"Well…I was going to see if she wanted it. Bilana bought it for me, but the darn thing was too big. I was going to give it to Casey, but I must have dropped it." Changing the subject, she asked Tanille, "How's the patient doing?"

"Well?" Elizabeth questioned Ann, not letting the matter rest.

"Well, what?" Ann asked, sounding annoyed.

"Are you going to give her the bra?"

"Oh yes, sorry." She yanked out the bra and tossed it to Casey. "Here you go."

Casey grabbed it, thanked Ann for her new undergarment, and shoved it under the sheets, out of sight.

"Are you all right, dear?" Fayrel asked Tanille, who stood with her hands crossed in front of her, covering her braless chest as best as she could. "You look flushed,"

"Yes, I feel fine, only tired."

"I'm sure you are. You've been on your feet since we arrived here. You should head to the estate and get a decent night's sleep," said her father.

"No. I'm fine, really. I plan to stay here with Casey until she's discharged."

"When are you thinking of releasing her?" Fayrel asked. He noticed Casey's electronic chart on the table on the other side of Tanille. "Mind if I take a gander?" He motioned for Tanille to retrieve it.

Tanille didn't move.

"Oh, I almost forgot!" Ann's shout was unexpected, making Elizabeth and Fayrel jump in surprise. She stumbled slightly with her words, as all turned to face her. "I…oh, I have to ask you two something very important. Yes, very important indeed."

The room grew quiet until Elizabeth finally spoke. "Yes?"

Ann moved to the door and waited. A reluctant Elizabeth and Fayrel eventually followed her. As soon as the door shut, Casey flung the bra to Tanille, who rushed to put it on. She finished fastening the last of the buttons on her shirt when the door to the room reopened.

"I wrote layered cake, but can't this wait until after we see to the girls?"

Ann peeked inside the room, obviously to make sure all was well before stepping in. "Silly me, of course it can. I guess I have a little pre-wedding jitters. Like both of you, I want everything to be perfect on their special day."

Elizabeth patted her on the arm. "It will be. Now stop fretting, and we can fill you in on everything the moment we arrive at the estate."

As soon as Elizabeth turned, Ann rolled her eyes. Casey had to stifle a laugh. She knew Ann would rather drive a nail through her hand than sit and discuss the wedding any more than she already had.

Once Tanille had the attention of the other two, Casey mouthed to Ann, "I owe you one."

Ann followed with a silent, "Yes, you do," before she joined in to hear about Casey's condition.

Tanille said, "We're not sure how it's happening, but her body is repairing itself at a phenomenal rate."

"Amazing," Fayrel said, marveling over Casey's chart.

Casey felt awkward while she lay there, watching them gather at the foot of her bed to talk about her. "So when can I leave?" she finally asked.

"In about three or four days. I still have some more tests to run."

Casey exhaled loudly, causing Fayrel to laugh. "Good luck keeping this one in bed."

Tanille covertly winked at Casey. "Oh, I don't think I'll have any problems there."

Ann was the only one who showed signs of understanding what Tanille truly meant. She snorted while trying to suppress a nervous laugh.

"You've done a remarkable job, Tanille. I'm proud of you." Fayrel handed her the chart. "I guess we'd better get on with it, so they can get some rest," Fayrel told Elizabeth, who eagerly agreed.

They positioned some chairs around Casey's bed. "First, the item you brought with you from the Erule ship has helped us out more than you could've imagined." Elizabeth thanked Ann, who handed her a glass of water. "One of the key components found was a backup drive which Chasel and Jasper decoded. One file held a list of names, or I should say, traitors inside our Universal Region who are under the rule of the Dayshires. We've captured many, but a few have fled."

Ann added, "It also held the locations of several uninhabited planets inside our region where they've built underground bases." The anger in her voice matched her disdain. "Seven in all."

"How's that possible?"

"We don't know. It appears the enemy has infiltrated key positions inside our own government. The list of names, though some go pretty high up, is still under investigation," Ann said, shaking her head. "The other items were collections of reports and files these traitors had stolen to give to the enemy. Information relating to our defenses, military bases, even blueprints for many of our weapons and scientific advancements. Intel we wouldn't want in enemy hands. And there's no telling what other data they've attained up to this point."

"The Hafite delegates were also on the list," Fayrel said.

"What?" Casey couldn't believe what she was hearing. The very people who her grandmother Elizabeth went to retrieve.

"That's how they got to you, Casey," Ann explained, growing more infuriated. "They kept Elizabeth away and sent you the phony distress call. They also swayed the vote to call off the Fleet when you were on your way home."

"The Fleet, but I saw all the ships with you."

"No, those were personal ships from other Assembly members. When they heard what had happened, they came to our aid."

Casey was having a hard time absorbing the truth. "How could they falsify a distress call? I saw Gran on my personal computer. The message was genuine. I'm positive."

Elizabeth said, "Genuine yes, but old. I'm not sure how they acquired it, but what you saw was the same message I'd sent when I went to save Hanna many years ago."

"How did they send it to my personal computer, and why couldn't I get a hold of anyone else on the team?"

Ann's tone was framed with venom. "They tapped into your computer. We're trying to find out how they got their hands on your security codes, but we'll take all measures possible to prevent this from happening again."

"I fell right into their trap." Casey felt like a fool. "They knew I'd be stupid enough to come."

"No," Tanille said. "They knew you'd do everything you could, including risking your own life, to save those you love."

Casey didn't respond, but inwardly she cursed herself for being so naïve.

"Tanille's right," Ann said. "They used your nobility and loving heart to their advantage. We have no clue why they're after you. We thought they wished you dead, but apparently we were wrong."

"They want to breed me with the Dayshire leader."

Elizabeth stared blankly at Casey. "General Morsen? Are you sure?"

Casey nodded. "Yes. They believe a child born to him with our abilities could win this war."

"But they don't know what our abilities are. How can they?" Ann frowned at Elizabeth, seeming suddenly uncertain.

None spoke, sending the room into an uncomfortable silence. The door opened and the head of council walked in. "I'm sorry to barge in like this, but I wanted to be the one to tell you…" he began, wiping his forehead with a handkerchief he retrieved from his breast pocket.

"What is it?" Ann asked, not losing her worry.

"Someone informed the Hafite representatives we were coming to arrest them. They've fled to Couhl Tabarr."

"The Hafite citizens will hand them over. I'm sure of it," Ann insisted.

"They have an immense influence with their people. If the Hafites refuse and we send troops in to arrest them, many innocent lives will be lost."

Ann narrowed her eyes. "How about ordering a covert extraction? They need to be questioned."

He shoved the handkerchief back into his pocket. "We ran the scenarios, and nothing showed us a favorable outcome. I'm afraid we might need to wait them out."

Elizabeth stood. "I have some close Hafite friends who are on their planetary committee. Let me see what I can do. At least we can get an idea of the atmosphere on each of their planets."

"We should go with you." Ann raised her eyebrow at Paraney, who nodded in agreement. The three said their goodbyes before heading for the palace to do what they could.

Fayrel groaned more to himself than to Tanille or Casey. "The safety of our region is becoming more unstable each day."

"It'll turn out all right, father. You'll see."

His downcast mood lifted. "You sound like your mother. She would be immensely proud of the woman you've become." He gave her a hug and leaned forward to embrace Casey. "I know you'll take good care of her," he said.

He bent close to her ear and whispered. "Please keep her safe and happy. She's the entire world to me." He stood, exchanged a flicker of understanding with Casey, and said his goodbyes.

Once he left, Tanille stared at her curiously. "What did he say?"

"I'm sorry," Casey said, patting the open spot on the bed. "It's between him and me. He's a good father and loves his daughter very much."

"Does he? Well, I love you." Tanille kicked off her shoes and crawled under the covers.

Casey held the tired healer close and gently stroked her hair. Not long after, Tanille fell right to sleep. Casey listened with contentment to the sound of Tanille's steady breathing. Enjoying the feel of Tanille in her arms, Casey stayed awake for as long as she could, until sleep ultimately got the better of her.

Casey wasn't sure how long she'd slept or why she was standing in the corner when she awoke, but she knew something wasn't right.

"Casey, please…I'm not going to hurt you. It's me, Tanille."

Casey inspected her shaking hands. At first, they appeared covered in red paint, but after a second glance, Casey realized it was blood. "What happened?" Her body was drenched with perspiration, several of her dressings were off, and her wounds reopened, with fresh blood seeping out. She could almost taste the metallic aroma of copper in the air.

"You had a bad dream," Tanille said, rushing to her side. "You started shouting. When I tried to touch you, you jumped from the bed and tore into your dressings." Tanille shouted to the ceiling, "I need some help in here."

She guided Casey carefully to the bed. Within moments, the room was swarming with medical personnel. Several individuals were assisting Tanille with cleaning and redressing the wounds, as Casey fought to control her trembling.

"I'll get you something for the pain as soon as we're done." Tanille sounded worried, even frightened, and she treated Casey as fast as she could.

"I'm fine." Casey did her best to smile, but her brain was spinning, trying hard to remember what had happened.

When they finally finished, Tanille thanked her colleagues and went to fetch Casey some medication. She returned with pills and a full glass of water.

"I really am fine."

"The manner of your care is not open for discussion. Now take them or I'll call the others back in here and we'll give them to you by force."

Casey did as she was told, not wishing to upset Tanille any more than she already had. "I'm so sorry," she murmured, handing over the empty glass. "I didn't hurt you, did I?"

"Of course not." Tanille scowled, as if offended Casey could think such a thing.

"I remember nothing."

"Do you recall your dream?"

"No. I'm not sure I had one. I remember closing my eyes. Next thing I know, I'm in the corner, bleeding all over the place."

Tanille stood. She inspected the monitor displaying Casey's vital information. Casey leaned her head against the pillows, wracking her brain for any detail to help her remember.

A loud crash echoed, followed by the sound of Tanille's heavy sobs. Casey instantly rose from the bed and sidestepped around pieces of her computerized chart which lay smashed on the floor. She cringed under the pain of her sudden movement, but she pushed it aside. She made her way over to Tanille, whose back was to her. Casey wrapped her arms protectively around the woman she loved. "Are you sure I didn't hurt you?"

"Please stop asking me that." Tanille rubbed her eyes. "You should be in bed," Tanille said, after taking a few deep breaths to ease her sobs.

"I'm fine."

"Of course you are!" Tanille's voice was bitter, and she spun angrily around. "Why must you play the hero, Casey? Why must you go in half-cocked not thinking of the consequences or what would happen to those of us who love you if you died?"

"Because it's who I am," Casey said honestly. "I've always had the impulse to protect others. It's in my blood. You know this, and that's not what you're upset about."

Tanille placed her hand over Casey's bandaged cheek. She took in a deep breath and asked, "What did those monsters do to you?"

Casey gazed evenly at Tanille. "Nothing I care to mention, especially to you."

"I'm your healer."

"No. You're the woman I love, and then you're my healer."

"I tried to stop you when you awoke, but you were so scared, so lost."

Casey sat on the edge of the bed and nervously rubbed her hands together.

"I'm sorry. I'll clean up this mess," Tanille said, gesturing to the busted chart.

Casey seized Tanille's hand, stopping her. She drew her into her arms. "What if it happens again? This waking up disorientated. What if it happens again, and it's worse?"

"We'll deal with it. You need to talk about what happened, Casey. If you don't want to tell me, maybe you should talk to Parrow or Queen Ann."

"I'm not sure if I can, but I'll try."

Tanille placed her arms around Casey's neck. "I'm sorry for my outburst. It's just—I feel so angry and helpless when I think about what you went through."

Casey placed a tender kiss on Tanille's lips. "It's over. I'm safe, right here next to you." She slid her fingers gently along Tanille's jawline and cupped her hand tenderly under her lover's chin for another kiss. "I never want to live without you."

"You won't, and yes, for the second time, I'll marry you."

The day of the wedding, Casey combed through the estate in search of Tanille. She had the yearning to peek at her, only for a second. An added dose of much-needed courage. She wasn't comfortable in crowds, and this gathering was monstrous. She passed many people she'd never met before and watched nervously as the vast stretch of land behind the estate transformed into a mighty scene for a magnificent wedding. She silently wished they could have eloped.

The last ten days leading up to the wedding had been overflowing with much to do. Not that anyone would let Casey do much, or anything at all, for that matter. Everyone kept shooing her away, telling her she had to conserve her strength to heal faster.

Vashee was the worst. She blamed herself for not being present when Casey received the bogus call from Elizabeth. She'd told Casey how she'd felt her dying and was helpless to do anything. More than once she lamented how if she'd gone with Casey, the Erules would not have captured her. Casey wasn't so sure. She believed the Erules would have killed Vashee without a second thought.

She eventually talked with Parrow regarding bits and pieces of her experience with the Erules, leaving out the parts still too difficult to discuss. Tanille was right. Sharing did help, but she still awoke with bad dreams every time she slept. Fortunately, she no longer feared Tanille's touch during one of these episodes or clawed at her wounds, which were starting to either scar or disappear, but she woke up anxious and shaking. Tanille would hold her until she fell back to sleep, or they would make love. Sometimes both.

"Why haven't you changed yet?" Bilana asked Casey after first removing her from the busy kitchen. "Hurry before Elizabeth sees you."

"Gran hasn't given me my outfit yet."

"Oh. You'd better go find her then." Bilana sighed, before quickly turning to scold someone, who apparently wasn't stirring something quite right.

Five minutes later, Casey finally ran into Ann and Elizabeth. Both women were elegantly dressed, Grandmother Ann in a pale-blue silky dress suit, and Gran in a matching glittery dress and robe. She was also carrying a silver box.

"Where's Tanille?" Casey asked.

Elizabeth frowned. "You can't see her before the wedding. It's bad luck."

"Trysals don't believe in superstition," Casey said.

"They don't, but we're also part human, and we need all the luck we can get."

"Elizabeth, don't be so dramatic. It'll all turn out fine." Ann took the box from Elizabeth and handed it to Casey. "Here, now go change. The wedding's going to kick off within the hour."

A mixture of excitement and fear washed over Casey. She returned to her room, feeling dazed. She didn't remember dressing, yet soon she stood in front of the full-length mirror, gazing at her reflection. She was grateful Gran had chosen a feminine-cut suit instead of the robe she'd first designed. If she could replace the pointy dress shoes with a pair of loafers, the white satin outfit would feel more comfortable. More like her.

The knock on the bedroom door made her heart skip. "Casey, it's time," Ann loudly shouted.

Casey anxiously opened the door.

"What's wrong?" Ann asked, fixing Casey's collar.

"I'm petrified to the point I may vomit."

The love in Grandmother Ann's eyes filled Casey with comfort. "You look more smashing in this than I did. But please, keep the nausea down until after the ceremony."

"You wore this at your wedding?"

"We had it tailored some, but yes."

Casey held Ann's hand. "Thank you for everything." Their exchange of silent understanding spoke volumes.

Ann escorted Casey toward the rear of the house where all eyes turned as if in one motion to the sound of far-off trumpets. "There are so many people," Casey muttered, stopping less than a foot inside the doorway.

Ann gave her hand an encouraging squeeze. "They're here to witness their future queen begin the first day of her life with the one she loves. These are your friends, your family, and your people. They love you, Casey. Allow them to share this with you."

Casey forced a nervous smile while giving Grandmother Ann a nod. Casey slowly inhaled, counted to ten, and gradually exhaled. Her fear subsided, and her hands were less shaky.

"Don't worry. Tanille is as anxious over the size of this crowd as you."

"I find that hard to believe."

Ann smiled proudly and gave Casey a loving kiss on her cheek. She escorted Casey to Elizabeth before leaving to take her seat in the front.

"Are you ready to get married?" Gran was standing taller and happier than Casey had ever seen her before. The sight warmed her.

Casey focused on her grandmother's eyes, feeding off Gran's internal courage. "More than you realize." A flicker of movement to her right caught her attention. She turned her head and saw Vashee, her black coat gleaming. Casey felt a sense of calmness flow through her. She marveled at how majestic Vashee looked wearing an ornate body harness decorated with the Royal House's colors.

Are you ready? Vashee's tail swished with excitement. *I hope you realize I would only wear this for you.*

Smiling, Casey stroked Vashee's back. *I know.*

Once the music stopped, as if on cue, Elizabeth motioned to Casey and they moved forward, sauntering arm in arm down the decorated footpath as Vashee kept pace beside them. There were vast rows of seating on either side. The entire mass of people stood. Some were smiling, some crying, but everyone gazed at them with warm, adoring eyes. Elizabeth left Casey at the front of the crowd with a kiss to her cheek and went to take her seat next to Ann, Bilana, David, and Ashonda.

Vashee growled low in her throat before jumping up to place her paws on Casey's shoulders and rub her snout against Casey's throat and jaw. Many tittered at the display. *I am so happy for you.*

With a small chuckle, Casey bumped her forehead against Vashee's. *Oh, go on, ya big baby. I love you too.* Casey watched Vashee join her family before turning toward Tanille.

The moment Casey and Tanille's eyes locked, she felt breathless. Fayrel was proudly leading his daughter through the stretched pathway, arm in arm. Her elegant, white dress was stunning, her free-flowing hair picturesque, her beauty unmatched by any. Tanille's eyes were as mesmerizing as they were the first day she and Casey met. The love they held as she ogled Casey was beyond conceivable. In every way imaginable, Tanille was the woman of her dreams. Her soulmate.

Fayrel placed a loving kiss on Tanille's cheek. He held out her hand for Casey to take before claiming his seat beside Elizabeth. Tanille and Casey stood next to each other in front of all in attendance, and the ceremony began.

Throughout the service, Casey couldn't take her eyes off Tanille. Her soul felt strong, at peace. She couldn't believe she'd been so worried today, when today had turned out to be the best day of her life.

"I now proclaim Tanille Beletal and Casey Malanight joined for all eternity." Casey scarcely heard the applause from the crowd. She didn't think about the approaching war, or the fact she would leave Earth and her loved ones soon for the Academy. She bent forward and kissed Tanille deeply, passionately. Nothing else mattered at this moment. For today, Casey's soul had found its better half.

To Be Continued…

About the Author

Michele Coffman lives in Kansas, has two wonderful adult children, and an adorable granddaughter. She is a passionate writer, has an untamable imagination, and enjoys writing sci-fi and speculative fiction—almost as much as she fancies reading them. For fifteen years she traveled around the world with the military, and now she takes a journey into the outer reaches of the Universe and invites you to follow. You can find Michele at http://michelecoffman.com/

Note to Readers

Thank you for reading a book from Launch Point Press. We have made every effort to edit this book. However, typos do slip in. If you find an error in the text, please email publisher@launchpointpress.com so the issue can be corrected.

We appreciate you as a reader and want to ensure you enjoy the reading process. We would like you to consider posting a review on your preferred media sites and/or your blog or website.

For more information on upcoming releases, author interviews, contests, giveaways, and more, please sign up for our newsletter and visit us at Launch Point Press: www.launchpointpress.com and "Like" us on Facebook: Launch Point Press.

Bright Blessings